Cracking America

'Deliciously offbeat and witty, Barbara Toner's sharply observed *Cracking America* is set in the idiosyncratic world of popular music. Taking the story of unknown Honey Hawksworth from Cockfosters and her attempt to crack Nashville to become a star alongside her beloved Dolly Parton, it's a pacey mixture of murder and mayhem . . . Bringing together a disparate, desperate but ultimately likable group of characters Toner skillfully ensures that even though only seen through Honey's eyes they are never merely one dimensional. All this and a perceptive insight into the country music industry makes for an excellent and at times riotous read.' *What's On*

'Barbara Toner is funny, sharp and uncomfortably perceptive.' *Evening Standard*

'Honey Hawksworth is just 21, yet she has the heart and soul of a country singer, a voice full of longing and a guitar to match. Nashville is calling in *Cracking America* by Barbara Toner, who captures the voice of her young narrator with satirical authenticity . . . Like the narrator of *Catcher in the Rye*, which this book cannot fail to bring to mind, Honey has her own way of seeing things. Funny, dark and original, this is a wonderful read.' *Sainsbury Magazine*, Book of the Month

'It is a real deep south tragedy, humour, baked apple dumplin' . . . Throughout you can just hear that guitar strumming and yearning voices singing songs of things that might have been. Expect to be truly mesmerised dahlin'.' *SW Magazine*

'A collection of all-too-human characters, a wealth of sharply honed, witty dialogue and a bevy of insightful asides on the heroes and songs of classic country music make *Cracking America* an excellent and entertaining read . . . Pacey and shot-through with a dark and delicious sense of humour. Barbara Toner's novel never misses a beat as the reader is drawn into the thick of the action from the very first page . . . Superbly written and sharply observed.' *Get Rhythm*

Barbara Toner

Cracking America

ARROW

Published by Arrow Books in 2003

1 3 5 7 9 10 8 6 4 2

Copyright © Barbara Toner 2002

The right of Barbara Toner to be identified as the author of
this work has been asserted by her in accordance with the
Copyright, Designs and Patents Act, 1988

First published by Hutchinson in 2002

Arrow Books
The Random House Group Limited
20 Vauxhall Bridge Road, London SW1V 2SA

Random House Australia (Pty) Limited
20 Alfred Street, Milsons Point, Sydney
New South Wales 2061, Australia

Random House New Zealand Limited
18 Poland Road, Glenfield
Auckland 10, New Zealand

Random House (Pty) Limited
Endulini, 5a Jubilee Road, Parktown 2193, South Africa

The Random House Group Limited Reg. No. 954009

www.randomhouse.co.uk

A CIP catalogue record for this book
is available from the British Library

Papers used by Random House are natural, recyclable products
made from wood grown in sustainable forests. The manufacturing
processes conform to the environmental regulations
of the country of origin

Printed and bound in Great Britain by
Cox & Wyman Ltd, Reading, Berkshire

ISBN 0 09 942821 0

Acknowledgements

I would like to thank the following for their enormous help and patience with my research: Barry Coburn, Stuart and Janet Colman, David Conrad, Jeff Green, Bob Moody, Ralph Murphy, Dennis Muirhead, Kerry O'Neill and Jana Talbert in Nashville; Alan Rafterman in New York and Tony Russell and Richard Wootton in London. They are in no way responsible for what became of the advice, opinion and information they gave me but I could never have managed without it. I would also like to express my appreciation and undying admiration for country music's all time greats, however old or dead they are.

1

This is what I know.

At 11.25 a.m. on 25 June, eight weeks to the day after I was signed by Moonshine Records, Rita Mae Rainbow (formerly Pinkerton), banjo slash fiddle player on both my single and my album, was walking past the apartment block where I was residing with my best friend and manager, Stella Maria O'Shea and our close friend Tom Sinclair, when a brick fell on her head and killed her stone dead. Splat! It crashed three storeys to five feet eight inches above the ground and smashed her brains out.

The police say bricks don't just fall. Someone must've picked it up and thrown it and that someone must've been Stella Maria who was seen by workmen on the roof not five minutes before. She had a motive. Insane jealousy. Everyone knows she had a motive and she's not denying it but she's saying she didn't throw anything. She's saying she wasn't on the roof. She was in the stairwell when it fell and they'll have to take her word for it. They say the evidence is compelling.

She needs an alibi.

Here's what I'm saying.

Stella Maria might have been on the roof at 11.20 but at 11.25 she was with me in our room going over schedules same as we did every day. We were going over schedules, we weren't expecting anyone to visit and Stella Maria was as shocked as everyone else to find Rita Mae had been taken from us by a brick. I'm saying her timing's all wrong.

She agrees she was with me at 11.35 but she won't have it she was with me at 11.25. Fuck off, she says. She knows where she was. I say she might know where she was but she doesn't seem to appreciate exactly where we are. She says she does, exactly, and she won't be party to another lie.

I tell her it's no lie. We were together. We are together. We always will be together in the eternal spirit of our lifelong friendship. Am I trying to make her laugh, she says. I'm lying to save my arse, not hers. That she could even think this shows how bad things are between us. They're at an all-time low. Which is tragic.

So here we are, driving along the Interstate from Nashville to be confined in the house of someone we don't even know in the East Tennessee hills, it's taking all day and so far she's uttered just two words. Drop and dead. 'You not speaking?' was all I said.

Doesn't bother me she's a sulker. She's always been a sulker. That's what she was doing in the stairwell. Sulking. And now she's in shock. Nothing in her life prepared her for seventeen hours in a prison cell. Not even twenty years being raised by a mother as stone-hearted and cold-faced as those old jailhouse walls. She sat in that cell and she cried and cried. I said, 'Come on Stella Maria. It's a laugh.'

'Are you insane?' she said.

Things must be different for an artist. Incarceration is rich pickings for a songwriter and nothing to an orphan. 'Want to hear a song?' I'm addressing the back of her head, which is a lump of knots dragged into a fluorescent green hair elastic.

She doesn't answer. I ask her again but she's staring out the window at the passing countryside like she wants it dead, so I sing to myself anyway.

> *'Girl behind bars*
> *Once she had stars in her eyes*
> *Now no matter how hard she tries, she can't blink away tears*
> *For all of the years she'll be wastin'.*
> *And da de de da de de . . .'*

'That's real pretty,' Archie says, taking his eyes off the road to compliment me. 'And real sad.' Archie's our janitor from the apartment in Nashville. He loves my music. But I hold it right there because Stella Maria turns to look at me with a face as friendly as rat poison and I'm thinking if she tries to get over the back seat to whack me, he'll crash this old rust bucket for sure and that will be the end of all our hopes and dreams, forget any old court case.

Boy, is she full of anger. We should be thanking our lucky stars for the twist our fortune has taken, but she's hating her life, hating my life, hating everything that's happening to us which she says is my fault and some of it is, I know it. I won't deny I caused her pain, but I'm doing my level best to make it up to her, I really am. Unfortunately, no amount of me saying it's going to be alright in the end is helping.

She doesn't want to be one of the most talked about people in Nashville today. She couldn't care less the record company's solid, the single's ready to go and the album is full of so many good things people are saying I'm the next Dolly. All she wants is for us to pack up and go home to Cockfosters, end of the Piccadilly line, London.

All she thinks she wants. I'm not having it. She's been my best friend for 15 years and I can read her like a book. She'll come to her senses any day now. We came to America to crack it and we're within inches of succeeding. All of us. Her, me and Tom. Our fortunes wind in and out of each others'

3

like the three gold bands on the wedding ring my mother wore, though she never married, may she rest in peace.

Stella Maria says she wants us to dump Tom but he brought us here for God's sake. We'd be nothing without him. I'm the subject of his documentary, *The Biggest Gamble In Nashville's History*, which is about life and luck but she's saying ours ran out the day we met him. It just isn't true and she's knows it.

We have these charges against us, but in ten days' time they're going to be sorted and all anyone will remember is how wronged we were. She's no murderer. We've been charged with crimes we didn't commit, not murder in the first degree, but reckless homicide and being an accessory to reckless homicide, Stella Maria being the alleged murderer and me being the alleged accessory. We wouldn't even be charged with this if Stella Maria and me could get our stories straight but we can't because she won't face facts.

Archie, crouching over his steering wheel like it's something we're going to steal from him, says, 'Nearly there, ladies.' And I won't deny it, my stomach heaves. I'm a person who welcomes new experiences but I'm only average on new places to live, new people to live with, and new rules to live by.

All we know about where we're headed is that we'll be in the care of this Betty Beecher and all we know about her is she's a prominent citizen as requested by the judge who also wanted our passports and $1.5 million to let us go. She's all the company we're going to get this next little while, unless she decides otherwise, so I hope she's decent.

We make a left, we make a right, and suddenly we're into country so fine, my stomach settles. In the fading light, the valleys and hills are golden and brown and violet and so beautiful there could be no better haven for the exhausted heart. 'Wow!' I say to no one in particular.

'Y'all oughta cheer up now,' Archie says, looking sideways

4

at Stella Maria and forgetting to steer for a minute. 'Y'all oughta relax a little.' And I want to hug him because soon he'll be leaving us and he's been a good friend since we hit town. He knows Stella Maria didn't kill anyone.

The road's about to dip to some place in darkest shadow where I'd rather not die, when he swings off it so fast he throws us into a 360-degree skid and I scream. So now my heart is pounding and I'm full of fear because we're heading up on to this mountain and the track's curving, straightening, curving, straightening and heights make me puke. There's no more than inches between us and oblivion and Archie's knuckles are white on the wheel as he struggles to stay on course.

I'm praying to Mammy, 'Send me a sign this isn't a nightmare', because it looks too freaky for comfort. And she does. We turn one more corner and right in front of us is the Tennessee mountain home to end all Tennessee mountain homes. Small for the house of a prominent citzen, and half hidden by undergrowth, but all covered in purple flowers and topped in gold where the sun is catching the roof. 'Look at that,' I say. 'Look at that, Stella Maria.'

'That'll be her,' says Archie. Waiting by the gate is a woman of maybe thirty-six, mid height, not fat, white blonde hair falling from under this battered brown hat she's pulled down over her face, and wearing a big check shirt over tight jeans which is normal. She's smoking a pipe which isn't.

'Betty Beecher,' she calls as we pull up. 'How ya doin?'

I get out, shake her hand and say we are doin' just fine, thank you very much and we are more than obliged to her for taking us in like this, but I'm thinking if anyone looks like a murderer, she does. I say I'm Honey Hawksworth, this is Stella Maria O'Shea and our driver is Archie. She says she's mighty pleased to meet us all and would Archie care to refresh himself before making the return trip.

'No thank you, Ma'am,' he says. He doesn't want to hang

round a moment longer than he has to, and I don't blame him. He looks up at the house and at the hills all around, he stares at the pipe Betty Beecher hasn't removed from her mouth and he says to me, 'Darn sight quieter out here than you're used to.'

'Looking forward to it,' I say as Stella Maria heaves our bags out of the boot.

Betty says, 'Mr Siegal talk to you about the need for discretion here, Archie?' He says there was no need for Mr Siegal to mention any such thing. He loves us like we are his daughters.

I give him a kiss and Stella Maria pats his arm, then he's in that car, revving the engine like some teenager when he's not a day younger than sixty-seven, and he's out of here, missing the gatepost by a whisker. He flies down the track like there are six buffalo on his tail, and I want to yell after him to come back. He's taking a bit of me with him, and it's a bit I know I'll need. I say to Mammy, 'Hope you know what you're doing up there because it feels mighty strange down here.'

2

Turns out she does. Turns out Betty Beecher's no weirder than the next person. I'm not saying her house doesn't smell weird, like pipe and something I'm guessing is goat from the scary white job with the crazy pink eyes tied to a tree outside my bedroom. But it has porches back and front with a breeze running between them and a feeling about the place that's pure sunshine and comfort. Betty herself is sunshine and comfort.

The echo of Archie disappearing was still bouncing about the hills when she called us in to eat last night. 'Doncha go worryin' about any unpackin' just yet,' she said. 'Y'all must be starvin' after such a long drive.' And I was just about hollow is the truth, having refused all food in jail on account of the injustice.

She showed us into the dining room all decked out with silver and candles and pictures of dead relatives from the bible business, then she brought in this big steaming pot of goodness like a farmer's wife with ten hungry children plus a husband with a crop in the field. She took a seat at the head of the table with Stella Maria and me either side, she said grace and she served up, all the while asking us about ourselves like we were the most fascinating people she'd ever met.

And that food was shite. I just about cried. 'Bean chowder,' she said when I asked her what we were eating. 'Sure hope you like vegetarian.'

Stella Maria mopped up her plate like it was heaven pie. I tried to give her a look, like how could you, but she was busy bonding with Betty. 'You have the most beautiful garden I've ever seen,' she said.

So now I'm delirious from hunger and not sure if I can concentrate on anything except the contents of my stomach. I missed breakfast so's not to keep her waiting on our first morning for a meeting on the dot of 11.00 but I'm just wondering if maybe I shouldn't excuse myself before we begin and grab something quick from the kitchen. Maybe not. 'Ah am not a stickler for rules but Ah favour a routine,' she said over dinner. 'A routine is a great soother of troubled feelings, doncha think?'

I'm just going to have to distract myself. It won't be so hard. The sun is shining in a bright blue sky, the air is sweet with hope, and here we are, Betty and me, sittin' out on her porch surrounded by history, and vegetation, and the places of famous people who've returned to their roots.

'You know why you're here, doncha Honey?' she says, and she both sounds and looks like the answer to an alleged accessory's prayers. She's sitting at a dinky little table with a white lace cloth on it, wearing a soft cream shirt and a long, patterned skirt and what's she remind me of? A gentle widder woman, pining for the sheriff so cruelly struck down by a bullet to the heart on their weddin' night. There's an air about her, a cheated air. Song: *The Cheated Air You Wear Upon Your Soft Pale Brow*. Wouldn't surprise me a bit to find she had a broken heart. There's no evidence of any man in her life.

8

Her tape recorder's whirring away and she's tapping her pen on the head of one of the big concrete lions that guard the front door. Her voice is all sweet and soft, untouched by tobacco, and full of southern hospitality.

'Sure,' I say. I'm in the canvas hammock attached to the porch rails, swinging to and fro, fanning myself with my stetson. Stella Maria thinks I can't see her but I can. She's hovering behind the billowing white curtains of her bedroom over Betty's shoulder, eavesdropping. 'Sure. Condition of our bail.'

'Right,' Betty says. 'And you know, doncha, that Harvey wants me to try sort things out between you and Stella Maria.'

Harvey Siegal is our lawyer. Best lawyer for murder in the state of Tennessee. I tell her I do know that and anything she can do would be greatly appreciated. 'Because what we can't have here,' she says, 'is you goin' back to the Nashville County Courthouse in ten days' time still not agreein' with each other.' I say right. 'It's mah intention to talk to you, and to talk to Stella Maria and find out jest what the problem is here.'

'Good,' I say. 'Great. You'll find the problem is Stella Maria's amnesia.' I wait for Stella Maria to object but she doesn't. Betty studies me, kind of squinting at me through eyes that would be piggy if she didn't have such thick dark lashes. 'What we have to get her to deal with is her loss of memory.'

'That so?' she says and she gives this some thought. Stella Maria will also be struggling with it. I'm almost tempted to call out and ask her what she thinks about that, but Betty has explained she wants to talk to us separately.

After a bit she says, 'Well, Ah don't think that's such a good starting point this mornin'. What Ah'm lookin' for this mornin' is some kind of thread, some little bitty thread Ah can pull to untangle the big knotty ball of wool that's come between you and your friend.'

'Title,' I nearly say, but *Knotty Ball Of Wool That Is Your Love* goes nowhere. The word wool has no place in a country song. 'You ought to ask me about Tom then,' I say. 'Harvey tell you about Tom Sinclair? He's a kind of thread.'

She shakes her head. She says Tom isn't where she wants to start. 'Why don't we start with what brought you to Nashville? Ah'd like to know all about that.'

And I think well that's just another way of getting round to Tom and I wonder how much she knows already. She said last night she knew the basics and I'd call Tom a basic but maybe Harvey wouldn't, even though it was Tom who hired him for us. 'Well I guess it was my destiny,' I say. 'Yeah, I guess you'd have to say it was always my dream to come here. Mine and Mammy's, may she rest in peace. And destiny brought me here.'

That's more than Stella Maria can take. 'What a load of shite. That's a great big pile of shite, Honey and you know it.' Her voice, let me tell you, doesn't know soft and sweet. She's lived in Cockfosters since she was four years old but her accent's as Ronanstown, Dublin as the day she left.

'It's not,' I say to Betty, who's picked up her notebook to swipe at a fly buzzing about her head. 'If I hadn't had the dream, I wouldn't be here. If I hadn't had the talent I wouldn't have had the dream. That makes it talent, dream and destiny. They all brought me here.'

'Sweet Mary Mother of God and her blessed son Jesus,' says Stella Maria. 'You never had a dream. You're so full of shite, it's pouring out your arse of a mouth.'

'You know what you've got, Stella Maria?' I call to her. 'No sense of place.' I apologise to Betty who's plainly not someone you insult with the language of the gutter.

She says, 'Forget it, Honey. Stella Maria's just railin' against her situation,' but she gets up and closes the window. 'You don't mind now, do you Stella Maria?' she says.

'Luck was another big part of it,' I say. 'Luck's on our side, thanks to Mammy. And I do. I thank her every day.' Then we sit in silence because I can't think of what else to say and Betty doesn't look like she can either. It's already so hot the fly that's been troubling her flops to the floor too knackered to move. 'You ever see a fly take a drink?' I ask after a while. She says why. I say I've only ever seen a wasp.

'Oh,' she says.

I'm embarrassed for Stella Maria. Really. Behaving like a fool in front of someone who wants only to help us. Eaten alive by rage and misery when rage and misery won't do us an ounce of good. Refusing to accept you can be amid great sorrow and still find joy.

I want to explain to Betty how I know this from experience. I don't want her thinking I'm this dose of pox crawling over the body of a poor dead banjo picker, may she rest in peace. I want her to like me. And I don't want her thinking Tom's a bigger shite than Stella Maria's probably already said he is. I want her to know he saved me from a future as sad as my past, which is why I'm not letting him down now.

She says, 'You wouldn't be thankin' Mammy for the death of Rita Mae though, would you, Honey?' And I have to dodge her gaze. The truth is, I do. Rita Mae was hell bent on ruining everything, most especially the happiness of Stella Maria, and it would be plain hypocritical of me to grieve for her. I hated her for what she did to Stella Maria and I wanted her out of our lives. We both did and fate said, 'Girls, me too.'

Betty's eyes drag mine back to her. 'You know something?' I say eventually. 'I loved Rita Mae like a sister.' It's only a small lie because there are sisters whose love is so small it's hate. 'We sang in perfect harmony. We had the same music running through our veins. It related us.'

Betty nods. She appreciates I was born with a powerful affinity for the US culture and that my poetry springs from the roots music of its southern states. She might not be overly fond of the genre but she isn't stupid about it the way people

11

in Cockfosters can be. 'I'll always be indebted to her,' I say.

This upsets Stella Maria so much, she comes bursting through the fly screen door yelling, 'For what, for what? Wake up, Honey, wake up and smell the frying.' Which would be shocking if it weren't stupid.

'You wake up Stella Maria,' I say. 'You've sent yourself to the chair already because you've turned your back on joy.' She's still wearing the clothes she had on yesterday. 'I'm sorry for you. You were born with a handicap called your mother . . .' I get no further because she's on top of me, her face inches from mine, spitting venom at me.

'Go. Fuck. Your. Grandfather's. Dog,' she says. I reply I would if I had a grandfather, or even a dog. Betty tells her to sit down and please could we stop talking about frying when the state of Tennessee doesn't fry anyone and the charge against us doesn't attract the death penalty, as we both know very well. And she says to me could I keep personalities out of it.

'Sure,' I say, 'Personalities aren't the point.'

Betty says what is the point? Stella Maria says the point is my stupid, ignorant self. I say no, this is the point. That every minute of every day you're this far, a centimetre, less than a centimetre, an eyelash, away from personal catastrophe.

One minute you're walking along the street thinking nothing, bits of food rattling around inside you, and the very next, something falls out of the sky, rips into your brain, splatters grey slime over the woman next to you and you're a vegetable. People are saying will we switch her off or spend the rest of our lives turning her.

'Whose tragedy's that, Stella Maria?' I say. 'Everyone's. But the biggest one is the brainless person not expecting it. She's walking down the street and she doesn't know how lucky she is. She's not thinking any minute I might be a vegetable, or a vegetable turner. She's not thinking is this breath my next to last so I'd better make the most of the time

I've got. She's doomed. Do you see that Stella Maria? After all we've been through?'

She shakes her head. She says what a liar I am and why don't I keep my goddam trap shut. But why should I? 'Look at you, Stella Maria,' I say, 'turning your back on everything we ever wanted from the day we met.'

She gives the hammock a great shove to make me fall out of it but I don't. She calls me a psychopath and she stomps off to the telly in the den to watch more news about us when all they're showing is what they showed yesterday, us leaving the courthouse, because nothing's happened since. Watching the news is all she's done since we heard about Rita. Driving herself crazy, as if we're all the news there is. I look at Betty and shrug. Betty has no comment.

Stella Maria's anger blows about the place like a fiery wind, changing the smell in the air, so Betty says maybe we'll wind up the session for today. I say OK. And she goes in as well, leaving me to my thoughts which are as follows. Stella Maria had better pull herself together or we'll never get our defence in order. It's a stress, no one's saying it isn't, she's hurt I'm not denying it, and it accounts for her being off her trolley. But she needs to be cool.

I swing back and forth, making a breeze for myself where there is no breeze and I think well I still love her very much, she is still my best friend and I'd do anything to make her life happy. Also, maybe at this very minute, I'm luckier than she is. I go to find her to make the peace. I stand in front of the telly so she has to look at me and has to listen to me. 'Stella Maria,' I say, 'You have to be cool. It's going to be fine because I'm going to make it fine.'

She says this just isn't possible. Actually what she says is, 'Are you out of your fucking goddam mind?'

3

God, the disappointment. The kitchen cupboard is full of seeds and stuff. Not a sliced loaf in sight. Only half tempting thing is the Froot Loops if you like a multi-coloured cereal. What's Betty doing with Froot Loops? She's got two king size boxes in here. I finish a bowl before I've even left the fridge so take a packet to my room, decide I can't eat them dry and go back for the milk.

It's a pretty nice room. Bare but OK. Walls and ceiling all white, curtains the same as in Stella Maria's and just the one picture on the wall. A tree. Painted by B Beecher 1996. Betty is a great lover of plant life. Only thing I don't like is the stink of moth balls coming off the mosquito net that hangs over the bed like some big-bummed bride.

I eat till I stop being hungry then I shove the dish, the Froot Loops and the milk carton under my bed and think what to do next when this is not a place where I've ever done anything. First thing is to open the window to let the pong out. What I let in is the smell of goat but I lean out the window anyway to clear my head of the mess of thoughts scrambling my brain and they're all about Stella Maria.

Rita Mae used to say, 'The girl's a leech. You'll never make it with her hangin' off your neck.' But Stella Maria said the same about Rita Mae so what does that tell you? Only that they hated each other.

Betty will be trying to get one of us to change our story but I'm not changing mine. Not for anything. Stella Maria might live her life on the edge of a tantrum but no way am I letting her go to jail. I can't believe she doesn't appreciate that's where she'll end up if her only alibi is a sulk.

I truly think she's gone deranged and if it comes to my word against hers, I'll sound saner. With any luck it won't come to that. With any luck, Betty will make her see reason. She'll talk to her, force her to see the hole she's in and show her the only way out is the one I'm offering her.

Meantime, I'm going to relax and enjoy the scenery. These hills are so still and quiet and so chock-full of stories you can hear them on the wind if you listen long enough. You can hear anything you want, once you stop hearing CNN from the den. 'Piss off, goat,' I say because the stupid animal has made a run at me even though there's a wall between us.

The difference between me and Stella Maria is where she's railing, I'm not, where I'm an artist, she's not. While she can only sit hour after hour in front of the telly fretting over the horror of our situation I can get on with my music. I write songs, sing them, make tapes, play them, just like I've always done. The difference between her and me is where her mother gave her nothing except life and sustenance for twenty three years, mine gave me my music.

Mammy was a cabaret singer from Cork but her heart was in country. I was tapping my foot to the country greats before I ever left her womb. My father was also a musician but I have no interest in his input. As far as I'm concerned he's a dead man. His name isn't even on my birth certificate. He and my mother met when they were working on a cruise ship and I was conceived at sea, so technically I belong to nowhere, which suits me.

I put it into *Take One Egg*, a song about life in a single parent family I wrote when I was no more than thirteen.

Take one egg, add mother's milk
Beat in tear drops and what you get is me
Born in a shack by a railroad track
But conceived somewhere at sea.

To be fair, I was borrowing from the life of Merle Haggard, most famous song *Okie From Muskogee*, who was born in a shack by a railroad track which I wasn't.

I was born in Euston and moved to Cockfosters when I was six. I met Stella Maria first day I set foot in the neighbourhood and I threw a stick at her to stop her staring. I had a ukulele slung across my chest and she couldn't take her eyes off it. Of course we had a dream. We had a dream from the very first day she heard me sing.

Wasn't she the one who told me to get off my goddam bum or die a lonely death from chlamydia in Cockfoster? Wasn't she the one who said music was a god-given gift not to be squandered? I love Stella Maria but I've been enduring her moods for fifteen years and this one has me at the end of my tether. I fish my fags out from under the pile of clothes on the floor, ferret about under the bed for my guitar, check my jeans pocket for my mobile and head out into the garden where the sun is high in the sky and no one's sulking.

The garden is Betty's pride and joy. She took me on a moonlit tour last night while we were enjoying our final smoke of the day and Stella Maria was clearing up. 'You always use a pipe?' I asked her

'Always,' she said. I waited for her to offer me a puff but she didn't.

There were a billion stars in the sky but you couldn't see a single one. You looked up and all you could see were trees and shadows of trees. It spooked me half to was like a pig in shit. 'Ah regard myself as custod finest work,' she said. She took me to her favourite spo a hundred steps to the bottom terrace which is where I h right now to sit on the swing that's looped over a big old cherry tree that never bears fruit. There's a table and bench down there which Betty says is a fine place to sit when the sun's going down.

I sing for company as I scoot through the jungle. I sing *Far As I Can See*, an idea I've been playing with which has two meanings, one about lookin' out and the other about lookin' in – *I love you far as I can see/ But far as I can see's not far/ Cos love is blind, don't you find, don't you find, don't you find?* – and I'm just thinking does this garden ever end or am I going in circles when suddenly I'm in sunshine and ahead of me are the steps which go down and down and down to where the land drops away to the river. I know at once what Betty loves. No one can see you except the birds swooping out of the valley and all you have to distract you is nature's beauty.

I climb on to the swing and push myself so high I can see the spire on the little wooden church Betty says has a sign out front saying Jesus Wants You For a Sunbeam. That could make you puke, if it caught you unawares, couldn't it?

I pick up my guitar and strum a few chords to see if I can make the melody work but I can't so I light a fag and dial Tom's number knowing he won't answer. Talking to him keeps me sane now Stella Maria's nuts. I phone him every day, sometimes three, four or five times and mostly just leave messages. I speak to him in secret, to spare Stella Maria.

'You've reached the phone of Tom Sinclair. Please leave a message.' Tom's voice is London with a bit of somewhere up North which betrays his roots though he never discusses them.

I leave a message. 'This is how you get here,' I say. I tell him how, where and when to find me.

...the style of *Kurt & Courtney* about
...t Cobain but he thinks my story is
...s its combination of guts plus tragedy
...s of my life. What drew him to it in the
...terrible luck and the chances of ever

...fe is just a series of possibilities and out-
com...........ick is what turns one into the other, doesn't
matter whe..... you do it all right or you do it all wrong. He
offered me the possibility of a lifetime, to make my mark as a
country singer in the home of country singing, and it was
Stella Maria who said grab it, the outcome is guaranteed. It
was Stella Maria who said 'Honey, look at the all deadbeats
you've trusted and tell me why you don't trust Tom.'

Now, she can't bear to see him or speak to him or have his
name mentioned in her presence. Now I have to pretend
there is no Tom in our lives. Not because he broke her heart
twice, she says, but because of his callousness. She can't, she
won't, she never will forgive his callousness.

Tom filmed the death. He filmed the brick falling. He was
on the roof at 11.05 but at 11.25 he was on the fire escape and
we know he was because he has film showing not just the fire
escape but Rita Mae in the last seconds of her life. He loves
that footage as much as Betty loves her garden. He thinks it's
a gift from God, a sign that he is destined for greatness
because it says everything he wants his film to say.

'It's perfect,' he said when we were viewing the rushes the
day Rita died. I could see from his face how big the break was
for him. But Stella Maria flipped. I thought she was going to
kill him she hit him so hard in the face. Personally, I don't
have a problem with it. It's not like he meant to film the
flipping brick. Police took it off him, anyway.

I yodel to warm up and my voice echoes around the valley
like the lonely lament of a miners' daughter from days gone
by. Woodman's daughter. This is logging country. I sing *In*

My Tennessee Mountain Home, words and music Dolly Parton, because it was Mammy's favourite and I know she's with me.

I close my eyes and give it all I've got so I don't hear Stella Maria creeping up on me until she says, 'You want to die of sunstroke?' She's standing right next to me, bottle of water in one hand, my hat in the other, not smiling exactly, but not scowling either and this is how quickly her mood swings these days. One minute she's wanting me dead, the next she's frightened my voice will dry out unless it's watered. She hands me the bottle and I take a swig, then she tosses me my hat and I put it on my head.

Stella Maria didn't become my manager officially until we came to Nashville but she's been managing me ever since my mother died nine years ago because this is what she likes to do. Even when I was sharing my house with Josie, Mammy's mother, Stella Maria was always checking there was food in the place and we didn't have rats. Her mood swings are taking us to hell and back, but she has a heart of gold, I'd never say she didn't. I hate it that she's letting herself go, like this.

'You had a shower since we got here?' I say.

'What's it to you?' she answers. Under normal circumstances, Stella Maria is meticulous about her appearance. Stretched out on the bench with her straw hat over her face, she looks soft and small despite the pounds she's put on these past few weeks from snacking in front of the telly. She isn't tall, five feet three, she has the very dark hair and the very blue eyes that run in her family. Also an overbite. Her features are small as well. Her boobs don't look small of course. Even flat on her back, they're her most striking feature. I have no boobs, being skinny, but I'm four inches taller than she is so we're probably covered by the same amount of skin.

'Play me something,' she says.

'What?'

'*Little Jim.*' I want to oblige her but I'm just not in a Little Jim mood. I start anyway. Key of D.

Twenty fours hours was all I knew you
Then God said come to Him, But Little Jim oh oh oh . . .

I stop because we don't need any more sadness here. Stella Maria's fists are clenched, she's kicked off her shoes and her toes are curling over the edge of the bench.

'Please be happy, Stella Maria,' I say.

'Why?' she says.

'The birds are singing, the trees in the valley are dancing, next month I'll be twenty-one and we'll have a great big party.' She says party her mother's fat arse. And it's true. Her mother has one big arse and a temperament so disgusting it puts hers well in the shade.

I give her a few lines of *Still Doin' Time*, words and music J Moffat and MP Heeney, best version George Jones, finest living country singer, and she says, 'Fuck off, Honey.' So without my fingers missing a beat, I slide into *Snowbird* (words and music G Maclellan), singing after the style of Lynn Anderson.

'*Spread your tiny wings and fly away/ Take the snow back with you where you came from on that day.*' Lynn's personal tragedy was losing custody of her two children to her ex-husband Spook Stream. '*The one I love forever is untrue, And if I could, you know that I would fly away with you.*'

'Would you?' Stella Maria says. And I'm saved from answering by Betty appearing on the top terrace with a couple of suits in tow and I'm so overjoyed I throw my hat high into the air and yell for joy.

4

I've been waiting for these guys without knowing I was waiting. 'It's Dick,' I say. 'Dick and that other guy.' Stella Maria jumps to her feet, tugging at her clothes to make her shorts longer and her T-shirt less tight.

'Jerry,' she says. She hates them both, and they're running down the steps towards us.

'Be nice to them,' I say but I can see from her face she's devastated to have the place contaminated by record people. She hates everyone at Moonshine because she thinks they hate her and I know she wants to hop over the fence and disappear down into the valley to escape them but she can't. Dick's A&R and Jerry's something on the business side, which is her department even though everyone, including herself now, is pretending it isn't.

Dick knows country backwards, which knocks me out when, until recently, I was the only person I knew who did. He used to be all picky about the early stuff but now he's my greatest fan after Stella Maria. I could love him if he wasn't so big and fat and sweaty. I know it's down to him that the label has been so great about our arrest. When I told him about the bail conditions, he said, 'Listen Honey, you take it easy,' which Stella Maria said was code for, 'You're dumped.' But Tom spoke to Merv Pickett, my producer, and Merv said no way was I dumped. People just needed to see me out of the judicial woods before committing themselves to a release date for *Bettin' On Your Cheatin' Heart*. November is still a definite provisional for the album which has the definite provisional title of *Sweeter Than Honey.*

I'm so happy to see Dick anyway that I put my arms around his neck and kiss him on the cheek. 'Beautiful as ever, isn't she, Jerrah?' he says. 'Doncha just love that peachy English complexion?' Maybe he's holding me a little longer than is necessary but that's Nashville. 'Nice to see you again, Marie,' he says to Stella Maria. 'You remember Jerrah, doncha?' He calls Jerry, Jerrah. I call him Jerrah too. Stella Maria calls him Jerry as her ear's not sensitive to accents.

I shake Jerrah's hand. He's typical Nashville. From New York. About forty-two with a grey crewcut, a lot of sharp teeth and a tanned face that has as much expression as a cow hide. Smiling, he looks like a hacksaw, but I bet he once wanted to be a singer songwriter just like everyone else. Dick's different. Dick is local. He grew up fifty miles from Pigeon Forge, no more than a hundred miles west of here.

I say it's great they've come to see us and he says you know what? He has this cousin over the way a little whose neighbour's a snake charmer and he reckoned he could do with some hints right now on the charming of snakes. I think this is hysterical but everyone else is looking at their feet and my laugh falls flat right by the cherry tree. Then he says, 'Will I tell her, Jerrah? Will I tell her or will I keep her in suspense?'

Jerrah looks like he doesn't give a shit either way so Dick tells me. It's the news I've been waiting for. The news every country singer would kill for. Radio loves me. Radio's had a truly magnificent reaction to the single and everyone can let out one great big sigh of relief. *Bettin' On Your Cheatin' Heart* is an out and out winner no doubt about it, didn't he always say, and I'm on my way to sure-fire stardom. *Bettin'*'s after the style of Harlan Howard, the most revered songwriter in Nashville. 'What do you mean, magnificent?' I ask him.

'What I say. Magnificent. You should be proud of yourself. Everyone at Moonshine's proud as they were when, well I can't think, but they're proud as Punch, anyway.'

I scream. I hug him. I hug Stella Maria. I hug Betty. I'd hug Jerrah except he's already walking back to the house. Stella Maria's grinning in a sick kind of way at her feet and Betty's patting me on the back saying good job, good job, why don't we all go back up the house when it's so hot out here.

Betty and Stella Maria head up the stairs together and I tag along with Dick who's puffing and panting owing to his weight. I ask if he's told Merv. He says Merv's out of town. I say has he told Tom and he hasn't. I ask Dick if radio loves the trailer Tom's made to promote the film and Dick says the trailer's not radio's concern. It's more Jerrah's, being part of the overall marketing campaign. 'What radio loves is you and your song,' he says.

Stella Maria has disappeared by the time we make the porch, which is sad when it's such a great moment for us, but I don't look for her. Betty says to make ourselves comfortable while she gets some refreshment, so I hop up on to the hammock and Dick rests his bum on the little table which isn't too clever when there's nothing little about him. Jerrah stands.

I'm smiling at them and Dick's beaming back. Then he stops beaming and says could we discuss something serious for a minute. I say hang on, I'll call Stella Maria out but he says no, no, no and he's looking over his shoulder like she's the last person he wants called. He lowers his voice so I can only just hear him. 'She's . . . now don't take this the wrong way, Honey . . . we couldn't be more excited about the way things are going for you, could we Jerrah . . . she's, Maria's a, well hang . . . Jerrah here's been speaking to Harvey about how the case is going, how it looks to the naked eye, and she's giving us this little cause for concern.'

'Stella Maria?' I say.

He nods. 'We're a little concerned about Stella's position.'

Jerrah says, 'Stella Maria.'

'You bet,' Dick says. I tell them well, her position is the same as it's always been. She's my manager and my closest friend. Dick says no, he's sorry no, this isn't what he means. 'Concerning the sad death of Rita Mae Rainbow. Her position in that respect.' I say oh in that respect, Stella Maria is very, very sorry.

'Ah'm sure she is,' he says. 'But this confusion over her whereabouts.'

I see where he's heading but I'm not letting this take away from my joy because you grab joy when it comes your way and you hang on to it as long as you can.

He says, 'Honey, your friend is bein' accused of murder. She denies it and we believe her, we really do, but she's got nothing that proves she didn't do it 'cept you saying she was with you. That would be fine, if she wasn't saying she wasn't.' I tell him I know. We all wait for me to say something else but I don't have anything else to say. 'The feeling is, Honey, that you're only saying that to protect her.'

I give the hammock a push so it swings into the porch then out into the clearing under the ash tree and I say well, she was with me, no two ways about it, but she has some kind of memory loss brought on by shock. Dick and Jerrah give each other a look.

Dick says, 'Your story, Honey, is all that connects you to this terrible crime.' I go to interrupt him but he won't let me. 'Believe me it is a terrible crime with this poor young girl just hurrying along the street to meet her friends, in the prime of her life, her talent as yet unfulfilled, everything to live for, and she's struck down dead, for no apparent reason.'

I say, 'Well her luck just ran out. It happens.'

Dick says, 'Pardon me?'

Jerrah says that's a very cool way of looking at it and I say what other way is there. A brick fell on her head. Dick says, 'Honey's an orphan,' so I say nothing. Then Dick clears his throat. 'It's not an event you want to be associated with – unnecessarily – when you are on the brink of stardom. This is what Ah'm trying to say, Honey. Radio loves your story but they don't love your best friend bein' a murderer. You want a record but not a record.'

Dick's made a joke and Jerrah goes heh heh heh. I start to say, 'You know she isn't,' but he's in such a hurry to assure me he wants to believe me that he leans forward and drags the table forward so for a minute it looks as if both he and it are going to pitch into me. He recovers at the last minute but the fright has made him pour with sweat. He takes a big, grey hankie out of his pocket and mops himself down. Jerrah's not sweating. Jerrah's face is dry as Oklahoma dust.

I tell them I don't really understand it. Radio likes me, they like my music, everyone likes Tom's film so the court thing is just a formality. And Dick says, OK, OK, and holds up his hand as if there's a jumble of thoughts to sort out here when there's no jumble. Am I sure Maria was with me, he asks, and I say totally. It's just a matter of time before she remembers. Betty is doing her best. I say they can all relax because at the next hearing, he has my word, the case will be dismissed. Dick smiles. 'Hear that Jerrah?'

Jerrah says, 'Rita Mae was a beautiful young girl. A fine banjo player.' I say I know, but Jerrah looks like I don't. What's his problem? I might cry now goddamit. Dick leaves the table and tries to put his arm around me, which isn't easy because hammocks are an awkward shape for that kind of thing.

Dick says last thing he wants to do is upset me. I'm a big, big, talent, a one-off, I'm going to be a big, big star, an unprecedented success given my place of birth. 'Isn't that so, Jerrah?'

'You got it,' Jerrah says. 'You just need to be aware, Honey, you and Stella Maria, that we would have difficulty marketing a product tarnished by the death of a lovely young musician who was not only a rising young star in her own right but a fine young American. You are, of course, not American.'

Now I really am pissed off. Rita Mae was no rising star. I say I thought her deal was that she'd risen a couple of times then sunk without trace. This is not what either Dick or Jerrah wants to hear. Jerrah says he thinks he'd better send someone from Publicity to talk me through my position. Dick says, 'You bet,' and at a nod from Jerrah, they get to their feet. Even though Betty has just staggered through the fly screen door bearing a tray spilling with local hospitality, they're out of here.

'You keep on practising Honey, you hear?' Dick says. 'You got a great loud voice. And we want the whole world to hear it.' Which makes me feel better. He bends to kiss me and his face is damp as a prairie swamp.

Jerrah says, 'You found an inspired collaborator in Rita Mae. I know you appreciate that.'

'May she rest in peace,' Betty says.

'Amen,' says Dick and he hurries down the porch steps after Jerrah.

5

I don't know how much Stella Maria heard but it almost doesn't matter. She'll be feeling betrayed again. She thought she was going to be safe from everyone out here but she can't be because life goes on. I'm wondering how to distract her when Betty says why don't we eat out tonight and everything immediately looks up. Stella Maria says OK, where?

She loves eating out. I'm not saying she's a lunatic we keep under control with food. Just if you read her right, you can snap her out of her misery, because she's a sulker but she's not a miserable person. I say, 'What about the Cracker?' We love the Cracker and I know there's one back on the interstate because I saw it on our way out and I bet Stella Maria did too. Archie, who introduced us to them, said it was the finest cuisine this great country has to offer and we agree with him. Stella Maria's favourites are the meat loaf dinner with potatoes plus two veg followed by baked apple dumplin'.

Betty says do we mean the Crackerbarrel Country Store and I tell her we do. She says well she's never eaten at one of those establishments and I say then she doesn't know what she's missing. I'm thinking however that their fancy fixin's might not be her cup of tea when she likes bean sludge. The Cracker's specialities are country ham and biscuits, country fried steak etc. But the chance is too good to miss. And this is another example of how luck works.

Betty's a stinker in the kitchen and it could totally suck having to eat her food day in day out. But if she gets into the Cracker the way we are, not only will we get to eat the food we like best in the world, we'll get to ride across the rolling countryside, twenty minutes there, twenty minutes back and that will bring great relief from the tedium of incarceration.

'Do they do bean chowder?' I say to Stella Maria.

She says, 'I'm going up front with Betty.' Like I care. She's let me off the hook for the time being only, is what I understand from this. She says nothing all the way there, slumping against the door of Betty's rattling old jeep thing and staring out the window, punishing me, even though I know all she's doing is going over in her head the vegetable choice of the day. The Cracker has a special veg for every day of the week. Saturday baby lima beans, Sunday boiled cabbage, Monday corn bread dressing. I can't remember Wednesday.

Just as well she's not talking because I can't stop. I want someone to appreciate what a huge deal it is that radio has taken to me. 'You can't get to be even a small country star without radio backing. It's the most sensational thing that's happened to me since I got here,' I say. Betty doesn't respond straight away and Stella Maria doesn't respond at all.

'Radio's the key. You think finding a producer is, then you find a producer, you think finding a label is, then you find a label, you think getting the label to like your song is then the label likes the song. Turns out all that really matters is what radio thinks. Radio likes you, then you get played. You get played, then you get heard. You get heard and the public likes you, then you're away.'

'Well that's great,' Betty says. She's doesn't turn to look at me and I know she still doesn't get the magnitude of the thrill.

'You don't get played and you're over. Even George Jones and Dolly. They don't get played because they're old. You wouldn't believe what it's done to their sales. And they're all-time greats.' Betty says well maybe they're not all-time greats but greats from a previous era.

'No way,' I say. 'An all-time great's an all-time great. Country radio just decided no one wants to hear them. Country radio doesn't know shit. I'm sorry Betty. I'd boycott it if I had a bigger fan base.'

Stella Maria suddenly whips round and I rear back in my seat in case she's going to bash me for saying shit when I had a go at her for her language, or to bash me for admitting I don't have a big fan base. 'You got your seat belt on? Put it on Honey, you idiot.' I do.

'I mean I'm grateful it likes me but truth is, Betty,' I say, 'country radio has betrayed its origins and it could break your heart. Couldn't it, Stella Maria?'

She says if you had a heart, but she knows as well as I do. When we first hit Nashville she spent weeks tracking radio play to see what we were up against and we weren't up against anything I admired. Just all this crossover stuff so people who like rock 'n' roll and pop get to like country without even noticing.

'You girls like the scenery?' Betty asks. I say it's great.

'It's amazing they like me when you think about it,' I say. 'I mean they must really like my voice because you can't get more traditional than me, can you Stella Maria?'

Stella Maria says, 'Radio's not the last word. The label has the last word. Label doesn't like you, then you're stuffed.'

Betty says this used to be black bear country. And buffalo.

Stella Maria says, 'Those the trees you were telling me about?' And I go to tell her I haven't discussed trees with her but turns out Betty has.

Betty says, 'White ash. Just beautiful, aren't they?'

I wish Tom would ring. He knows what it means to me. I have the conversation in my head I expect to have with him on the phone and I spend the rest of the trip just thinking about stuff, like the A&R man from a company I've forgotten who said music like mine put country back thirty years. 'Good,' I said. 'It's where it belongs.'

Stella Maria perks up at the restaurant once the menu's in front of her. We sit side by side like the best friends we are and she bends right down over the menu to read it because the light's not good and she's blind as a bat. She goes over and over it from start to finish, thinking first she'll have the fried shrimp platter, then the turnip greens cooked with ham hocks, then the chicken pie and I pretend I don't know what I'm having just to keep her company but already I've settled on Ruby's Dressed Up Chicken Sandwich Platter. Betty's having beans 'n' greens with corn bread.

In the end Stella Maria settles for the meatloaf. I can feel the heat coming off her body which is comforting and familiar and I think how much I want her to be back to normal. I want her to be pleased with the way things are, to trust me when I say the worst is over, and to forgive me. That's what I want most of all because we're a team. We always have been. I give her a nudge. 'Breaded fried okra,' I say.

'Breaded fried oprah,' she goes.

'Yum,' I say.

'Excuse me?' says Betty.

'Oprah,' I say. 'She's big in England.'

'She's big everywhere,' Stella Maria says.

'No way. She's skinny again,' I say.

'Then she'll be stringy,' says Stella Maria.

'Better have the carrots,' I tell her. Betty says she would recommend the carrots. As well as there being no men in her life, I don't think there's much television.

Stella Maria and me used to love watching Oprah. And

Ricky Lake. Stella Maria would head straight to my house from school, we'd fix ourselves a big plate of snack-style food, then we'd lie on the sofa in front of the TV and tune out. That was a lifetime ago.

'You never watch Oprah or Jerrah Springer?' I say to Betty. She says not that she can recall. Stella Maria orders carrots and corn then says why don't we check out the shop while we're waiting for our food and Betty says by all means. I hold my breath in case she's wanting to have a shout at me in private, but she just wants to check out the shop, which is mostly full of candy and cookies and her expression is calm and friendly, even if it is mainly in the direction of the candies.

Walking back to the table I put my arm through hers to show her how much I still care about her and though she shakes it off, I think we must look like a happy family group out for dinner even if Betty is Mammy's opposite. Maybe she's given herself to the Lord. My mother, may she rest in peace, loved sex. I never used to say rest in peace but people say it out here and I like it. Stella Maria says no way is she at peace. If she's in heaven, she's shitting herself, not an argument I choose to have with her.

Our food is hardly on the table when my mobile goes and we all jump away from it like it's exploded. I feel every heart at the table stop plus every drop of blood freeze. I pretend it's someone else's phone. We all know it's not Betty's. She doesn't have one. And it can't be Stella Maria's because hers is in bits after she chucked it at a wall the day we got taken to jail and she found all the messages on it were from Tom. We know it's my phone and we're pretty sure who's calling.

I keep eating, lifting food to my mouth, sticking it in, swallowing, waiting for it to stop, praying it will stop at once. Betty's watching Stella Maria who has put down her knife and fork and is glaring at the phone on the seat between us. She says, 'Turn that thing off, Honey will you?'

'Take the call,' Stella Maria says.

'Not while we're eating,' Betty says.

'Not while we're eating,' I say.

Stella Maria says, 'I know you talk to him. Talk to him in front of me.'

'I don't talk to him,' I say. Why upset her? The people in the next booth turn to take a look at us.

Betty says, 'Switch it off.' Stella Maria picks up the phone and hands it to me. I switch it off. 'Give it here,' Betty says. So I do. She drops it into her bag.

Stella Maria doesn't take her eyes off it, willing Tom, it looks to me, to come swooshing out like a genie trapped in a bottle even though she swears she hates him. Then she gets up and leaves the table, with her food hardly touched which is a terrible sign.

I ask to be excused and follow her to the car park where she's sitting in the gutter, her face all white and miserable, another terrible sign. Stella Maria making a spectacle of herself is a frightening thing. I sit down next to her. 'He asks after you every day.'

'You said you wouldn't speak to him ever again.' I tell her I didn't. She says, 'You promised.'

'I couldn't have, Stella Maria, because I can't and you know I can't.'

'You're a liar, Honey. You've been a liar all your life.' We've been speaking quietly but now she's on her feet. 'You call yourself my friend, you beg me to forgive you but how can I when I can't believe a word you say.' I'm on my feet too, telling her to shush. I touch her arm but she recoils, like my hand has leprosy. She's shouting. 'What's it take Honey? What's it take to make you see reason? You want me to hang? Well, I will. I will.'

People are staring and I know any minute a crowd will form so I tell her again to shut up. 'I won't fucking shut up,' she yells. 'You're a liar and a traitor not just to me but to everything we set out to do and I want nothing more to do with you.'

She's shoving me in the chest and I thank God when Betty appears at the restaurant door. I give her a look like help, help, but her eyes don't even flicker in our direction. She walks straight to the jeep, starts the engine and looks as if she's about to leave without us so I race across the car park and jump in the back. Stella Maria, torn between one hell and another, jumps on at the very last minute and we drive home in total silence.

I'm feeling bad. Bad but not choked as when it comes down to it, I have an optimistic nature. I stop feeling bad in any shape or form when I remember how happy I am in my professional life. But then I'm aware it doesn't feel so good, feeling this good when I know she feels so bad. *Doesn't feel so good/ Feelin' this good/ When I know you feel so bad . . .*

I work with the line the whole drive back. I lose myself in the thought so it's a great bolt from the blue when Betty, without warning, turns on both of us like a mad coyote. She pulls into the drive and switches off the ignition without a word, jumps out of the jeep and confronts us at the porch steps, her hands on her hips. She's so angry I think at first she's joking.

'OK you two, listen up. Y'all are goin' to your rooms and y'all are goin' to be makin' your minds up one way or the other. Either you buckle down to sortin' this thing out or Ah'm telling the judge to stick you in the penitentiary.'

6

She wouldn't mean it. She couldn't mean it. But what if she does? What's she want me to do? Say Stella Maria wasn't with me after all and leave her without a leg to stand on? She's the person I love second in the whole world and the person I love best would never forgive me when saving her is so, so simple. What's it matter, anyway, whether she was in the stairwell or whether she was with me? She didn't chuck the sodding brick and that's all that counts.

It's not even properly dark yet but I strip to my knickers and T-shirt, feeling sick then hungry because I didn't get to eat my chicken and I've only had Froot Loops in God knows how long. Also, pissed off that Betty has my phone so I can't get hold of Tom to confirm our date. Am I brave enough to ask Betty for it back given the mood she's in?

I practise a few microphone moves in front of the mirror while I think about it. Movement's not my best thing. 'Great oaf,' Stella Maria always says. She's an excellent mover, herself. Very light on her feet from years of Irish dancing. Only thing she ever did to make her mother proud, but she gave it up when she was eight and who could blame her?

An artist needs to see herself as an audience would. I'm kind of tall and gangling, with long auburn hair and an unusually wide mouth which I try not to open too wide when I sing. I do minimal movement. Even so you need to get it right. OK, I'm going to get the phone back.

'Come in,' Betty says. She's in the study tapping away at her computer and doesn't look up even though I'm standing right by her shoulder. Her study reeks of tobacco. Smell's hanging off the walls.

'Just came for my phone.' I say.

Now she looks up. She swivels her chair to face me and I see she's still pretty grumpy. 'You know, Honey,' she says. 'Ah don't think Ah'm going to give it back to you right now. Ah don't want you on the phone every two minutes to Mr Sinclayuh. Ah have nothin' against him personally, Ah don't know the man. But he's gettin' in the way.'

'He's not,' I say. 'I promise he's not, Betty. He's just doing his job.'

She says that may be but he's gettin' in the way of her doing her job. 'Ah don't want you on the phone to him, Ah don't want him callin' here, Ah want him out of the frame for just as long as it takes us to sort this out.' Then she gets up and opens the study door so I leave without putting up a fight. Bugger. She never gave me the chance to tell her what was already going to happen and she never gave me my phone back so I could stop it. Therefore, too bad.

I give it maybe an hour and when I hear her bedroom door close, I creep down the hall to have it out with Stella Maria. Her room's in darkness, apart from the moonlight shimmering through her curtains and she's flat on her back, snoring softly.

I pull the door behind me, creep across to her bed and grab her by the shoulder. She lashes out with her leg and I go flying. I try to land quietly but fall hard anyway, in a heap halfway across the room, like a Gatling boy in *Coward of the County*. I hold my breath and stay very still, waiting for the sound of footsteps in the hall, and I hear Stella Maria holding her breath as well.

I bury my face in my arms and lie still as a cat. Stella Maria clambers off her bed and tiptoes across the room. Before she reaches me, I bare my teeth into a horrible death smile, fill my eyes with anger then turn slowly towards her with a low growl.

'Get up,' she says, her anger all gone as I knew it would be. She nudges me with her foot then gets back into bed.

I say, 'Penitentiary? Who says penitentiary? I thought it was called the county jail.'

'That what you woke me up to say?'

'Betty's not bluffing,' I tell her. Stella Maria slides down under her sheet. 'You have to say you were with me. It's the only way.'

'But I wasn't,' she says. 'You know I wasn't.'

'You'll go to jail,' I say.

'So will you.'

'Is that what you want, when we're so close to making it?'

'Making what?' is all she says. I want to give her a good hard slap. I say what did she think the dream was then, when we got on that plane to Nashville? Who was she kidding? Herself or me?

She doesn't answer and I wait a couple of minutes and soon she starts to snore again so I tell her to drop dead. I can't be bothered with her, I really cannot.

I go back to my room, so cross I don't care if Betty hears me or not. I give my bed a couple of kicks which calm me down, then sit on the floor to think. 'Help,' I whisper. But the only advice Mammy gives me is to put on my headgear and get into bed because I have to wake up early.

I hate the sodding headgear. It's a wrap round brace thing with bits sticking off it and I'm wearing it to get a perfect bite.

'You sure have terrible teeth,' the dentist said when he first met me. Stella Maria laughed herself silly first night I wore it.

'The lonesome alien,' she said.

I set my alarm for 4.23, arrange the mosquito net so it hangs properly over the sides of the bed, then I strip to my skin and slide in. 'Please sort it out for me, Mammy,' I say, then I close my eyes and think of Paddy, my lost love, my only true love who helps me make it through the night. We can never be together. Fate has decreed it. And it would be a tragedy if I hadn't turned it into my inspiration.

Paddy is Stella Maria's brother. I wanted to marry him from the day he shoved me out of the path of a speeding car when I was ten and he was fifteen. He pushed me so I fell over, then he helped me up and brushed the gravel off my face. 'Stupid eejit,' he said. 'Watch where you're feckin' goin'.' I made him kiss me on my sixteenth birthday. He said, 'Honey I love you like a sister', but the kiss he gave me wasn't so brotherly.

Stella Maria said, 'Stay away from her, Paddy. Stay away from her or I'll get your legs broken.' She didn't know anyone who could break his legs but even so, we both knew not to inflame her. Ours was a secret love, stolen kisses over household jobs that he'd do for me whenever I could think of one and later, a whole week of passion that will live in my heart forever. For as long as I'd known him I'd dreamt of that week and of us running away to marry. But it's never going to happen now.

I imagine his arms about me, pulling me to him. I imagine him kissing my hair, my neck, my lips, I hear him calling me his gorgeous sweet thing and I let the tears roll down my cheeks because he never will again. I can see his beautiful face inches from mine, feel his long black lashes on my cheek and my fingers in his dark curly hair, like Stella Maria's but shorter. He's not tall but he's very strong and I miss him. 'I thought you loved me,' he said last time he held me which is five months and two days ago. He was smiling like he'd never believed me anyway.

'I do love you,' I told him. His blue eyes pierced my heart, searching for its true intention.

'But not enough,' he replied.

Then his blue eyes shone
And he was gone and my heart broke forever.

I ache for him, I truly do. But I've ached for my mother and I've ached for my brother Jimmy who died with her and I've even ached for silly old Josie, who died when I was sixteen. Josie loved Paddy almost as much as I do but she knew he'd never be mine. She took my hand in hers, mad old thing, and she said, 'Destiny doesn't deal the cards you want, just the cards you're meant to have.' And I screamed at her.

I can live with aching. An artist learns to turn pain into dreams and dreams into music or she'll end up a lunatic. It's what the great songwriters have always done. Harlan Howard and so on. Harlan Howard, best songs *I Fall To Pieces* and *No Charge*. I turned Paddy into the man of my dreams. And I dream of him every night.

7

I wake up because something's making my head my vibrate, but I can't find the alarm clock under my pillow, then I do and can't remember how to turn it off. It's pitch black outside. No moon on my side of the house, which is a title. I stagger to the bathroom to pee and am tiptoeing back when Betty calls from her room opposite the den, 'That you Stella Maria?' though I haven't even made a floorboard squeak.

'Honey. Just peeing,' I say and wish at once I'd said 'Yes' because she'd never have known the difference. I take my brace off and lie on my bed for two minutes to give her time to settle back down, then I pull on jeans, a T-shirt and my boots, whack some mascara on my lashes, gloss my lips and climb through my open bedroom window. I'm half in, half out when I see the goat. Not ten feet from me, head lowered and pointed in my direction.

I'm not a goat person even if I do have a special feeling for the poetry of the great outdoors. Betty keeps her for milk and she's on a long rope to give her plenty of scope for moving about, but what I can't decide from here is how long the rope is. She's looking at me, I'm looking at her, I'm breathing deep so's not to let her smell fear and then I hear a noise outside my room, Betty going to take a pee herself, so I have to make a move one way or the other.

Surely to God Mammy would protect me from a dangerous animal. I drop out the window. The goat runs at me and stops at the point of strangulation. I hug the wall and scamper to the edge of the house, looking like an escaped psycho except for my make-up. The dark's giving me the creeps but I dive into the far right corner of the jungle garden where there's no path and I trample my way through; I go like the clappers until I reach the top terrace and see Tom's outline down by the fence. I give myself a second before running down the steps to meet him. No point arriving in a state. He's sitting on the bench. 'Get back over the other side of the fence,' I say.

'What?' he says.

'You have to stay off the property. Betty says.' He frowns. I give him a kiss on the cheek but he's still unhappy so I put my arm about his shoulders and explain how Betty doesn't want us to have any contact with him for the time being owing to Stella Maria being so crazy.

He says, well how's that going to work? How can he film me if he doesn't see me? How can he film me when he's half dangling off a cliff?

I say I know. We're going to have to work something out but right now, it's dangling or nothing. I know he won't settle for nothing. 'I mean it,' I say. I lift his kit back over the fence.

'Jesus, Honey,' he says, 'who's going to know where I am this time of the morning?' But I tell him I wouldn't feel right so he climbs over as well. Then he studies me the way he always does, wanting to see if how I look is how he wants me to look. I'm used to him examining me in this manner even if it is weird. I just stare back. Once that stare was pure passion but not any more.

He's not handsome. You couldn't call him handsome because his face is too big, and he has a kind of stoop, like his head's too heavy for his body. Also he has no real style. His jeans are shapeless, his boots are dirty, his T-shirt's just a T-shirt. But he has something. He has a look that says money, a look that says confidence. Like he's a winner. It's appealing and he's changed for the better since we got to Nashville. His hair's blonder and shorter and his face is kind of sharper. Success must be doing something to him or for him: *Is what you're doing/ to me or for me/ are you . . .* nah.

He lights a smoke, gives it to me, then lights one for himself and sticks it in the corner of his mouth. 'You OK?' he asks. I nod. 'You talk to Stella Maria?' I say nothing. 'Why not? You said you would.'

'I talked to her.'

'Well what did she say?'

'She won't see you. She doesn't want me to see you. Nothing's changed from last time.'

He takes a big draw on his cigarette and stares up over my shoulder to where the dawn in breaking. 'All you have to say is that I love her.'

I'm sorry for him, but if he's missed his chance, he only has himself to blame. 'D'you talk to Merv?' I ask. He shakes his head. 'Why not?' He says he couldn't get hold of him. 'Did you try?' I can tell he didn't.

Last time I spoke to Merv was before we were arrested when he said *SweeterThan Honey*, featuring Rita Mae on twelve of the sixteen tracks we're considering, was the finest tribute a banjo picker ever had. 'Take care now,' he said. 'These are sad times.' Poor Merv thought he was Rita Mae's boyfriend but so did about fifty other guys. I told him to take care too but I haven't heard from him since and I hope he hasn't drunk himself to death from grief. I want to shake Tom for not seeing how important that is to me, but why bother? Getting tetchy with him is a waste when I'm so starved of his company.

'Hey,' I say. 'What about us? What about radio? Isn't it brilliant?'

He grins and reaches over the fence to hug me. He wants to know what it's like out here so I tell him while he's setting up his camera. It's a Sony DV Betacam with a mike stuck on the front plus many additional features which don't interest me. I'm a front-of-the-camera person, not a behind. He says, 'Bring the table closer to the fence.'

I say, 'No. It'll make me sweat. I don't want to look all sweaty.'

He says, 'No one minds a glow.' So I do and it's heavier than a water buffalo and I do feel myself go all moist on my forehead and top lip.

'Now look,' I say.

He tells me I'm perfect. But he climbs up on to the fence to arrange me so the view behind is exactly the one he wants. Then he gets behind the camera and says, 'Go.' Which could strike a person dumb if she wasn't used to it. I know what's required of me. He wants me to catch my story up from where we left off and where we left off was packing our stuff to leave Nashville with Archie and Stella Maria waiting downstairs ready to go.

I don't look into the camera right away. I save that for important moments like the one I get to when I've done the drive out and first impressions of Betty. 'Biggest news is that Dick and Jerrah turned up yesterday to tell me radio loves the song. They've had fantastic feedback and they came all the way out here to tell me. Getting radio backing is the dream of every country singer and the biggest blast for me since I was signed.'

'They bothered about the trial?' Tom asks. I say does he want to get on to that right now? The radio thing's so important. He says we covered it pretty well last time, when our hopes were up. I say OK. I tell him to go again. He says again, 'They bothered about the trial?'

'Dick and Jerrah are bothered about Stella Maria. They want me to say she wasn't in my room when Rita Mae died. But I'm not going to. And Betty's getting real mad at us for not agreeing. She says we have to get over it because we could both end up in jail and it's crazy.'

'Well it is,' he says. 'I mean she either was with you or she wasn't. And if she wasn't, you'd better say so or it'll blow your chances with Moonshine.'

'You think so?' I say, because he's never said this before, not on film. He's only ever told me to stick to my guns. No one would hold integrity and guts against me. In the faint light of the dawn, he winks at me and I see what he's getting at. He's looking for a good line. 'Everyone wants me to dump Stella Maria,' I say. 'But I won't. Not ever. It would break her heart.' Then I turn and look back up to the hills which, to me, is a nice touch.

'Shoot,' he says softly but he doesn't move from behind the camera. He just changes its focus so it's trained on a spot above and to the left of me.

I turn to look. A banshee in a white nightie is belting down the terraces, waving her arms and finally finding a voice like she was just too mad to locate it for a while there. 'Git off mah land,' she's yelling. 'Git off mah land. What you playin' at Honey when Ah expressly forbid it? Kindly git back to the house and Mr Sinclayuh, Ah presume you are Mr Sinclayuh, if Ah see you on mah land one more time without mah express invitation, Ah'll . . .'

I think she's going to say, 'blow your brains out.'

She says . . . 'get a court order.' But the words blast from her face like a mouthful of bullets.

8

Finally. Betty's study door has just opened and closed which means any minute she'll call me in. She's had me sitting out here on the porch till she was good and ready by which she meant until she'd finished with Stella Maria who's been carrying on like I'd dropped a brick on her stupid head. There's been a major scene here. Huge.

Didn't matter Tom said how sorry he was and I said how sorry I was. Didn't matter I said I hadn't disobeyed her on purpose, that she made the rule after I'd arranged to break it and there was nothing I could do about it when she had my phone. She said, 'You went behind my back.'

Tom tried to make it OK with her. He said, 'Miss Beecher, I was just doing my job. Honey was doing hers.' He pointed out he wasn't trespassing, being on the other side of the fence as requested by me out of respect for her wishes.

But Betty went, 'Mr Sinclayah, thayah is the letter of the law and thayah is the spirit of the law.'

I don't know what she went on to say because when I tried to make her see reason she turned on me so fierce I just ran, fast as I could, up the terraces and back through the jungle, scratching my arm really badly on a sodding branch. And I'll tell you what. She might look sweet but she is only sweet to a point.

As I got closer to the house, I thought if I could make it to the shower without Stella Maria seeing me, the whole thing might pass unnoticed because surely Betty wouldn't want to inflame matters. But I spotted her through the kitchen window soon as I rounded the corner and she saw me. I slammed the fly screen door so's not to look like I was creeping about the place and crossed my fingers she'd be sulking, but no chance. When Stella Maria's out of her mind with rage, she couldn't button her lip if she was in an attic, the Germans were coming and her name was Anne Frank. She was slathering peanut butter on slice after slice of the white bread Betty has bought for us specially. 'Y'all want coffee?' I said, relaxed as could be.

'Y'all?' she went, copying me. 'Y'all?' She was just about vomiting. She turned towards me with the knife raised and peanut butter dripping from it.

'Don't start,' I said, backing away. 'Put the knife down,' I said. She was coming towards me. 'Stay back.'

'Scared of dying, Honey? That your problem?'

'Put the fucking knife down,' I screamed. OK it looked blunt, but you get one of those butter knives in your eye and you know about it.

Betty, hearing my panic, flew into the house screaming, 'Stella Maria, no. Stella Maria, no.' But Stella Maria had dropped to her knees with her face in her hands and she was sobbing and sobbing and I was thinking sweet Jesus! I never once saw her cry before Rita Mae entered our lives.

When Betty saw the state of play, she turned on me like it was my fault. 'Oh Honey, Ah am so bitterly disappointed in you.' And I was disappointed with myself as Stella Maria's sobs were so pitiful I could hardly stand it. I moved towards

45

her. I wanted to hold her. I wanted to tell her there was nothing to cry about and I wanted to make her see the logic of it.

She's in love with the guy, right? Been in love with him from the day we met him according to her, love at first sight, one and only love etc, and here she is, treating him like he's her very worst nightmare in human form. 'He loves you, Stella Maria. Honestly,' I said. But Betty said to hush up at once and Stella Maria began this lunging as well as howling so I retreated to my room but Betty said please to go to the porch until she sent for me.

I'm so hungry I could be sick. I'm desperate for a bowl of cereal but don't dare leave the porch in case Betty calls me, finds me gone and thinks I'm disobeying her again. I could have another smoke but I don't believe my lungs could stand it. Stella Maria's been in there so long I've gone through half a packet. I'm itching to put the record straight. I have this very big feeling Betty's barking up the wrong tree.

First, I want her to know these aren't normal relations between me and Stella Maria. These are strained relations. Our usual relations easily accommodate Stella Maria's bad temper and all the stuff she complains about in me – laziness, self-centredness and blah. What she mightn't know is we love each other very much and our current situation is making it seem as if we actually don't.

Also what I want to explain to Betty, if she's calmer, is that if Tom can't keep up his filming on a regular basis, then all our hopes and dreams are down the toilet, including Stella Maria's and this will be a bad thing, whatever Stella Maria is saying. Dick might have said radio isn't interested in Tom's film but that's only kind of true. Tom told me Moonshine is in love with the package. My record, my life and his record of my life.

Stella Maria's just switched on the TV so I get to my feet but Betty doesn't appear at her window. I tiptoe over to look in.

She's at her desk and I know she knows I'm here. What's she playing at? I have feelings as well. Things might be going better for me than for Stella Maria but that's mainly down to our temperaments. I'm not coasting here. I'm having a small struggle what with one thing and another.

Just as I'm thinking sod it, I'll get my guitar and hop it, she calls me in. She says, 'Sit down, Honey' and I do, on the armchair with the floral upholstery, under the window. Betty's study is so cosy a body can't help relaxing. The walls are lined with books, there are lamps all over the place, including one that looks like a house on the corner of her desk. You expect to see photographs of her family, of some kids with a smiling husband, but there are none.

She's writing notes so I wait in silence, my hands getting clammy even though I'm enjoying the surroundings. Then she swivels on her chair to face me just like she did last night. 'This is how we're going to proceed,' she says, giving me no time to explain anything. 'We are putting this morning right behind us. Mr Sinclayuh is banned from the house. You will respect that or leave.'

I'm about to say may I phone him but think better of it. She says, 'Since we've made zero progress with the informal approach Ah thought would be most appropriate, Ah am now goin' to formalarz our relationship.' Then she begins this speech that you'd swear she's rehearsed she has it down so pat.

'Each of you will have two sessions a day with me, one in the morning and one in the afternoon. In between, you will think about what was discussed in the first session and report back to me in the second. You won't discuss with each other what you have said to me and nor may you ask me what the other has said, though Ah may, from time to time, ask you to comment on something the other has said. The point of these sessions is for me to discover what has gone wrong between you in the distant, medium and recent

47

past that has brought us to this truly wretched present. We'll start right now.'

I burst into tears, which is my usual response to anything I can't find words for and I disgust myself but not her. The robot goes out of her voice and she hands me a tissue. 'Honey, there's no need for tears now. Ah can help you but you're goin' to have to help yourself as well.' This makes me cry more. It's what comes of so much early tragedy. When you have a well of sorrow in your heart, it runs over any old time someone drops something in it, even if you have an optimistic nature.

First up, she says, she truly believes neither of us murdered Rita Mae so that's not an issue and I'm relieved to know it. Second up, she says, we have to face the fact that one of us is not telling the truth. If one of us has something to hide, the obvious question is why and the judge will want to know.

I say I know that. It's not like we haven't heard it a million times before.

She says, but do I? Do I really understand the significance? I say I do.

'OK,' she says. 'Then we're going to get to the bottom of it.'

The dynamics of our relationship are central to our defence, turns out. Betty wants us to collect our thoughts so she has all the information she needs to resolve things between us. 'That OK with you?' she asks. I can't exactly say no and, to be honest, it's a relief not to have her yelling at me or threatening me with the judge. 'Sometimes it'll be hard. Some days you'll breeze through it but what we want in the end is a clear picture. Clear as the view of the valley from the bottom terrace,' she says.

I tell her I'll do my best and I will. I really will.

9

Now I'm sitting on the swing, with proper food at last, a tuna sandwich Stella Maria left on my bed with a note saying Eat This. Collecting your thoughts is OK. It's like collecting mementos from places you've kind of forgotten and seeing them differently. *From A Distance* was a great title but the song sucked.

This morning was fine in the end. 'Let's look at the big picture,' Betty said. But we ended up talking about Mammy. She thought the big picture was me and Stella Maria but now she knows you can't look at me and Stella Maria and not see our mothers.

I explained Stella Maria and me had this love/hate relationship and she said hate could be as binding as love. I told her that was so right. I was frightened she hadn't understood our real closeness. She said she wasn't sure she did but she hoped she soon would. I said our relationship had always been complicated.

'By what?' she wanted to know.

'Our mothers,' I told her. 'Hers is a devil. It comes between us.'

'What else?' Betty said.

'What else what?'

'What else complicates it?' And I couldn't really tell her. The truth is everything complicates it, but what's the use in telling her that when she only has eight days. Eventually I said, 'Well, it's complicated by Stella Maria thinking she's superior when she isn't. Her thinking I can't get by without her when she can't get by without me.'

Betty said, 'How's that?'

I said, 'You can't be a manager without someone to manage, can you? Without me she isn't a manager.'

There was a noise at the study door at this point and I jumped out of the chair. Betty went to check it and found nothing, but I was scared enough to lose my train of thought and when I found it again I wasn't so sure I wanted to pursue it. 'That the only way she makes you feel inferior?' Betty asked finally and it sounded rude saying nothing, so I settled for telling her stuff Stella Maria already knows I think. Telling anyone stuff she doesn't already know I think would be off.

'I look at her and I'm just grateful there's no family in my background. I've put my suffering into my music and I take comfort from that. Title, anyway. *The hate in my heart for the man that I love.*'

Betty wanted to know if I always saw my life in song titles. I told her I did. She said had it occurred to me that it might be distorting my perspective. I said no, it cleared my vision. Was she implying I was a freak? She said of course not. It was obviously in my blood. Then we got on to my blood and how I came by my cultural affinity with country music.

And now I'm reflecting, I'm looking at the gorgeous view and I'm thinking it was lucky for both of us Mammy wasn't too fertile because she was terrible about birth control. I've never once found myself unexpectedly expecting. *Unexpectedly Expecting You* is great title.

Betty wanted to know about my father, but I said there was

nothing to tell. He was a bag of sperm attached to a guy who doesn't even know I exist. I don't have any thoughts about him and I don't want to. Mammy met him when she was young and healthy and looking for love. 'You can fall for anyone in this condition,' I said, but I don't know that Betty understood me.

My mother never stopped looking, never stopped hoping for her own true love. She had many bad experiences as a result of her capacity for giving, but she stayed true to her hope. 'And she wasn't the slag the O'Sheas say she was either,' I said. 'She didn't shag about.' I waited for the door to fly open but it didn't. 'Shagging about,' I said to Betty, 'is a matter of opinion. A shag might be a shag but about is open to interpretation.'

Betty said, 'Not shag, Honey. Shag is crude. Intercourse is better.' Which I guess it would be for a virgin.

Fatima O'Shea had it in for my mother from the beginning because they were both Irish and Fatima was scared witless the neighbours would tar them with the same brush. She thinks of herself as middle class which is the danger if you live in Cockfosters.

Maybe Mammy did go looking for pain. Josie said she did and Josie was her mother. But you think about looking for and you think about coming your way and where's the difference? This is the kind of thought that tantalises a wordsmith. In my view, the only difference is how soon you see it in your general vicinity.

Mammy fell for my father because he was like a god to her, but by the time they hit shore, she was pregnant and off him so she never told him. It would be nice to think he searched high and low for her for many years, his hard heart breaking for the love he'd been faking, but I know my mother's taste.

My father would've been the standard pig, even if I do have his genes in me. Mammy must've got on a pig roll when she was a teenager and she just never got off it. She went for pigs the way other women go for broad shoulders and she always thought they were different until they hit her. I loved my mother. I loved her very much and I miss her to this day. May she rest in peace, Amen. We're right in tune Mammy and me.

Always in tune with love's sweet mandolin
You opened your heart and you took me right in.

It's not easy to find the proper balance between bitter and sweet in a lyric about the death of a loved one. Not easy to find a balance between love and hate in a relationship with someone like Stella Maria. Sometimes I think would we have been friends if fate hadn't thrown us together but we are and that's that.

Betty wanted to talk more about mothers but I said could we do it later because I was faint from hunger. She said sure, but the family angle was interesting. She'd like to look at it some more.

A bird soars up out of the valley and circles in the jungle garden. 'OK with you?' I ask the bird. And it must be because Mammy sends me a sight for sore eyes. A boy working on the garden up in the middle terrace with a bum to inspire the stupidest poet.

10

I have to wait until dinner to ask about him. The afternoon session was a dead loss all round because Betty wanted to talk about Mammy some more and I didn't want to so she asked me about ambition. She wanted to know was I always ambitious.

The thought had never struck me. I said I supposed so. She said how but I couldn't explain it to her. Just that I always knew I was a singer and writer of songs and that singers and writers like their songs to be heard, so I always knew that one day I would be looking for an audience.

'So you came to Nashville in search of an audience, just like you always wanted.' I said yes, kind of. I came to Nashville because country music and the place that inspired it and the people who inspired it were in my heart and soul. 'It was like ... a calling,' I said. 'Know what I mean?'

She kind of didn't but I couldn't explain it any more than that so we sat there looking at each other in case I tried. I said, 'Maybe we should have a smoke to relax us.' Betty said she never smoked when she was working and not in the house anyways. I said well the room sure smelt like tobacco and then realising this could cause offence added how much I liked it. 'Beats goat,' I said.

She said, 'Ah am unaware of Marigold havin' any particular odour.' I said it wasn't particular, just hers, and no way bad but I preferred pipe and then I shut up. She waited and waited but nothing else came out of my mouth so I asked if I could go to my room and she said yes. I appreciated that.

I flopped on to my bed all tuckered out by the conversation, put my headphones on, listened to some tapes and tried not to think about stuff. You've got to give your brain a break. Josie used to tell me that. Her brain was on permanent holiday.

Now we're back in the dining room and Betty's made this rice dish for dinner. It's the same colour as the beans but I see vegetables in it and burnt bits plus some kind of herb that must be used in hospitals to make people throw up. Stella Maria's getting it down. She'd eat a dog's turd, if she were hungry enough. I can't. I say, 'I'm allergic to rice.'

Betty says she doesn't think so when rice is so bland. I say I think it's the bland I'm allergic to. She says we need to eat complex carbohydrates so try it, at least. I put some on my fork and hold it near my mouth but I'm thinking my own mother never put pressure on me to eat and Josie certainly didn't so what's going on here? I ask her about the gardener boy I saw on the bottom terrace. She says, 'Abraham. What about him?'

I say 'Well who is he?' And she looks like she's only half interested in telling me.

'He's someone who comes every day to do work about the place. Ah give him a list of duties and he carries them out. Don't you go distractin' him now.'

'Why?' I say and laugh. She says because he's the preacher's son. I laugh again. I say he sure doesn't look like it from the back. Then Betty asks Stella Maria how long since she painted anything and I say, 'She never paints' but Stella Maria says, 'About a month.'

Well that's a lie. Stella Maria never paints. She's sucking up to Betty because she knows it's Betty's hobby. So let her. Nothing to do with me. 'How old is he?' I ask pleasantly.

Betty says twenty-three, she guesses. Maybe twenty-six. Then she asks Stella Maria what kind of paints she likes and Stella Maria says watercolour. She's going for it, truly. But I'm sorry. I'm going to have to talk because I honestly can't eat. The food on our plates is pigs' swill, no it's the bits of swill the pigs couldn't stomach.

'Eat something, Honey,' Stella Maria says. 'Skipping meals is pathetic.' She says this to get at me. She knows I don't have an eating disorder. She does. She's the one with the mother who tells her she's too fat which makes her binge then starve.

Betty looks alarmed, as intended. She says, 'Come on now, Honey, you stop talkin' and eat.'

I put some rice into my mouth and chew, but it makes me want to heave so I shove the mouthful into my cheek to spit out later. 'He live in the valley?' I ask.

'Who's that?' Betty says.

'Abraham. With his parents?'

'With his mother,' she says.

'I thought his father was the preacher.'

'He moved away.'

'God,' I say. 'With another woman?' Betty says this is enough so sharply I shut up but then she studies me to see if I'm eating and I can't so I have to make more conversation because I sure as anything can't take another grain of this.

'How long have you been a vegetarian?' I ask.

'Eat,' Betty says.

But I can't. I give up. 'Sorry Betty,' I'm forced to say. 'Wet rice makes me puke.' Stella Maria tuts and Betty looks so hurt, I wish I'd fainted instead. She tells me to go make myself a sandwich and then she excuses herself, leaves the table and locks herself in her study for the rest of the night.

'Now look what you've done,' Stella Maria says. I haven't done anything but to avoid a fight. I tell her I'll clear up, even though it's her turn. She doesn't say thanks. She just buggers off to the den, which leaves me wondering why she isn't lonely when I am now I don't even have a phone. She must miss my company. I'm missing hers. I'm missing us making plans, talking over how the day has gone and having a big laugh together. I can't think how long it is since we did that.

A phone's ringing in Betty's study. 'Please make it for me,' I whisper and sure enough, Betty calls me from the study door.

'Mr Merv Pickett would like to speak with you, Honey,' she says. 'Make it snappy, if you don't mind. Ah'm waitin' on a call.'

I tell her she's got it and I get to the phone in record time. My heart's pumping so hard with relief that it's Merv and he hasn't ditched me that I can hardly get the right words out. 'Howdy Merv,' I say. 'Howya doin'?' He says he's doin' just fine and how am Ah doin'. I tell him Ah'm just fine. What with the radio thang an' all. Then I see Stella Maria in the doorway and say, 'I am just fine. Stella Maria is fine too. She says hi.'

'Hello to her,' says Merv then he pauses and I know he can't remember why he's called as he has no short-term memory from too many drugs and he can't even remember the last thing I said which was about the radio.

'Did ya talk to Tom?' I ask. 'Did he tell you about the radio?'

'The radio!' he says finally. 'Well hang! Isn't that the best news of the century? But I knew it. I always said so. Tom says you're lookin' real well too, Honey.'

'Have you finished the mix yet?' I say because I know we don't have much time. And he tells me he hasn't but it's goin' well and he pauses again which doesn't bother me because I'm just so happy to hear his lovely, lazy, growly voice.

'Oh,' he says, remembering. 'One liddle thing. Jerrah came by today. You remember Jerrah, doncha Honey? Tall guy. Tan. Ladies man.' I say sure I do though I'm thinking 'which ladies'? 'He just had one verra small suggestion which Ah took to and Ah reckon you will too. It's kinda cute. And it's kinda fitting.'

'What would that be?' I ask and a chill runs right down my spine because something tells me any liddle suggestion of Jerrah's isn't going to be fitting anything that's to my taste.

'He says why don't we set aside *Your Blinkin' Eyes* for the time bein'. It's soundin' a liddle too like *Cheatin' Heart* anyway. And why don't we give a liddle more credit, a liddle more ac-knowledge-ment to poor little Rita Mae. He's suggestin' you come up with a new song to replace *Your Blinkin' Eyes* that could be a tribute to poor little Rita Mae.'

Whoa! goes a voice in my head. What is going on here? What is coming at me here from the grave? Rita Mae will get her due acknowledgement. She did some harmonies, she did some arranging, she played some fine fiddle but mainly she was just the person on banjo and that's that.

'What?' says Stella Maria in the doorway, catching my expression which I guess is repulsed. She comes into the room to stand next to me. 'What's up? What's he saying?'

'How's that take you, Honey?' Merv's enquiring.

'Well Ah don't know,' I say. Truth is, I hear no choice in the offer and I think it's in my best interests not to say what I want to say which is forget it. 'Do we have time?'

'All the time in the world, Honey,' Merv says. I say aren't we aiming for November for the album and he says sure we are but with something like this, something as sensitive as this, you need to get it right and radio loves me which is just great, isn't it? Hadn't he told me from the beginning that they would?

Betty's come into the room now, wanting to know if there's a problem and I tell her there's no problem. I tell Merv there's no problem. Betty says would I mind very much ending this call as the one she's waiting on is urgent and I tell Merv I have to go. Then I say I'll get to work on something and maybe call by his office later in the week to try it out on him.

'Ah knew the idea would tickle you,' he says. 'Rita had her faults but you and I loved her, didn't we? We loved her so much Ah think this is the least we can do for her.'

'Absolutely,' I say. 'Definitely. You take care now, Merv.'

'You take care too,' he says and we hang up.

'He wants me to write a tribute for Rita Mae to go on the album,' I say. Stella Maria laughs. She laughs like a drain. I ask her what her problem is. I say what's so funny? She says it's flaming hysterical. I say I guess it is. I don't know if I can do it.

'You can do it on your ear,' she says and you'd swear from the sound of her that she was still my manager and cracking Nashville was still her dream. I join her on the sofa in front of the telly and say what happens if I can't come up with anything. 'Course you can,' she says. 'You were so far up her arse you could write a love song to her bowels.'

11

Where can you go except to your room, even if it isn't one that feels like home? Back in Cockfosters, my room has the curtains from when my mother was alive with suns and stars on them and on the walls, posters of Emmy Lou Harris and Tammy whose faces bring me comfort in the dark hours. Emmy Lou has a beautiful face. She was only born a few years after Tammy but look at her, younger than springtime and a cult figure. I'd settle for being a cult figure.

A tragic love affair with the brilliant but allegedly drug plagued Gram Parsons in her youth has helped to make Emmy Lou great. Tammy Wynette, may she rest in peace, was also assailed by tragedy in love. George Jones was both her heaven and her hell. Song there.

You're my heaven and hell
You know darn well etc.

I have great admiration for Tammy but she's not a major influence. Only reason I have posters up of her is someone gave them to me. With the exception of Dolly and Emmy Lou,

59

I preferred the men of that generation. Funnily enough, of the new men, only George Strait and Ricky Skaggs really impress me. The Skaggs version of *Rank Stranger* is excellent. Backwards and forwards goes the pendulum in country music, as in life.

Nothing in this room reminds me of me. Forgetting my make-up on the dresser and my clothes on the floor, there's just the four track I brought from London and my photos on the bedside table in the silver frame that opens like a book. One's of Mammy singing at The Silver Flamingo in south London and the other's of me, Tom and Stella Maria, taken by Archie the day we moved into our apartment.

I give Mammy a kiss. She's wearing the red dress with sequins on it which is still hanging in her wardrobe and she looks as beautiful as Emmy Lou. I'm the dead spit of her, except she's blonde, I'm not, she has a small nose, mine's long, she has blue eyes and mine are green. Also she's curvy where I'm more or less straight. It's in the expression, Josie used to say. I don't kiss either Tom or Stella Maria but remembering how we were that day makes me happy.

We were larking about on the roof in cowboy hats, all bursting with excitement, I know we were. Stella Maria as much as anyone. The roof had a fantastic view of Nashville, city of our dreams, and Stella Maria had decided she could make it a terrace. 'All it needs is plants,' she said. A simple thought maybe, but her undoing, as it turns out.

I mean she was just not a gardener in Cockfosters. She didn't have a place to garden. The O'Sheas have gravel out the back and front of their house because Fatima can't tolerate mud on the carpet. But we hadn't been in the apartment more than a week when Stella Maria was out getting all these pots with ferns and trees and flowers in them. She set about turning that tacky old roof with a great view into a leafy oasis fit for an Opry star and it became an obsession with her. Like she owned the roof. Like only she could say what went on there and who could go there. Who knows what drove her to it?

No one else in the block was that bothered but Archie was pleased as punch. Gave him somewhere to snooze that felt like a park. Stella Maria set up a special corner for him with a lounger and a little side table she built out of bricks the workmen had left about the place. Only other people you ever saw up there were the workmen, sodding Jed Wilcox, Henry Linklater and Marty Dodge, who are lined up against us at the hearing that is pending.

They had no respect for Stella Maria's decor and no understanding of the joy it brought her. They trampled all over her finer feelings just like Rita Mae. I curse them all for ruining it for Stella Maria who was as joyful as I was back then. I have nothing good to say about Rita Mae in any song. I refuse to give her more credit than she's due. She doesn't deserve a tribute.

I'm thinking how to tell this to Merv when Stella Maria bowls into my room just like it's old times and sits on the end of my bed. I smile at her. She smiles back. 'Fag?' I say, reaching for the pack under the bed. She's not a big smoker. Back in Cockfosters she'd clean her teeth before going home in case Fatima smelt her breath and went for her.

She shakes her head. 'What'll you put in your song then?'

'Dunno,' I say. 'Rita Mae couldn't last, what a blast!' Well I think it's funny but Stella Maria puts her hand across her mouth like she has to, to stop herself crying or screaming. I can hardly believe it. Her happiness has lasted less than a second.

'I keep seeing her body lying there, all by herself with her head smashed in,' she says.

Oh God! I want to be sympathetic but I'm so sick of this. I won't be tormented the way she is. 'I know. But Stella Maria. She didn't suffer and now she's dead. End of story.' I want to change the subject and I want to pluck her eyebrows which are so overgrown she's looking angrier than I can stand. 'Want me to pluck your eyebrows?'

She runs her hand across them but she couldn't be less interested. She doesn't want to look in the mirror I hold in front of her. She shoves it away. 'A girl has died and we have to take responsibility.'

I'm ignoring the saintliness in her voice. 'Why?' I say. I fish about in my make-up purse for tweezers. 'Why, Stella Maria?' I put my hands on her shoulders to hold her still and I tilt her head back so I can concentrate on what must be done. She's rigid under my hands, so I start plucking and shaping as deftly as I know how and after a sec, she begins to relax. 'We don't have to take responsibility because neither of us could have stopped what was always going to happen. Rita Mae died the way Mammy died – prematurely. That was her lot.'

Stella Maria's eyes are closed but there's a big furrow down the centre of her brow which deepens, despite my touch and the soothing tone in my voice. 'We couldn't have known she'd be coming to find us. We couldn't have known she wouldn't see the brick and jump out of its way. We couldn't have known it wouldn't just bounce off her. She was always going to die like that. It was her destiny, wouldn't have mattered what we did.'

We've been over and over it. Same words. Same thoughts. Same great chasm between us. She fills it with anger. 'We could've known that coming out here on such an idiotic mission would end in disaster. I should've put my foot down. It's my fault for not putting my foot down.'

'Which foot would that have been?' I say. 'Both yours were occupied getting us here as fast as you could.'

'And yours weren't?' She pulls my hand away.

'Just a bit more across the nose,' I say. She lets me get back to work but she's tense again. 'Stop fretting over what's done. Fret about what's happening now. You're letting her destroy your life and where's the sense in that?' Her eyes are watering. 'Be pleased the music's going well thanks to you and be pleased Rita Mae died happy.' I stand back to inspect the improvement.

'She didn't die happy,' she says.

'She died delighted,' I say. 'Because she'd just made you as miserable as she'd hoped. If you want to dwell on anything, dwell on that.'

I couldn't have sounded more reasonable but she jumps up from the bed like she's been scalded and she leaves the room with me wishing she'd never entered it. What's she mean put her foot down? I follow her into hers where she's standing in front of the mirror like she's searching her face for the mark of Cain.

'You know what's sad?' I say. 'What's sad is that you don't remember how we felt when we got here. How happy we were that your years of planning were paying off. What's sad is that you can't see how close we are to having everything we ever wanted. Rita Mae didn't die because of us. She probably died to get at us.'

She just stands there, looking at me in the mirror like I'm speaking to her in Russian. I'm half way out the door when she says, 'What's sad is that all you can think about is you. Rita Mae will never crack America and God knows it's what she wanted. Her life's over and all you can think about is whether it's going to work for you. It's all that's bothered you since we set foot in this feckin' country. And if we're looking at who's made me miserable then look at you're feckin' self.'

Back on my bed, I take a few deep breaths to get my spirits back to their normal level and I take another look at the photo of the three of us. Stella Maria's staring up at Tom, her eyes glued to his face like it contains a message from the Virgin. If that's love, I'd never have picked it. She says it is and maybe it is but how was I to know? She never said. All she had to do was say and I never would have slept with him.

I slept with Tom because I was missing her brother and here was a man who saw something special in me just as I saw something special in him. I put the photo down and close my eyes to clear my brain.

I don't get what's going on between them now, I truly don't. I can't believe she's stopped loving him when she loved him so much. First thing tomorrow, before we talk about anything else, I'm going to tell Betty she's on *A One Way Track To Nowhere* (Words and music Honey Hawksworth), keeping him out of the frame.

I don't hear the door open. I just sense someone in the room. Stella Maria's looming over the bed, peering down at me like a ghost in a down-at-heel beauty salon. 'Where are the tweezers?' she says. I reach for them on the bedside table and pass them to her. 'Thanks,' she says.

And now I'm going to bed. I ask Mammy what I can say in a tribute to Rita Mae when she was such a bad person but she draws a blank. I tell her not to bother then. Instead, I ask would she mind winging her way to Paddy with all my love and all my thoughts. I thank her for looking after me this day, though it had in it more tribulations than I like, and she tells me tomorrow will be better.

12

First thing I hear on waking is Abraham, spreading his garden tools out on the ground before he heads off to the terraces. I go to the window to watch him and he truly is a joy to behold. Tall and broad, with a body that tapers inwards all the way to his feet. His check shirt is open at the front and his chest is a cowgirl's dream. For the son of a preacher man, he sure wears his pants tight.

I stick my head through the window and breathe. The day's as pretty as a cornfield and its sweet fresh smells are enough to make me dizzy. 'Hey!' I call. 'Great morning.'

Abraham spins around like a grizzly's tapped him on the shoulder. 'Yes Ma'am,' he says, seeing it's only me.

'I'm not Ma'am,' I say, laughing. 'I'm Honey.' But he rolls his tools up in a sack, slings them over his shoulder and takes off like the grizzly's snapping at his head.

I remove my brace, then hop out the window for my first fag of the day. How great would it be to have a husband whose life is the soil? I wonder if Abraham's got an education and whether he eats grits. Betty isn't one for grits, thank the

Lord. She's a fruit, yoghurt and cereal woman which is just as well because I hate grits even when they're cooked properly. I'm not a breakfast person full stop. It's all I can do to keep coffee down.

I get myself a cup of instant and take it out into the yard. No sign of Stella Maria or Betty which is hard to believe when they're early risers and I'm not. I finish my smoke and wander through the house looking for them.

Stella Maria's voice cuts through the air like an arrow to my heart. 'I wanted her dead. I wanted her dead.' And then there's this sob like someone with too many tears stuck in their gullet.

I fling open the fly screen door thinking I can say well good, be pleased she is, but Betty says 'Leave us, Honey. Ah'll call you when it's your turn.' Stella Maria, in the floral chair, is slumped forward with her face in her hands. I ask her if she's OK but she doesn't answer so I go and fix myself some Froot Loops which I eat without noticing that I have. We all wanted Rita Mae dead. Well not dead, maybe, but gone. And here's the first line of my tribute: *Now you're dead and gone Rita Mae*.

I hear the tune in my head like I wrote it yesterday. A A A C D C B A. Key of C sharp. This is how songwriting goes. You think you've given up on an idea but all the time your brain is worrying away at it, teasing some thought into existence without you even knowing it. I go straight into my room to work on the melody, knowing I have to keep it simple and pure because the lyric will be haunting and true.

I'm so lost in the possibilities that Betty calls me before I know it and it takes me a minute to hear her. I put *Now you're dead and gone Rita Mae* plus all the possible lines that could follow it aside, not sure where it's taking me anyway, and think maybe I need to explain in this session that Stella Maria isn't usually so emotional and maybe it's hormonal, or dietary, or being Catholic.

Betty's sitting at her table, looking fresh as a daisy. She has excellent skin. I can't believe no one has ever loved her. 'You had breakfast, yet Honey?' she asks. I say Froot Loops but I'm hearing the song in my head, a good sign, and it reminds me that I already planned what I wanted to say and it wasn't about diets.

'Excuse me, Betty,' I say. 'Could I say something on behalf of Tom?' She flicks her tape off. She says now isn't the time. She wants to proceed chronologically. I say. 'We've done a deal and a deal is a deal. We all shook on it. We're all in it together. It's not his fault we're stuck out here so he can't get to us. It's not his fault Stella Maria won't see him. They're just having a . . . moment.'

Betty sighs. She stares into the garden where there's no sign of Abraham and she switches the tape back on. 'OK,' she says. 'Let me ask you this so you know what Ah'm thinkin'. In doin' your deal with Mr Sinclayuh, did you ever ask yourself what his motives were?'

'His motive was to crack America, same as mine.'

She says, 'Same as yours. Did you ever ask yourself how he wanted to accomplish it?'

'With his film. He wants his film to be the best thing he's ever done.' Surely Betty can't be dim.

'Did you ever ask yourself why he chose you as the subject of his film?'

'Because of my story. Which you don't know but I guess you're wanting to.' She nods, but she's thinking something else altogether.

'Mr Sinclayah is tellin' your story. About how you fare in your attempt to break into the country music industry in Nashville.'

'Right.'

'And where does this leave Stella Maria, who has no wish to crack America, who only ever came along for the ride? Do you ever ask yourself that?'

It's so wide of the mark I have to laugh. 'Betty,' I say. 'Stella Maria's more ambitious than I am.' She looks surprised, like she doubts me. 'She was even more desperate to get out of Cockfosters than I was. I was our ticket.' It's such a given I can hardly believe Betty thinks there's another side to the story.

Stella Maria's actual words, prior to us making what looked like an overnight decision were, 'You'll die of chlamydia in this godforsaken house if you don't use your measly talent to get out.' And when I said I was biding my time, she said, 'What time? You have no time. You come from a family with a short life span.' I can only guess at what she's telling Betty.

'She was ambitious enough for both of us,' I say. 'I didn't know what I wanted to do with my music but she always knew it was our fortune.' I can see from Betty's face she still needs persuading and I know Stella Maria has told her only what she thinks Betty wants to hear. 'She tell you she only came along to keep an eye on me?'

Betty says, 'You know I can't answer that.'

I tell her all our lives Stella Maria has seen us as a partnership with me performing and her managing, and she wasn't going to rest until she got it up and running because it was her best chance of making something of herself. It was the only way she was ever going to get away from her mother. If she's now saying she only came along because she felt sorry for me, she's fibbing. 'She practically forced us on Tom.'

Betty says, 'That so?'

'If you don't understand that, you won't understand anything,' I say.

She raises her beautifully shaped eyebrows, so I tell her about the night we met him, a major moment in history for all of us. Like we'd collided at this random point in time, our lives disintegrated and then reformed as something better than we'd ever imagined. Maybe Betty's never yearned for something the way we all have. Yearning is what gives my songs their special dust-bowl quality.

'England's piss. Crack America or forget it,' Tom said. And for Stella Maria and me, a great big light appeared in our foggy end-of-the-line lives and suddenly we could see our future as big and bright as a star-spangled rodeo. Just the way we'd always hoped. OK, it wasn't as obvious to me as it was to Stella Maria but pretty soon I got the picture. Tom was exactly who she'd been looking for.

We'd been heading up west every Friday and Saturday night for months to blag our way into places where people from bands and films hung out so we could meet movers and shakers and one night, there was Tom moving and shaking in our direction and she was in there before you could say 'Don't take your love to town'. We were trying to get into Puncinello, a Soho venue popular with the international show business fraternity, which had never been my favourite because they always chucked us out.

This night Stella Maria reckoned we couldn't fail. We were all tarted up with our boobs hanging out and all we had to do was con the girl at the desk. Except the girl on the desk took one look at us and maybe remembered us and said no way was she going to let us in. Whose guests were we, she wanted to know.

'Olly's,' said Stella Maria.

'He's not in,' the girl said.

Stella Maria told the girl to go and look because maybe he'd crept in without her noticing. The girl wouldn't. Stella Maria said well we'd just sit here and wait for him then and the girl did this big sigh. She said why didn't we leave now without any fuss. This was a club for members only, we weren't members and no one was expecting us. She smacked the signing-in book. 'No Olly,' she went.

It was the tone of voice she used. Stella Maria leant across the desk and gave her a hard shove in the stomach. 'We'll

69

wait,' she shouted. The girl squeaked really loud three times and in a flash, two blokes with muscles bursting out of their skins appeared from nowhere. They grabbed Stella Maria by the arms and dragged her to the door. I was whacking them and kicking them and we were half in and half out of the stupid place when Tom turned up and Stella Maria, nature's tribute to quick thinking, yelled, 'Olly!'

He got it in a flash. He took one look at Stella Maria, another one at me and it was like he truly did recognise us, not from his past but from his future, just as Stella Maria had recognised him. 'Hey girls,' he said. 'Sorry I'm late.'

'They're looking for Olly,' the receptionist said.

Tom grinned. 'That's me. Tom Olly Sinclair.' Just thinking about it now makes me laugh. 'You've got to admit it, Betty. He's got something. And lovely manners.' Betty frowns. 'Well what do you admire in a man?' I ask.

'Honey!' she says.

Actually, I went off him almost immediately because he is such a big-notes when he's socialising. We went through to the bar, he ordered us vodkas and he couldn't shut up about himself. Even in the dark his expression was cheesy. It's the exact same one you see around Nashville on the faces of weasly dudes with new contracts. He wasted no time telling us he'd had an overnight success and it took us no time at all to see it had gone right to his head and he was throwing his weight around like he was Steven Spielberg. A few creeps were all over him so we knew he was a bit famous, but we'd never heard of him and lots of people had forgotten him because he'd had his success years ago.

'Like Kitty Wells,' I tell Betty. 'First lady of country for years but now only famous in the industry or with people in their eighties. I'm not saying she isn't revered. Just she's not cutting edge anymore.' Same was true of Tom. He'd had it and lost it. Trouble was he didn't know why and it was eating away at him.

Betty wants to know how old he is and I say thirty-five. She wants to know what grounds we had for trusting him and I say none but that's not the point about this part of the story. 'The important thing is, he'd been called a genius when he was twenty-three, now he was called a nothing, and he was going mad trying to be at least a someone.'

Betty doesn't look impressed. 'Why exactly was he called a genius?'

I'm wishing for something that sounds finer. 'A great film about pigeons,' I say. But it came, it was a masterpiece and it went. It didn't matter what he did or how well he did it. 'When we met him, twelve years of downhill slide were gnawing away at him like a hungry rat in a rotting house.'

I'm remembering how edgy he was, his eyes all over the place like a bar room hustler's, like he was too frightened to blink in case he missed the single opportunity that was going to make his fortune. After a while he was boring me shitless. But then he said about cracking America and Stella Maria saw a golden opportunity sitting at that bar and she grabbed it. 'Jesus,' she went, like Our Lord had appeared before her very eyes. 'You two are made for each other. Honey's a country singer.'

Tom did not see golden opportunity as he was having a great time with the sound of his own voice. 'Country and western? Yee ha!' he went and began to sing *D-I-V-O-R-C-E*, taking the piss. Stella Maria roared like she'd never been so amused and I wanted to smack their heads in.

'The late Tammy Wynette's enormous hit,' I explain to Betty but she knows. 'It's something I won't tolerate. People slagging off Tammy.' She was an all-time great. On the road so long that in the end, she looked like her face was melting and she was only fifty-five.

I thought no way were we on the same wavelength. I dragged Stella Maria to the Ladies to tell her he was a total dick but she said no way was he.

'Maybe she was attracted to him,' Betty remarks.

'To what he could do for us,' I correct her and I'm trying to recall exactly what it was I did think so I knew for sure it wasn't love we were discussing but to be honest, it's hazy. I know I said no way should she shag this guy as he'd have genital warts, and she said no way was she going to. She might also have said it wasn't her he was interested in, but maybe she didn't. She says she didn't. What I do know is that she was never going to let him slip through her fingers.

We went back to the bar and I told him he sang like a pig with a stick up its bum. Stella Maria asked him what he was working on now and he said a documentary in the style of *Kurt and Courtney*, a searing account I tell Betty, of the relationship between Courtney Love, the singer and actress, and her long-time lover, the musician Kurt Cobain, who died mysteriously after a desperate struggle with drug addiction.

Betty says, 'Ah think you'll find they were man and wife.'

'Right,' I say. 'Right. I never saw it, just heard about it.'

Tom told us his idea was about how luck influenced possibilities and outcomes, how luck was his obsession owing to his unfortunate experience with it and he was planning a project about what made a miss and what made a hit. Stella Maria, thinking so fast on her feet that all I saw was bull dust, said, 'Then it should be about Honey.' She said he'd love my story when he heard it, it was every bit as good as Courtney's and my music was easily as interesting. It was shot through with stuff about luck and it would make a truly brilliant film.

'He went, "Cool," as in "Now I'm bored".'

'Stella Maria said, "Tell him, Honey," so I did.' Stella Maria has always had total faith in the story-telling skills I inherited from Mammy, just as I've always had faith in her judgement. She asks me to tell my story, I tell it.

To begin with Tom was only half listening, mainly looking at Stella Maria's chest, then my legs, his eyes wondering

72

between her tits and my legs but after a bit the story started getting to him. I didn't linger on the details. I mainly told him how I used the story to write my songs and after a bit he was going, 'You fell over her corpse?' I apologised to Josie for that but a story teller needs to shock now and again. 'It inspired me to write *I Touched You But You Weren't There.*' I didn't sing him *I Touched You.* I sang him *Take One Egg* and it just about brought the bar to a standstill.

He was knocked out. It was obvious. My narrative was simple. An orphan girl from an end-of-the-line suburb of London, with only raw talent and passion going for her, heads to Nashville to peddle her poetry. To try her luck in the country music arena which thrives on passion and tragedy.

'By the time we left him it was 3 a.m. he was calling me his little love and we were all on kissing terms. He was going to take us to America and the idea was we'd crack it together. That's how it happened.'

Betty says, 'You dropped everything, just like that.'

'Not just like that. We'd spent our whole lives thinking about it. All we'd been waiting for was the right opportunity and Tom was it.'

That's a song. *Take you, take me, we're a perfect opportunity.*

'Anyway, next day, I woke up and I was totally off the idea. It wasn't until Mammy said, "Run, run, run" that we did.'

Betty looks up from her notepad. 'Run run run,' she repeats. She's dying to know more but she looks at her watch. 'That's it. Time for lunch,' she says. She turns off the tape and gets to her feet.

I say, 'Do you understand better about Tom?'

She says, 'You're not in love with him, are you Honey?' And I say God no. And I definitely am not, even if I once thought I was. But we're on this roller-coaster journey together and we're clinging to each other with every pitch and spin of the car, welded by hope and faith. Betty says she likes to place her faith in something more substantial. I say, I know. The Lord Jesus Christ. And I'm not comparing Tom to Him. All I'm saying is we've got these tickets in the lottery and what we are hoping for is a brilliant outcome. 'Which is?' Betty asks.

'For the album to top the country charts with unrivalled airplay in the history of radio, for Tom's film to be celebrated globally but mostly in the US because that's what he's set his heart on, and for me to find true love in the arms of a man as true as the mountain I'm looking at right now.'

'Does Stella Maria's interest in Mr Sinclayuh feature in your brilliant outcome?' she asks.

I say to Betty, 'You know what, Betty? I hope so, but it's so long since I saw them in each other's company.'

'D'you have a contract with him?' she asks. 'A written contract?'

'No,' I say and I get the feeling she's disgusted.

I want to tell her how much worse it could have been. He could've been some drunken lech who chatted us up and forgot us by morning. But I knew he wouldn't be because when I got home that night three light bulbs popped one after the other, hallway, kitchen and landing, signalling my mother's approval. Light bulbs are among Mammy's favourite means of communication. I was always grateful Paddy showed me early on how to change them myself.

13

Betty's taken a salad into her study, Stella Maria has several plates of something in the den and I've brought toast and honey into my room to work. *'Now you're dead and gone Rita Mae.'* I play the line on my guitar and hold it in my head while I eat and stare out the window for inspiration. The hills send me nothing about Rita Mae which is understandable. Composition's hit and miss, anyway. Some days no trouble. Other days all the trouble in the world. Usually I don't write songs to order.

I give up and begin a letter to Paddy on paper from my song book. I've kept him informed about the state of my heart and my life since we hit Nashville, but all I've had back is one postcard from Portugal saying, 'Lisbon. Weather sunny.' He drives a pantechnicon across Europe, delivering goods to countries like Romania. He's been a bouncer, a scaffolder, a robber and, for two days, a milkman, but he could turn his hand to anything except writing. There he's like Stella Maria. More a speaker.

Last letter I wrote said, 'In jail, please come.' Today I tell him how miserable Stella Maria is and how fat she's getting from depression. I also want to explain about Tom, as I don't know that he has the full picture. I say there's a love issue with Stella Maria but I don't go on about it. He doesn't need to hear that Stella Maria thinks I'm a whore like my mother.

I used to send my letters to Cockfosters but Fatima would've burnt them for sure. Now I send them care of The Moon on the Green, a pub in Wood Green where the land-lord's a mate and there's some hope of them being passed on. I enclose a new song called *No Signposts* about two blind people who find love when they fall into each other's arms on a honky tonk dance floor. It was a breeze to write. If I could turn it into a tribute I would but I can't.

Betty comes to find me. She says, 'What time do you call this, Honey? You were due to meet with me at 2.45.' I say I don't call it any time as I don't have a watch. She says time-keeping is important in sessions of this nature and I say sorry. She says, 'All you had to do was refer to the timetable.' She's referring to the timetable which she's stuck to the fridge door. In the study, she asks me what I've been reflecting on.

'Love,' I tell her. I ask her if she'd be interested to hear my theory on it and she says why not as she arranges her stuff and changes her tape. 'It's a triangle,' I say. 'When you fall for someone you're at the top of it but in the bottom corners are joy and tragedy only you don't know which is which. You can shoot down one path or you can shoot down the other, but you take your life in your hands because there are no signposts.'

I sing for her a snatch of the song I've sent Paddy. I'm watching her face and it strikes me that maybe she's taken the tragedy path once too often. She says well the song's very interesting but now we're going to pick up my life from its early days as she wants us to get back on track. 'Maybe find a signpost or two ourselves,' she says. She looks at her notes and asks me if I find it easy to talk about my mother's death.

'Sure,' I say. 'It was ages ago. I was twelve. It was fine. She had the baby and they both died.' She's watching me hard while I tell her this, searching for something in my face, don't know what. And she keeps her eyes on me when I finish speaking so I have to look out the window.

'That must have been very shocking.'

'We all gotta die some time.' Betty wants me to say more but what is there? I'm not so interested in that period of my life anymore. To be truthful, I'm trying to figure out here how I can get the conversation around to my mobile phone. My life's on hold without it. 'I think you appreciate that Mammy being dead isn't a final thing for me,' I say. Betty looks up but says nothing. 'She's with me day and night, guiding me. Like I said, she guided me to Tom.'

Betty fiddles with her pen and I guess she's going to tell me she doesn't want to talk about anything that's not chrono-logical so I tell her meeting Tom was pre-ordained and Mammy ordained it. 'We used to dream about her coming over here and singing in the Opry but the Opry just couldn't offer the security of Cockfosters. So it was up to me.'

Betty wants to know how old Mammy was when she had me. I tell her twenty-two, just a year older than I am now. 'And she called me Honey because I was the sweetest thing she ever saw. She would've put it to music but composing wasn't in her. She just had this great range vocally. Different from mine which is a lot like Willie Nelson's. She was higher.'

'How did you know she said "run run run" the night you met Tom Sinclayah?' she asks, putting us right on track, mine not hers.

'She sent a butterfly to circle three times.' If Betty's not smart enough to embrace the notion of the dead returning as insects, we're sunk anyway.

'But why run run run?'

'Because Micky Besant was going to kill me.'

She asks how to spell Micky Besant and I tell her, then she

says we'll get back to him. What she wants to know right now is the name of the baby's father which confuses me.

'Which baby?' I ask.

'The baby who died with your Mammy,' she says, so gently my heart starts to race because I know this gentle territory and I don't want to visit it right now. 'Was his father your step-father?'

'He was Morgan Finch,' I say. 'I hated him. He did nothing for us. He took off when he found out Mammy was pregnant.' Betty sits back in her chair and looks out into the jungle, where funnily enough I see there are many butterflies, though I don't believe any of them is related to me.

'Did your Mammy have lots of boyfriends?'

'She wasn't a slapper.' Betty says she isn't suggesting for a minute she was. What she's trying to do is form a clear picture of the quality of my early life. I tell her I had a fine quality of life. My pulse slows. 'Mammy did the very best she could. I was given an excellent start in life. Breast fed. The works. And great music. We had a brilliant record collection.'

I was raised on the music of Dolly, who I resemble artistically and temperamentally, Patsy Cline, Hank Williams, Tammy Wynette, Johnny Cash, Kris Kristofferson, Kenny Rogers, Kitty Wells and George Jones who are like kin to me. When Mammy wasn't listening to country songs, she was singing them. And if she wasn't singing or listening to them, she was making up stories from them. She knew loads because books on the stars arrived every year on her birthday from an old geezer who signed himself Barney Noble. He sent books from Kentucky regular as clockwork.

Betty writes on her pad, 'Barney Noble.' I ask does she think it will rain. She doesn't. She says what were the stories about. 'Broken hearts. Lost love. Hardship. Gambling. Divorce. The usual.'

'Tell me about your house,' she says.

'It was a mock Tudor semi.' Betty thinks I'm describing

some sort of caravan. She has the impression Cockfosters is a kind of trailer park and I laugh. People in Cockfosters would perish at the thought, even though the lives they lead are practically non-existent. I couldn't tell you the number of songs I've started called *End of the Line*. I never finish them because Cockfosters is a bugger to rhyme. The closest I can get is Blockbusters but I've never been able to find a story where the twist depended on video rental. Mammy loved it being so respectable. I, personally, have never hankered after respectable. I hankered after the life in the songs she sang. Not the sorrow and heartache, but the love and the triumph.

By the time I was seven or eight, the backwoods, the mountains, the cottonfields and the dust bowl which drove the farmers from Oklahoma to the coast were more real to me than the Three Bears. I believe Mammy was drawn to them because they reminded her of her own life. I believe she sang the songs to give her life a sweeter melody.

'Her stories were even better than bible stories,' I tell Betty, which I know will impress her as we have a common bond in the Bible. I studied the Bible with the Baptists on Sundays when the O'Sheas were at Mass and I wanted to get out of the house. Sunday morning was when Mammy gave her boy-friends bacon and eggs in bed to show them what a great home-maker she was. She'd stink the place out with flowers and cooking smells and be so full of laughter that I'd think how could anyone not love her. I can hear her laughing even today, clear as a bell.

'She was dead unlucky in love,' I say. 'She needed a man with big calloused hands, looking like a mountain. The husband Lucille ran out on in Kenny Rogers' hauntingly tragic ballad.'

Betty can't place it so I sing it for her. 'Right. I know it,' she says before I finish the second verse.

Mammy and I knew he was the man for us. We'd never have run out on him. We were never going to run into him either as he hung out in a bar in Toledo across from the depot and Mammy had given up on travel. I'd say, 'Don't you want to visit old Barney in Kentucky?' And she'd always say yes but no, which I understood. 'Most things are yes but no, aren't they?' I say to Betty. 'Or no but yes.'

She asks who was Barney Noble again and I say, just someone from the US Mammy met through work who stayed in touch. She met loads of Americans on the cruise ships. I used to tell Stella Maria that one day Mammy and me were going to live on his ranch even though I didn't know if he had a ranch. Then, the very first day we were in Nashville, Stella Maria went, 'Look Barney Noble.' I said where, not thinking, how could she know what he looked like when I hadn't even seen him but she was pointing to the book store, Barnes & Noble. I say to Betty I guess Barney was someone pretending to be a book shop.

She makes a note. 'Did your Mammy know you hated Morgan Finch?'

'Yes,' I say. 'But he was the only one we had at that time.' I wanted a man for Mammy almost as much as she wanted one for herself. Morgan was never going to be it. I did my best to take care of Mammy but she was a handful.

'Do you remember how you felt when she died?' Betty says which stuns me. What's she expecting? I was sad. I was so sad my stomach and chest and lungs and brain were full to the brim with it. I was stuffed stupid with it.

'I didn't try to kill myself or anything,' I say.

'I guess you were too young to mourn the death of the baby,' she says.

And now I feel sick. I pour myself a glass of water from the jug on the table. 'I guess,' I say. We called him Jimmie after Jimmie Rodgers, the father of country music. 'He died. Mammy gave him a couple of hours to get wherever he was going, then she took off after him. I don't want to talk about it. I was twelve.'

Betty says, 'Maybe we'll end it right there.'

'OK,' I say. But I'm thinkin' why's she doing this? What's any of this got to do with the hearing? What's it got to do with anyone? I want my flipping mobile.

14

The sun's setting behind me so there's a big shadow over the valley making the spire of the church look grey and sorrowful, which shows what a shadow can do. That spire is pure white and joyful in the light of day. I've been trying to work this thought into my tribute, seeing as Rita Mae was a shadow over our lives and now is a shadow in death, but it's not happening.

Rita Mae never struck me as a good subject for a song when she was living and though her dyin' is fine material, I don't know's how her dyin' is what Jerrah is looking for. I wouldn't mind asking him what he's looking for but my guess is he doesn't know himself. He's just of a mind to have us pay tribute to her and now I've reflected on it, I can see the wisdom. To ignore her when she's featured on so many of the tracks would be insensitive.

Trouble is, I can't recall anything I'd like to say about her. I remember how she looked. Tall, long black hair to her arse, wild eyes that shone with malice whatever she was feeling, and teeth so white we had to ask Merv where she'd had them bleached. But where will this get me with a lyric? I'm trying to think of qualities that will make some kind of appealing narrative and I'm struggling. All I have is a feeling of her and that feeling is of misery and dread. What I remember clearest is a scene I never saw. Of her in bed with Tom, grinning up at Stella Maria with triumph lighting up every bit of her spiteful face. It makes me ill.

Now you're dead and gone Rita Mae
A A A C sharp D C sharp B A
On lonely nights I try to hear you play
E A A A C D D C B A

To give me inspiration I sing a little of Dolly Parton's fine song *Coat of Many Colours* about the coat her mother made her from rags and think how shite it is for Stella Maria that Fatima has turned her back on her since our arrest. I wonder if she's told Betty about that. I wonder if I should. It's a big, big sorrow for Stella Maria when she needs her family about her. As a mother Fatima O'Shea has always sucked.

My mother even looked like an angel with her pale frothy curls, her dreamy expression and her floaty way of walking, as if supported by invisible clouds. Sometimes I think her coming to earth was a mistake God realised He'd made only after thirty-four years. Now she's like a summer breeze, gently stroking me, looking out for me in accordance with her dying promise. 'I'm not leaving you, Honey,' she said.

'Ever?' I was holding her hand, wearing my cowgirl outfit to cheer her up even though it was three years too small.

'Ever,' she said.

'Give me the next line, Mammy,' I whisper, but nothing. Just images Betty has summoned without knowing the pain they bring.

I tried to climb up on the bed next to her but someone held me back even though all the tubes she'd had in her were gone. I got her hand and I pressed it to my face. Her eyes kept closing though she was trying her hardest to keep them open. She was wanting to look at me, to keep me in sight. I was holding her to the earth.

'Wake up, wake up,' I screamed. 'Don't leave me.' But she had to go. Jimmie had gone already and he couldn't go alone. Thinking of it drives me crazy. It's a bad memory and I won't dwell on it. I smoke three cigarettes fast as I can and make myself dizzy.

Mammy has no thoughts on Rita Mae. She never liked her anyway. What she puts into my head is *Jolene*, also by Dolly and a diamond of its kind. Stella Maria and I used to love it. Now we can't hear it without wanting to punch each other's faces in. It's about this girl who's desperate she's going to lose her boyfriend to the local scrubber. Dolly is a truly brilliant poet and my bet is she has lived the life we all live, one way or another.

Stella Maria's view of my mother is that if she'd stuck around a bit longer, the scales would've fallen from my eyes as mothers are all the same and idolising them the way I idolise mine is unhealthy. She says she looks at hers and just thinks oh no! which is healthy. It is healthy as well. Any sane person would look at Fatima and think oh no!

Had Fatima O'Shea been my mother, scales wouldn't have had to fall from my eyes because it would've been crystal clear from the minute I dropped out of her revolting womb that she only had self-love in her veins. A mother like Fatima would've killed me, or I would have killed her. I thank God I never had to live with her. Stella Maria wanted me to when Mammy died. The social worker asked Fatima was she up for it but Fatima said no way. No flipping way. Even though Stella Maria begged.

We were in a room where the bereaved were taken and Stella Maria had her arm around me which was unusual as she's never been a hugging person. We were sitting next to each other on this couch, she had her arm round me and

every so often she gave me a kiss on my hand. And sometimes she pushed my hair out of my face. She never did it
before and she's never done it since. The social worker was
saying, 'Would you be prepared to let her stay with you, Mrs
O'Shea?' I suppose she thought Fatima wouldn't be able to
resist me.

'She can sleep with me in my bed,' Stella Maria said in this
matter-of-fact voice so I thought well that's all right. That's
settled. I'll be safe in bed with her.

But Fatima did her nut. 'Out of the question,' she went.
Like a mad woman. 'Completely and utterly out of the
question. It's unhygienic and the woman was never a friend.'
Then she pulled Stella Maria off the couch and dragged her
home. I stayed in hospital until they located a relative, Josie,
a woman I could barely remember.

The dusk is so beautiful I could live in it permanently.
Mammy would've loved it here. I reckon here she would've
found a gentleman to love her who was decent and true.

In the lengthening shadows, I look back towards the house
and blow me if I don't see Abraham collecting his bits and
bobs on the middle terrace. Like a boy in silhouette. Decent
and true or I'd eat my hat. So here's my choice. I could hop
right off the swing and hurry back to the house, striking up a
conversation with him as I pass, lingering with him maybe in
the jungle garden, I could just sit here looking and sounding
lovely in the hope that I catch his fancy, or I could make him
come to me.

'Oi,' I call. 'Hi there.' He doesn't hear. 'Hey Abraham.
Quick, I need you.' He looks up, sees me waving, but hesi-
tates. 'Quick. It's an emergency,' I scream to get him going
since my personal allure doesn't seem to be enough. Christ,
Paddy wouldn't have wasted a second and he's turned out in
all weathers.

Abraham's thinking about it. He begins to walk slowly in
my direction, then goes back, picks up his shovel and breaks

into a run till he's going full pelt down the steps towards me. I climb up on to the swing because he thinks I'm frightened and I don't want to disappoint him.

'Where is it?' he asks. There's no getting away from it. He's a fine looking boy. High cheek bones, lips that are sweet and curved and a head that looks noble from the back. The back of the head is Stella Maria's and my acid test. I don't know what he's talking about. I just look dumb with fear. 'Which way'd it go?' He's looking all about, his spade half raised as if to strike.

'That way,' I say, nodding towards the fence. He stabs the ground as he goes, imagining that whatever it is is hiding between the blades of grass waiting to pounce. 'Guess it got away,' I say. He guesses so himself. He has a fine mellow voice.

I sit back down and and play a few chords on my guitar, to show my appreciation. 'I was just down here trying to write a song about this woman who's died and I was having trouble with the lyrics and then . . . oh boy!' I'm speaking a lot because I know he won't speak at all and I don't want him to go. He's going anyway.

'Hold up,' I say. He stops. 'Just give me a hand here.' He's keen to go but I begin to sing and manners prevent him from turning his back on me.

Now you're dead and gone Rita Mae
On lonely nights I try to hear you play

'That's it,' I say. 'I'm stuck.'

He says well I don't need to worry too much about snakes as they'd prefer to keep well outta my way and I say, 'I sound that bad?'

He smiles. A small, shy, manly smile. 'You sing alright,' he said. 'You sure sing loud.'

'Thing is,' I say, 'I can't get the next line. Writer's block.' He's backing away. 'Come on. Give me a word. Give me any word.'

He thinks, then he says, 'Banjo,' and I feel such a rush of warmth for him I think it could be love. He vanishes in a trice but I hug myself anyway. I'll be Paddy's forever and ever Amen, but Mammy knows our love can never be so she's sent me a man who'll allow a corner of my heart not to be his.

I pick up my guitar and play some lovesick chords. I don't even have to shut my eyes to see us in a log cabin in the valley, surrounded by many children all dressed in ragged rainbow coats singin' their hearts out for the sheer joy of being alive. Might even be grits on the hob.

I can't wait to tell this to Stella Maria but I guess I'll have to. Last thing to interest her is a good laugh these days. Back in Cockfosters we could talk about love for ever. I'd make her tell me about the man she wanted marry, then I'd tell her about mine. She'd say, 'Mine's loaded.'

I'd say 'What else?'

She'd say, 'How the fuck do I know?' She wasn't bothered about getting married, just about getting rich.

I'd say, 'Mine's a man with diamonds in his eyes.'

She'd say, 'Blind then.' I guess you never see your brother's eyes the way others do. I couldn't live my life the way she and Betty lead theirs, without sex or companionship or undying admiration from a man for whom I'm everything. I don't regret any of the intercourses I've had. Not even Tom who was crap at it anyway. We weren't meant for each other, turned out, just overwhelmingly attracted to each other's talent. I want to run my tribute past him.

The light's just about gone so I head back to the house through the jungle which gives me the creeps. All sorts of weird stick noises are coming from inside the bushes and up in the trees. I'd feel safer if I had my phone with me. I start to run, slip a bit on the mossy path and think I can see eyes rolling about in heads deep in the shrubbery. I really want my phone back. I'm going to tell Betty I have to have it. I need to talk to Tom even if I can't see him.

There are cooking smells coming from the kitchen which means Stella Maria hasn't talked Betty into taking us to the Cracker. I can hear Betty clunking about with utensils that never look safe in her hands. 'Hey,' I say, finding her red in the face with a whole lot of pulses or whatever on the go. 'Want some help?' She says could I put knives and forks on the table. 'Plants are great, aren't they?' I say.

She stops chopping whatever she's chopping. Green stuff. And she looks at me in a way that makes me think there must be another word for plant in the American language. 'One of God's finest creations,' she says.

'Just been admiring them,' I tell her. 'In the garden. Abraham sure does a fine job keeping yours up to scratch.' She says that's why she employs him. I say my own garden was your basic dirt, weed and a marijuana plant. She says she hopes that's an exaggeration.

And I gather from this that maybe now isn't the time to raise anything tricky in a light-hearted manner. I set the table then check out Stella Maria who's watching a report on tidal waves. 'Alright?' I say. I plonk myself into the armchair so I can see her face as well as the TV and wonder if Abraham fancies her. I hope to God she doesn't fancy him. I couldn't stand that all over again.

'That Abraham's a decent guy,' I say. 'Saved me from a rattler down on the bottom terrace.'

'What kind of rattler?' she asks. She's turned to look at me, interested even if she doesn't want to be.

'Spotted,' I say. 'Didn't get a really close look at it. He saw it when he was digging on the middle terrace and came screaming down to kill it, but it got away.'

'What's a rattler sound like?' she asks. I make a rattling noise and she laughs. For a minute we both watch the tidal waves together swamping some poor community which will never recover and I think maybe I could tell her I think I love him. 'He's got a dumb face,' she says which is the kind of remark she always makes about men I fancy, a point I will mention to Betty in the morning.

In the end, I settle for not raising anything with her or the matter of Tom and the phone with Betty and the night passes without incident. I go to my room early so's not to upset anyone and do some work on the four track:

Now you're dead and gone Rita Mae,
On lonely nights I try to hear you play'n
Sweet and low
On your old banjo

Blah blah blah more words to come. Something about harps and angels is the way I'm thinkin'. Go to sleep thinkin' it and wake up thinkin' it but still without a line that works for me.

15

Another sunny day. A day closer to the hearing and what's getting to me is how much is riding on this flipping song. Well I'm not sure how much is riding on it but my gut's telling me everything. And what am I supposed to do? Dream up a work of genius overnight?

I ask Betty if we can have this morning's session down by the cherry tree so the fresh air can clear my head. She says provided I don't get distracted and I say I won't but in my heart I know I can't guarantee it because I welcome all distractions at a time like this.

'Stella Maria hated Micky Besant, by the way,' I say when we're settled. 'The Micky Besant who tried to murder me.' I'm hoping I can work my way round to Abraham via Micky and how Stella Maria has it in for men I like, then on to Tom, collecting the phone on the way.

Betty says sounds like Stella Maria's a fine judge of character in that case. However Micky's not on her agenda for this morning. 'Any reason he's on yours?' I say none in particular. It can wait. She's down to work at once. 'Your mother dies and the authorities send for your grandmother? How'd you feel about that?'

I want to go, 'Hang on, Betty. You can't just plug into my tragic past and switch it on like a toaster.' But my intention today is to be as pleasing as I can so I take a deep breath. 'Josie was OK,' I say. 'I don't think a lot about her. She was in my life for four years and then she wasn't. We never had much to say to each other.' Truth is, I didn't speak to her for months even though she talked to me and left food out for me. Potatoes mostly. 'She cooked mash,' I say. 'We should have that some time.'

Potatoes aren't on Betty's agenda either. 'Was she a good homemaker?' she wants to know and why's that helpful?

'She was great,' I say. There's no point in trashing her memory now. She showed up with all her belongings and not a single tear for the loss of the daughter she hadn't seen for fifteen years. It made me so angry I couldn't eat. I said if she wasn't in mourning she ought to get the hell back to wherever the Social Services had found her because I was so sad I was dying and I didn't want anyone living with me who didn't understand that.

Something like that, I said. I can't remember the exact words. Whatever you say when you're twelve. She said she wasn't crying her eyes out because she'd seen it coming when Mammy was no older than I was and she'd done all her grieving then, but what was she saying, that she'd written her own daughter off when she was no more than a baby?

I took myself off to bed and tried to sleep my way through the disgustingness. Then I got out of bed and told her to fuck right off out of it because I hated her, but then she did cry because she'd had a hard life and what could I do? I felt sorry for her.

I still didn't talk to her because anything I had to say I said to Stella Maria or to Mammy. I had such a vivid image of her it was like she'd never gone anywhere and I held on to it hard as I could for as long as I could. It breaks my heart that the image is fading. People say time makes loss easier but it just makes it harder to hang on to the details you want to remember forever.

After a while they said I was too thin and maybe mad and if I didn't eat they'd have to hospitalise me, so I ate. And once I'd got round to deciding that speaking to Josie wasn't a betrayal of Mammy's memory, we got into the music together. She loved Patsy Cline. She loved only Patsy Cline and I never thought you could have too much of a woman with a voice so fine but you can. I went right off Patsy at that time.

Josie'd say, 'Stay out of trouble,' then off she'd go to the pub knowing I'd do exactly what I wanted because the only person in my life whose opinion mattered apart from Mammy's was Stella Maria's, whose opinion has always mattered.

My thoughts drift towards Abraham. If he's the man I think he is then maybe one day he'll make me happy. All I've ever wanted is a man who'll crush me to his chest and protect me forever. I shiver at the thought.

'Would you agree, looking back, you went a little haywire about that time?' Betty's saying. Agree with who, I ask her and she says with the general proposition.

'You mean sex?' I say and I'm blushing. The sex with Paddy was perfect.

'OK. Let's talk about sex,' she replies, like it wasn't what she meant but I know it was. And we may as well when I want to tell her how it's always come between Stella Maria and me. Sex, men. Men, sex. Doesn't matter whether it's Paddy, Tom or Micky.

'Truth is, Betty,' I say, 'I don't think Stella Maria's all that keen on intercourse.' And the face Betty pulls makes me think she's not either which maybe accounts for the book I saw in her study, *The Risk to Reward Ratio of Romantic Love* by Betty Beecher.

She says, 'Is Stella Maria to blame for you going off the rails when Josie died?'

'See?' I say, 'She calls it going off the rails. I call it having a lovelife. We just see anything to do with sex differently and we always have, from day one.'

By day one I mean the day we lost our virginity which happened to be on the same day because that's how we planned it. Stella Maria thought she might as well get it over with and I was so in love with Paddy and ignored by him, I was up for anyone. If anyone was to blame it was my own sweet Paddy.

He'd come over to the house, do any chore, fix the roof in the pouring rain, find fuses in the dark, but he never so much as peck me on the cheek and I was dying. Josie spotted it. She said, 'He's not for you, darlin'. He's a fine boy but he's not for you.' I hated her for saying it. She said, 'Your destiny's over the water.'

Anyway, being desperate, I said to Stella Maria we might as well get on with it because death could take us any day and who wanted to die a virgin? We picked up a couple of guys she thought looked less repulsive than the rest.

I'm trying to see how much of this Betty knows and turns out she knows enough. She says, 'Honey, remind me. How old were you and Stella Maria when you lost your virginity?' I tell her I was fifteen, remember that wasn't legal, so say sixteen, then realise Stella Maria probably told her the truth so I say I was fifteen and Stella Maria was seventeen. She makes a note of it.

'Were the boys your sweethearts?' Betty asks. I want to say we met them at church but what's Stella Maria already said?

'Busking friends,' I say. And to get us off the subject which certainly doesn't look like taking me in the direction of my mobile, I describe to Betty how we went busking from the time I was fourteen in the hope of being discovered.

There's a trick to it. Energy. You get those poor sods on street corners looking as if they're singing an apology for living, and you think God, join a queue so you can have some fun. I'd get out there and hammer it, being a natural perfomer, a fact recognised by Rita Mae who was technically brilliant but had minus energy. George Jones began his singing career as a busker and I'm proud to have this in common with him. Lots of guys tried to pick us up but Stella Maria would see them off. She chose Boris and Karloff because they didn't look violent.

I suggest to Betty that we draw a veil over them because they can't have much bearing on anything and she says, 'And how were you gettin' on with Josie at this time?'

I say, 'Same as usual.' A couple of months later she dropped dead at the kitchen sink to the tune of *Crazy*, words and music by the one and only Willie Nelson, and I was all alone again. Shit! I'm going to cry. I really don't want to cry. I really don't need this at the moment.

'You OK?' Betty asks.

I say I am, then sob for two minutes and she lets me. She hands me some tissues from her pocket. 'I wasn't that sad. She wasn't someone I cared for that much.'

Paddy came round. He gave me a hug, first time since he'd saved me from the car. He said, 'I'm very, very sorry, Honey. She was a fine woman. D'you need anything?' I wanted him to hug me for ever but he let go after a brotherly length of time. 'Who's going to organise the funeral?' he said. I told him me and Stella Maria. He said Stella Maria might be an idiot but this was the kind of thing she'd do well and I want to bawl my eyes out just thinking about it now so I do.

It's Mrs West's fault I blub all the time. And Mrs West was Stella Maria's fault. She decided after Josie died that I'd gone round the bend and organised for me to be counselled because she thought the way I was going, I'd end up on the streets. Idiot.

Of course it's a shock to fall over your grandmother's corpse when you think she's in bed and you've crept in from town when she thought you were in bed. Of course it makes you jumpy. But Mrs West was well out of her depth, trying to make judgements about stuff she couldn't even begin to understand. All that crap she spouted about giving in to the sorrow of the moment. 'You must cry when you want to.' Now I cry all the time and I never want to.

Stella Maria said she did it because I was carrying on like a prostitute. I wrote *Laying Down and Looking For Someone to Love* so she'd see I wasn't and sang it to Mrs West who said had I thought about the flute which was a nice instrument for a girl. Despite everything Fatima has told the neighborhood I have never, in the whole of my life, had sex for money. The sex act, to my mind, is an expression of emotion, and that's how I've always embarked on it even that first time when it was expressing my fear of death.

'Do you fear death?' Betty enquires. I say all I know is it's waiting around the corner. Otherwise I don't think about it. She says even now?

'Sure,' I say.

She raps her pencil on the table – tap tap tap tap tap – and she looks out over the valley. She says do I think much about the hearing that's ahead of us.

'I worry what the label will make of it,' I tell her. 'I don't know why they want this Rita Mae song.' She says is what the label thinks more important than what the hearing is about. 'The hearing's about the workmen,' I remind her. 'That's what I thought it was about. Harvey having a go at the workmen.'

Betty says this is the case, but I see she thinks I should be fretting about Rita Mae, the way Stella Maria is. Well I'm not. I know how to control my thoughts so that I only worry

95

about what's worrying and I'm not worrying about the hearing because Harvey's on the case. He just has to make those guys see they got it wrong. And he will.

They're not saying they saw Stella Maria chuck the brick. They're saying they saw her on the roof near the brick. Stella Maria should've been nicer to them is all. They wouldn't be incriminating her if she'd been nicer to them. I was pretty nice to them but I hadn't spent ages watering the stupid plants. No way would Stella Maria tolerate them leaving their crap all over the place. She told Archie to make them keep their mess to themselves and he did but they took no notice. I told all that to the police. They made nothing of it.

'So how do you think the brick fell, Honey?' says Betty. 'You ever applied yourself to that question?' She's looking at me like she truly believes I mightn't have.

'God willed it,' I say. 'That's how it goes. It was an accident. A life can be short, a life can be long, but it's going to end one way or the other and some end in an accident. Stella Maria never threw it, whatever anyone says.'

'Fact remains, Honey. You are saying she was in your room. She's sayin' she was not.'

'Right,' I say. 'I'm hoping you'll help her recover her memory.' Tap tap tap she goes again, staring at her pencil and not at me, then she lets out this short sharp sigh.

'Oh Honey. You're real nice girls. Ah cain't bear to think what will happen to you.' I say nothing will happen to us. It will all become plain in light of the facts.

Poor Betty. Lucky for her she won't be called to give evidence herself. She's not an expert witness, just a prominent citizen. 'The hearing'll be fine,' I say. 'Once you make Stella Maria see reason. All she needs to know is that I only care about what's best for her.'

After that we say nothing for a long time, then Betty says, like this will help me remember something better, 'Many crimes have been committed in jealousy's name, Honey.'

And I say I know that only too well. Look at Micky Besant. 'Maybe later,' she says, so I guess that's that for the morning and dammit, I'm no closer to getting the phone back than I was when we started.

16

Abraham's appeared on the top terrace so lustworthy I can't take my eyes off him. His muscles are running with sweat. 'Abraham!' I yell. 'Wotcha doin'?' He half lifts his hand to wave then goes straight back into the jungle again.

Betty hasn't waved. She's looking puzzled, maybe that I'm treating the gardener like a friend which is plum snooty, if you ask me. I say, 'A hot-blooded male on the premises sure does relieve the strain of murder in the second degree.' She gets to her feet right away and gathers up her stuff.

'That's it, 'she says. 'That's enough for one morning.' I say I've had enough too and if she doesn't mind I'll hang about down here for a while. She says 'Make sure you fix yourself some lunch.' Nice as pie, as if she likes me and the weight that's been gathering about my heart lifts. I think how fine the world can be even when the going is hard.

I sing what I've so far written of my ode to Rita Mae and wonder if he can hear me up in the jungle.

Now you're dead and gone Rita Mae
On lonely nights I try to hear you play'n'
Sweet and low on your old banjo
But I cain't. You're dead and gone, Rita Mae.

I sing loud but it doesn't lure him from his work. Maybe he's not musical. Paddy has such a store of music in him. Micky was tone deaf but he loved me to sing for him. Micky and me were never right for each other, no matter what I told myself or he told me. We were wrong, wrong, wrong but I set out to make Paddy jealous and suddenly we were so involved I couldn't get uninvolved. I could've ended up Mrs Besant. I thought it was what I wanted. Stella Maria just about flipped.

I said, 'Plenty of people get married at fifteen in the US. Priscilla Presley to name but one. It's usual out in Tennessee.'

'Only in backward families,' she said.

The big joke is I'd never even have met him if I hadn't known her. He played pool with Paddy and I used to make Stella Maria go to the pool hall any time I thought her brother might be there. She thought I'd get over it. Paddy wanted me to get over it as well. He said he didn't want to take advantage of a poor orphan girl when he was so much older and not in her best interests. But a boy with diamonds in his eyes says this and do you believe him?

Not long after Josie died, my love for him was so out of control and so not being returned, that I'd have fallen for anyone. You just can't live with that much love to spare.

Little house in the valley, a girl lives there,
Hair of gold, lips like wine and so much love to spare,
Little house on the hillside, a boy lives there,
Lonely as can be—

You know what doesn't work here? *Family eaten by a bear.*

I never liked the line and I never thought it was one of my best. But Merv heard it, his eyes lit up, he said, 'Now this we can work with.' Rita added some banjo, Merv told the label it was a classic because of the hillbilly storyline and moving retro sound not to mention the irrestistible boy-meets-girl theme. Record companies can't get enough boy meets girl. They say it sells. But what do they know about what sells? No one knows what sells till it sells.

Paddy was my inspiration for the valley song and when I sing it now, my heart churns. You'll never see anyone as handsome as my gypsy boy. Abraham looks as if he's spent the whole of his life ambling between valley and hill making things grow which is magnetic for someone craving serenity but Paddy's a poet prince. His hair is black, his skin is white, he moves like a panther and he has eyes the colour of the sapphire ring Mammy took to her grave.

Stella Maria believes even today that Micky cured me of the crush I had on her brother. She thought the reason Paddy was so much at my place was to do good works to make up for his sinning elsewhere. I don't think it crossed her mind to wonder why one house had so much go wrong with it. He was never that sinning anyway. Just did the one armed robbery and he was only the look-out. Father O'Mahoney spoke up for him in court and kept him out of jail. You'd think that might alert Stella Maria to her need for an alibi. She's got no priest here to save her. Just me. Micky, who knew the wrong side of the law better than anyone always said, 'Trust no one with the truth, Honey. They never know what to make of it.'

The O'Shea children have all been a sore disappointment to their mother. Stella Maria couldn't hold down a job to save her life and now she's charged with reckless homicide. Paddy was off the rails as soon as he realised they led straight back to Cockfosters and their little sister Clover could pass for a mute. But Fatima should count her lucky stars she never had Micky for a son.

Micky had loads of charm and eyes that lit up every room he was in, turning every girl who saw them into a sick weedy thing with no will of her own, excepting Stella Maria. She made puking noises at the very thought of him sticking his lips on to anyone.

One day he wasn't in my life and the next day he was, and then he took it over the way people do when they have incredible charm, like Johnny Cash, who I understand was mesmerising when he was on speed. Stella Maria and I dropped into the pool hall one night when it was so terrible out almost no one was. Stella Maria had tried to talk me out of it. She said a) her brother was physically repulsive, b) I wasn't his type, and c) we would get pneumonia but I said I was going anyway so she tagged along.

She was dead wrong as regards a), but as for b), it sure looked that way. Paddy spoke to me the way he spoke to her. When we pitched up at the pool hall with our faces blue from cold, our noses all red and wet and our hair glued to our heads, he didn't even look up.

'You here because someone's dead?' he said to Stella Maria and they started getting at each other in a way I preferred not to involve me. Any minute, I knew, Stella Maria would make me agree that he had a face like a pig's anus so I wandered away and there was Micky. A young, short, blond Johnny Cash, all gaunt and mean, his voice in a slightly higher register.

'Hey!' he said and I knew I could make him love me. 'Hey babe!' he said and I thought, in the absence of Paddy, he'd do. A bolt of lightning boinged out of his pupils rendering me senseless. I say boinged. I'm going for the word that looks like lightning.

I wrote *Tall Broad Hunk of Danger* that night, even though Micky was neither tall nor broad, and I still love that song. It's in a minor key, because a boy who's in and out of jail lives in a minor key, right?

> *Tall, broad hunk of danger,*
> *Lead me where you will*
> *Your life is surely stranger*
> *Than a paradise that's hell.*

I wrote it hearing Johnny Cash's voice in my head but it's a girl's song. When I sing it, I try to make my voice vibrate so that the receiver of the song will get the picture I'm attempting to deliver, of a female Johnny Cash maybe on speed delivering a bolt of lightning to some girl's heart.

It doesn't matter 'will' and 'hell' don't rhyme. 'Speak' and 'sleep' don't rhyme in the first verse of *The Gambler*, Kenny Rogers' classic, loved across the world by all generations. *'On a warm summer's evening, on a train da-de-da da, I na-ne-na-ne-nana . . . we were both too tired to SLEEP. So blah de blah de blah blah . . . out the window at the darkness, till boredom overtook us and he began to SPEAK.'* Some writers ignore rhyming altogether but theirs aren't proper ballads, in my opinion.

I was fifteen and nine months the night we went to the pool hall and Josie had been dead eight weeks. I'd dropped out of school, I was living alone, and the house in Cockfosters was full of ghosts. Josie and Mammy and Jimmie, who'd wail in the dead of night for the life he never had. Stella Maria said I was sleeping too much in the day and it was why my imagination was out of control at night. She thought I was letting myself rot and needed to take myself in hand. She said get a job but I didn't want a job. I had an allowance from the compensation I got from losing my brother and mother. It wasn't much because the trustees, especially Bundy the bank manager, were mean as hell, but it was enough to live on. And what did I want a job for when all that interested me was my music? I worked on my music, I worked on my vocabulary and I read. I knew just about everything there was to know about the great country artists. Less about the new, since they are new and we have no way yet of knowing if they're great.

Stella Maria had Saturday jobs. Job after job after job. Always being fired for giving cheek. She'd get the sack and she'd go looking for another job right away because she really loved the money. Sometimes she'd only hold a job down for a matter of minutes. It was a joke. She thought the money made me lazy but having money doesn't make you lazy. It just makes you choosy. She said I was unfocused. She was focused on making money. I was focused on nothing. I said I was focused on higher things. 'Oh right,' she said. 'Dicks.'

Maybe I didn't look into my future and see a career path like Dolly who knew when she was ten that she was going to be a singer. But I wasn't doing nothing. I was waiting for life to move me on, waiting for signs from Mammy to tell me what to do. I'd see an ant and wait to see what message it brought me. I'd say if it runs here, she wants me to do that, if it runs there, she wants me to do something else. I'm less insect-based in my relationship with Mammy now.

Anyway, Micky Besant says, 'Hey!' I go, 'Alright?' and even if I still looked aimless, my day-to-day existing all at once had a point. I totally threw myself into loving him. Paddy came round to put a washer on the kitchen tap and to tell me to stay away from him. I said to him 'What's it to you?' as he himself at the time was seeing a fat girl who called herself a glamour model. Then he told Stella Maria to tell me to stay away because Micky was trouble and I thought, who needs a brother?

It's too hot down here now. I head back up to the house, seeing neither hide nor hair of Abraham. He must've gone home for lunch. No sign of Betty, either. Her study door's open and inside I can see only Stella Maria who's on the phone.

'Get me out of here,' she's saying and she's crying like a baby. 'I want to come home. Please get me home.' Whoa!

17

Can't be Fatima. Can't be her Dad, who's only ever said to her, 'Ask your mother.' I know it's Paddy even before she's turned to find me standing in the doorway. I want to grab the phone from her and pour all my love into it even though he doesn't want it anymore but she sees me, she says, 'OK, OK,' and puts the receiver down before I can take a single step in her direction.

'Harvey,' she says. 'That was Harvey. He's coming tomorrow to take us through our evidence.' She brushes past me and goes to her room, closing the door behind her, slamming me out of her life.

That's not how we speak to Harvey. I'm halfway down the hall to her room to say so when the phone rings again and we both make a dash for it. I get there first. 'Is this the correct number for Miss Honey Hawksworth?' Merv says.

'Hi, Merv,' I say. And he hears the disappointment in my voice.

'You expectin' someone better lookin'?'

Stella Maria disappears, not interested in Merv. I want to

haul her back and say who did she think it would be, but Merv wants to know how I'm doin' with the tribute and I'm sensing an urgency that's rare in him. I say it's going fine, real well. And I concentrate hard so's to reassure him. 'Kind of with pathos but sinister,' I say.

'Sinister,' he says.

'Not exactly sinister. Kind of dark.'

'Dark,' he says.

'Not dark. Light,' I say. 'Light and dark. Sinister and not sinister. Same as she was.'

'Great,' he says. 'Not sinister. Not dark.' We have a long silence while we think about that. He says he has a mind to come and visit with us and I say well we could come to visit him. I'd been hankering after a trip into Nashville. He says haven't I been away only three days? And the truth is I can't remember. I just want a break.

He says well he has a cousin down the way from us a little. I tell him Dick's got a cousin down the way a little as well. He says he's not related to Dick and I can feel the conversation falling in on itself when he says. 'You know one thing you might like to be thinkin' about? You could be thinkin' about how much Rita Mae had to give. That little gal had so much talent. Maybe you could be addressin' the loss of that talent. Light and dark.'

This fills me with so much disgust I end the conversation there and then. I say Ah'll see him tomorrow or maybe the next day and Ah'll be looking forward to that, I truly will, then I hang up.

Rita Mae's horrible tentacles are reaching out from the grave and getting me by the throat. She was always wanting to grab the attention I had won on my own account when she'd never been able to win any on hers. She wanted to have the Honey album called *Bluegrass Babes* and never stopped pitching for equal billing when no way did she deserve it. The songs are mine and I'm the singer. The life in the songs is mine. Christ, she'd never even heard of *Wormwood Scrubs*, my tribute to the man in black's *Folsom Prison Blues*. And *Wormwood Scrubs* is the best thing on the album, Stella Maria says no question. And what's scary is that now I doubt her. Now I'm wondering if she does think that or if she has a reason for saying it I don't know. Am I losing faith in her or me?

It's hot. It's stinking hot. I wander out on to the porch, drop on to the hammock and light myself a fag. Deep in the jungle garden I can see the life Betty wants me to recall, all hazy and ghost-like and Stella Maria's in there, every inch of the way, even when she was trying not to be. Pulling me here, pushing me there and I went along with her because I trusted her. Just the way she should now be trusting me. She put an end to Micky and me, even if that was a mercy killing.

Funny thing. I've hardly thought about Micky since I got to Nashville but here he is now, real as he ever was, breathed into life by Betty's plan for keeping us out of jail. I feel bad for him now. Sad for him now. He thought I loved him for four years. Off and on. But now I know I only ever loved Paddy.

Sometimes Micky'd disappear because he was in hotter than usual water with his business acquaintances, once he went to jail for three months for bashing someone, but mostly I sent him packing. Stella Maria sent him packing the time he smacked me in the face and broke my jaw. I remember how chuffed he was I'd written something just for him.

Hard men go to the Scrubs to die,
Turn their face to the wall, say they'd sooner fry etc.

I kissed Paddy on my sixteenth birthday and he kissed me back. There was a party for me at the pool hall and I was supposed to be with Micky. Well I was with Micky but it was early days and there was Paddy, on his own, having a quiet fag outside and thinking it was time for him to leave. There I was, looking for him but pretending all I wanted was air. He said, 'What are you doing, going around with Besant? He's a madman.'

I said, 'You available then?' And he ruffled my hair and laughed. Pretending he was my brother. So I kissed him and he kissed me back. His mouth received my lips like they were a dentist's drill but I kept them there and I pressed my body into his and soon he was kissing me for all it was worth until he pushed me away and laughed. He said what was he thinking. I said that I was irresistible. He said he could resist me. I said I loved him and he laughed again. He said he loved me too, like a sister. So I kissed him again and said did he kiss Stella Maria like that? He said OK not like a sister. Not love either. He was fond of me, but not like that. So I kissed him again and Stella Maria turned up and threatened to break his legs. This made him laugh so hard I had to hit him.

Next day I told Micky I loved him. OK it was on the rebound but I just thought that the kiss had cleared my head and it truly was Micky I loved. He loved me. I made Cockfosters into a love nest for us with home-cooked meals, the smell of Pledge and flowers all over the house, the way Mammy did for her boyfriends.

He never moved in on a permanent basis. He just stayed the night now and again which is how he liked it. When the police came looking for him, he was never there and I never knew where he was so I couldn't tell them anything even if they tortured me. But when he wasn't there my arms ached for him and my heart thumped with fear for him which produced a whole pile of songs. *Missin' You At Night Most of All*, *The One You're With* and of course *All You've Left Behind You Is Your Smell*. Stella Maria said, is that meant to be funny. No, I said.

Sometimes the Social Services popped in to see how I was doing and comment on how clean the house looked. They'd say had I thought about going back to my studies but I'd say no. They weren't that impressed with my domestic situation.

They said did I know this boy's background? I said sure I knew his background. He was raised on a council estate five miles from Cockfosters where two policemen had been killed and there was a crack problem. His family was poor and he was like any boy from any ghetto, looking for a way out. I played them *In the Ghetto*, another song Dolly has made her own.

They said, 'Don't romanticise him, Honey.'

I said, 'I'm facing facts. The facts are I love him and he loves me.' I knew he felt bad for hitting me. *The Things You Do* is a song I wrote about domestic violence: '*Hand, why do you/ Do the things you do?*'

From the hammock I can see back down the hall and I keep looking for Stella Maria who worries me when she shows signs of mental illness. I don't think she'll do anything stupid but you never know. She sure is crying a lot for someone who never cries.

I hop off the hammock, stub my smoke out on the heel of my boot, put it into my pocket, then stand outside her room singing *In The Ghetto* because she can't stand it. I wait for her to yell 'Shut the fuck up,' but she doesn't which proves how deep this sulk is.

In the kitchen, I fix myself some carrots and stuff and remember the worry she caused me when I was with Micky. I'd worry she was alone and sad because I wasn't with her but I couldn't forsake my man for her. I tried to make her come over when he was there, but she'd say, 'Why?' And it would have been rubbish. All she and Micky had in common was me.

When he wasn't there I'd phone her up and say come over and she'd say did I think she was a fucking doormat, but she'd turn up anyway and we'd slip right back to where we were before he entered our lives. We'd have a great laugh. She'd say, 'Don't you think you're worth more than that steaming pile of shite?' She didn't know how safe I felt curled up in his arms in my little bed. We never slept in Mammy's room. It wouldn't have been right.

I'd say, 'I love him.'

She'd go, 'Oh, for Christ's sake.'

Overnight though, I stopped being happy with Micky, hardly remembering why I ever had been. It must've have been because I'd wanted to be which is all an optimistic nature needs. A big enough want. There had even been days when I'd forgotten I wanted him to be Paddy. But in the end, I knew I was just pretending. Like Mammy used to do.

One day he went away somewhere, up north, don't know where, and I thought I might go mad with longing for Paddy. If you haven't experienced it, you won't know the pain of yearning like that. Your flesh aches with it. Your throat bursts with wanting to scream. I pulled out all the nails holding a kitchen cupboard to the wall, I let it fall and when the mess was total, I phoned him to come and fix it.

He said, 'Can't it wait till Micky gets back?'

I said 'No, Paddy it can't. There are cockroaches and stuff.' So he cursed me because he was expected somewhere, then over he came. That was that.

He looked at the cupboard, he looked at everything all over the floor, he looked into my eyes then he put his arms around me and he touched my lips with his. Oh God, the memory of it chills me, even in this heat. Being a secret just heightened every sensation. I nearly went mad with sensations. Our world was this private place where passion dwelt. Title, if I wrote an opera, *Where Passion Dwells*.

He stayed that night and the next and no one knew he was there. I told Stella Maria I was working and even though she came over, he stayed in Mammy's room and she was never any the wiser. Even when she said she thought she could smell him. I told her he'd been over to fix my cupboard and God what was he wearing as aftershave these days?

It lasted a week, then it ended. It was always going to end.

I asked Mammy was he the man for me. I reached for a falling leaf and thought if I catch it, he's mine; if I can't, he's not, and it fluttered away. I said send an insect, even a cockroach, but she didn't. I said get the barking dog to stop. The dog barked all right.

I can recall the feel of him, the touch of him, the sound of him whispering in my ear. The sound of the door closing behind him. We'd talked and talked, about sorrow and joy and dreams and nightmares, our past, our present, but it was when we got to our future that our world collapsed. 'So when will we get married?' I asked him, snuggled warm and cosy in his arms.

'You don't want to go spoiling things now do you, Honey,' he said. That's what he said. I told him marriage spoilt nothing. Married was a fine thing to be for two people who loved each other and wanted children.

He said, 'Not necessarily.'

I sat up and looked him in the eye. 'You want to marry me, don't you?' And he looked back at me like I'd asked, 'Can I plunge a knife in your chest?'

He said, 'Honey, I can't marry you.'

'Why?' I asked him.

He said, 'Look at you. You have to have a life before you marry anyone.' And after I'd cried a billion buckets and he'd said a few more hurtful things about me getting a life, I told him to sod off then. He looked at me from under those long black lashes for what seemed like an hour. Then he said, 'If you like.' And he did.

Micky came home and I knew at once it was over between him and me as well. I just didn't know what to do about it. I went up to town with Stella Maria, first time in months, and having done it the once, we did it all the time whether Micky was in town or not. I told him I was young and needed to get out more. 'OK,' he said. 'Just remember who's waiting at home for you.'

We hit the Soho clubs because Stella Maria knew that's where the record industry hung out and she thought if she met a guy from a band, I could become the band's singer, she'd get to be the manager and one way or another, we'd make it. I didn't want to marry any old cheese in an English band. And I always thought who could she manage when she couldn't even hold down a job at Our Price? But I went along with her because she was my buddy and I understood her dream. I shove a couple of carrots into my pocket and bang on her door, 'Let me in,' I say. 'I'm sick of this now. I'll do whatever you want. Let me in.'

18

She's gone. I knew it. You can hear a silence louder than a scream. Window's open. Room's empty. I run out on to the porch yelling her name but I can't see her and one thing I can bank on is her not saying, 'I'm in the jungle, come and find me.' I want to kill her because sulking's one thing but giving people heart failure is another.

All around the kitchen garden I run, calling, calling, but quietly so's not to alarm anyone else, then through the jungle, expecting any minute to run into her body dangling from a branch because she has given in to despair. I also look under bushes in case she's winding me up, then out on to the terraces where I collide with Betty who's bent over a garden bed with Abraham at her side. They're so engrossed in the dirt they nearly fall into it when I trip over them.

Abraham jumps to his feet. He says he's mighty sorry. I say how mighty sorry I am. Betty says, 'Where you off to in such a hurry, Honey?' And I'm about to make up a story but think Betty's on our side and if Stella Maria's legged it, she could fall down a ravine or any damn thing so I'm going to need her help.

'Looking for Stella Maria,' I say. 'You seen her?' Betty says she hasn't. Abraham shakes his head.

Betty says, 'You looked in the house?' which I consider to be a pretty dumb question given I'm in the garden looking. I tell her she's nowhere in the house and nowhere outside the house either.

Abraham helps Betty to her feet and she brushes the soil from her hands. She says when did I last see her and I say maybe twenty minutes ago. She says well she can't have gone far but she's looking up the mountain and I know she's worried. She's hurrying back through the jungle, she's telling Abraham to hurry and pretty soon we're all running and covering the ground I've already covered with the same result.

'Take the jeep, Abe,' she says. 'If you find her, don't you frighten her now.' Then she grabs my arm and says we'll take the valley path to the village because she's almost certainly gone to the Post Office to send a card to her family. I'm thinking she most certainly hasn't but I don't know where else to say we should look. Betty says, 'Don't look so worried, Honey. We'll find her.' But my heart's pounding anyway. Stella Maria never runs away from anyone or anything. Not ever.

The Post Office is two miles there, two miles back, past just three other places set so well back there's no point troubling the householders about the casual sighting of a rank stranger who's an escaped alleged murderer having a breakdown. Betty's not talking much, concentrating on speed, and I'm having some trouble keeping up. I'm trying to force images of a dead best friend out of my head best way I can which is by counting. At six thousand and two, Betty wants me to tell her the names of other close friends we have back in London. 'Can't think of any,' I say.

She looks at me as if I'm joking, but sees I'm not. 'None?' she asks.

I say, 'Stella Maria doesn't like other people.' And this is the truth. She's honestly never wanted any other friends and I didn't care because we were great together.

She was so happy when we got shot of Micky her face changed. Like someone had tugged all the skin from behind to create a permanent smile. Getting shot of Micky coincided of course with us landing the Nashville gig. She's not in the Post Office and we're in and out in a flash, which I'd regret if I wasn't so worried. The lady who runs it has a halo of white hair, cheeks like apples and a voice as southern fried as you're ever going to get. 'Bye y'all' she calls after us.

'Bye Ma'am,' I call back.

Betty says even less on the way back and I don't have the breath to talk. I study the road beneath my feet which is what you do when you're walking uphill.

Downhill clutching you,
Uphill no view.
Lead me to the even ground
Where we can be at peace together (words and music HH).

Betty suddenly says, like there hasn't been three miles and a Post Office between comments, 'So it was always just you and Stella Maria.' I say we knew other people, but we never hung out with them. And I can hear it sounding nuts.

'Funny though,' I say. 'Where no one liked her back home, plenty of people in Nashville do.'

Not necessarily Dick and Jerrah, but loads of others. She certainly has a future in star management as I've tried many times to tell her. Thing is she's depressed. It accounts for her behaving like a great gobshite when she's a positive thinker by nature. Oh God, oh God where is she? I pray to God she hasn't topped herself. I pray to Mammy and every saint whose name I can recall. I can tell Betty's worried. I'd like to ask her about Stella Maria's depression but not if she's going to tell me is it's all my fault.

Betty's just about running up the hill and now she's asking me how much money Stella Maria has, if Stella Maria has credit cards and whether she knows people in Nashville she might call on. I say, 'She has all our money. She could contact Merv maybe. But probably Tom.'

She says, 'Shoot. Of course.' And she sprints away, leaving me for dead, unbelievably fit for a pipe-smoker. If she's implicating Tom in Stella Maria's disappearance I'll never get my phone back. And if I don't get my phone back, the film's stuffed. If the film's stuffed, I'm double stuffed. I wouldn't even have a film to dedicate to the memory of my dear and only friend.

I curse the fact that Betty's a virgin and unable to see the way love goes. If she knew anything about risks and rewards, she'd know you've got to put your money on the table before you can win. I'm looking at Betty and Stella Maria and I'm seeing them bonded by disappointment in love but mainly because they kept their investment down to nothin'.

Betty thinks Tom's not meant for Stella Maria. What she doesn't get is that Mammy would never have put him into my path if he'd been all bad. She never would. When she finds for me an instrument of progression like a pile of money, a rhyme from nowhere, or a boy to love, she chooses carefully.

I ask Mammy to send Betty someone to love but first to find Stella Maria safe and sound because I need her and I love her and even if I did say different to Betty, I can't do without her. And Mammy sends her back to me. By the time I get to the house, Betty has her closeted in her study and I'm so mad at her I could bash her. I charge in there and say as calmly as I can manage, 'So where were you?'

She's in the chair, her face is green, her eyes are red. Title –

but only if the song's about martians. 'Nowhere,' she says so sulky I can't imagine that I was bothered worrying.

Betty says, 'Honey, will you excuse us?'

I tell her no I won't. Stella Maria has just given me heart failure and I want to know why.

'I went for a walk,' Stella Maria says. 'That's all. What was the big fuss?'

I tell her the big fuss was her disappearing and me not knowing where she was when there are wild boar out there. Betty tells me to calm down. We were all worried but it's over now. I say I'm not leaving the room till I know what's over so Betty tells me as Stella Maria can't bring herself to.

Her story is that after talking on the phone to Harvey about the hearing she panicked and took off. She just ran and ran, in a circle as it turns out, because Harvey was pushing her to remember exactly where she was at what minute during that fateful morning and she completely spun out. Now she's spinning out for Betty. I leave the room but only as far as the door so I can hear what else is being said even if it is only snatches. Stella Maria's going over the morning of Rita Mae's death.

We went to the dentist, we parted company, she went to the office, she came back home. She was upset. She's upset now. She was on the roof. She left it. She sat in the stairwell. That's all she knows.

'Tom was on the roof, right?'

'On the fire stairs.'

'Was anyone on the roof?'

'Maybe Archie. Archie was.'

Betty says, 'Just Archie?'

'The workmen.'

'Did you speak to any of them?' I don't catch Stella Maria's reply. 'Why was that?' Betty wants to know.

'Because I'd taken their fucking ball away.' I hear Betty's silence. I know how she's looking at Stella Maria. Like she's never heard the word fuck before. I hear Stella Maria take a breath because she can't really be fagged with this talking. 'They'd broken my pots.'

'OK. How long were you on the stairs?' No answer. 'Well do you know what time it was when you joined Honey in the apartment?'

'No.' she says. 'No, no, no.'

I jump away from the door just as Betty opens it. 'Honey, would you care to join us?' She smiles but it turns out she doesn't mean it. 'I want you to tell me why you are persisting in a story Stella Maria insists is a lie? I want you to understand just how much damage you're doing by telling such a story. If that's what you are doing.'

19

I want to say OK, I'll tell you. Because Stella Maria hated Rita Mae with a passion so fierce they couldn't be in the same room, that plenty of people knew it and thought one day she might snap and kill her, that those same plenty might get up in court and say that very thing unless someone proves she couldn't have because she was elsewhere. That someone is me.

I'm looking at them both looking at me and I'm seeing the two most naive people on the planet. What can I do when they know zero about love and its consequences? Rita Mae slept with the man her alleged murderer loved and Rita Mae alienated the affections of her alleged murderer's best friend, business partner and protégé, me.

Maybe I also slept with the man the alleged murderer loved but all that says is maybe the alleged murderer will come after me. And some days I think she is. I say 'It's no lie. Stella Maria knows it isn't a lie. We were in my room talking over the schedules like we did every day and we didn't know Rita was dead until Archie knocked on the door and told us.

Isn't that true, Stella Maria?' She says nothing. I say, 'That's the truth.'

'Archie doesn't say he saw Stella Maria,' Betty says.

'He doesn't say he didn't either. He heard her because she was there.' And she was there. When he knocked on the door, Stella Maria had been sitting on my bed for three full minutes. Archie's no idiot. He loves Stella Maria and he loves me and he sees the value in what I'm doing. He never had any time for Rita Mae. He thought she was a child of the devil. He can't say he saw her in my room but he can say he truly believed she was there. Only reason he didn't see her was he was in such a state himself.

'Well what did he hear?' Betty's asking.

'He heard her crying,' I say.

'Over Rita Mae?'

'Yeah.' Betty turns to Stella Maria. Stella Maria looks out the window. 'She'd just caught her in bed with her boyfriend for God's sake. Of course she was crying.'

'So what did Archie say?' Betty asks. And all I can tell her is not much. His face was the colour of concrete. He could hardly string three words together. It was the most shocking thing that had happened to him since his wife ran off with the gasman. A brick falls off the roof of a building where you're janitor and kills someone, then you're in trouble.

'He just told us. He didn't hang about. It was a bad time for him,' I say. 'Stella Maria and me felt really terrible for him.'

Stella Maria snaps. 'You're not helping. You think you are but you're not.'

'Nor are you,' I say. Then I ask Betty if I can go and even though she doesn't want me to, I'm out the door before she can stop me. But I remember Merv and have to come back to say he'd like to visit tomorrow if it's alright with her.

Betty thinks on it then says well she's not sure it is. Harvey would like to call on us tomorrow. The prospect of this makes

Stella Maria go, 'Oh no', so Betty says maybe she'll ask Harvey to come the next day and I say thanks.

I just can't believe this is happening. Before we left our native shores there's no way Stella Maria and me would be burrowing our way down different tunnels to get out of the same hole. We'd be hanging on to each other for dear life and drawing comfort from each other's strength and company. The two of us together against the world.

Look how solid we were on Micky. Maybe I wasn't so happy with the way Stella Maria sorted it at the time, but now I believe she was doing it for my own good. This is how it's always been and how I thought it would be when we were both good and married with a hundred kids hanging off our heels and record contracts coming out of our ears.

It's not like this is a big hole. Someone's died in an accident and we're accidentally being blamed. What's beginning to get to me is how big a deal it's become. What's upsetting me is why the people who should be making everyone see it's a small deal aren't, and this should be the happiest time of our lives.

I get my smokes and guitar from my room. I'm going to lose myself for a while, deep in the jungle garden where animals hide when the harsh light of the day gets too much for them. I find a fern to lean against, I light a fag, stick it in my mouth and sing with it dangling from my lip.

Now you've gone to God Rita Mae.
I try to grieve but only hear you say . . .

. . . what? What can I hear Rita Mae say? She'd be saying, 'Why bother? The girl's an idiot.'

Rita Mae taught me a thing or two about human nature. Maybe I should be grieving for her. Maybe I should be crying over the loss of my musical soul mate. But you can only do so much grieving in a lifetime, and then only for people you've loved. Stella Maria's grieving for her lost dream which she loved more than she hated Rita Mae.

She was so revved up when we met Tom. So sure we were on our way to fame and fortune. I never liked to point out to her that my life story wasn't something she could take credit for when Fate, not her, had made me an orphan who could be plucked from obscurity, propelled towards the limelight by talent and obsession and would now take her chance on life's wheel of fortune in the land of her dreams. But why spoil it for her? She'd been spot on about its appeal.

She sold it so well to Tom that even when he woke up the morning after we met wanting to forget he'd ever met us, she managed to persuade him we were worth a trip to Cockfosters. She was only sorry I hadn't grown up in Lonesome, a place we'd heard about in south London.

I'd also woken up that morning thinking just forget it. I didn't want to sell my life to anyone for anything. 'What's he know about country music. What's he know about me?' I said to Stella Maria when she turned up before I was even out of bed. She had to use every bit of self control not to scream.

She said, 'He can tell your story like it is.' I composed on the spot the first two lines of *Telling It Like It Is*.

Just telling it like it is, the facts are sweet and true,
There's sun, there's moon, there's rain, there's shine
So why don't I trust you?

Then she flipped. It had only been a matter of time. 'Get your lazy arse washed and dressed,' she yelled, 'or you'll never get to Nashville.'

I said I wasn't leaving Mammy. I wasn't ready.

She struggled with that. She said we could take her with us. I said that still left Jimmy and Josie. She said them too. But that's not how ghosts work. They cling to walls and ceilings and doorways and we couldn't bring them with us.

She wanted to kill me. Her brows formed a thunder cloud over eyes that would've rained buckets had she been the crying type at that time. She wanted to be understanding but she couldn't manage it. She yelled for five minutes so I put my head under the pillow. She grabbed the pillow and beat me with it.

'You stupid cow. Don't you know this is the only chance you'll have to get out of this stinking hole? Are you going to fester here until you're beaten to a pulp by a useless thieving punk?' I said nothing. 'The only man who'll ever get you out of this dump will be here in one hour so, please get up, Honey, please, please, get up.' I did, because she was begging.

Funny thing about plants. They give off feelings. This fern scraping my neck, looks all soft and welcoming but it's bloody aggressive in point of fact. I play a few loud chords to accompany the memory of that day and the fag falls out of my mouth and between my legs. I have to move quickly to stop myself catching fire.

I thought Tom wouldn't turn up, whatever Stella Maria said, but he did and he loved everything he saw. He loved my room being jam packed with items of country memorabilia for a start. 'Brilliant,' he said.

The big surprise was how boring he suddenly wasn't. It still surprises me because he can be a bore, right, but when he's working he never is, unless of course he's explaining what's in his kit. Then he is.

He sat on my bed telling me why even against his better judgement, my story was so appealing to him. 'It's your turn to have a win, Honey,' he said. 'Your life has been nothing but losses. We could tell the story of how your terrible luck becomes your great good fortune.'

I wasn't sure. My interest, story-wise, has always been tragedy. Writing tragic songs puts my life into perspective. He said he hoped I wasn't frightened of good fortune because I'd had so much bad. I said all I was frightened of was leaving Mammy in the house without me.

This stopped him in his tracks. He said, 'Why do you think your mother died?'

'The hospital killed her,' I said.

He said, 'That's not why she died. That's how she died. I'm saying why do you think she died.' I didn't know what he meant. He said, 'Listen, Honey. We all die. But some of us die before we've taken a proper breath like your little brother and some of us die when we're young and beautiful and we haven't finished what we started, like your Mum. Why do you think that is?'

'They're called,' was all I could think. He said maybe. But the reason they were called when they were called was down to one thing and one thing only and that was luck.

'The woman in the bed next to your Mum didn't die. The baby born after your brother didn't die. No one expected your Mum and your brother to die but they did because of shit luck. And you know what was good luck? They left you behind. So all their money's on you. You've got your ticket in the lottery and now you've got theirs as well and it's up to you to make the most of them.'

I said, 'A ticket doesn't make you a winner.'

'Wrong,' he went. 'Your ticket's already won a whole pile of stuff. More time. A gift for music. A friend who's talked me into coming out to this godforsaken place. A hundred more tickets, that's what I'm offering you. A hundred more tickets in the lottery of life, if you come with me to Nashville to see if you can crack it.'

He sat there, watching me with eyes which truly sparkle when they aren't fogged by the shite he shoves into his body and I thought but do I trust him? I wanted to. Stella Maria said, 'You want to hear her sing again?'

She was wearing a dress which came so far down her chest you could just about see her knickers. She was pretty clever here because she knew how much I liked to sing for an appreciative audience. I did *I Long For You* which I wrote on a lonely night without Micky but it was about Mammy.

124

I long for you, this song's for you
May angels bring my voice to you
I'll walk across the world for you
Oh please come back to me.

That's the chorus. The verses are about a woman who goes in search of her lover who's been hit on the head and has died in a ditch though she doesn't know. She finds him in the end. Too late. When I'd finished Tom sat there struck dumb. 'Great,' was the only word he could utter.

He and Stella Maria began talking about a schedule which would include filming in London prior to our departure, some filming round and about Cockfosters and meetings with US labels a.s.a.p. I wasn't listening because I was still hearing my voice in my head and thinking I could've sung even better and what he would have said if I had. I tuned back in to hear him say we'd leave for Nashville as soon as he felt everything that could be lined up was lined up. Stella Maria said, 'Like what?'

He said, 'Production details, money.' He said we could have a contract if we wanted but he thought at this stage a loose arrangement was better. I said could we please stick to no arrangement as I hadn't agreed to anything which made them both sigh loudly together as if they'd rehearsed it, which was weird.

Stella Maria said, 'Think how proud you'd be making Toni.' And it was a fair point. I could see it was a great chance for me to do what Mammy should always have done. Gone with her music to find love in the Blue Ridge mountains. But I just couldn't see how I was going to cope.

Then Tom said, 'OK, one thing we have to get clear. This will only work if you trust me. I don't know what I can do to make you trust me but if you can't, the thing's dead in the water.'

I said, 'Well the truth is I don't trust you. I don't think I can confide in you because I don't know the sort of person you are but the sort of person you seem to be gives me the creeps.'

Stella Maria went, 'Honey!'

Tom laughed. He said he knew how I was feeling. Trust was a very hard thing to give, especially for an artist who has so much to protect. But an artist has to trust people, or in the end their art ends up a secret and what kind of art is that? 'You can't be an artist if you're not a gambler,' he said. 'And I know you're an artist, Honey. I know you're a real artist.'

He said making this film would be the biggest gamble of his life. It was going to cost him a fortune in time and money but that was his investment. Mine would be placing my life story and all my talent in the hands of some cheese promising me the chance of a lifetime. If we didn't trust each other, if we didn't roll our dice together, we were both blowing the chance of a lifetime so please would I trust him to give it his very best shot.

I was finding his interest endearing, I'm not denying it, and I knew we were clicking on some level Stella Maria could never understand. She was trying but she couldn't.

Telling It Like It Is never had that many words to it. I try to think of a few more, and am mucking around with *Big rig rolling down the interstate,* when the day suddenly looks up. Through the foliage, I spot Abraham fishing stuff out of the little pond right on the far edge of the garden.

He must know I'm here. I've been making enough noise. My heart's pumping so hard he has to hear it. He looks up as I crunch twigs and leaves underfoot. 'Hi,' I say. He nods. He gets back to what he's doing which is tying a green thing to a stick. I watch him. Stella Maria must have recovered because I can hear CNN in the background.

I'm racking my brain for some conversation. 'What kind of pond life inhabits the Smokey Mountains?' I enquire. He has just about nothing to say on the subject. I have truly never met anyone so silent who wasn't called Clover O'Shea. Could

I stand to be married to anyone with so few words? But would he be here if Mammy didn't think I could?

I'm standing here, he's standing there and maybe something's going to happen, maybe it's not, but suddenly Betty's beating her way through the shrubs to find me. She wants me back at the house for my session which I have apparently forgotten again. I tell her how sorry I am but she's not mad. She's too relieved.

'Stella Maria has just had the nicest chat with her brother,' she says. My breathing gives up on me.

'When?' I manage.

'Just now.'

'What did he say?'

'He said it to Stella Maria.' I'm hurrying ahead of her, knowing he's no longer there, but wanting to be in the room where his voice was. Betty has to yell after me. 'I wouldn't spoil it for her. That would be a real shame if you spoiled it for her.'

20

Due respect to Betty, but I know good times for Stella Maria just as well as she knows bad times for me, and right now we couldn't give a toss for either. She's in the kitchen, piling food on to a plate. Salad, I see. I calm myself before opening my mouth. 'Is he coming then?' Casual. I'm going for casual. So's she.

'Why would he?'

'Because we're in trouble.'

'You admit we're in trouble?'

'You're in trouble,' I say. 'You don't have to be but you are.' I take a tiny finger of carrot off her plate. Her face is giving nothing away. Not a message she's keeping from me, or that the last thing she'd expect from him was a message for me. 'Did he say he checked my house?'

'What's your house to him?' she replies and she picks up her plate and heads into the den, knowing she's tormenting me because the one thing she knows he's always done for me is kept an eye on on my house.

Out on the porch, before we even start the session, I tell

Betty I need my phone back. She says all in good time and I want to yell at her that I want it right now, it's mine and she has no business keeping it. Instead I say that's a song, *All In Good Time*. She says write it then, but I don't have the same interest in titles that are other people's. It was a problem I had with Rita Mae who was always coming up with crap ideas and getting furious when I said they didn't work for me.

Now you've gone to God Rita Mae
I try to grieve but only hear you sayin'
He loves me, it was meant to be
A dirty lie so you had to die, Rita Mae.

My head's starting to ache. I'm parched but the jug of water Betty keeps on the table is empty. 'I'm going to fill the jug,' I say to Betty.

She says, 'Take it from the tap, Honey, not from the fridge. Water kept in the fridge is cooler, but not so good for you. Maybe you should get something to eat as well.' I tell her I'm not hungry. The smell of peanut butter in the den is enough to put anyone off their food. I catch a whiff of it on my way back and just about heave.

Betty's changing her tape. I say does she know, incidentally, how terrible it is for a film-maker not to have access to his subject? Tom will be just about mental with it. Please, please will she let him visit or please, please can I have my phone back? She snaps the tape into place and her expression is so kindly I'm sure she's going to give in. She says, 'Ah'd much rather he didn't. And Ah don't think havin' the phone does you even the tiniest bit of good, Honey, you know that?'

I say, 'But it's not fair to put a spanner in the works now.' I can hear a song in my head called *Spanner In The Works* and am looking for a first line when Betty spots Abraham leaving the jungle and says could I hang on just for one minute, she needs to speak to him before he leaves for the day.

She stands very close to him which makes me think he has a hearing problem. It's true that unless I stand right in front of him and make him speak to me, he won't. Betty's practically in his ear.

From this angle he has a look of Paddy. Noble, though he's taller. And bloody bugger, there are tears spilling down my face and my nose is running. Betty will wonder what the fuck is up because I don't have a handkerchief even though I always try to travel with tissues about my body. I may have a hormone deficiency. Definitely I need a Panadol.

You know what I think? That it's just as easy to fall in love with the wrong man as it is with the right. That's the truth of it. But what can you do unless you test your luck? Stay a lonely spinster for ever. Not me.

There are never any guarantees for anything. No guarantees that people will live, or when they'll die. No guarantees that the man you pick is the right one, or the wrong one, or that you'll ever get another chance at anything.

How unlucky was Rita? How unlucky is Stella Maria? How lucky am I? Micky was the wrong man for me. Tom was the wrong man for me. Paddy was the right man at the wrong time. But Mammy has sent me to this land to find the right man at the right time. I know he's the right man because he's the opposite of Micky.

I'll tell you something though. Micky was hard but you never saw anyone as sad as he was when I sang *Little Jim*, which I wrote when I was fourteen and trying to get a lump of pain out of my chest. You turn pain into music, then you can see it and hear it and touch it, and so you can bear it. He'd ask me to sing it some nights when I was curled up in his lap and the light was fading on the posters of distant hills on the wall in the front room.

When I sing it now, I don't think about the words because they commemorate such a terrible event. The worst. Not even closing my eyes gets rid of it. Fatima was stamping up and down the corridor, terrified they'd force her to keep me, wanting only to distance herself from her tart of a neighbour even if she was dying in childbirth. She'd had a seizure about me wanting to go to the hospital in my cowgirl outfit. She'd said, 'Sweet Jesus, what are you thinking, d'you know what you look like, put your school uniform on if you've got nothing better to wear.'

I said, 'Why's he blue?' The nurse said he'd been in distress. I couldn't believe they'd let a baby get distressed. He was the tiniest thing you could imagine. I covered him in kisses and I kicked them when they tried to take him off me. I began to cry and I couldn't stop. They gave me an injection so I wouldn't heave my intestines up. It stopped me crying for three years. Remembering makes my head pound so much it could explode.

I strain to hear what Betty's saying to Abraham, but make out only three words which are, 'In my study.' They're enough to get me out of that hospital and I'm grateful. It's not a place you want to hang about. Micky'd had a brother who died as well. Run over. Something we shared. Probably it was all we shared. It wasn't just Paddy that finished us. It was everything. The stupid thing was that him hanging on so hard only made me long even more to be free.

The day after Tom came to Cockfosters, Micky pitched up from wherever he'd been, off his face on something, but pleased to death with himself. He had this great surprise for me. 'I'm going to make you a star.' I laughed because what a rubbish thing to say. He said, 'I know a man who owes me who knows a man who owes him and he can fix it.' I thought what the hell is Mammy up to. Sending Tom, mucking about with Micky.

The man was Freddy Barlow, landlord at The Moon on the Green. He couldn't have owed the man who owed Micky much because all he'd said was I could sing in his back bar provided I didn't expect to get paid. He wasn't mad about country music, but he thought it might appeal to the older clientele as a one-off.

'It's your big break,' Micky said, grinning like an idiot, wanting me to be blown away. I wanted to be since he'd gone to the trouble, but you line up cracking The Moon on the Green with cracking America and who'd bother? The Moon's just a funny old pub on the high street that'll do anything to get punters in. Curry nights. Fruit machines. I didn't see myself as the musical equivalent of a curry night.

Micky spotted it on my face. He said, 'What? It's a great venue.' I said I wasn't sure I was ready. He said I had plenty of songs and some of them weren't bad. 'Christ, it has to be better than a street corner, doesn't it?' he said. His eyes had gone mean. He said, 'Think about it, then.' Then he pulled me to him, gave me a kiss and we went to bed.

Next morning he said he hoped I wouldn't pass on it as I wouldn't want him to look like a dick, would I, in front of Freddy. I said it wouldn't make any difference when everyone knew he was a dick anyway. He laughed. You could have a laugh with him.

It was Stella Maria who talked me into it. She said, 'I hope you bloody well said yes, you moron. It'll be great for the doco.' She was totally in there with Tom already. Didn't matter a scrap that I hadn't agreed to anything.

It wasn't a gig I'd have chosen to do in the normal run of things and it wasn't even a gig I wanted to do in this not normal run of things. But she was seeing another window of opportunity and she wanted to put me right through it, even if it meant picking me up and shoving me. I don't know what persuaded me in the end. A bee or something. Some sign from Mammy. I thought if I flopped that would be another sign and I'd decide what it meant when the time came.

Betty's back in her chair with the tape running asking where we were and I tell her I haven't got the foggiest. I've got a headache actually, I say. Her face relaxes, like a mother's would. She turns the tape off. She says she just is not surprised to hear that, given the stress Ah am under. She studies me for a while then says did Ah know that near to here is an old town called Rugby that was built to look like Rugby in England? I say I didn't.

She says well what she's thinking is that when Merv comes tomorrow, we could do whatever business is required and then Abe could drive us all there as a special outing. How would that be? I think groovy. I could sit up front, next to Abe, and map read. 'I think it would do Stella Maria the world of good,' I say.

21

By nightfall my head's so bad I tell Betty I have to go to bed. She gives me herbal pills that don't make a scrap of difference and says she'd like me to eat dinner first. It's pumpkin pie. I tell her I don't think I could manage it, I truly don't. I go to bed.

Can't put the stupid brace in. Too sick. Can just about manage to get the stupid net from round my face and pull the sheet back. Stella Maria comes in. I know it's her even though my eyes are closed because she shuffles everywhere in her stinky sandals. She says, 'What do you expect if you don't eat?'

I can't answer her. She says what did I have for breakfast. I say, 'Coffee.' The 'C' in coffee bounces off my brain. She says what did I have for lunch. I can't think, then I remember. It was the smell of peanut butter.

She says, 'No dinner last night. No dinner the night before. You trying to starve yourself to death?' She sits on the bed next to me and puts her hand on my forehead. It's cool and smells like shampoo. 'You worried about the song?'

'Bit.'

'You missing home?'

'Bit.'

'Paddy sends his love.' Tears leak from my head. I mop them with the mosquito net. 'He has a great new girlfriend.' I can't even whack her for meanness. This is Stella Maria cheering me up with news from home. Which now feels a long, long way away and a long, long time ago.

I keep my eyes closed to block out all light and I pray for sleep. The mosquito net lets in just about no air and all these thoughts are charging about my head, noisy as stampeding cattle. It might be cooler in the hills than in the town, but I'm baking.

In Cockfosters, I'd get Stella Maria to sleep over. It suited us both. She hated living with her family. But even after Josie died, Fatima would put her foot down most nights and say Stella Maria had a home of her own to go to. She reckoned if I were lonely, I should put myself in the hands of the local authority.

I used to freak sometimes at thoughts I couldn't put away. I'd see my family, not happy and smiling and saying it's OK we're in heaven. But dead, how they looked when they were dead. Well I'm not having those thoughts tonight. No flipping way. I concentrate on other thoughts, like Stella Maria and Micky falling out massively at the Moon audition.

Boy, did he do his nut. If I could, I'd remind Stella Maria now sitting by my bed. The smell of the shampoo hits my stomach. I feel how I felt back then. Sick to my stomach. Full of dread at so much change in the air. 'What's she doing here?' Micky said when she got off the bus with me.

'Managing her,' Stella Maria said before I could tell her to keep her trap shut.

'I'm her manager,' Micky said.

'Who's your manager, Honey?' Stella Maria went, shoving past him in the pub's doorway. 'Him or me?'

Freddy Barlow must've wondered what in God's name was going on. He didn't care one way or the other if I lived or died. While they were scrapping he kept on wiping tables, a smoke behind his ear, taking not a blind bit of notice and I was with him. Last thing I wanted was to get involved in a brawl between Micky and Stella Maria. Either of them was capable of pulping me.

Stella Maria said was this the room I'd be singing in and Freddy, not even glancing at her, said oh, where was the stage, he could see no stage. Stella Maria said how did she know he'd have a stage in a crapola junkyard like this and he said she doesn't have to sing here, you know, she looks like she can't sing anyway.

Micky said, 'Jesus.' He was finding himself in a difficult position with Freddy showing him minus respect and Stella Maria showing double minus. A nerve beneath his eye was jumping like crazy. I gave him a kiss. Stella Maria glared. He said how I looked wasn't the point. I said what's wrong with how I look and everyone stared at me as if I'd farted. Micky said Freddy had better be able to pack the place out because it was a big night for me and I was a huge talent. Freddy laughed.

I said, 'Shut it, will you, Micky.'

Stella Maria asked if a fee had been arranged and Freddy went, 'Fuck me. Who is this? Hoe-down Spice?' But he put down his J-cloth, sat at one of the tables, looked me up and down and said, 'Go on then. Let's hear you.' I knew then it was between him and me which is a lesson I took with me to Nashville. Know your audience.

I tuned my guitar and the other two shuffled about, not talking, looking everywhere but at each other and I thought this is showbiz. I was about to do *In The Ghetto*, about poverty trapping boys into lives of violence and crime just like their fathers before them, when it struck me Freddy was more of a singalong type so I did *Rawhide*, after the style of Frankie

Laine, not a household name these days but a very able singer.

OK, the song is western and not country and there's a major difference but everyone knows *Rawhide* and I like the striving in it. *Through rain and wind and weather*, I mean that's how life is, isn't it? The acoustics were shitty but this song suited my voice. I gave it everything I had in terms of technical ability and passion. *'Rollin' rollin' rollin' Keep those wagons rollin','* imagining how well it would go down with the pensioners.

Freddy's face was a picture of blank. Nothing. Then he stunned me, saying. 'Know any Dolly Parton?' I gave him *In The Ghetto*, not in Dolly's key, naturally, but it works just as well in a lower register. Maybe better.

The reason I sound so like Willie Nelson is not just a matter of pitch. I hold the final sound of each word just a fraction longer than normal somewhere between my tonsils and my sinus so it sounds like a note played on a comb through paper. Comes naturally to me. Guess it does with him too. Also I pay a lot of attention to words ending in 'N'. Many lines in a country song do. Pain, again, train, rain, soon, moon, run. Willie works an 'n' like nobody's business.

You might think *In The Ghetto* isn't country either, seeing it's set in the back streets of Chicago but country is about story, melody and gut wrench, all abundant in this particular song. *'People doncha understand, a boy needs a helpin' hand / He's gonna be an angry young man some day.'*

Stella Maria began to clap in time which didn't work for Micky so he gave her a punch in the arm, a mistake, as she whacked him back and just about killed him. She doesn't look much but she has a lot of power in her arms. I pretended nothing violent was happening. Freddy said, very flat, very unemotional, 'The lady is singing.' So they shut up and when I finished, all you could hear was the sound of Freddy breathing. He said, 'What a load of cobblers. Thursday at ten, before the main act.'

Stella Maria and Micky fought for three days about what I should wear, what I should sing, how they'd get the people in, who they should be, and on and on and on and I let them because it was pointless not to. In the end, I knew I'd do what I wanted because that's what I've always done.

And all the while Stella Maria was talking to Freddy about the best way for Tom to film me. Freddy thought being in a documentary was a blast. She didn't breathe a word to Micky, Freddy didn't breathe a word to Micky and I didn't either because I figured it was out of my hands. I wanted to concentrate on the performance. All I said to Stella Maria was, 'Just you make sure he doesn't cock things up.' She thought I meant Micky. I meant Tom.

Pleased though I was with his interest, in the back of my head, a voice, not Mammy's, probably Josie's, was saying, 'The guy's a flake'. I was beginning to rehearse ways to tell him once and for all to get off my case, I was sorry we'd troubled him, I'd crack America in my own way in my own time, thank you.

It comes to me now how many people have told me what a worry he is. Everyone except Stella Maria who's only recently changed her tune. But now I'm fond of him. I feel loyal to him. I know how hard he works. We've come this far down the track together, I want to keep going till it takes us to the end, whatever the end is.

Even then, Stella Maria and I were travelling on different journeys though we were both going by train. I was chugging along my little track with its platform running alongside for boarding and leaving at the drop of a hat and she was charging full blast along hers, which was in a long, long tunnel. I think already I was feeling detached from her, but I didn't clock the difference and she didn't either.

She was ignoring me having reservations. She fixed everything so Tom could film my performance without interruption or irritation and she did a great job. Tom loved the tacky stage, the pathetic lighting and the shitehouse tables and chairs. Obviously. If you're filming an orphan starting at the bottom, you need to see the bottom. But I intended to shine, bottom or not, and I didn't want Micky or Stella Maria or Tom distracting me.

Day of the gig Stella Maria said, 'You told Micky about Tom?'

'Not yet.'

'You better tell him. We don't want any brawling.'

I said, 'I will.' And I meant to, but I'm a performer. I was concentrating on my act. It's a simple acoustic one. Just me with my songs, my guitar and my harmonica, but even so, I had to decide what to sing, what to say between numbers and whether I wanted to wear a T-shirt with sleeves or no sleeves. I wrote a couple of new songs. One to Micky. *'Spurn it/ return it/ just don't make me earn/ your love, mountain man'*, but my heart wasn't in it.

I settled for no sleeves and black rather than white because my skin is dead white and I think that black suggests vulnerable as well as menace in a girl singer. The rest was standard. Black jeans low on the hips, black boots, hair shiny. I've never been tempted to bleach my hair even though red isn't maximum cool. I saw what long-term bleaching did to Josie's.

I wanted the lighting to be soft, yet dramatic, picking me out of the darkness like a lonely beacon of song. I said so to Micky and Stella Maria when I got each of them alone. Stella Maria said to leave it to Tom, Micky said to leave it to him. I hoped between them they'd get it right.

There are singers who want to control every inch of their careers but me, I can see the benefit in letting other people do stuff. Why do everything when you need all the time you can get to write, play and sing? That was my thinking then and it is now. But what I've learnt is that leaving stuff to others requires complete trust in others' ability to do just what you want and that trust should not be given lightly. At that time, I totally trusted Micky and Stella Maria when I had no real reason to. What did they know about lighting? What did they know about artistic? I didn't ask myself.

That night I sobbed my heart out for Mammy. I wanted her in the front row where a mother should be. Micky held me and said, 'She'd have been proud of you, baby, honest,' and I was grateful as he is emotional cripple. Stella Maria said not to be fooled. He was terrified I'd leg it and maybe he was. Losing face was a very big deal for Micky. But I had no intention of legging it. Once I stopped crying, I wanted only to get out there and do it.

Stella Maria met me in the car park, carrying a clipboard. 'You told him yet?' she asked.

I shook my head. 'You tell him.'

She said, 'Really?' She was so up for it. When things are going her way, she's hard as nails, which Betty has yet to understand.

'Only what he needs to know,' I added. And she now says what she would've said to me next, if Micky hadn't caught up with us and body-blocked her, was that no way would she withhold information from him because that would've been lying and she didn't lie. She was always going to put him in the picture totally. For everyone's good.

Micky pretended she was no one he knew and we jostled into the saloon together where I was relieved to see no sign of Tom. Micky said why didn't I order us a couple of beers while he made sure everything was up to scratch out the back. Stella Maria said no need for him to do that as she already had and everything was fine. He gave her a death look and disappeared anyway. She took off after him, to protect Tom, she said afterwards.

I went to the Ladies. To be honest, I just couldn't face the scene I knew was coming. I wanted to keep myself intact for the performance. And when I came out everything was so quiet and calm, I thought a complete bloodbath had been avoided. Now I know calm and quiet is the sound of a bloodbath.

I walked through the door of the back bar where everyone was waiting and the picture that hit me in the face was of a crowd staring down at someone on the floor, trying but not managing to get back on his feet. Micky. At the front of the crowd were Stella Maria, Freddy and Tom with his camera trained on Micky, which was, like, suicide. Micky didn't even bother to pull himself upright. He was still bent double when he charged.

People were going hey and whoo because it was a great laugh, but he'd have killed him for sure as no one was going to stop him. Then Stella Maria, seeing her window of opportunity about to be smashed by Micky's bullet head, threw herself into his path, making the ultimate sacrifice. But in a movement so quick and graceful I hardly saw it, Freddy shouldered her out of the way, grabbed Micky by his neck, smacked him twice in the head and bundled him across the room, through the bar and out on to the street. I didn't even have time to think what I wanted to scream. My heart was crying, 'Go after him,' but my legs didn't see the point so I stayed where I was. Tom's camera was now on me and Stella Maria was by my side.

'I told him,' she said.

'What?' I asked.

'That he was dumped. That we're going to Nashville with Tom.' And that was how she did it.

This is the story Betty needs to hear, about the slow collapse of a lifelong friendship as trust leaves it like breath from a balloon. 'Stella Maria?' I say, reaching out for her. But she's gone.

22

I dream I've got a headache, I wake up and my head's pounding. I can't even stand to go and find Betty so she'll give me a pill that works. At 9.00 she comes to find me. 'How ya doin', Honey?' she says so bright and shiny I can't bear to look at her. I say too sick to get up. She says well it's a glorious day, Merv will be arrivin' in two hours exactly and she has planned the most excitin' excursion.

I remember she has and that I'll be next to Abe in the jeep which is almost a healing thought. But next I remember is I haven't finished my tribute. Merv'll be expecting it and I can't even remember how it goes. Betty says, 'Stella Maria's makin' a stack of pancakes that'll do your little ole skin and bones the power of good.'

I open my eyes and see her face is all soft and smiling and gentle and happy. Thrilled to bits that Stella Maria is making such a friendly gesture. She really doesn't know Stella Maria for this to surprise her. Stella Maria cares about my welfare almost as if she can't help herself. Unfortunately, at the moment, she also hates me. Song: *Can't help hating you/ cos you're the one I love.*

I say can she give me an aspirin because my head's splitting open and I truly can't get up just yet. She says she'll go lookin' and back she comes with an Anadin that looks like someone trod on. I take it.

She says, 'Rest up a little bit but not too long now. Those pancakes are best eaten hot.'

I say, 'Compliments to the chef, Betty.'

She rolls her eyes. She's going to make a joke. 'Save them till you've eaten,' she says. 'They don't look like any Ah've ever cooked.'

I close my eyes and remember at once what I was thinking just before I went to sleep, which you do. A trick of nature. God's own narrative. I remember the night at The Moon was the night my childhood ended once and for all. Bits broke off the day Mammy died and the night Josie died but what was left gave up the ghost there and then. It was the exact same feeling. You see your life all shattered at your feet, you kick the bits out of your way, try not to give them a second glance, then you go make a new one. This is how it has to be.

Freddy said, 'Right, you're on. Where's your hat?'

I said, 'I don't wear a hat.'

He said, 'A country singer without a hat! Great!' And up he went on to the stage to introduce me to the crowd which was now massive, as people had come from all over the place at the sound of trouble. He blew into the mike, and said without any attempt to sell me to anyone who wasn't a pensioner, 'She sings as good as she looks. North London's answer to Olivia Newton John – Honey Hawksworth.'

Olivia Newton John! I've got nothing against the woman. She's had breast cancer and a difficult marriage. But she sings like a strawberry milkshake tastes and I'm your Baileys-plus-nicotine addiction. I gave Stella Maria this what-the-fuck look, but she shrugged her shoulders and gave me the thumbs up.

I didn't run on to the stage. I walked on quickly and saw

at once the lighting was a mess. I thought OK, move the mike and the stool to be in the light, but the audience was already so jumping, the last thing they wanted was an act making a cods of getting started. This is when I knew for sure that I was blessed with a natural instinct for working an audience.

I sang nine songs – six covers and three of my own including *Saving The Fare To Heaven* in honour of all the deceased in my family. Of the covers, four were old favourites but I didn't do the old favourites in the tried and tested manner. I gave them a real Honey spin, making them, for those three minutes, totally my own.

Kenny Rogers' all time hit, *Me and Bobby McGee*, went down best of all. Totally rocked, Tom said. I made it into a sexually ambiguous anthem, like Bobby could've been a guy or a girl and maybe I was a girl who liked girls, and the audience went wild. Especially when I sang, *'Holdin' Bobby's body next to mine.'* I just closed my eyes and crooned it all low with longing and I could've meant anyone.

I look back on it as a night of wonder, far surpassing my expectations for a country performance at the end of the Piccadilly line. It wasn't just the performance that rocked. It was the whole night. Cataclysmic is the word for it. Like a cry in a canyon that echoed long and loud. Started a landslide though. Started an avalanche.

Micky came back with a few mates while I was singing *I Never Promised You A Rose Garden* and trashed the saloon, getting himself trashed in the process. Freddy called the police who'd been waiting outside judging by how fast they turned up and when we were all being herded out by this arse-faced police woman, I saw Micky propped against the door, bleeding, and my heart ached for the good times we'd had together. I wanted to wrap him in my arms and say goodbye Micky, I love what you have meant to me, but the police woman wouldn't let me anywhere near him. She said,

'Keep out of it, girlie,' not appreciating the incident she was attending was an earthquake in my personal life and that keeping out wasn't an option.

I looked up and saw Tom filming me with Stella Maria at his shoulder. She was glowing with joy, not appreciating the trouble coming our way, seeing only plain sailing all the way to the top in the US of A because she'd had no experience of tragedy and no understanding of the power of luck.

Anyway. Might as well get up. The pain in my head's faded. Not gone, just faded. And I don't feel like heaving at the smell coming from the kitchen which is definitely pancake. You get a headache that's not on the mend and the smell of eggs and butter together is just not acceptable.

Have a shower and wash my hair. My pulse is blasting away in my forehead and at the top of my neck to prove the headache's just on hold. I put on my most cheerful face to show I too am up for a fine day out and bounce into the kitchen like a painfree person. The effort's wasted. No one's in the kitchen. Just this pile of pancakes and a jug of maple syrup. Yuk!

Back down the hall I go, looking for signs of human life and I can hear Betty and Stella Maria in the study with the door closed. I go back to the kitchen, put a couple of the pancakes on a plate and take it to my room to work. Merv would just not be happy with a verse and a half not properly thought through. He rates me as a songwriter.

I get to work on the four track and when he pulls in the gateway an hour and fifty-five minutes later, I have something for him that I'm pleased with. This is the mystifying thing about the creative process. Headaches are just the sound of the wheels turning, gettin' ready to roll.

'Merv, you remember Betty,' I say. I've given him this bear hug and he's given Stella Maria this bear hug and I'm so happy to see him I can hardly keep my hands off him. He's the most gorgeous man ever and Rita Mae wasn't worthy of him.

First time we met him he had his feet on his desk, his head in a cloud of smoke, and half a bottle of whisky in his stomach. I spotted two things straight away about him. One, he was more relaxed than a true professional ought to be and two, we were out of the same mould. Willie was blasting from his sound system and he was singing along so loud you only heard him when he got the phrasing wrong which was practically never.

He sized me up and said, 'You're the manager, right? And you are . . . who?' he said to Tom. Tom said he was the film-maker and Merv gave this great bellowing laugh. 'Ah ha, myth-making already.'

He's about sixty and seen it all. Almost a mountain man, given his size and his deep Tennessee accent, but more stoned old cowboy. Mammy would've fallen for him in a flash, with his sweet heart and talent bigger than the prairie. He would've been wrong for her, given his interest in the likes of women such as Rita Mae, but had he been saner and less ridden with booze and dope, he could've been my stepdad. Maybe Mammy wouldn't have liked his beard or the great big shirts he wears flopping out over his jeans but I reckon she'd have loved his old worn-down riding boots which Rita swore he never took off.

Betty's drawn to him, I can tell, and I think fantastic, they can get in the back of the jeep together and I'll make sure Stella Maria's not squashed in between them. Merv has his arm around Stella Maria's shoulders and that makes me happy too. She needs to feel safe somewhere, even if Merv would fall over if he tried to be a knight in shining armour. Actually, studying him, I reckon he's pretty sober today.

'Stella Maria, you look like a sight for sore eyes,' he says. 'Ah don't believe Ah've ever seen anyone look as purdy as you look today. But Honey, what's happened to you? You gone all scrawny on me.' We all laugh. Betty offers us the study for work but I say the porch's better. Everyone's welcome. I'll give them a live performance and send Merv away with a tape.

'Come an' join us, Abe,' I call. 'Ah'm givin' a concert.' Everyone arranges themselves around the place. I stand by the fly screen, tune up and let rip, knowin' in my heart that this song will tear the nation apart.

Now you're dead and gone, Rita Mae
On lonely nights I try to hear you playin'
Sweet and low, on your old banjo
But I cain't, you're dead and gone, Rita Mae

Now you've gone to God Rita Mae
I try to grieve but only hear you sayin'
He loves me, it was meant to be
A dirty lie so you had to die, Rita Mae

It's goin' down a storm I can tell. They're transfixed. Into the chorus where I go up an octave and I'm staring into the jungle, giving the words everything they are due.

But God loves me, Rita Mae
In Heaven the angels will say
There's mercy for all, and even those who fall
Will rise and find glory some day.

I hope you're happy now, Rita Mae
The jury found me guilty so I'm payin'
With my life, not as a wife
But a girl who loved too much, Rita Mae

Chorus again. Repeat last two lines. Finish. Bow. Wait for applause. Wait for applause. Look up. Abe's clappin'. No one else. There are tears pouring down Merv's cheeks. He can barely find the words. Eventually he says, 'Well it has great ... insight,' he says. 'It really has. It tells a mighty interestin' story. But you know ... Ah feel it's not exactly what they're lookin' for.'

147

Stella Maria is hangin' on to Merv's arm, her face rigid, her eyes wide as wide. Betty says, 'Honey, you sure have a fine loud voice but the words are confusin' to me. They wouldn't be an admission of guilt, would they?'

A what? I go, 'A what?' I say, 'It's a tribute. I've used Rita Mae's tragic death as inspiration for a love story. This is called song writing.' God. My mouth is dry. My head's aching. My stomach is rejecting the stupid pancakes.

'Ah can see that,' Merv says. 'Ah can see what you're doin'. But what Ah believe Jerrah had in mind was something more . . . more heroic. Somethin' to capture the public's imagination. But we'll let him decide. We'll play it to him and let him decide.'

I say, 'What do you think Stella Maria?' She's always been my best critic.

She says, 'Sure it will capture the public's imagination. You ever sing that in public and we're as good as dead.'

Tears from nowhere spurt from my eyes. Betty says, 'Well let's not spoil a lovely day. Honey's so clever she can write another song. Why don't Ah lock up the house and why don't we forget all our troubles and head off to scenic Rugby for the day.'

Merv says, 'Rugby? Rugby is God's own country. Wow! Wow! Let's go.'

23

Betty sits up front with Abe which someone should tell her is precisely the kind of arranging that leads to the failure of relationships. You don't stick two potential wives for the best looking boy in the valley in the back where neither can get a go at him. But I don't care. I can't stop snivelling. People long ago gave up trying to shove tissues and stuff at me because I told them all to leave me be, I was just upset, and I had this headache. So now they are leaving me be.

What would they know, anyway? That song's great. I got that song right. What the fuck are they talking about? I'm not writing another one. What do they think? That you just sit down and a new thought comes to you complete all over again saying the same but better? I've said what I want to say about Rita Mae and that's it. This is the trouble dealing with people who don't understand creativity. God knows what's up with Merv. I thought he had an instinct that was in tune with mine. Maybe he's lost it. He's pretty old.

I sing the tribute to myself under my breath as Merv and Stella Maria chat away about distribution deals like they are her life, and Betty and Abe say nothing at all in the front. Turns out he doesn't need anyone directing him anyway. Knows the way like the back of his hand.

After an hour or so I manage to stop sniffing and decide what I'm going to do is pretend that performance never happened. I'm going to sing the song for Dick and see what he thinks. Historic Rugby sucks, anyway. Once it had seventy buildings and now it has almost none, just a few English-style houses in a Tennessee-style landscape.

Betty and Abe are as excited as one thing and so's Merv, blown away by the thought that they've brought Stella Maria and me, their English visitors, to the site of the last English colony in the Unites States. 'Oh my,' Merv says. 'Oh my, isn't this great?' You'd swear he'd never seen anything so astonishing in his life but I know he has. 'Yippee, butter,' I've heard him say. A simple slice of bread can excite Merv.

Betty and Abe are watching us for signs of being thrilled and Stella Maria is smiling like a wolf. I want to be fascinated, but the Moon on the Green is older than this place. If it's old they love, then it's just not old. Betty's giving us a lecture, sounding like a school marm takin' poor farm kids on an outin' paid for by the town miser.

'The colony was founded in 1880 by Thomas Hughes who attended Rugby, the great British public school for the impoverished second sons of wealthy families who failed to benefit from their fathers' wills.' Her reading voice would make me laugh if I had a laugh in me.

Stella Maria's been smiling so hard she can't smile any more so she's wandered down the road looking into the buildings for some new adjectives to describe her thrill and for a minute she seems to have found some. 'Hey,' she calls, when she gets to the Harrow Road Café. 'Look what this is called.' She wants to have a joke with me because she feels bad for me and because the Harrow Road is so not what this is like.

I smile a little bit, seeing what they serve inside. 'Bubble and squeak,' I say. I had two mice called Bubble and Squeak.

'Rats,' Stella Maria replies.

'Rats plus bangers.'

'That an English dish?' Betty asks. I say definitely. Then I notice I'm hungry and could eat anything, even mashed up old cabbage or whatever the bubble is that goes with the squeak. And I say so to Betty who says she's not surpised and maybe we'll drop in for somethin' after we've toured the historic buildings. She's talking to me like I'm damaged and that could totally piss a person right off if she let it so I won't.

Off she leads us, into the historic buildings, and I do my best to look as if nothing appeals to me more. It's not her fault my heart isn't in it. To prove I'm no sulker, when we get to the library I declare nice and loud that I've never seen anything as fine.

Merv, relieved, says far louder than is necessary, he hasn't either. Abe has because he's been here before but he wants to explain the full significance of it to Stella Maria in sentences of two words or less. 'Verra old.' 'Great pictures.' 'William Shakespeare.' 'Brown.'

We wander about looking at the books and so on, me tagging along with Merv, the others going their own ways, and I say to Merv does he have any news from Dick or Jerrah or radio or anyone. I'm walking ahead so he doesn't see from my face how badly I need to know.

'No dream is dead that leaves an afterglow,' he replies and I'm thinking is he nuts when I see he's reading from a brochure. He's so transfixed by the thought that he's standing stock still, staring into space, figuring, I bet, how this notion could come to life with a bit of banjo and fiddle.

'Sounds like sex,' I say which doesn't make him laugh. Makes him just about cry. He turns his big red eyes on me.

'You say some mighty wise things for such a slip of gal,' he says and means it. He's remembering Rita Mae. I try to come up with something even wiser but can only manage dreams are excellent.

'Cracking America's my dream,' I say. 'Mine and Tom's.' He smacks his head with his hand.

'Clean forgot.' He ferrets about in his trouser pocket. 'Clean forgot all about it.' He looks this way and that to see no one's watching, and I look too, terrified he's going to hand me a spliff which he might think I've asked for even though I haven't and never would as I hate drugs and the plant in my garden was Micky's. But he slips me a folded piece of paper and whispers so loud people in Rugby, England could've heard. 'From Tom.'

It rests in my palm like a smouldering thing, and when we catch up with Betty and Abe with their heads bent over a book, I whisper, 'Betty, can I have the car keys? My head's still bad.'

'Sure,' she says, hardly looking up. Abe fishes them out of his shirt pocket.

'Ah'll go look for Stella Maria,' Merv says as I take off.

I can hardly get the keys in the lock and myself up into the driving seat I'm so desperate to read what Tom has to say. I pray he hasn't decided to abandon me, given all he's had to endure.

'Sweeter Than Honey,' he's written. 'I hope you're getting on with the tribute. Dick and Jerry want to run with that and not *Bettin' On Your Cheatin' Heart*. Will also be fab on the soundtrack. Getting great feedback from Hollywood. Give my love to the girl who rolls my dice. Tom.'

I sit there with the bit of paper in my hand, appreciating there isn't anyone right now who can hear how sick this makes me feel. I feel the way I felt the night after The Moon gig when I thought I'd give the performance of a lifetime but was having a whole different response from Stella Maria and Tom.

Stella Maria was saying that Mammy's work for me that

night was better than anything else she'd ever done. 'She got shot of Micky, she launched your career and she got Tom some great footage. God bless her,' she said. 'She wants you to go to Nashville, Honey, you better not deny it now.'

But that was bollocks because Stella Maria had seen Micky off, not Mammy. I said Mammy'd never have been so hard on him and I reckoned I would pay for it. I definitely didn't see any omen to go any place. I saw only an omen to stay.

We were on our way to a casino to celebrate. Stella Maria was sitting in the front with Tom I now recall, while I was jammed in the back between his kit and the door. She was high as a kite over what had come to pass and she wanted me to be. 'Honey, enjoy it,' she said. But I couldn't.

I'd hated Tom's reaction to Micky being bounced out of my life. 'Great metaphor,' he'd said. 'Your old life booted out the door to make way for the new.' No 'Poor old Micky', or 'Was that fine by you?' Neither of them had asked if it had been fine by me. Stella Maria swore she thought I knew what was going to happen, but how? How could I have guessed what she'd do to please the camera? I've seen the tape. I've seen how she played to the camera.

She was half a step ahead of Micky when they'd bowled into that back bar and found all the lights in their faces. Micky being Micky, didn't bother with what was happening but who was making it happen.

'Who's that geezer?'

'Tom Sinclair.'

'What's he up to?'

'Filming Honey.' Stella Maria's face had been so smug, she could've just won the lottery. 'He's the guy taking her to Nashville. You know about her going to Nashville, don't you?' She'd watched the shock register on his face then said, 'You're dumped, Micky. She's way way out of your league.'

It still makes me cringe. He grabbed Stella Maria by her jacket and she decked him. It was the thrill of her life, she said, whacking the man who'd whacked her best friend. 'I paid him back for you,' she said. She thought he'd had it coming and maybe he did but not from her. While we were at the casino watching Tom lose a bomb, Micky was being shunted between the police station and the hospital and the police station until they charged him with affray and stuck him in the cells.

I wasn't even slightly surprised he went off his head. The minute the police let him go which was the minute his mum paid his bail, he totally lost it. Overnight he turned into a stalker who didn't seem to care if he became a vicious killer. 'I gave you everything,' he screamed down the phone at me. 'You whore, you bitch.'

'That was his everything?' Stella Maria said. I told her it was no joke. He could get us both. But she thought it was great. She couldn't wait to tell Tom. That's how quickly she learnt to look at my life through his eyes. It was like she turned into someone else the day she met him. She was Stella Maria with an eye transplant from Tom.

Who knows if this was how Mammy planned to get me here but whether she did or she didn't, I'm here, with a bit of paper on my lap that's telling me I have to come up with the goods right now or lose everything.

I'm still sitting here when the others come back. Betty takes a look at me and says she thinks we should get home as I am awful pale. Stella Maria has a good look at me and she thinks I'm pale as well. I'm feeling pale. Still hungry but kind of exhausted by it all. Betty says we'll have a picnic on the terrace and we travel home the way we travelled out, with Merv between me and Stella Maria.

To break the silence and to prove I'm not dying, I say, 'I've been singing that song over to myself and you know what? I like it.'

Merv says, 'Well Ah like it too, Honey. It shows great flair. Just what Ah think we need more of is . . . Rita Mae. That's it.

We want more of Rita Mae in it. And you can do that because Ah know how much you loved her.'

He heads off the minute we get back to Betty's, not interested in a picnic and I'm not either. I get myself a bowl of Froot Loops which I take to my room. What I'm thinking is that your dreams are your own, no one else's and you pursue them solo, doesn't matter who looked like they were coming along for the ride. I'm thinking maybe the plan all along was for me to get used to being a solo act, in my private life as well as my public. And I'm thinking well I can handle that. Sure I can handle that.

I play the tribute back to myself on the four track. It's good, whatever anyone says, and I don't see any need at all to make it better. If radio loves me and my sound, Nashville should take me as they find me, a theory I would like to test on Tom.

I stretch out on the bed to rest my head which has developed a permanent throb over my left eye. Through the billowing curtains little shafts of light dart across my body, and dreams being what they are, my thoughts being where they're directed, I'm straight back in Cockfosters, in a single shaft of sunlight. Lying on my mattress on the kitchen floor, picking out notes on my guitar to block out the sound of Micky hammering on the door.

I was scared out of my wits. My fingers were sticky on the strings. Stella Maria had been going to stay the night but when we pulled up at the gate, the lights had gone on across the street and we knew what that meant. 'You be alright?' she'd said.

I put furniture against the back and front doors and sat up all night. First thing in the morning, I called out the swindler locksmith to change the locks. Cost me £120. I stuck a note on the front door that said Gone Away. I pulled all the curtains closed in all the rooms, and I set up a camp in the kitchen which Micky could only reach if he clambered over several back fences and risked spearing himself to death on broken palings. I brought down a mattress, my sleeping bag, my musical instruments, my make-up and some clothes. I thought if I was going to be frightened, I'd rather be frightened in one room than all over the house.

All I could do was wait. I wrote an excellent song called *Over The Moon*, which I definitely was. I didn't put the telly or the radio on, in case I missed the telltale sounds of glass being kicked in or doors being smashed. I just sat there and when the tension freaked me out completely, I wrote *Waiting To Die*.

Hear the birds, hear the rain, smell the flowers . . . then all I could think off was *'smell the drain.'* You can't rely on inspiration.

I knew he'd come. Even so, I just about had a heart attack when the phone rang late that afternoon. I prayed it would be Stella Maria but it wasn't. I put the phone down when he said he was going to kill me. I prayed to Mammy to save me. I didn't want to be dead like them anymore. I said, 'Please Mammy, send help.'

An hour later she sent Stella Maria. I said, 'You great arse,' when she phoned. 'Where've you been?' She'd been meeting Tom. We worked out a code so I'd know to unbolt and unchain the door. She'd knock to the rhythm of *Mind Your Own Business*, words and music by the one and only Hank Williams. *'I may tell a lot of stories that may not be true – but I can get to heaven just as easy as you.'* A classic. She made it to my house four minutes before Micky did. I said, 'How long can you stay?'

She said, 'As long as you need me.' Title. Taken. *As Long As He Needs Me*. In a different genre.

Hank Williams died aged only twenty-nine of drink, despite the loving care and attention of June Carter, later the wife of Johnny Cash, who must be an addiction expert by now. This was it with Micky. Couldn't hold his drink. Got drunk, got mad, got arrested – story of his life. Tried to get me.

Stella Maria had just wormed her way into the sleeping bag next to me when he banged on the door like an insane man, so drunk he could barely pronounce the obscenities he was shouting. 'We're trapped,' I said to Stella Maria. I wanted to say, 'Get Paddy, get Paddy,' but how could I when Paddy and I hadn't spoken in months and I didn't want her to know how on my mind he was. I said, 'Get Tom.' She phoned him, but all he said was call the police. Amazing, when you think of it, that I went on to throw my hand in with him. But isn't this the way affection goes? Never in a straight line.

24

Micky was banging at the door, hollering filth, going away, coming back. Stella Maria and I didn't dare move. I said maybe we should phone Paddy. She said forget it. He wouldn't come, she didn't know where he was, she didn't want him involved. She didn't want him involved because she hadn't told Fatima that she was taking off for America with a stranger she'd picked up in a Soho club and she didn't want her brother snitching on her. Which he wouldn't have. He's an honourable man and totally appreciative that his mother's a toilet, though he respects her. I said well we needed help from somewhere and who else was there? 'Need help,' was the message I left. 'Micky's trying to murder me. Please come.'

Stella Maria went, 'If that works, I'll take a vow of poverty.' I said he's more likely to save us than flipping Tom. She said, 'Flipping Tom is a flipping film-maker not a hero.' I said no way was I going to be his flipping heroine. She said, 'Well flipping die then. You don't have a future without him.'

I have to explain this to Betty. It definitely affects our

current position. I told Stella Maria I'd be a fool to hook up with anyone so gutless. Someone so gutless would have no feeling for me and no feeling for the music. 'Here we go,' she said. And she was right. I wanted to have a go.

All the stuff that had been bugging me spewed out of my mouth and into her face only inches from mine. I said I couldn't work with someone so ignorant. Did she think he'd even heard of Rose Maddox, whose family headed east from Alabama when she was a tiny girl, hitching lifts and dodging guards on freight trains and who only found fame with her brothers on radio after endless toil in the fruit fields of California? Did he know anything about Johnny Cash's anguish at the untimely death of his brother? Even Micky was familar with that. She said, 'Shut up. No one's heard of Rose Maddox'.

I said, 'She's my life. They're my songs. It's my music. Nashville's my dream.'

She said, 'And without me and Tom, your talent will rot. Whatever Rose Maddox did or fucking didn't.'

There was silence out the front. Micky had stopped hammering but we had no idea where he was. He could've been crawling on his stomach to the kitchen door to get us with one of the big iron bars he carried up his sleeve. He could already have broken into the house. His career was burglary so we couldn't be sure. We should've been planning how to protect ourselves. Instead we were arguing about Tom. 'Can you hear anything?' I said. I thought I could hear stabbing noises.

It makes me sweat to think about it. We listened hard as we could and when we'd heard nothing for five minutes I was angry all over again. I said my gig at The Moon wasn't letting my talent rot. That audience had liked me. Stella Maria gave a repulsive little smile. Letting me know there was more to that than I knew.

'What?' I said. 'What?'

She said OK, since I insisted. That audience had been ninety-five per cent Micky's biker mates who'd cheered and whistled and carried on as if I was Whitney Houston because he'd paid them which she couldn't believe I hadn't guessed seeing everyone else had. She might just as well have torn my heart from my chest and jumped on it. I went, 'Really?' She knew I was hurt, but she didn't care. She said what did it matter for God's sake? That's what everyone did at The Moon. It didn't take away from the fact that I'd given the performance of my life and she personally had loved every minute of it.

That was when Micky threw a brick through the front-room window and screamed at me from the street. 'I know you're in there.'

Stella Maria and I yelled blue murder right in each other's faces. Then we screamed laughing because we were in such a panic we couldn't get out of the idiot sleeping bag. We were grabbing each other's boobs, falling over each other, and all the time we could hear more glass breaking and the sound of Micky bursting through the smashed front window. I was screaming, she was screaming, half laughing, half crying, rolling about the floor, terrified.

'We're dead,' I said.

'We're not,' she replied. She scrambled to her feet and grabbed a kitchen knife. She shoved the frying pan into my hands and said get behind the door. That's where we were when we heard the screeching of car tyres and the sound of Paddy coming to rescue us in his beaten-up white van. He jumped through the front-room window after Micky who was now bashing the kitchen door with something that sounded like an iron bar. We heard thumping and walloping and cursing, then more glass breaking and more footsteps in the hall.

Paddy called 'Honey, Honey,' and I burst into tears with relief and joy.

Stella Maria gave me a big whack between the shoulder bladers and said, 'It's not Micky, you blinking eejit, it's my brother,' as if I didn't know. She dragged the table away from the door but I couldn't stand to follow her into the hall. I just couldn't bear to see whatever was out there. I heard her say, 'Tom! Thank God you came.'

This is where the man's a weasel. He's happy to pretend he saved us because he was the one who told Paddy Micky was inside. He couldn't get involved himself because he is a film-maker and needed to be a neutral observer. I froze when I saw Micky. His face was grey and twisted under a black beanie pulled down over his forehead. He was dressed all in black, like a big black angry cat and he looked like a murderer. He would've killed me, I'm sure of it. He was out cold. Tom said, 'What are you going to do with him?'

Paddy said, 'Who the fuck are you?' and to Stella Maria who plainly knew him, 'Who the fuck is he?'

Tom, still filming, stuck out his free hand to shake Paddy's. He said, 'Tom Sinclair. I'm making a film of Honey's life.'

Paddy ignored the hand. 'Holy Mother of God,' he said. He had lifted Micky to his feet and was half dragging him out of the house. 'You got somewhere to go?' he said to me.

And maybe I knew what I was going to say, maybe I didn't, but you spend as many years as I have watching for clues from the grave and you get to be very sensitive to the presence of messengers. A brown butterfly had flown through the open front door. She circled, she looped and she landed without a second's hesitation on Tom's head. There was no doubt in my mind who she was.

'Nashville,' I said to Paddy. 'Stella Maria and me are off to the States.' I waited for him to grab me, to clutch me, to say I couldn't, he'd never let me go, I was his and his alone. But he didn't.

'Right,' he said. 'Look after yourself.' And I smiled and said thanks though my heart was breaking.

25

Stella Maria's standing by the bed, looking down at me, telling me I have to get something into my stomach and this is it. 'Is it runny?' I say.

'Tomato sandwich.' She puts the plate on to the bedside table and grabs my arms to pull me up. 'You're making yourself sick,' she says.

'What's it to you?'

She hands me the plate. 'I don't want your corpse stinking the place out.'

'If I die,' I say, 'you could tell the court what you liked.'

She said, 'I'm telling it what I like anyway.'

'What did Merv say about distribution?'

'I wasn't listening,' she says.

'You were,' I say. She shrugs. Stella Maria's silent act is better than anyone's because she still talks. She just doesn't tell you anything you want to hear. 'Well Tom's doing OK, anyway. Got a lot of interest in Hollywood,' I tell her. She says nothing but she doesn't stomp off. 'Can I ask you something?'

'No,' she says.

'Did you tell Betty you were the one who made us come to Nashville? That you persuaded me?' And she looks guilty. I swear she looks guilty. 'What have you been telling Betty?' I say. 'Because sometimes I get the feeling she despises me.'

'We're not allowed to talk about it,' she sniffs.

'But Stella Maria, this is you and me. Not you and Betty, or me and Betty. You and me. We're in it together. We have to talk about it.'

'Eat the sodding sandwich,' she snaps and then she slams out of the room, only to come back a second later with a glass of milk. 'And drink this.' It'd be laughable, if it wasn't pathetic. She's torn between mollycoddling me like I'm this useless half baked person, and wishing me as dead and gone as Rita Mae. Torn between punishing me and forgiving me.

What strikes me as I force the sandwich down my throat, is it's misery that's making her mean. I'd work on the melody if I felt up to it because the words come to me in a perfectly formed song.

Wrong road down the love triangle
Wouldn't ya think she'd've seen the way?
Neon sign flashing at the cross road
Sorrow ahead, sorrow ahead, delays!

It sucks I can't try my stuff out on her. I've always tried everything out on her. I played her *Sayin' Farewell To The Home Of My Childhoood* in the back of the taxi heading out of Cockfosters up the A10 in peak-hour traffic.

In the end, we didn't so much leave as escape. Paddy dragged Micky away before he had a chance to come to his senses, and the minute they were out the door, Stella Maria said, 'Right, go go go, Honey. Let's get out of here while we can.' I went upstairs to pack, all the time asking myself what in God's name I thought I was doing. Tom filmed me putting stuff into a suitcase and Stella Maria watched me, going, 'You won't need that, or that, or that, for God's sake, Honey.' She was all out to impress Tom with her efficiency and insight into the world of documentary making.

I hardly knew what to take and what to leave. When the whole of your life is being abandoned in ten seconds, how do you know which bits to take? Stella Maria said, 'Just get your songs, Honey. That's all you need. Plus your guitar, your harmonica and some knickers.' As if I could leave it at that. But I only had one suitcase and when that was full, we just loaded piles of stuff into the taxi and Stella Maria sorted it into Tescos bags while I sang to stop myself from thinking.

I took underwear, jeans and T-shirts, make-up and so forth, all my songs, the four track, a pile of tapes and CDs and in my special box three photos of Mammy, her rings, the lock of Jimmie's hair, a pair of Josie's tights, Mammy's and Jimmie's hospital tags and the last letter from Barney Noble written after she'd died. I also took the cowgirl outfit which is hanging in my wardrobe here. Stella Maria said, 'No, Honey.'

I said. 'Fuck off.' It's the last glimpse Mammy had of me, the one she took to her grave. She will remember me for eternity in two small studded scraps of pretend leather. Black.

Tom asked me questions as I packed, like why I was taking this or that, how I felt and so on but I didn't have much to say. I'd shut my feelings off like a dripping tap or they would have drowned me. Drowned me in dread and fear about leaving the home that had protected me for so long to face the challenge ahead.

You can tell Tom is a professional because he never pushes it. He doesn't make you talk if you don't feel like it. And the camera never bothered me. It's just like an extra bit of his shoulder. Like he's got two heads. His face asks the questions and I answer his left eye. I don't bother looking at him, I just get on with what I'm doing. If I don't feel like talking, the camera just watches in silence.

164

While I was packing, Stella Maria tried to make up for my silence by saying things like well, I'm really really excited and eventually it got on Tom's wick. He said, 'Do you mind shutting up, Stella Maria?' which must have hurt her feelings.

I said, 'What about the gas and electricity? What about security? The window's smashed.' If you're a householder, you have to worry about things like that.

She said, 'Worry about your skin.' She was dead worried about hers for no reason.

The light outside tells me hours have past since Stella Maria was in the room and it must be dinner time at least. Either they're letting me survive on a tomato sandwich or Betty's going to be madder than mad that I'm showing such disrespect by not getting to the table on time. My head's trying to tell me it might just still explode but I get up from the bed anyway, and tread in the sandwich which is half eaten on the plate on the floor. I scrape it off my foot, shove the plate under the bed, slide my feet into my boots and go to the dining room where Stella Maria and Betty are eating but not speaking. I say 'Sorry, Betty. I lost track.'

She says, 'Ah hope you are feelin' better, Honey. Please help yourself to somethin' to eat.' The food's in dishes on the sideboard which runs along the dining room's back wall. Baked potatoes in one. Tuna in another, grated cheese in another, beans in another. All stuff I can just about manage. My feet make this loud clunking noise as I cross the floor and I wish I'd done the zips of the boots up. I wish I'd brushed my hair.

'I was composing,' I say. No one's interested. We eat in silence. If I had more energy, I'd ask Betty if she'd like to hear the truth about Dolly and Porter Wagoner, long-standing compere of The Grand Ole Opry but I can't be bothered.

You can eat baked potato really fast, provided you're not Betty. I start half a plate after her and finish when she still has a quarter to go. She looks up to say tuna canned in water doesn't always have a lower fat content than tuna canned in oil because the fat content is in the fish itself. She gets zero response from either of us. Maybe she has an eating disorder. She watches what she eats, no doubt about that. Maybe she's a tub of lard in real life. Hard to tell when she gives away so little.

'Was your Mom a good cook?' I ask her.

Stella Maria says, 'Mam. We say Mam or Mother.'

Betty says her father was the cook in their family. I have nothing to say on the subject of fathers and nor does Stella Maria. I say to Betty what does she mean by risk-to-reward ratio? She looks surprised. 'Saw your book on the book shelf. Something for you to think about,' I say to Stella Maria.

'Something for us all to think about, when life in general is a trade off,' Betty says. I say *Trading My Love For You* is a great title.

The phone rings in the study. Betty says why do people always phone at meal times? She doesn't get up. We hear the machine click in and her smooth southern tones thank the caller, apologise to the caller, invite the caller to leave a message and the caller turns out to be Tom.

We hear him plain as one thing and we're all stunned by his cheek, given the last thing Betty said to him. 'Tom Sinclair here,' he says. His voice has a husky quality that women find attractive before they notice he likes himself more than he likes them. He apologises to Betty for troubling her and asks if she could possibly contact him on his mobile as he has something to tell her which he believes may have significant bearing on our defence. Then he thanks her and hangs up.

Stella Maria excuses herself from the table and Betty says of course, as if they have an understanding that any mention of Tom is the cue for her to have an epileptic fit and it's better she goes off to have it on her own. 'Wonder what that could be?' I ask.

Betty says she can't begin to imagine, implying by her tone

she's not interested either, but I'm definitely intrigued and my heart lifts at the thought of him applying himself to getting us off the hook. I ask Betty if I can help myself to more tuna. 'Go ahead,' she says. Then she turns all her attention to what's left on her plate and I can see she doesn't want to be interrupted.

Tom came into his own once we'd left Cockfosters. He has great staff at his disposal. They organised the hotel in Regent's Park for us until everything was ready for our departure. Stella Maria tried to involve herself but couldn't work out how.

The only thing we managed between us was to see the bank manager. Getting money out of Bundy was like getting blood from a stone which is ironic when Mam bled to death for it, but he agreed to what he called 'a significant advance' which Stella Maria called a pittance. And Tom gave us £500 as down payment on my story and our time, so Stella Maria came to be in charge of the money which was fine by me. My heart still wasn't in it. It was aching for Paddy.

I called him when Stella Maria was at the office filling in forms. I said I was worried about the house. The window was broken. He said he'd fixed it. I said well my heart was broken as well. He said, 'Honey, you have a very strong heart.' I begged him. I needed to see him. I needed to say good-bye. So he came and I guess he regretted it.

He looked around and said, 'Who's paying for this?'

I said, 'Tom.'

'Tom. Who is this feckin' Tom anyway?' I said he was a famous film producer and Stella Maria trusted him. He said, 'And since when did Stella Maria know pig shite from dog spit?' He sat on the bed. He looked up at me and sighed, not with sorrow but irritated. 'What are you playing at, Honey?'

'It's the chance of a lifetime,' I said.

'What chance? Whose lifetime?'

I sat on the bed next to him and took his hand. 'I have to

167

go.' He wasn't convinced. 'If I stay Micky will only murder me.'

He smiled. 'I'll save you.' And he would have. But – and how mad is this – even as he was being all I'd ever wanted him to be, I knew I had to leave him. With all my heart I wanted him to save me. But with all my soul, I knew I had to go to Nashville and if it meant sacrificing him, I would.

He said, 'I'll even marry you.' Oh boy! The minute's sitting there in the front of my head like a horrible sharp object boring into my brain. I so wanted to marry him, I so did. And here he was asking and here I was, knowing I was going to refuse because he'd been right the first time.

'I love you,' I said. I couldn't look at him. He didn't need to hear anymore.

'Right,' he replied. He stood up, he took me in his arms, he kissed my forehead and left.

His blue eyes shone and he was gone
And my heart broke forever

So there I was, with nobody. No Paddy, no Micky. I didn't even know where Mammy was. I said so to the camera and Tom said, 'She's never deserted you yet, has she?'

26

That fucking goat's gone mad. Keeps running at the house and butting the wall under my window. I fed her a whole pile of food from under my bed last night, old crusts, left over cereal, apple cores and a few tissues and she's gagging for more but there isn't any more. What I want is for this stupid animal to knock itself out so I can go back to sleep but I'm forced to open one eye and once that's done, I have to get up.

The sun's shining again. I stick my head through the window to tell the goat to fuck off and the air's as clear as . . . well I don't know what it's as clear as but it's later than I think because the shadow has crept to the side of the house which means it's mid-morning.

'You up and about, Honey?' Betty calls. 'You spare a minute?' I put my head out my bedroom door and see her head around the study door. 'Join us, will you darlin'?' she says. I pull on some jeans and yesterday's T-shirt so I look like I haven't just this minute left my bed.

Stella Maria's sitting in the floral chair, all upright and tense. The room feels funny. Betty says, 'You mind sittin' on the floor, Honey?' I sit on the floor. She swivels her chair so she can study me, checking if I'm ready for whatever it is she's about to say. Not crying or snivelling or any such thing.

'Ah spoke this morning to Tom Sinclayuh in Los Angeles and he has made a proposal which Ah feel Ah must pass on to you,' she says in her widder-woman voice, so I guess she's treading carefully. Stella Maria's staring at her feet so I can't tell whether she knows what he's proposing and I can't think what he might be proposing that he proposes it to Betty and she tells Stella Maria before me. I say what is it.

'He'd like to go lookin' for your father.'

For a minute I think she's confusing me with Stella Maria whose father is a shadow of a man. But the idea floats towards me like a deformed object that wants to claim me even though I don't want anything to do with it. I knock it out of the way. It's a joke.

'Is he mad or what?' I say. 'My father's dead.' I look at Stella Maria but she won't look at me. 'Why does he want to do that?' I say.

Betty says, 'He hopes he might speak up for you in court.'

'He can't if he's dead.'

'Mr Sinclayuh doesn't seem to think he is. Do you know he's dead for sure?' And I know for sure that I don't. Mammy just used to say he was as good as and that was good enough for me.

'Tell him to forget it,' says Stella Maria. She's full of outrage on my behalf. 'Tell him to stop meddling with stuff he doesn't understand. It's an obscenity. Orphan girl kills friend, finds father, cracks America.'

And I can see it is. Tom and I have talked into the night about the power of my story and I can see straightaway how the finding of my father will only improve it. I'm repelled by the idea. Tom can't have any idea how disgusting it is, or he'd never have suggested it. But I don't say so. Not to Betty when she hates Tom so much already. I say, 'I have to think about it.'

I get an apple from the kitchen, take it to my room and bite into it so hard my teeth smash into each other. Shite, you know. Who needs it? The dream is me triumphing with my songs. The idea of looking for my father was never part of it. Not even when Mammy died and I had no one except Josie. Not even when Josie died and I had no one except Stella Maria.

I'm not saying I've never wondered about him. I've imagined him coming to find me and me having to break the news that Mammy, the love of his life, has died. I've imagined him sending out appeals on the radio for the daughter he was longing to meet before he died of something ugly and agonising. I've imagined him sitting at a lonely desk piled high with letters to me he'd never sent. But I've never wanted to look for him because Mammy never did. She didn't want him. I don't want him. I chuck my apple core under the bed and reach for my guitar

The terrible thing about a seed like this in a head like mine is once it's in there, it grows of its own accord, sending shoots in all directions so soon you have this jungle, much darker than Betty's, with images of all sorts strangling each other as they fight for light. I play random chords but I'm not hearing them, I'm fighting to see stuff in the jungle.

I'm seeing the man Tom could find if I let him go looking. I'm seeing the handsomest, strongest, wisest, richest, most loving man in the whole of the US. Kris Kristofferson, best song *Loving Her Was Easier*. I'm seeing this low-down piece of scum who hasn't been the same since Mammy walked out of his life and who stinks of old fart and sweat and clothes that haven't been washed since he put them on a hundred years ago.

I play extra loud and make my fingers ache. *Dang me, Dang me, they oughta take a rope and hang me high from the highest tree. Woman would you weep for me!* Words and music Roger Miller, who is one of the few artists I admire for cross-over appeal because of his natural country sound.

I play till my arms ache, same song over and over because darn right, dang me! Then I get undressed and into bed to stop the aching, but I can't sleep because it's 11.00 in the morning. I try to remember what I was thinking last night before I went to sleep and I get to it easily enough.

I'm back on the plane that brought us here, soaring into the blue and feeling the load drop from my heart. Not frightened or anxious. Full of excitement and joy because I suddenly had so many tickets in life's lottery. I certainly wasn't thinking I was heading to the land of my father. I was going to Nashville to crack it.

What makes him think my father's alive? What makes him think he's American? Did I ever say so? Did I ever discuss it with him? Only person in the whole world who knows as much about him as I do is Stella Maria. And there you go. Thank you Stella Maria.

Tom travelled business class, something to do with his tax, and Stella Maria and me travelled economy. It was the first time we'd ever flown and I'm remembering the thrill. The best feeling. Running, running, running, then up and away and free. We were laughing our heads off, knowing we could crack anything now we'd cracked the law of gravity.

Tom brought us two glasses of champagne. 'One for you,' he said giving me a kiss on the lips as he passed the glass to me. 'Girl of all our dreams. And one for you.' He didn't kiss Stella Maria. I was just beginning to appreciate how attractive he could be. I said so to Stella Maria and she said, yeah, he really is, but if that was unusual for her, I put it down to her being so pleased to get out of Cockfosters.

She should've confided in me. I wouldn't have given him a second glance, just been happy she was over hating sex and saving herself for marriage. Her silence on the matter was the beginning of the end. Betty's anxious to discover when the end began and Stella Maria says it was Rita Mae barging into our lives, but it was Tom.

We met Tom, he lifted us from the skins we were in and brought us to Nashville where we were both born again into the skin that was meant for us. I became the person I was meant to be before tragedy, in the way of so many deaths in the family, turned me into someone else. I think that can happen.

I must be falling asleep because my thoughts are breaking up. My friendship with Stella Maria became money based and you know what? Love and money are like cheese and burger to me. I sit up and write *Love and money/ cheese and burger* on the pad I keep by my bed to see if it inspires a narrative, but it doesn't. Instead, I go from narrative to story and from story back to father. I'd have to be an idiot not to appreciate Tom's interest in him. I know the value of narrative better than anyone. And the label would love it. Maybe me being part-American would make up for the loss of Rita Mae. I wouldn't have to see him. I could let Tom find him and refuse to see him. That'd be a twist.

I look at my photos of Mammy, may she rest in peace. I say, 'What do you think, Mam?' Her face is as soft and pretty as a spring day, looking up at me, smiling at me, loving me. The fucking goat takes another run at the wall. Is it crazy or what?

27

Wake up feeling so great, I climb out the window for a smoke and find Betty's come out for a quiet pipe herself. Betty loves that goat. I say she's not vicious, is she, and Betty has to remove her pipe she's laughing so hard. She says she's gentler than a lamb still suckin' from its mother which is what pet owners always say when their animal would rip your heart out. 'Let's walk,' she says and we head down to the terraces. 'You're not lettin' things git you down, are you, Honey? Frettin' never did anyone an ounce of good.'

'I'm not the frettin' kind,' I say, and sing snatch of a song to make my point

> *'I'm not the frettin' kind*
> *Don't think you're on my mind*
> *Ah gotta better things to do*
> *Than sit here frettin' over you.'*

She gives a small smile, which I take for appreciation, but she says nothing more until we get to the bottom terrace and I see why we've come. Abraham's been working like a Trojan.

174

Newly dug beds run all the way along the fence to where the land drops down to the river and Betty's itching to inspect them. 'Beautiful, isn't it?' she says.

I say it is. I breathe in that fine dirt smell, and wonder how Abe and I would go, running a market garden. There are plenty out in the countryside near Cockfosters. She strolls along peering into the newly dug earth, proud as anything of the the way it looks, then gets down on her hands and knees to pull up a speck of something green she chucks over the fence.

I lie down on the grass next to her. Clouds have come up since morning and maybe it's going to rain. 'Those new plants will enjoy a spot of rain,' I say.

She says maybe, but they won't want a downpour. 'You thought about what you want me to tell Tom Sinclayuh?'

I say yeah, I've thought about it. Betty says well there are two things I ought to be asking myself. One: do I want to find my father? Two: what are Tom's motives in wanting to find him? I choose my words carefully. 'If Tom's telling my story, tracing my destiny, finding my Dad makes sense.' This isn't when she was expecting, I can tell.

'Why's that?' she says.

'I'm here for a reason,' I say. 'Maybe I'm here for two. Maybe I just can't ignore it.'

She gives this some thought. She finds another tiny green shoot which she nips from the soil. 'Well would you be ignorin' it if there was no film? Would you have given your father a second thought if it wasn't for the film?'

I say maybe not. But if there wasn't a film I wouldn't be here and then my destiny would be different. 'Maybe, you know, I owe it to myself.'

'Well Ah don't know 'bout that,' she says.

The more hesitation I hear in her voice, the more I think, well, I do owe it to myself, and to Mammy. If finding my father makes my dream come true, the dream I'm cherishing for both Mammy and me, then I owe it to both of us.

'I'm thinking he should look up old Barney Noble,' I say. 'If Barney was on the cruise ships with Mammy, he probably knew my dad. If Tom finds Barney and Barney knows where to look for my father, then it's meant to be. That's what I'm thinking.' Even as I say it, my chest tightens.

Betty says, 'All righty.' But she's not happy. I shut up in case the next thing I say makes her even more unhappy. After a bit she says, 'And how's he goin' to find Mr Noble?'

'I've got a letter with his address on it,' I say. 'Up in my room.' I know that letter by heart because I look at it all the time to remind me of Mammy. I hear it in my head, spoken by the Barney I've always imagined, an old, old man with a sweet face whose grey moustache is streaked in brown from the tobacco that's made his voice all rusty. 'I would like to say I'm pleased for you but I won't because I'm not. He'll never make you happy. Let me know when you wake up to the fact. Barney.'

'Meeting him would be OK. It would be good to meet someone who was fond of my mother.'

'Maybe you need to give it more thought,' Betty says. 'It's a big thing. Ah don't know if you understand how big.'

I say I'm clear on it. If Mammy wants me to meet my father, she'll point us in the direction of Barney Noble who'll know where to find him.

'OK,' she says. 'Let's get Mr Sinclayuh to the house. Now might be the time for me to sit down and talk to him in a civilised fashion.' I would like to hug her but she has to run. She has a session with Stella Maria, she says. 'Maybe you should get on with your song. Maybe you think about what Rita Mae gave to the world while she was here.' She looks down on me and her face relaxes. '*The World While She Was Here*. That a title?'

'Could be,' I lie, and I flop back on the ground. I watch the clouds move slowly across the valley to their doom. And that's a possible. *Across the Valley to Their Doom*. A song maybe, for Stella Marie and me.

Tragedy has always inspired me. Like *Now That You're Dead I Can Say That I Love You*, which turned out to have a creepy significance when I wrote it well before we met Rita Mae. That song is true country. I sang it at a couple of auditions when we first started doing the rounds and I wanted it for the flipside of *Bettin' On Your Cheatin' Heart*, but Moonshine hated it. They loved the song I subsequently wrote, called *What Makes You Think You're The Man For Me?*

What makes you think you're the man for me
With your diamond eyes and your careless ways
The man for me is a million miles from the man you are cos he's
A mountain man

Man for Me is more upbeat than I like but this is what they wanted. I said upbeat works best when it follows a downbeat. You go downbeat then upbeat to maximise narrative. And sometimes you don't need to go upbeat at all. I think it was Jerrah who said, 'That so? Well morbid isn't working.'

Many people in Nashville think tragedy in the country lyric was OK before but not now, as if tragedy comes in and out of fashion like happiness. What's that saying about our life and times? It means the people flogging the songs have turned their minds from life's harsh reality. I said so to Tom one morning after I'd sung *Now That You're Dead* to a music publisher who'd heard I was interesting but then decided I wasn't. Tom went probably, but sing something else next time.

He was just beginning to think recording me being a big flop mightn't make such a hot documentary when it would be one more sad thing in my life. We needed an upbeat. He never said so, but I could tell because all the advice he was giving me was with a view to me making a good impression. Which I didn't at first. Not by a long way.

I'd say, 'What happens if I'm a flop?'

He'd say, 'Doesn't matter. Our story's the random nature

of luck. We're just following the ball whichever way it bounces'.

He did a great job keeping that ball rolling. He made big and powerful contacts who saw us straight away. Managers, producers, agents and so forth, who knew people he knew. They took a look at me because they loved the idea of the documentary. They figured I had to be pretty interesting if this hot-shot producer was spending so much time and money on me.

Those first couple of weeks in Nashville, when everyone was saying 'Let's see her, then,' were the best of my life, not counting the first twelve years and my week with Paddy. I even loved the long, long line of people queuing to get through Immigration in New York, which is where we landed before getting another plane to Nashville. I looked into their faces for signs of hope and joy like mine, and saw mainly desperation because the queue was moving so slowly, but who knows what hopes they nursed in their breasts?

We touched down in Nashville at 8.00 p.m. on an early spring night and I was jumping with excitement. Tom's office had laid on a limo for the drive into town and the driver turned out to be a songwriter who was only too pleased to point out landmarks. Mostly he pointed out the offices of all the people who'd stolen his songs which I thought was his personal tragedy until I realised every second person in Nashville thinks every first person is a song thief.

That driver could talk. I was the only one paying him any attention which was a shame. I'm still not certain that the others know Nashville has a Parthenon like the one in Greece, or that its major industry is Bible selling. I was all eyes on the way in from the airport but nothing was familiar until we were on Fifth Avenue and the driver went, 'Ma'am, the Ryman Auditorium.' I screamed and Stella Maria sat up like someone had stabbed her.

She said, 'Looks like a dump.' I told her this was no dump,

this was the home of the Opry from 1943 to 1974. She said, so? I said Stella Maria, the Grand Ole Opry is the world's longest-running radio show which hasn't missed a broadcast since 1925 owing to the dedication and worldwide enthusiasm of its fans. She went, 'Oh piss off.' She was knackered.

I said, 'You piss off. My mother was a member of the Opry's Fan Club.' Stella Maria has a mega blood-sugar problem as a result of her bingeing and starving. I said 'Let's go via Music Row.' But Tom said he was wrecked so we didn't.

We checked into the Hilton and that was the last we saw of him for the night. Stella Maria and I shared a room on a different floor from him. She wanted to go to bed. I was way too excited to sleep. I ordered a hamburger on room service which was as big as the plate. An all-American hamburger. My first all-American meal. It made my eyes water for Mam. She'd have loved that hamburger. And she'd have screamed her head off if she'd seen the Ryman. She'd have made us drive right to Opryland.

Stella Maria, who was eating my salad and fries because the smell of food had woken her up, said, 'You crying?' I said I wasn't. She said, 'She'd be happy just to know you got here.' And she patted my arm. That was the kind of friendship we had. So close we didn't need words.

I love Stella Maria. I believe where we are now, on the verge of triumph, is where we were always headed. Everything we did together and everything we did separately was bringing us here and it's not the vale of tears she thinks it is. Vale of tears is when you lose your mother before she's ready to go. Then there aren't tears enough, just grief like nails in your heart. A father could be an upbeat. I think she'll understand that, eventually.

28

I race up the terrace steps to find her. I want to explain to her that finding my dad could be great for all of us. She's in the den glued to a report of a mass shooting. When she doesn't yell or sling cushions at me, I sit down but can't fathom the mood she's in, which is quieter than I'd been expecting. 'What kind of an arse shoots up a school?' I say.

She says, 'A sick one.' We watch the disgusting action replays and I listen for the sound of her marshalling her thoughts. She's crunching her way through her lunch of Oreos but she has to be churning over the conversation she's just had with Betty.

'Betty say about Barney Noble?' I ask.

She nods, not taking her eyes off the screen.

'Good idea?'

'You never wanted to find him before.'

'Never thought about it before.'

'Guess you needed Tom to think of it for you. Guess you have to keep Tom happy.' She's swinging her leg back and forth, a sure sign she isn't as calm as she'd like me to think she is, even if she isn't drooling with fury.

'I don't have to keep anyone happy,' I say. 'I please myself.'

'That so?' she says.

'Right.' I say.

'Who are you pleasing when you please yourself?'

The words bounce towards me from another time. It was a fight we had over Rita Mae. Why Rita Mae was in my life when Stella Maria said she was someone we'd normally run a mile from. She couldn't get around the fact that I'd never have run away from a good song-writing partner, whoever she was. She was accusing me of selling out, without understanding I was buying in.

I can see where this conversation is headed so I'm going to stop it right now and find something better to do, but she says, 'He's got no right wanting to find your dad. You hate your dad.'

'I don't know him.'

Her leg starts to swing faster. 'You don't know him because you never wanted to know him. The idea of him made you sick. Made your mammy sick. And Tom knows that because you told him. Think about it, Honey. Try to remember how you felt before you started feeling stuff for the camera.'

I think well she's not raising her voice, a miracle, so I'm not going to raise mine. We'll discuss this calmly. 'I'm not feeling it for the camera,' I say. 'I'm just plain feeling it. Where do you get off, telling me how I feel? You stopped knowing how I felt the minute we got to Nashville. Maybe I want a future with a father in it now I'm here. Maybe we need an American father to get us through this court case.'

'Bollocks,' she says. 'Bollocks, Honey. All you want is a future with your name in lights and it doesn't matter what you do to get it there.'

I say, 'If getting my name in lights includes me finding a father to love me, then where's the harm in that? Where is it, Stella Maria? Just tell me so I know.'

'The harm's in what it's doing to your immortal soul,' she says, which is what she said the day Rita Mae died. She said we had to pull out and go home. There was blood on our hands. But I told her, and Tom told her, there was no blood on anyone's hands. Just on the path where she fell. Then we got arrested so going home wasn't an option but stopping the film was. For her. Not for me.

'He brought us here to see what happened,' she is saying. 'He slept with you to see what happened. He slept with Rita Mae to see what happened. He wants to find your father to see what happens.'

This is what she does. She tells half a truth but she changes it by making up its other half. I think how could she kid herself like this when she was up for everything he was suggesting such a very short time ago?

'And why's he paid our bail? To see what happens? He's mortgaged everything,' I remind her.

'Jesus wept,' she says. 'Look at what's unfolding here and ask yourself what's going on.'

'What's going on,' I say, 'is that I'm within inches of doing everything Mammy would've wanted to do and I'm not backing off now.'

I leave her to it, hardly believing we've had a conversation so horrible and neither of us shouted or physically attacked the other. In my room I think maybe it is all over between her and me. She might be blown off course but I won't be. If she wants to pull out she can. All Tom has to say in his commentary is, 'At this point Stella Maria stopped talking to Honey so she isn't in the rest of the picture.'

If I have to soldier on without her, I will. I'm just sorry she has so little faith. If she stuck with it she could be famous, not as a murderer but for managing the English girl who topped the charts with a return-to-roots rendition of her own song and we could all have good times again. We had great times. Before Rita Mae turned up, we had great times.

I'm putting that conversation right out of my head. I pick up my guitar and get to work, trying to have heroic thoughts about Rita Mae, even though I don't see why I should when I've aready finished a tribute I'm happy with.

Rita Mae oh Rita Mae, how I loved to hear you play

Christ! Sounds like the singing nun Mam said she'd met once. This is stupid. I ask Betty if I can use the phone and I ring Dick because Merv has definitely got it all wrong. Dick will love my finished version.

I hear him sweating down the line. 'Verra steamy, verra, verra steamy,' he says when I ask how Nashville is today.

'Want to hear my tribute?' I say.

'Now?' he asks. I say well does he have a minute? He says he always has a minute for me. He wants to know if this is the first version or the second version. He says Merv said I did a version that needed a little work and Jerrah said he didn't want to listen to any old thing that needed work. He wanted to hear somethin' that's perfect. 'You know Jerrah,' he laughs.

I tell him this is the version I like. I think it's good. It's what I want to say. 'Well OK then,' he says. So I sing it, I finish and he goes, 'You know what, Honey? You gotta listen to Merv. Merv knows what he's talkin' about.' I tell him goodbye. They can all fuck off.

First gig I ever had in this country without any help from any accompanist was at The Black Door, a groovy little place on the edge of town which had an open mic on third Sundays. It wasn't even as big as the back room at The Moon, just one small bar that served food and drink to people sitting at three or four tables around the stage. I had to audition. The owner said, 'You guys are British, right?'

Tom said, 'Right.'

He said he'd had a couple of British performers come by before but they never worked out. Too British. I said I was less British than Irish. He said I didn't sound so Irish. I said what did it matter how I spoke when how I sang was what counted. He said there was no call to be rude.

I sang *Little Jim* and he said, 'Yeah, right, you sound British when you sing.'

Stella Maria said, 'You're just hearing British, she doesn't sing British. She sings country.' Which floored the bloke because he couldn't understand her accent which is Irish.

So I sang him *Lonely For You* in an accent so like his own he could only say, 'Well you sure sing loud.' He gave me a time slot for the next weekend and told me not to miss it because he was doing me a favour here. I wasn't upset by the experience. It was what I'd been expecting. You know you're going to get a hard time from people who don't know you from Adam and would just as soon not.

Stella Maria spent ages working out what I should sing and what I ought to wear and she took me through some movements that looked slick but not stupid, given I was never going to be graceful. Mainly a step back and a step forward. We settled for songs that expressed yearning with sex appeal, like *I Long For You* and *I'm Lost Without Your Lovin'*.

The place was a packed out when we got there, mostly the acts watching each other to see if anyone was nicking anyone else's material. They all knew each other. Like one big, happy, suspicious family. Stella Maria took a quick look round and said, 'You're best-looking by miles.' Tom had his camera on his shoulder and the barman wanted to know what was going on. Tom told him about the doco and he nodded, like it went on every day, and he said he'd be available for an interview afterwards.

Three acts in and we knew it was no ordinary night. All the songs were about Jesus. Stella Maria turned to the guy next to her. 'These people singing from the Nashville hymn book or what?'

He said, 'It's Christian night. You got a problem with that?'

And we did. I had no Christian songs to speak of and I didn't want to go home without performing something.

'Fuck,' Stella Maria said. She said to Tom to see if I could sing anything that wasn't Christian and Tom came back and said nope. It had to be Christian. So Stella Maria had this great idea that I should sing a few standards but put Jesus into them like *Me, Bobby McGee and Jesus*. And *Stand By Your Lord*.

Maybe I would've got away with it, if she hadn't started laughing real loud halfway through the *Bobby McGee*. A couple of people clapped when I got to the end. But when I started *Stand By Your Lord*, someone booed and after a bit everyone was booing so we had to pack up and go home. 'Thang is,' I said to the owner, 'no disrispek intended hayuh but Ah ain't a Christian singer perrrsay. Ah sing all mah songs for the Lord.'

My tapes need sorting. I can't find the one with *Gypsy Woman* on it. *I Recall A Gypsy Woman*, words and music Reynolds/McDill, about a man remembering his night of passion with an exotic woman when he was seventeen. I've been looking all over for it.

Betty calls through the door. 'Can I come in, Honey?'

I say, 'Sure.' I don't look up. I reckon I know what's coming.

She has to tread carefully to avoid the tapes scattered over the floor to get to the bed so she can sit on it. 'Honey,' she says, 'you know ethics prevent me from discussin' with either you or Stella Maria what the other one tells me in confidence.'

I say 'Yep,' and I continue sorting, sorting, head down, not checking her, looking for *Gypsy Woman*. 'I know all about that,' I say.

She says well in view of the circumstances, she's had second thoughts about the wisdom of inviting Tom on to the premises. 'Things are at such a delicate stage with Stella Maria,' she says.

'No kidding,' I say.

She says, 'Ah know you're disappointed.'

I say not disappointed just really pissed off because things are at a delicate stage with me as well. I mean what is it with Betty and Stella Maria? I thought she was supposed to be impartial. It's really getting to me now. She gets off the bed to look out the window. I say, 'Don't tread on the sodding tapes, for God's sake.' I want her to know how I feel but she doesn't comment. She just says she knows I'm feeling delicate as well. And either I'm going to cry or I'm going to shout so I shout. I get to my feet so I can shout in her face which is a trick I learnt from Stella Maria and Micky. 'You're not being fair. Doesn't matter what I say, doesn't matter what I tell you. All that bothers you is if I took into account the feelings of poor Stella Maria. Well she didn't always matter. Sometimes I mattered more. She's not the injured party. I don't know why you're treating her like she is. She's tough. She can be a cow. It's my father we're talking about.'

Betty drops her pen, bends down to pick it up and catches sight of the mess under my bed. A whole pile of stuff I was saving for the goat. Froot Loops, a sandwich or two, some clothes. Shit. Now she'll despise me even more. 'Don't raise your voice, Honey,' she says. She's not raising hers. She's leaning against the window frame, watching me the way you watch a dog chasing its tail.

'I'm raising my voice because I'm angry. You ask me all about myself and I tell you. You make me remember all these times I don't want to remember and then you make me feel like crap. Tom wants to find me a family and you say think about it. I thought you were supposed to be helping. Well you're not helping. In fact you're not helping so much I'm going.'

I wasn't thinking of going before but now I am. 'I need to get back to Nashville and I'd be very grateful if you would let me phone for Archie.' I'm starting to sling stuff into the carrier bag I was using for dirty knickers and she's watching me, not saying don't go or anything. 'I have work to do and Nashville's where I need to do it.'

'You know what, Honey? I think you need to count to ten,' she says. I tell her to sod off I'm not counting to anything.

She says, 'The law requires that you stay with me, Honey, so Ah don't reckon you will be goin' anywhere.'

'I'm going anyway,' I say and I'm out the door and into the hall where Stella Maria, who's been sitting on the floor outside my door, listening, suddenly jumps to her feet. 'I'm going,' I tell her.

She says, 'You can't. You know you can't.'

'Try and stop me,' I say.

'You're going to have to walk down that long winding mountain road all on your own.'

Betty's followed me into the hall. She says, 'If you really want to go, Ah'll call Harvey and arrange it. Ah don't see any point in me wasting mah time, or mah energy, though Ah cain't say Ah won't be sorra to see you go. Wait in your room, if you please.'

I go back to my room. Stella Maria follows me and closes the door behind her. 'What your fucking problem?' she says. I tell her. Betty favours her. Everything I tell her, Betty says what about Stella Maria. I've had enough.

'Well everything I tell her, she says what about Honey,' Stella Maria says. 'You think she doesn't know what she's doing?' And I think she doesn't.

Stella Maria doesn't hang about. I have nothing to say to her anyway. Soon as I can, I'm finding another place to be where no one thinks I'm some kind of skunk's arsehole. I lie on the bed, I stick my headphones on and I listen to *He'll Have To Go* sung by Jim Reeves, one of the great country figures of the 1960s, when the genre was producing its finest. But I'd rather be listening to *Gypsy Woman* and feel cheated right up to the end when I realise the song that follows is great.

Deportee, written by the very great Woody Guthrie and sung by Nanci Griffiths, about South American illegal immigrants who get thrown out of the country but their plane crashes before they get home. They die nowhere. It grabs me by the throat with its lyrcial combination of feeling and story. I think to die in the air is a fitting end to a body born at sea and I call upon Mammy to free me from the choking stench of my sorrow.

29

Where's Woody Guthrie today, anyway? Nashville in the year 2000 wouldn't know its own face in the mirror. All it wants is to be mainstream. All it wants records to be is crossover. All it does is break your heart. First people to listen to my songs just rolled their eyes and said, 'Listen Honey, people aren't buying songs like that anymore. People stopped writing them way back in '65.'

I said well that had to be stupid because these were the songs that people like me who really love and understand country music like best. Nothing fancy. Simple songs, sung loud and tunefully to the accompaniment of an acoustic guitar. With maybe a bit of banjo and fiddle. They said well there were people who liked that kind of thing. Some alternative people and some of the oldtimers like the one and only Dolly were favouring acoustic these days, but if you wanted sales, you needed something a mite more sophisticated. I said well who were they selling and they'd rattle off the names of a few young babes, and I'd say well they sang something real well but I'd never call it country.

Nor did Rita Rainbow who'd been busting her gut for the best part of three years but hadn't cracked it, despite her enormous talent, and wasn't even looking like it, whatever Jerrah says now. She favoured simple as well. Being a banjo player who could also turn her hand to the fiddle. It's a battle for a banjo picker, it really is.

I hit town, landed way out on a limb, walked just a little way along that limb and there she was, a really talented mean-spirited failure. Rita Mae was lower than a corn snake but she was a great banjo picker. And she agreed with me that the best songs are stories about ordinary people in hard times struggling to find happiness where they can. 'Songs without stories deny the genre,' she said the day we met.

'Dang right,' I said.

Rita Mae and me were a great team musically. Everyone could see it. Even Stella Maria, eventually. She had this great ear for melody. My own melodies are pure and clear but she could listen to a lyric, go 'What about this?' and come up with something so perfect tears'd be pouring down my face before I knew it.

What she was drawing on I do not know. The only tragedy in her life was a past so dull she'd had to invent one. Dullness is as tragic as you can get. I think she was trying to pass herself off as part Native American but Nashville already had its part Native American in Shania and Nashville adores Shania Twain. Whatever Stella Maria says now, I never tried to pass myself off as anything other than what I am. An orphan girl from Cockfosters, end of the Piccadilly Line.

Deportee ends for the third time, my gloom's lifted somewhat and what's bothering me all of a sudden is where will Betty send me? What happens if I end up with a cruel person who says I have to work for my keep and doesn't care what happens at the hearing? I go knock on Betty's door before she gets to Harvey.

'Come in,' she says.

'I guess I was just disappointed,' I say. 'Sorry.'

'Apology accepted,' Betty's voice is neutral.

'I think maybe I won't leave after all,' I say. She does her pen tapping thing. Not speaking. She could send you mental, she really could.

'Why Honey, Ah don't think this is your decision to make,' she says. 'It's mine. Ah listened to what you had to say and Ah suspect you may be on to somethin'. We're not making much headway and time is short.'

'So what are you saying?'

'Ah'm sayin' maybe you do need a change of scenery.'

'I don't. Not now I think about it,' I say. 'I was just confused.'

'By what?' Betty says.

'All the stuff you're asking me to remember. Sometimes I can't see what it's got to do with a brick falling on the head of a girl we didn't know so well.'

Betty swivels in her chair like she's giving herself a small thrill but I can see her mind's not on it. She sighs. She says, 'Ah guess Ah'm goin' to have to tell you and Ah guess this is an admission of failure on mah part since you didn't get to it yourself which is what Ah'd been hopin'.' The look on her face, all disappointment and maybe anger, makes me feel sick.

'Ah have been explorin' your life lookin' for patterns of behaviour and what Ah have unearthed and what Ah have been wantin' you to see for yourself is that you find it verra, verra difficult to accept responsibility for your actions.' She's staring at me hard, like she thinks I'm a lost cause, and she's hurting my feelings. She must know she's hurting my feelings but she barges on anyway. 'It's either Mammy, or Stella Maria, or a butterfly or Tom. You just about never say you did somethin' because you thought about it and it seemed like the right thing to do.'

There's sweat running down my back and I'm thinking what a cow she's being. Hasn't she heard a single thing I've said? Haven't I been responsible for myself since I was twelve? Haven't I just told Stella Maria that what I'm choosing to do is for me? I might as well leave right this minute and I would if I knew where I'd end up.

She says, 'Ah'm goin' to have to give this some thought. You oughta take a spell in the fresh air. Get some colour in those pale cheeks of yours.' She's smiling but she sounds offensive. 'You got green fingers like Stella Maria? You could try some weedin.'

I give her a look like, 'You know nothing even if you are prominent,' and I get out of there. Sod weeding. I hate gardening. And when did Stella Maria get to be so good at it I'd like to know? She stuck a few plants in some pots on a roof terrace and now it's like she invented dirt.

Betty thinks gardening is this gentle pastime but I can tell her there was nothing gentle about the way Stella Maria took to it. She should've heard the way she went for Archie when he told her maybe she'd gone far enough now. She unbuilt his brick sidetable to punish him.

I grab my guitar and go looking for Abe to cheer me up. If I'm going to be evicted I might as well have a quick intercourse with Abe before I go. The more I think about it, the better I like it. He's not in the jungle garden or on the top or middle terraces but there are signs that he's somewhere about. The table on the bottom terrace is covered with his stuff. He'll have to come back for it sooner or later so I hop up next to it to wait.

Hey hey hey, Rita Mae

No.

Maybe you thought you were someone else Rita Mae,
Maybe you wanted more than you could see
But Rita Mae what you didn't see was what you held in your hand
The person you could be took her promise to the Promised Land

Look at that. Came to me in a rush. Thing is, does it make sense? Does it matter? Sense doesn't always count in a country song. Anyone understand *After The Gold Rush*, words and music Neil Young? I don't think so.

As a writer, you can concern yourself with story or you can concern yourself with emotion or, best of all, you can concern yourself with emotions roused by the story which is where Bobbie Gentry hit the spot with *Ode to Billy Joe*, my favourite song of all time, best version, for my money, sung by Tammy Wynette, may she rest in peace. Tammy made that lyric ache with the heavy grind of working in the fields, the longing for love, the stifling smallness of the country town and one boy's total insanity. What I admire most about it is the way the tragedy nestles into the narrative.

There's this everyday family, out doing everyday things, choppin' cotton and balin' hay, and just nearby someone they've known all their lives has ended his by chucking himself off the Tallahachee bridge. The mother of the family breaks the news over lunch which she's spent all morning cooking. She's saying can you believe it? Eat up. Why would he do a thing like that? How come you're not hungry? And we never get to find out why. Only the singer knows and she's not saying.

I love that song but I wouldn't presume to record it because it doesn't suit my voice which does better with a tune. To be truthful my voice needs the discipline of a tune. This song doesn't need a tune because it's more like a dirge. Also the phrasing's funny. But you can't beat it for capturing the way tragedy will slap you in the face just when you think your life will go on forever like it always has.

Possibilities and outcomes are at the heart of the country song, for sure. How luck can love and leave you when your guard is down then swoop you up when you least expect it.

My take on the song, incidentally, is that the singer had said Billie Joe, I love you like a brother but I don't want it to go any further than that, and Billie Joe, who'd been in love with the singer all his very short life, just couldn't handle going on without her, so having chucked the ring into the river – the preacher saw him do it – next day chucked himself after it. Smashed to death on a terrible risk-to-reward ratio. It has echoes for me in my own life though Paddy isn't the suicidal type. Paddy is a man of steel.

You wonder where Bobbie could have taken that song if Billy Joe had plummeted off the bridge and landed on a rock. Straight into *Ruby Don't Take Your Love To Town*, words and music Mel Tillis, best version Kenny Rogers, where a paraplegic war veteran whose days are numbered but who still needs the love of a good woman, is tortured by the tarty ways of his girlfriend, Ruby. Or what would have happened if Billy Joe wasn't meaning to take his life but just going after the ring because it was his mother's and she'd said where is it, I need to sell it to put food on the table? Tragedy can take you any old where. As can a shit risk-to-reward ratio.

I see Abraham before he sees me. When he does see me, shyness overtakes his very, very handsome features. I watch him realise it's too late to avoid me. And this is insane. I know he's attracted to me. I've felt the burning and the longing from the first time we were in touching distance of each other.

He walks slowly towards me, looking at me, staring into my eyes and I think he's going to put his arms about me, so I let my body go slack. I gaze into his eyes. I see the strength in them. He gets to the table. He puts down his tools and his bag. He opens his mouth and says, 'Ah thank yo'll farnd yo sittin' orn mah seeds.'

I jump off of the table and find I'm doing no such thing. The seeds have fallen under the table. But the remark leaves us with nowhere to go. Body language has to work better. I cross to his side of the table and pick up a spade from his pile of tools. My small white hand brushes his strong brown one as he also bends to pick up a cigarette stub that's fallen out of my pocket. The nearness of his body makes me tingle. We stand up together, so close I can just about feel his heart pumping. 'Excuse me,' he says and leaves. Anyway.

I give him a couple of minutes and head back to the house myself, not sure I can stand a romance that goes this slowly. Don't even know if I want to. I'm writing to Paddy to ask him to come and get me. I don't want to go anywhere that isn't with someone who loves me.

Where Rita Mae and me could fall out was over the use of rhyme. She said a song doesn't need to sound like a limerick. But I love to rhyme. Several publishers looked at my songs and said, 'I see you like to rarm,' and I'd just say yes. No point in trying to justify it. The great painters of the sixteenth century never had to explain their fondness for brown.

'Dear Paddy, Times are tough out here, right now. I'm being asked to leave the house where SM and I are being given refuge and am v. unhappy about it. Can you come? Love Honey.' I need to post this quickly or I never will. It's not the sort of letter he'll be expecting.

'Can you post this for me?' I say to Betty who's admitted me to her study even though it's not for a session and this is the second time I've interrupted her today. She looks at the address on the envelope and says sure. I say, 'It's confidential,' meaning don't tell Stella Maria and she shoves it into the folder on her desk.

She says, 'In the morning.'

I say, 'Have you made up your mind if I'm going?' She shakes her head. She's thinking, she says, she's thinking. Then she opens her desk drawer, gets out my phone and hands it to me.

She says, 'I know you're strugglin' here, Honey.' And I thank her and get out of there before I fall into her lap from joy. She's not so bad.

Just the feel of the phone in my hand restores my faith in human nature. I find Barney Noble's last letter and scoot out the back, checking Stella Maria is where I left her in the den. I light a fag and dial Tom who picks up which is the best omen I've had all day. I'm so happy to hear his voice, my own comes out of my mouth too loud.

'Why didn't you ask me about finding my Dad, ponce?' it says.

'Hi, Honey.'

'You still in LA?'

'At the airport. With a lot of very positive feedback.'

'What's positive feedback?'

'A lot of interest. We need a song,' he says.

'Great,' I say. 'That's great. Why didn't you talk to me before you asked Betty?'

'To protect you. I was being sensitive.'

'Huh,' I say. 'You got any proposition regarding me, you put it to me.'

'So what's the answer?'

I say hasn't Betty told him and he says would he be asking if she had? I say 'When've you ever heard me say I wanted to find my father?'

He knows, he knows, he says, but listen Honey, it's a terrific opportunity. He saw it in a blinding flash when he was looking at stuff we'd taped about my early grieving and he thought to himself maybe I was pining for a dad. It stood to reason I might be, especially now, especially in such challenging times.

He's talking fast, like he's pitching. I think well he is pitching, but my mind's open. 'I remembered Stella Maria had said he was a musician and he was from the States and I thought, we'd be mad not to look for him. I think you'd like a father to love you. I think if I can find the man I'd be doing you one great big favour.' The gentleness in his voice gets to me.

'You OK, baby?' he says.

I tell him piss off, he can forget looking for my father

because I know he's only thinking how great it would be for his narrative. He says he's not denying it's an interesting story line. But he wouldn't go there if he thought it would be bad for me and I think he means it, self-centred git though he is. Stella Maria's wrong. He does care for me and he'd never do anything that would harm me. This is instinct, based on sleeping with him. Sex alters stuff, like it or not.

I didn't like it much, actually, because Tom's a dud in bed which is eerie. He just doesn't go at it the way you'd expect from a fit young man. It's not that he doesn't know his way around a woman's body. He just doesn't give it enough oomph. 'You there, Honey?'

'Maybe you can look for Barney Noble,' I say. 'Ask him if he knows my father and if he does and he's not a jerk then maybe I'll think about it.' I have to remind him who Barney Noble is. I read him the letter and give him the address at the top of it.

He says, 'I need to see you. You're going to have to make Betty see reason. Can you do that, Honey? Of course you can. You can do anything.' And he hangs up before I get a chance to sing the tribute to him.

30

Terrible sex isn't why I ended it with him. I ended it when Stella Maria finally told me he was the passion of her life. I just about died. Truly. It came from nowhere. I said she could have him. She said she didn't want him. I said sure she wanted him, if he was the passion of her life. She said why would she want anyone who didn't want her just because I no longer wanted him? And we were getting nowhere, so I said she was missing out on nothing anyway. I thought it would cheer her up.

How could I have been betraying her when I had no reason to think she was interested? I guess that Stella Maria has never understood the signals. There always are signals but some people never work out how to read them. Like music.

Tom and me both knew the score. Maybe even as far back as the night we met when I thought he was such an idiot. Stella Maria might have been doing all the talking, but it was my eye he kept catching. It wasn't as if we meant to fall in love anyway. I wasn't even sure I liked him. Some minutes I did. Some minutes I didn't. But you can fall in love with someone and not like them much. I had this in mind when he took me in his arms and said, 'You are mesmerising, you know that?'

The risk-to-reward ratio of Tom and me taking that step into the bedroom had to be crap. But sometimes it just happens and to be honest, I was mesmerised by him too. Working together the way we were was like seeing into each other's souls.

Maybe he wasn't my type. Maybe he is Stella Maria's type. But type didn't come into it. We'd forged an artistic bond and I went to bed with him because I thought sex could only bring us closer together. Tom thought the same. From the time he'd kissed me on the plane we both knew something was smouldering between us. It didn't need much to make it catch fire.

'Strike me, set me on fire/ You are the perfect match for me' isn't a country lyric. It's a pop lyric, though I wouldn't put it past certain recording artists in Nashville to give it a country spin in an attempt to enter the mainstream market via the back door.

What lit the fire between Tom and me was us falling out over the integrity of his piece the day we took the apartment in the block that became our Choctow, the ridge in *Ode To Billy Joe* where nothing ever came to no good. I never heard anyone talk about integrity in regard to pieces before but once he'd raised it, I knew exactly what he meant and what it came down to was his versus mine.

We'd been in Nashville three days and someone had lent Tom the truck he's still driving so we could go apartment hunting. Archie showed us around this fantastic place, bright and airy, well fitted out, and no more than ten minutes walk from Music Row which, as far as he and Stella Maria were concerned, was perfect. I was going, 'Forget it'. They looked at me like I was some kind of brat who couldn't be made happy even though they'd raised her from the gutter. Which I resented, you know?

I wasn't saying the place wasn't great. It had three bedrooms, a big lounge and this dinky little kitchen etc. but it was no more right for me than a hailstorm is for a hayrick. I was a semi-penniless orphan, hoping to make her way with her talent and her hope in a strange land and the plain fact was, I could never have afforded this place if I'd been doing it the regular way. Toni hitting town, for instance, could never have afforded it and I was no better or worse than Toni. Moving in there was going to be a lie. In my life history which was the subject of the film, it was a lie.

I said, 'It's too posh. I can't live here. We should be in something we can afford. This is crap.' And sparks were suddenly flying everywhere. Verbal foreplay, Tom said later. We spent a lot of time afterwards explaining what happened between us because writers do.

He said oh for God's sake, he was paying so what was the problem? I said any half-interested viewer would know it was wrong and the whole thing would look pathetic because the deal was I was testing myself in a hard, expensive and unfamiliar world. 'With a trust fund,' Stella Maria chimed in. I said I'd never use my trust fund to pay for accommodation like this. Not in a month of Sundays.

Tom's eyes glittered and his mouth went all sulky and miffed. First time I ever saw it. Usually he's charm itself but you set your will against his and you rouse from his inner depths this creature of jagged steel whose shadow transforms his face. The creature said, 'Let's get this straight. The film's mine. The song stuff is yours, but the film's mine.'

I said, 'Well up yours. The life is mine.' And his eyes bulged like I'd kicked him in the balls.

'Listen, Honey,' he said, and in brackets I heard you moron, 'Listen, Honey, the story isn't about hardship and grinding poverty. The theme isn't going to be hardship and poverty. The story is the gamble. What shortens or lengthens the odds in a high-risk situation. The struggle isn't the issue.

Your chances of cracking it when the odds are stacked against you is the issue. Don't you worry about the integrity of the piece. I'll take care of that.'

He expected that to shut me up because Stella Maria had a shut-up look on her face. But I said, 'No, you listen to me. My integrity's in there as well. I'm your subject and I'm just not having you tell a story about me that isn't me. I'm not having you make me look like a liar. Any idiot knows that if you come to Nashville to make it, how you survive is a big factor in the odds. People give up because they can't afford to stay.'

That didn't shut him up either. We were both charging up and down the hall waving our arms about and Stella Maria was, not for the first time, out of the frame. This had nothing to do with her, which maybe she was registering and maybe she wasn't.

Tom said, 'We're not going to tell the story of some no-hoper from any old place pitching up on the off chance. That's BORING. And I'm not pretending you don't have an edge because I'm opening doors for you. We don't have to apologise for cutting to the chase. What's interesting is how your passion and your past and your talent work for you. Where you live is incidental.'

I said, 'That sucks.' And I was heading for the door but Stella Maria was standing in front of it. He grabbed me by the shoulder and spun me about to face him which shocked me.

'Sucks,' he repeated, like he couldn't believe I'd uttered the word. The corner of his mouth was a hard little knot. Sexual tension was zinging between us like music down a banjo string.

I gave him a shove to get him out of my face. I said if this was the deal, we didn't have a deal. He banged his head against the wall. He said why was I being so thick? Why couldn't I see what he was trying to do? He could open doors for me but he couldn't force people to like me. We were talking powerful, intelligent people here whose fortunes relied on market forces. Did I truly believe he could make an industry ignore market forces?

Stella Maria butted in. 'Are you insane, Honey?

I said, 'I'm not going to be in any film of my life that's a lie.'

Tom said, 'Fine. If you two want to make a go of it on your own, working your passage like most people, spending years waiting at tables, struggling, starving, freezing and having doors slammed in your faces, then I'll just have to say goodbye because I want to crack it before I'm eighty.'

And then we all yelled at once with Stella Maria going 'No way can we manage on our own', and sticking her finger between my shoulder blades to make herself clear. 'Where do you get off, anyway, being so up your own arse?'

I was yelling at her to get off, it was my story, then Tom suddenly yelled he wasn't so sure it was anymore when he'd given us £500. That shut us up. Stella Maria and I stared at him, thinking what had we done because who wants to sell so much for so little. Tom, being a gambler, saw his mistake and immediately tried to fix it. He took all the anger out of his voice.

'Come on, come on, you two. Let's calm down.' He said I'd be taking my chances the same as anyone else. I'd just be taking them faster. Rejection or triumph would come my way in months instead of years. What was so wrong with that? And I tried to think. I wasn't sure. I hated arguments.

I pushed past him into the lounge and sat on the couch with my head in my hands and cast my thoughts to Mammy. The words I heard in my head, which I believe were hers, were, 'Anything for an easy life', which I guess was the lesson she had learnt from hers.

I told myself she must mean go with it, so I did. And I have no regrets about it because this is also true. Everyone's stories can end in a billion and one ways, whatever strings are pulled. No one can write the ending which is what we're all finding and what I should have understood at the time, but all I could hear was the anger in his voice.

We compromised. I'd be the heroine of the story he wanted to tell but he'd have to be the narrator and explain why my story wasn't the same as the story of any other singer/ songwriter who bowled into Nashville same day as us. That he was opening doors that normally wouldn't be opened so fast, if ever. We agreed on that, then he said, 'Fuck,' like he'd walked through the desert for forty days and forty nights. We were all kind of wrung out and we sat there for a bit without speaking. Then he leapt up from the chair he was in and gave me a kiss on the cheek. 'Brilliant,' he said. 'Let's take this place then. Let's all set up house together.' And my heart jumped. His did too. I saw it. We looked into each other's eyes and knew that any minute we were going to sleep together because we were in love.

Stella Maria didn't see it, naturally, because she was blinded by what she thought was a lucky escape. On the way back to the hotel, she said, 'Idiot. You nearly finished it then.' But I knew it was just beginning.

After dinner, Tom said maybe she should take a walk after putting in so many hours on the phone and laptop, lining up appointments and so on. He said he wanted us to work on the new film structure that was involving him and we might as well do it in his room so's not to disturb her.

Stella Maria said she didn't feel like a walk. Tom said he didn't want to offend her but he thought I sometimes worked better for the camera when she wasn't there. Stella Maria looked to me to tell him to forget it, I needed her there as she was my manager but I looked away.

Maybe this was treachery. Maybe it wasn't. It didn't feel like it. It just felt like it always did when I wanted to have a sex life and Stella Maria couldn't stand it. I said to her, 'I worry you're thinking I'm rubbish.'

She said, 'Thanks.' And she left slamming the door behind her. Tom stood there looking at me for half a minute, then he said, 'Right, let's get on with it.' But I never for a moment thought he meant it. He pulled me to him and kissed me.

We didn't sleep together though. Not for ages. We just had a really good snog and got down to work. There's no doubt in my mind I was in love with him at that time. I know how I feel and in love was how I felt. Gooey, paranoid, a bit sick, wanting to be with him every minute, all the usual.

I didn't think about Paddy or Micky. They were part of another existence. I floated back to the room I was sharing with Stella Maria that night but said nothing about anything to her because I knew from experience it would leave her cold.

I felt only real happiness because this is my natural tendency and I remained happy until the circumstances arose which subsequently killed Rita Mae. Right now I have feelings which aren't happy welling up in my chest and if they don't come out, my chest will explode all over Betty's goddam white curtains. I have to struggle to remember why, I'm so lost in my memories. When I do, I realise I've had enough. Betty's going to have to let me see Tom. If he's going to go looking for my father, I need to talk him through some ground rules. I'm going to tell her that.

She comes to her study door and opens it a fraction. 'Oh, Honey,' she says. 'Come in. Ah've been expecting you.' She tells me to sit. She asks me how I am.

'Oh you know,' I say. She says well maybe she can cheer me up a little. She's talked it over with Harvey and they've decided to allow Tom to visit, but only under supervision. He can stay one hour only, that one hour is to be in this very room and that she'll decide how to proceed after that. Does that help me? More than she can know, I say.

I ask if I'll have to move away after that. She says she hopes not. I say, what about Stella Maria? She says she'll explain it to Stella Maria. I say what I mean is how does Stella Maria feel about me not moving out. Betty says Stella Maria was always opposed to me moving. She was going to leave with me. And the load in my chest melts away. Betty gets up from her desk and checks her watch. She says, 'How 'bout we dine at the Cracker?'

31

Stella Maria's agonising over the menu, toying with the notion of Spicy Grilled Catfish Dinner served with your choice of three country vegetables. She's thinking turnip greens, fried apples and pinto beans. I know she'll have the meatloaf. I say, 'You'll have the meatloaf.'

'Maybe I won't,' she says, not a trace of rancour in her voice though her system has been chock full of it. I'd sure like to know what Betty's been saying to her to make her this calm. I hope she'll stay cool once she knows Tom's coming to visit.

'You eat up good and proper, Honey,' Betty says, scanning the menu and I guess trying not to vomit at so much meat. 'Why don't you try the Roast Beef Dinner or maybe the Cracker Barrel Sampler?'

Stella Maria says maybe she'll have the Cracker Barrel Sampler which is a hearty sampling of their own Chicken 'n' Dumplins, Meatloaf etc etc and I tell her to go for it. I'm not so hungry. I order Homemade Beef Stew 'n' corn bread. Betty has beans 'n' greens.

Food comes, we start to eat it and I don't speak just to be on the safe side. I'm actually wondering who's left messages on my mobile while it's been in Betty's custody. 'You have five new messages' was all I had time to hear before Betty yelled from the truck and I had to go. I tucked the phone under my pillow for safe-keeping.

Betty's trying to engage us in civilised conversation so I do my best. And Stella Maria does hers. We discuss the weather which we all agree is perfect. We discuss the food which we all agree is very filling. Then I think, shoot, I can do better than this. I say, 'Does Abraham have a girlfriend?'

Betty, picking at a green like it could be a slug, looks up. She's interested, I can see, as much in how I'm asking as what I've asked. This is how it is with psychologists.

'Why?' she wants to know.

'Just wondering.'

'Well he's never brought any young lady to my place but Ah suppose he must, bein' such a fine looking boy.'

I say to Stella Maria, 'Don't you think he has a cute bum?' And for a minute I think she's about to lose it, but she takes a deep breath and tells me no, but he is a fine looking boy, like she's practising to be Betty in the next life.

I say, 'I fancy the pants off him,' and that puts the lid on all conversation for the rest of the night. Except for stuff about the sunset. They are both weird, weird, weird women when it comes to sex.

Minute we're home, I thank Betty for the lovely meal, she says she wishes I'd eaten a little more of it, I say well I sure as anything am full up and she says why don't I join Stella Maria in the den to watch some TV. I say thanks but I have stuff to do that's work related, then I go to my room to make calls. Stella Maria hits the den, Betty takes to her study. No one looks pissed off so this is pleasant.

Messages are: two from Tom wanting to know why I haven't called him; one from Archie askin' how we're doin', saying he's still waterin' the plants; one from Dick sayin' he looks forward verra much to hearin' the tribute as does Jerrah; and one from this girl, Cindy, wanting to know if I need a new fiddle player now Rita Mae is no longer with us, may she rest in peace. I remember Cindy. Met her at The Bluebird one night with Rita Mae when the word was already out that we were hotter than hot. Blonde, skinny, thinks she should be the next Alison Kraus who's a truly great singer and fiddle player, which this girl sure ain't. She said, 'Love your stuff,' but everyone loved our stuff. Not calling her back. Don't remember giving her my number.

Actually, now I'm lying down, I don't feel like calling anyone back. I'm not sure what I want to say to anyone. Stick my earphones on to listen to some George Jones. Close my eyes and go to sleep.

Must've woken some time in the night because next thing I know the sun's up, my earphones are on the floor and I'm under the sheets having spent the night fully dressed which is something I don't like. And I really don't like forgetting to put my brace on. Rats. I check my teeth in the mirror to see if they've gone crooked in the night but they're OK. I want them white and straight for the album release even if they do miss the single.

Meet Betty on my way to the shower. She says, 'You have a session with me in . . .' she looks at her watch '. . . six minutes. In the study this morning, Honey.'

Seven minutes later and I'm in the floral chair with her raring to get on with it. She gets straight down to the subject of me and Tom so she can be well acquainted with the details before he gets here. 'You going to interview him about the death?' I ask.

'That's a matter for the police, not me,' she says. 'What Ah want to know is how you two came to be lovers.'

'Er,' I say.

'Ah hope this isn't too embarrassin' for you, Honey, but it

is pertinent.' She's trying to put me at ease but she can't because it's like discussing intercourse with a nun. 'You'd put Micky right out of your head and you found yourself in love with Tom.'

But I'm looking out into the garden where to my astonishment I can see Stella Maria on her knees looking hot as a chilli pepper, digging, digging and it's only 10.00 a.m. I can hardly believe Betty has managed to get her off her arse and out of the house. Does she know about Tom? Is she out there digging to work off her rage about Tom?

Then I see Abraham behind a bush that's covered with big white flowers. He's just standing there, watching her. Saying nothing, obviously. I wonder if he spies on me the same way but know he doesn't because I've been so carefully watching out for him. I say to Betty, 'Do you think that's healthy?' But she won't even look.

'Come on now Honey, no procrastinatin'. We don't have too much time.' But I'm desperate to know what's going on out there. I force myself and tell her, after a short think, that Micky remained in my heart – *The Bit Of My Heart That's Forever Yours* – but I was now in love with Tom. They were just different loves. 'Love is a coat of many colours,' I tell her.

'Dolly Parton,' she says to encourage me. I laugh and shake my head.

'Did you post my letter?' I ask, thinking suddenly of Paddy.

She says, 'Are you goin' to be able to concentrate or should we leave it right now and try again later?' I say sorry. She says the letter's posted.

I tell her that the colour of my love for Tom was purple and the colour of my love for Micky orange. The purple represented its intellectual content. 'My heart was engaged elsewhere.' This is the truth. My heart was engaged with Paddy in a scarlet way which isn't something she needs to know.

'With whom?' she asks.

'With Nashville. I was falling in love with my home from home.' It's the sort of remark that makes you puke in London but over here sounds as natural as the falling rain.

Getting to Nashville, living in Nashville, was like getting it on with a boy you've fancied all your life, I explain. Betty isn't too interested in me falling in love with Nashville. I explain I didn't have time to be so devoted to Tom because of everything else that was going on. We were both completely taken up with everything we had to do to get our careers off the ground.

We had to keep an eye on the competition. Tom was always checking what was rating on TV, or how movies like his were doing at the box office and I had a similar regard for the competition in Nashville. Hardly anyone was in direct competition with me, however, as what I was offering was unique.

'So he was just someone in passing as far as your love life went,' Betty says. And I go *Someone In Passing* – song – and she says please. I agree. Looking back, he was just someone in passing. There's no point in making him out to be more. Love-life-wise, he never was, despite the intense feelings we had for each other. 'So how would you rate your love for him one to ten?' she asks. I tell her three.

'I learnt a lot from it though,' I say. 'He taught me a lot about my craft which isn't so different from his. About themes and metaphors, the kind of stuff you learn at university.' Having a man as smart as Tom interested in my mind was sexual beyond belief. The physical side was secondary. Mostly snogging if we ran into each other and no one was looking.

Betty writes down snog and I think Betty, what are you like? I say we snogged on a regular basis which was dead sexy and made even more sexy in that neither of us was in a hurry to get into bed. First, we were exhausted by the day-today business of cracking America and second, there was Stella Maria, though her name was never spoken by either of us in the context of 'What will she think?'

'And what was she up to durin' this time?' Betty enquires. I hear in her voice a protective interest which both upsets and pleases me. I'm pleased she's concerned for Stella Maria but I want her to be protective of me too.

I say Stella Maria was busier than both of us. On the phone all day long, setting up meetings, organising photographs, stylists, studios, dentists, editing suites. Really getting on with it. Bossing me about. Tom was following up the contacts and immersing himself in all these books about the music business.

Betty looks up from her note pad but says nothing. She looks out the window where she now has a good view of Stella Maria but not the boy. The boy is still behind the bush and I can see, but Betty can't, that he's chatting to Stella Maria who's not looking at him even a little bit but digging away as if she has a purpose that isn't just working off a jar of peanut butter.

I think 'How come he talks to her and not to me?' Maybe he's less shy with her given the chemistry between us. Betty gets up and crosses to the window where she has a full view.

'Stella Maria is preparin' the ground for some seedlings,' she says.

'She wouldn't know how to,' I tell her.

'Abraham's advisin' her,' she says.

Jed Wilcox told Stella Maria her plants would die from the heat on the roof anyway so why was she bothering. He told her this was a work space for maintenance not recreation and she told him to fuck off, he had a face like an anus and if her plants died it was because he'd breathed on them.

She checked on them three or four times a day, pouring love and nutrients and buckets of water on to them and it got so even Archie wasn't sure if his deckchair was fun. He wasn't sure about the rockery she'd built out of the bricks that had once been his table.

Betty goes back to her desk. 'You never told Stella Maria how you were feelin' about Tom and she didn't tell you how she was feelin', even though you were best friends since you were six.'

I tell her I just put it on the backburner. Maybe we never discussed it for the same reason Tom and I never hopped into bed together. We had so much else on our minds. We were creating this new life for ourselves in a strange land and we were having to create new selves which, in my case, wasn't just time-consuming but uncomfortable because I was getting my teeth fixed.

Stella Maria, I tell Betty, was right across the scene in next to no time. The new self she was finding was a clear-headed businesswoman who knew not to bite peoples' heads off the minute they said something she didn't like. I believe she was seeing the world and everyone in it in a whole new light at that time and she was enjoying herself. She didn't come to all the meetings Tom and I were having because she had so much else to do.

Mostly Tom and I were meeting people who weren't Nashville's major movers and shakers but people who knew the movers and shakers and could explain to us how to get on with the movers and shakers. After a bit however, all those sessions started to merge into one long meeting with guys who all looked the same, saying the same sort of thing. They were interested that I was from the UK, which was becoming such an important market for any local artists prepared to risk the food poisoning, and they were interested that I was already the subject of a film in the making.

'Nashville artists don't like European food,' I explain to Betty. 'Raised on grits, addicted to grits, can't hack a steak-and-kidney pie.'

They said there's no reason you won't crack it with the

right song. 'How do you know a right song?' I asked them. And they laughed themselves stupid, like it was the dumbest question in the world.

There was only one who said it'll plain just never happen. He was the only one I out and out hated. He said it would never happen owing to the crap delivery of British singers who could never master the accent, but he just hated foreigners. I said well I deliver country like it should be delivered. I deliver in good ole country style because that's my style. My favourite days are the good old days.

He said did I mean Roy Acuff and Ernest Tubb or maybe Kitty Wells and I said I meant Rose Maddox and he went, oh poor old Rose, what a life she's had. Rose was famous for having a really loud voice and I said I had that in common with her. He said, 'Let's hear it then.'

Stella Maria was at this meeeting as luck would have it. I watched Tom's camera move from me to her as we exchanged a look and she said, 'Hold it,' knowing instinctively how much I was hating this guy. She said, 'You up for it, Honey?' I said definitely.

I sang *Roaring Into Town On A Train Going Nowhere*, words and music HH, which Stella Maria has always considered a classic. It's a narrative/feeling combo, relating the tale of this wayward girl without hope or money or friends suddenly finding joy on a train from the cotton to the orange fields.

Tom was filming, Stella Maria was sitting tight in her chair, willing this plonker to hear my great accent and I was relaxed as could be. When I finished the geezer said, 'Close, very close,' because he was never going to admit he was wrong, was he? Then he said but you'll still end up a novelty act.

'We won't remember you when we're famous,' Stella Maria said and we left.

Everyone wanted to know who I liked and when I told them Emmy Lou, Dolly, Patsy, Willie, they smiled and said well they're wonderful but who in the current market? Which made my blood boil. Someone always said, 'Garth Brooks sells 12 million. George Jones sells 400,000. Garth gets played on radio. George doesn't.' And I'd say how totally crap that was when George Jones has a voice like warm caramel and Garth Brooks doesn't.

This is something I feel passionate about. If you're famous for music beloved by the entire world, then you don't water it down with every other goddam kind of genre you think might turn a buck. 'You know something, Betty?' I say. 'Nashville's full of greedy blighters who don't give a tiny toss for the place's heritage.'

She says, 'What Ah am trying to get to Honey, is what happened when Stella Maria discovered you and Tom were lovers? What Ah'm working towards is the reason for the rift between you which is placing you in such mortal peril.'

32

Truth is, the recollection upsets me and I just don't feel like going there. I look back now and can't see it was worth it when we'd been having such a great time, all three of us together. What Tom and I had seemed special for a minute or so, but wasn't. All it turned out to be was respect for each other's craft. The song is as distant from the documentary as corn meal is from buffalo hide but what they share is a love of story.

Tom was blown away by the confidence I had in composition but it was as natural to me as laughing and crying. He used to say, 'Don't you ever get stuck?' But the last three words of any sentence can always start a song. *Ever Get Stuck*, for instance, could take you somewhere interesting if you put your mind to it.

I say to Betty it was pretty straightforward really. One night I went into his bedroom and didn't come out.

Betty sighs. She's disgusted. I don't want her to be disgusted. I say, 'Will you pray for me Betty?'

She says she prays for me every night already. I tell her I'd meant to creep back into our room but I never did. I'd fallen asleep and woken up only when I heard Stella Maria banging around in the kitchen. I mean BANGING around in the kitchen. Betty wants these details. I spell them out for her.

'I jumped out of bed, and went to find her. She took one look at me and ran, so I took off after her.'

'What were you thinking?' Betty asks.

'Better get some clothes on.'

'Apart from that?'

'I was thinking here we go again. Bloody nightmare.' Betty taps her pen on the tape recorder. 'She tried to close the lift doors in my face but I forced them open. There were other people in there but we ignored them. The doors hadn't even closed when she went for me.'

'With her fists?'

'With her voice. She called me a tramp who fucked anyone she could her my hands on, who was sick, who was depraved, who sang like a shagging donkey and basically any other repulsive thought that came into her head. She said I was a carbon copy of my mother. By the time we got to the lobby I wanted to kill her. You know I don't mean that literally.' Betty nods. 'I said, "Stella Maria, shut it. Shut it right now or I'm on the first plane out of here and you will have no one left to manage." '

'We were walking along the street and I was having to shout to make myself heard. She said, "Go away. Get lost!" I said, "OK" and I headed back, pretending I was going to pack. I don't know if you've found this, Betty, working with crazies, but ignoring them gives them a chance to change down a gear.

'She calmed down. She followed me back. She said how could I have slept with him when I knew she loved him. "You knew I loved him and you slept with him just because you could." Like Jolene,' I say to Betty. I grab a tissue out of the packet on Betty's desk in case thinking of it sets me off. 'I burst into tears from shock. I was so shocked. I mean it had just never occurred to me. On my mother's life, may she rest in peace. I told her I truly had no idea. But she just wouldn't believe I hadn't done it deliberately.'

Betty now taps her biro on her tooth. 'Would it have changed things if you'd known?'

I say, 'Betty, if I'd known, Tom would've known and everything would've been different.'

'Why would Tom have known?'

'Because I'd have told him. Nothing would have made me happier than to encourage a romance between them.'

'Did you talk about your relationship to the camera?'

'No.'

Out the window my best friend has stopped digging and is getting to her feet to admire what she's done. Which is turn the soil into a garden which I have to admit looks beautiful. The soil is rich and brown and the seedlings are tiny and green and hopeful.

'Anyway,' I say to Betty, 'we were all over it pretty soon so you don't need to get distracted by it. Stella Maria came to see that the pain I'd caused her was unintentional and we went back to being as happy as could be. I gave her advice on how to make him love her.'

'Bet she enjoyed that,' Betty says, and I know it's a joke from her face.

I admit it got on her nerves. 'The point I'm making is we went back to where we were before.' Which is more or less true. We did it the way we always have done after a fight. I let her yell at me until she had nothing else to yell and of course I dumped Tom.

Not at once. I went to bed with him a couple more times but never when she was around, then I said it wasn't working for me owing to us being three in a flat and the awkwardness of it and he understood at once. There was no tantrum – well the guy has a low sex drive. He gave me a hug and said if that's what I wanted, it was what he wanted, which I think showed sensitivity as well as a low sex drive. Then I fell out of love with him. I didn't miss his warm and tender loving even a bit. There's tender and there's useless. We all put our heads down and got on with our work but now it was official that Stella Maria was in love.

'Did Tom know?' Betty asks.

'It was obvious.'

I wrote *Mad, Sad And Goddam Glad* about a girl in love with a boy she can only communicate with via her best friend. It's on the demo tape along with the original version of *What Makes You Think You're the Man for Me, Down and Outa Love* plus *Ballad of a Poor Boy*. Funnily enough, *Bettin' on Your Cheatin' Heart* wasn't on the demo. It was Merv who discovered it on Honey 44, a compilation tape I made more than three years ago. The honest truth is I can't remember whether I told Tom or I didn't tell him. Maybe I did, maybe I didn't.

I hear Stella Maria come into the house and ask Betty if we can finish. I want to talk to her. I'm hoping she'll want to speak to me. Betty says, 'OK. Hop it.' She's made a note on her pad I can see plain as day. 'Father fixation?' it says.

33

If there's one thing I don't have, it's that. Stella Maria would kill herself laughing if I told her and I'm tempted. She's at the kitchen sink, running herself a long glass of water. Her cheeks are pink. Her hair is damp. Her T-shirt's clinging to her back. She'll be in a good mood for sure, given her new mellow temperament.

'Hot out there?' I say.

'What do you think?' OK so not in a good mood.

'What were you up to with Abraham?'

'What did it look like?' She's not mellow. She's crabby. Betty must have told her about Tom.

'Looked like you were showing him your tits.' She's getting on my wick. She stomps off. I call after her. 'You should save them till tomorrow for Tom.' I don't mean to upset her but she's upsetting me. Maybe I do mean to upset her. This has, anyway. She's back in a flash to confront me and underneath the pink are patches of pale. Betty hasn't told her.

'What do you mean tomorrow?' She looks so distressed, I want to back off.

'Harvey said he could come. Because of the film.' She's paralysed by the information. Standing there with nothing moving, not even her face which doesn't know what expression to pull for the best. 'Didn't Betty say?'

How come Betty didn't say? Was she hoping she'd get away with not saying? Did she just forget? I try to make less of it. 'It's not the worst thing that can happen. It'll be a chance to sort things out between you.' Stella Maria says nothing.' 'You might as well.' She makes a sort of you-what noise in the back of her throat. 'He loves you.' Now she flips.

'For God's sake, Honey.' She's just about crying. And I'm thinking how pathetic it is. If she's over him, fine. She can still see him. I could see Micky without having hysterics and he wanted to kill me. Then all at once, I know.

'You think he did it, don't you? You think he killed Rita Mae.'

She looks up into my face. 'He did. As good as.'

'What's that mean? As good as.' But that's it. She's off, leaving me nowhere. Title. And you know what I'm thinking? I'm thinking stuff it. 'As good as' equals not at all. She's winding me up because she's so wound up. Stella Maria acts like queen of tough but she has minus resources to fall back on. You'd think she'd know, just from watching, that horrible events glue themselves to your life but you learn to live with them.

I need air. I'm going down to the cherry tree. She'd be a darn sight better off if she used the energy she's devoting to her suffering to do the job she came here to do. I still need managing for God's sake. The wagon train's still rolling, even if we are tucked away behind a boulder while Harvey fights off the Indians.

And she's a great manager, forget everything Rita Mae had to say on the subject. Maybe Dick and Jerrah don't respect her as they should but I ought to know. Workwise, she fights my battles for me better than anyone.

Tom couldn't believe how tough she was with the guy who produced the first demo, 'You know something?' she said, walking right up close to him so he had to take a step back and the only step he could take was into the wall. 'I hate this sound. We hate this sound. We don't want any old chee-chu-chu-chee-chee happening. We want clarity of voice. We want clear, pure, like in a waterfall.'

The guy said, 'Where y'all from again?'

I said, 'London.'

He said, 'Knew you were some sort of foreign.' He said nothing about the calibre of material he was hearing or my talent so I've wiped his name from my memory. But after that, he treated us like we were someone, until Stella Maria sacked him. And look how she nagged and nagged Tom until he found us Merv who was recommended by people who knew people, just like everyone else we saw. Stella Maria knew we needed a special sort of producer and she hunted him down and made him listen to the demo then she talked and talked until he agreed to listen to me.

Tom's contacts might have opened doors for us but it was Stella Maria who did the selling once we were in. 'What you have here,' she'd say, 'is a gorgeous babe with the soul of Patsy Cline, the heart of Emmy Lou and the tonsils of Dolly who can sound like Willie Nelson.' It took people's breath away.

In next to no time, I stopped having pangs about our inside track. It's how the business works. There's an outside track and there's an inside track. You get on to that inside track any old way you can. Rita chose the shag route and she sure as hell wasn't the only one.

Everyone's out there hustling. Everyone. Everyone needs to get in with someone because there are ten thousand song-writers in Nashville and all of them think the song in their pocket is a hit. Those stories you hear about unknowns getting discovered in honky tonks by big shots who blow in with ten babes on their arm and suddenly drop down in a dead faint when they hear the voice of an angel? Forget it.

The music's one thing. The industry's the opposite. It might have started with simple folk writing simple songs about heartache to relieve their stress but now it's about contacts and contracts and how to make people think your song is the one they've been waiting for.

Sex is a big help. Course it is. But Stella Maria was never going to sleep with anyone and nor was I, unless I loved them. Once Stella Maria got going, people just had to sit up and listen. I'm not saying it was an easy ride. It was a short ride, but it wasn't easy. People don't want to like you. Saying no is what they want to say. Saying yes is a whole pile of trouble ahead. So people'd have us in, then they'd tell us pretty well what they told everyone else.

'There's two lots of people in this town,' they'd say. 'People with dreams and no talent, people with talent. Your girl (me) might have talent or she might not. Being English might work or it might not. Her voice is interesting, being so deep and so loud but her songs are shallow. We'll pass.'

Stella Maria would say, 'Then you're crazy. She's already the star of her own movie,' which of course they could see because Tom was recording everything. And they'd say, 'Really impressive', which pretty soon got right up her nose. She got to realise that impressive was another word for goodbye. Title there. *You Say You Really Like Me But What You Mean's Goodbye.*

Only person totally not impressed by any filming was Mamie Potter who runs Low Down and this was kind of shocking as she was the single person I wanted to impress (not counting George Jones and Dolly). Low Down is *the* alternative country label. She wouldn't even listen to my songs, she hated the pitch so much. Stella Maria had gone in on the film angle because it had worked best for everyone else and she just laughed in her face. She said why would she listen to someone who thought they had the edge on every-one else just because they were in some irrelevant movie. She was interested in musicians and poets, not film stars and she definitely wasn't interested in some creep from London thinking he could barge through her door expecting her to pick up a no talent he was peddling just because he thought he knew someone who knew her.

This was how Stella Maria reported it. Maybe these words weren't the ones Mamie Potter used. But they chilled me to the bone. Stella Maria just never stopped to think how much or why they'd upset me. Someone I respected was accusing me of having no integrity. Stella Maria said she wasn't doing any such thing. What she was doing was cutting off her nose to spite her face. And Tom said who gave a toss anyway. Her label was the smallest, no account outfit in town. If I wanted to get to an audience, I had to concentrate on the big guys. Stella Maria said, 'That's what we're doing.' But even so. It was a regret.

Every day before we finished work, the three of us would get together to analyse what progress we'd made, where it left us, and what we needed to do next, like it was a serious campaign. Which it was. Stella Maria made lists, ticked things off and put stars alongside some meetings and crosses alongside others and Tom added sequences to his story board, which was the way he kept track of the narrative. He did these fantastic drawings of Stella Maria and me. He always sketched her with giant bazoombas, proof I used to tell her of his interest in her.

We were working our arses off. Forget father fixation. If anyone was carrying on like a parent, it was Stella Maria, controlling every area of my life – what I ate, when I ate, where I slept, how long I slept, what I wore, how I wore it, who I saw and what I said to them. She confirmed all my appointments, ordered my taxis, briefed me before all my meetings. She worried about my voice.

I yodel across the valley to see how it's sounding today and it's shite. I clear my throat, try again and it improves.

She could get really spiky, if she thought it wasn't being appreciated enough. 'You've got raw talent,' someone might say. 'But that's it – it's raw. You need to get yourself played in.' By which they meant do all the crappo venues in town until people stopped throwing things at me. Arse to that, Stella Maria said. None of us was up for that anymore. Didn't matter what Toni would have had to do. If she could've avoided it, she would have. 'Everyone does open mic to begin with,' they said. 'You gotta pay your dues in this town.'

We were in town maybe two months, and we had a couple of labels sniffing about the place, but Stella Maria wanted a producer with influence who liked my sound, was prepared to swim against the tide and whose feeling for the music harked back to its roots, as mine did. Tom came up with Merv. We met Merv, then we met Rita, and our fate was sealed.

No sign of Abraham. I might leave a note asking him to meet for coffee in the greenhouse before he goes home. On the other hand, I can't be fagged going up to the house for a pen and paper. I'll have another smoke. The motion of the swing soothes my troubled spirit and I could nod off except that there's this major cacophony from somewhere behind me and when I look I see it's Betty ringing a bell and waving from the top terrace.

'Honey?' she's yelling. 'Honey, git yourself up here now. We have a visitor.'

34

Betty says I remember Morris, don't I? And of course I do. Who could forget him? Morris from the Siegal office looks at Stella Maria and me like we owe him an intercourse for everything he's doing for us and he is repulsive. He's smiling so wide, another man would have great news, like the charges against us are dropped, everyone says they're sorry and here's a million dollars. But not Morris. 'Hi Morris,' I say.

I have no good feelings about him, even though he turned up at the police station the day we were taken in for questioning and told us not to say a single other word concerning the events to anyone and especially not the police. At that time I was so grateful, I could've kissed him and maybe I did kiss him. He's always looked like I should kiss him again every time we've met since and it's disgusting.

Betty says, 'Come on into the study. Ah'll bring you somethin' to drink. Iced tea?' I say we don't need any iced tea, thanks Betty. Morris says he'd love some iced tea.

'Where's Stella Maria?' I ask. Morris says he's looking forward to seeing Stella Maria again and I want to slap his

225

face. It's a pink face with a very small nose and he looks like a pig. Betty says she believes Stella Maria could be resting and why don't we chat while she fetches her. The minute she leaves, Morris starts his smiling all over again.

I say, 'You got cousins out this way?'

'What do you mean by that?' he says.

'You just passing by then?'

'I'm here by appointment,' he says and I think is he? Did I know that? Did Betty tell me he was coming? He takes Betty's seat at the desk. I sit in the floral chair. Sun's pouring into the room and into my eyes so I have to squint to look at him and it's no improvement. He says he's here to clarify a thing or two before the hearing.

'Like?' I'm not sounding friendly but there are men for whom friendly is just out of the question.

'Like your relationship with the workmen, for instance.' I say what relationship and he says come now. 'You were friendly with those guys. More than friendly.'

This shocks me. I say we didn't have a friendship with them. They were just painters and people about the place. He smiles his horrible smile. He says, 'Well you're not denying you knew them.'

I say, 'What I'm saying is we didn't hang out with them. Stella Maria had most to do with them.' He's studying me hard now. Like there's this big fraud being perpetrated by me in particular.

'Would you say she was closer to them than you were?' I say she spoke to them more. 'Why did she speak to them more?' The answer to this is she wanted to kill them. She hated their noise, she hated their mess, she hated them being on the roof when we wanted to be there. She hated most of all them chucking their flipping ball about the place.

'She's a friendlier person,' I tell him. 'All I knew was one was called Jed.' Morris grins at me.

'So you don't deny knowing Jed Wilcox?'

At this point, Stella Maria comes in bringing the tea tray and Morris leaps to his feet to take the tray and grin all over her. 'Honey didn't know Jed,' Stella Maria says. 'She didn't know him from Adam. I knew Jed better than she did.'

Morris looks like he doesn't believe either of us. 'But you knew Jed was in love with Honey,' he says. What? Jed was about fourteen with spots all over his neck and a head too small for his body. 'I can totally understand it because she is a fine looking girl. You are a fine looking girl if you don't mind my saying so.'

I do mind him saying so and so does Stella Maria who says where did he hear that pile of shite, she'd like to know and he says from Jed himself. Stella Maria says well he's talking through his backside and I'm looking at her and looking at Morris and I can hardly make out what they're on about, as no one's ever mentioned any feelings Jed has had for me, not even Jed. We had one conversation, maybe two, three tops and all about nothing.

'And is Tom Sinclair talking through his backside as well?' Morris asks, simpering because he's come as close as he ever will to saying something rude. 'Tom Sinclair told me, no two ways about it, that Jed formed an attachment to you the minute he saw you and he thought maybe you liked him too.' I look at Stella Maria and she's as mystified as I am. 'Tom Sinclair has it on film,' Morris says.

'Has what on film?' I'm now so lost, I wonder if Stella Maria has been living a parallel reality.

'One interview,' Stella Maria says.

'What's he talking about?' I ask.

She shrugs. She says to Morris 'All you need to know about the workmen is they were pains in the butt. They were slobs. And they saw me on the roof five minutes before the brick fell on the head of Rita Mae, may God have mercy on her soul. Anything else you hear is bollocks.' I agree with her.

Stella Maria leaves the room, I tell Betty Morris is done and the minute he leaves I ask Stella Maria to explain what's been going on. All she says is, 'Ask Tom.'

The worst thing about sulkers is the space they leave around them. It feels empty but it's full of anger that cuts into you like broken glass if you try and reach across it. I spend the night in my room working on my tribute but I'm so distracted all I can come up with is:

Was there ever such a day Rita Mae
As the one that put you in my way
Was there ever such a tune Rita Mae
As the song in your heart that I heard you play

Merv would laugh in my face if I sang that load of old shite to him.

If I'd been going to fall in love with anyone at that time I'd have gone for someone of substance like Merv, despite his great age. I didn't need Tom to tell me a romance with Merv would be a powerful strand to my narrative but it was a non-starter. He was Rita's, along with every other person with a penis in Nashville, according to her. Every other person with a penis who could further her blighted career. Anyway, I didn't need to have sex with Merv to love him. I loved him for himself. He was the man who understood my talent and saw how throwing in a dash of Rita Mae's could turn it into magic. He's a legend in Nashville. A man after my own heart.

We met him late one afternoon after I'd spent a couple of hours warming my voice up, practising what I'd do for him and generally getting myself into a state because Stella Maria had said this was the man we absolutely had to impress. I'd settled for three compositions – early Honey, middle and late – to show my artistic progression. He closed his eyes to listen, nodding and smiling to himself when he liked something in particular and when I finished he said, 'Well that was cool.' Then he appeared to go to sleep but all he was doing was looking for connections. 'I hear Willy, I hear Patsy and you know, goddam it, in the phrasing, George Jones, which I never have in a woman before.' I could've cried for joy but I made myself not by blowing down my nose as hard as I could. 'Tell you what you need, girl. You need a writing partner to get a couple of those old English edges off and I have the very one for you.' Who was Rita.

I see her now, striding into the room with one hand stuck out to shake mine and the other resting on the banjo she carried with her at all times. Dressed in black. Tall, broad-shouldered but also kind of frail, like a big gust could sweep her clean off her feet. But nothing ever blew Rita off her feet until she encountered that brick.

She'd groomed herself to look like a coal miner's daughter whose grandfather was an Apache, whose voice had been honed in a church choir in the valley and who'd learned the banjo at her mother's knee. But she was raised on an army base by parents who loved each other and she'd had a really good education.

She knew from the beginning I was worth latching on to. An English hillbilly girl starring in a movie about her own life and whose songs were getting to be the talk of the town. She set out to be what she reckoned I'd be looking for in a writing partner and I fell for it. Stella Maria reckoned if I'd have said nursery rhymes were my genre she'd have said hers too.

'What about *Ode To Billy Joe?*' I said. People don't like *Billy Joe* then I'm never going to understand them.

Rita said, '*Billy Joe* is art giving tragedy its due.' I couldn't have put it better myself. Stella Maria said it was how I put it, Rita just repeated what I'd said but that's not how I remember it.

Her own favourite was Emmy Lou's version of *When We're Gone, Long Gone* and I said well that practically made us sisters as the sentiments of that song are the very ones I've carried through life and will value always. This woman's saying to her life's partner that even though they've struggled through shite together, when they're dead the only thing that will matter is that they loved each other. Completely beautiful in my opinion, soft on story, but as powerful as anything on the word picture which is the only substitute for a story I can accept in a song.

Rita said we could do a fine harmony on it. I said maybe. I never wanted to harmonise with anyone after my mother died. And being truthful, I wasn't so confident about my technical ability. I'm not like those chicks who blow into Nashville from music school where they learnt opera but have decided rockabilly's their gift because it'll get them into pop. My music's from my gut and heart. Not my head.

Was Rita Mae beautiful? Well she had this big hooter and wide-apart eyes that were always moving. I guess she was. But it's hard to be beautiful and always on the look-out for something you think you ought to have because someone else has it. Rita walked into Merv's office and her scurrying eyes took us all in in two quick sweeps around the room. She didn't need Merv's introductions which were useless anyway. 'Ah. This is, er, Honey, and Sally Mary and Tony. Just wait till you hear this little girl sing.'

Merv was besotted by her. He tried to pull her on to his lap but she dodged his outstretched arms and gave this laugh that said no way was she involved with him. This was how she always played it. No allegiances to anyone in case it put off people who might be more useful. She kept her options open until she decided they were closed then she slammed them shut, not even caring a tiny bit whose feelings were busted in the process. I saw her do it over and over.

That day, she wanted to get us right. She wouldn't hate me until she'd drained from me every ounce of use I could be to her. I have no illusions about her. None at all. But I did at first because she had a winning way she never wasted. What she did that first meeting was decide who to use it on, me or the main man in my entourage. She ruled Stella Maria out within seconds. Maybe because Stella Maria tried to rule her out within seconds. They looked at each other and it was like this repel bomb exploding between them. Instinct is a funny thing.

Instinct tells me right now I've smoked more than is good for me. And sure enough the room's in fog even though the window is open. I need air. As I pass the den, I hear Betty soothing Stella Maria. I think she must be soothing her. She's doing all the talking, which she mostly doesn't, so I stop to listen.

'A heart can recover,' she's saying. 'Believe me, Stella Maria, Ah know the pain. Ah know it goes away.' I'm shocked out of my skin. I want to go in. I want to join in the conversation. I don't want to be left out.

How come Betty's never told me about her pain? Footsteps move towards the door so I duck back to my room and fall on to my bed, sick with injured feelings. To be excluded is a painful and lonely thing. 'Like it was for Stella Maria,' I hear in my head. 'Like it was for Stella Maria.' Sometimes it would be better not to have an angel for a mother.

I knew all along it wasn't easy for Stella Maria but what could I do? If I was going to crack America I needed a writing partner and Rita Mae had all the qualifications. It wasn't like she was a new boyfriend. But even as I explain this to myself, I can hear Mammy telling me it was like a boyfriend. Rita walked through Merv's door and, if she'd been a man, she'd have charmed the pants off me. It took her two seconds flat to decide I was the one who needed charming. She gave Tom as much attention as she thought he needed to keep him on hold.

Merv said, 'This little girl's got one helluva voice.' And he nodded to me to play something, so I sang for her *Time Will*, which I'd written when I knew I was growing out of Micky.

Stand still

Time will
Pick you up and carry you away
Stand still
Time will
Get you to the next stop day by day.

And by the time I got to the second chorus, she had her banjo out and was playing along, singing a high sweet harmony which sounded finer than anything I'd heard since Mam sang *It Wasn't God Who Made Honky Tonk Angels*.

Stella Maria, Tom and me went straight home from Merv's office, so we could talk about it, and I remember Tom filming the conversation because he was under my feet. Alarm bells were already ringing in Stella Maria's head. 'How's it going to work? How big a partner is a writing partner? I don't want her in our life,' she was saying.

She was sitting on her bed and I had clothes everywhere. I said, 'Let's talk about it later. After I see how much I like her.' I was off to meet her at the Thai restaurant on Haywood Lane. I'd said let's meet at Shoneys but Rita had done Shoneys. Every single sucker who drifts through Nashville with a pocketful of songs ends up at Shoneys. She didn't want to look like a sucker.

I didn't want to look like a sucker either and I wanted to impress this on Rita who was so impressive herself, given the dues she'd paid. She was twenty-three and they were some dues.

She'd played every damn club in town, Douglas Corner, The Bluebird, every damn club and she was admired by everyone, Merv had said in the five seconds before she turned up. 'All she's short of is a deal.' I couldn't wait to talk to her about how she wrote, where she wrote and what she wrote. I'd spent so much time in isolation and Tom had whetted my appetite for a fruitful exchange of ideas.

'You going to be a double act or what?' Stella Maria nagged

as I pulled boots on then kicked them off. I told her could she just piss off for a single minute because until I actually sat down and talked to the girl I didn't know what I wanted. For all I knew I might come back and never want to clap eyes on her again. Stella Maria didn't believe for a single minute that's what would happen, but she knew not to call me a liar.

Tom said from behind the camera, 'What'll happen if you do hook up?'

I said, 'Listen, I'm a solo act. End of story. If she comes along with me, she'll only get noticed by the audience if I invite them to notice her.'

Serves me right for being so cocky. You only needed to take one look at Rita Mae to see she was sick of being anonymous. Well Stella Maria did. 'She's trouble,' she said while I fussed with my hair.

'Maybe, but she sure knows her onions on the banjo,' I said. I gave Stella Maria a kiss and Tom a pat on the shoulder as any form of lip contact was now out, then I left.

'Have fun,' Stella Maria said and I told her you too and showed her crossed fingers. She had a night alone with Tom ahead of her and I understood that despite her being so full-on with me she was well excited, sifting through the uplift bras on the floor.

35

It's 9.15 a.m. I've been awake since 7.00 not just because the goat hates me sleeping but because I spent the whole night keeping myself awake in case I overslept, Tom arrived while I was still in bed, and Betty did her nut. The tension in the house is unbearable. I got out of there as fast as I could and came to the gate to wait.

Betty's glued to Stella Maria's side in case she panics and tries to suffocate herself in the fridge. She regrets ever saying Tom could visit, because Morris freaked us out and Betty just doesn't need anyone else freaking us out. Stella Maria looks like she's trying to decide whether to freak out or not. Freaking out isn't what her new calm self does but she's tempted I know.

My sympathy for her is all over the place, sometimes overflowing like a river in full flood, sometimes dry and hard like a river bed that hasn't seen rain in years. *No Rain For Years* is rattling about my head, like some sad old chorus to my life but I hum loudly to block it out. Betty has said I must bring Tom into the house by the front door and take him directly into the study. We can stay there exactly one hour, then I must lead him out of the house and straight back to the truck so's to cause miminum disruption to the household, i.e. Stella Maria.

Due respect to Betty but if I were an expert in human relations I wouldn't be giving her this kind of leeway. I'd be saying just get on with it, Stella Maria, because this is life. Beats me why she isn't. Must be the terrible thing that happened to her that's making her believe Stella Maria's suffering is fierce. It would be so much healthier if Stella Maria, Tom and I could sit down over a civilised cup of coffee plus a peanut butter sandwich, and chat like we always did about how to sort it all out. We used to be so good at it. Here's a problem. How will we fix it? I don't suppose we'll ever do that again. A broken heart is a broken heart and there's no getting away from the fact that Stella Maria's heart is just not ready for repair. When I think about it, why would it be?

I thought she'd do herself in when she found out Tom had slept with Rita. I thought she'd throw herself under a bus. But then Rita died and her own would have been one death too many.

One death too many
In this lonely old town
Diggin graves
Can really get you down.

Stella Maria had just begun to let herself believe she stood a chance with Tom and I'd been telling her she definitely had because I thought she did. He certainly seemed fond of her. I was saying see how he looks at you? See how he puts his arm around your shoulders? Hear the way he speaks to you? I was saying if she did without intercourse one more week she'd end up with a vagina withered like an old pea pod. Take a chance. Go on. Take a chance, I said to her. And

235

though this is all love ever is, and though I knew she was staking her whole life's happiness on it, I never took Rita Mae into account.

Rita got into men's pants the way Stella Maria hoes into meatloaf. She'd decided to get into Tom's as soon as she realised he was turning my life into a cinematic masterpiece for a global audience. And he was just so easy.

I'd been saying to him, 'You've got to admit Stella Maria's a good-looking girl' and so on and he'd been agreeing because she is but making any kind of move towards romance isn't in him. While Stella Maria was hesitating, Rita pounced and suddenly we were all in this great stinking bog of treachery which oozed from her heart, through her every pore, bringing misery to us all like a disgusting pestilence.

No song there, by the way. *Disgusting Pestilence* isn't a thought that goes anywhere.

Rita Mae didn't sleep with Tom for the sake of a pleasant shag. She slept with him to get rid first, of Stella Maria, then second, of me. She believed she was more entitled to be the star of Tom's movie than I ever was and she deserved the breaks I was getting since I'd done nothing to earn them.

Stella Maria, being Stella Maria, smelt a rat the minute Rita looked straight passed her in Merv's office and said to me, 'Why don't you and I go get a bite to eat,' excluding both her and Tom, and also excluding Merv though he was used to it. I don't believe he ever feels excluded or included in anything but just goes his own merry way and is happy whoever's there. A gift. Merv is a man of many gifts.

Rita had no gifts apart from her banjo playing and her excellent ear and you know what? Though I remember how well she played, I can never hear her. She's left no melancholy echoes in my life and I'm someone given to the melancholy echo.

A big old hawk is circling above the house and I'm

thinking what does this mean? Is a hawk a good or a bad sign? And why be a hawk? On the other hand, why be an ant? A soul takes the form of life mostly likely to attract the attention of the person it's guiding. That's what I think.

And now I'm feeling furious with Tom, not because he's so late but because he gave Stella Maria such a great time that night, her fate was sealed. Finally, in the distance, I hear his battered old truck and when it appears, I'm overjoyed.

Tom looks so normal. He looks like he comes from an everyday life where no one's charged with murder and people are taking it easy which is not how we're taking it here. His hair's all over the place, his white T-shirt has a black mark down the front and his face is mostly tan and stubble. He leaps out of the car, lifts me off my feet and his very tight hug makes me burst into tears which upset him even though I've told him a thousand times they're nothing to be upset about. He holds me even closer so in the end I have to knee him in the groin to get him off. His head looks smaller because his hair is even shorter and he's dyed it black. 'What did you do that for?'

'You want the truth?' he says. I tell him of course I want the truth, unless it's cancer. He says, 'Because I hate being stopped in the street and told I'm the guy those English girls killed for.' He sees the look on my face. 'Joking,' he says, as he unloads his kit. 'Where's Stella Maria? Where's Betty? I'm looking forward to meeting her again. I think I can make her like me.'

He truly has no idea of the shit he's in with those two. I say Stella Maria is hiding from him, that he's not to make a single sound she might hear or put himself anywhere she might see, and he's to pretend that he's dead to her now and possibly forever. I tell him Betty's waiting for us in the study as she doesn't trust him.

There are just no nice ways to say these things and he's crushed. 'Christ,' he says, slinging his bags around his shoulders. 'Christ.' He's so thrown he can barely speak as we head up to the house.

I'm about to confront him on the subject of Jed when blow me if Abraham isn't suddenly right in our way, fiddling with bits of plants in one of the beds, and I think well is this a heaven-sent moment or not? Tom can see me meet the man I know is the man for me. But Abraham buries his head in the dirt as we approach and I think, later, then.

I put my finger to my lips so Tom knows to keep his trap shut. We tiptoe up the porch steps. The telly isn't on. All you can hear is nothing. Creepy nothing. Tom says, 'This is spooky.' I ask him what. He says, 'That boy, this place. Can't you feel it?' I tell him the place is beautiful. He shudders. 'Poor Stella Maria,' he says and I just can't be bothered asking him what he means by that because I'm finding the whole Stella Maria issue a big burden right now.

Betty says, 'Enter,' when I knock at the study door and since this isn't something she usually says, I know this won't be the usual style of session. 'Hi,' she says to Tom. Her face gives nothing away. 'Pleasant journey?'

Tom beams at her, says the scenery is spectacular. 'Is this bear country?' Betty's not having anymore small talk. She wants to knows does he require anything in the way of power points and such and for a little while there they are both pre-occupied by that, but if Tom thinks this is his charm working, he's wrong. Betty's doing blank. I have to offer him coffee. He says thank you.

There's no sign of Stella Maria in the den, in the kitchen, or in her bedroom. Her door's wide open to prove the room's empty, like a magician's hat before the rabbit pops out, and I'm so frightened of Tom messing things up by saying stuff he doesn't know is out of order, I don't even let the jug boil. I'm into the kitchen and back so fast, the stuff in his mug looks like drowning ants.

He's moved the floral armchair so the camera is looking

into the study, and he's trying to manoeuvre Betty into the shot, but she's not having it. 'Ah am no entertainer, Mister Sinclayuh,' she says. 'Carry on as if Ah'm not here.' I do my best, I truly do. I want them to impress each other. My aim is to instill trust into their hearts which won't be easy, given I want to tackle Tom about Jed.

While he's arranging me with the light across my face in the armchair and Betty on her seat at the back of the room in the shadows, I try to let him know via my expression that he has to make this good for Betty as much as me. 'First thing I want to say is what's going on with Jed? We had that Morris out here yesterday and he was saying you were saying there was something between us when that's tripe and you know it.' I wait for a sensible answer and cringe when I see it's not forthcoming.

He looks uncomfortable. He says, 'You knew about Jed. You knew he had a thing for you.'

'I didn't. You made it up. And you'd better unmake it, Tom. You'd better unmake it fast. Morris thinks it's a big deal and it's just a big lie.'

He keeps his eye behind the camera. He says, 'It isn't. He said he fancied you rotten, so I thought it would be fun if he turned into a romantic interest. That a problem?'

Is it a problem? Tom knew I was looking for romance when I came here. He can't truly ever have believed Jed might be it. 'How come he never told me to my face?'

Tom shrugs. The camera goes up and down on his shoulder. 'You never gave him the chance,' he says.

'He found the time to tell you. And now he's finding time to give evidence against Stella Maria.'

'Not against her,' Tom says. 'I thought he was your type. He looks like Paddy, don't you think?'

'Paddy who?' is all I can say. And I have to ask for a breather because I don't want to know anymore about Jed and what the fuck's Tom doing raising the subject of Paddy when what the fuck does he know about Paddy? What's anyone know? I can't stand to look at Betty but I feel her eyes like darts to my soul.

36

I ask Betty if I can have a smoke and she says certainly, provided I appreciate it will cut down the time I have with filming. Oh boy! I say to Tom, well I need a smoke, and he says I can have two minutes, so we go out on to the porch, Betty too, though she doesn't light up. To bring us to neutral ground, I tell Tom this *is* bear country for his information. And Betty, who can't help having social skills, says you will also find otter, boar, skunk and coyote. 'Gosh, really?' Tom says.

On closer inspection I see he's looking thin, and it's not just his haircut. His eyes are sunk. 'You eating properly?' I say. Now and again, he says. I tell him he oughta split his appetite with Stella Maria's who's eating for the nation. Neither he nor Betty find this funny.

I'm so on edge I can't think of anything else. I draw long and hard on my fag to calm myself. I didn't know he knew about Paddy. I didn't know any of the Jed stuff. I didn't know he knew more about my father than I'd told him. There's too much here I don't and didn't know, but how do I confront him when Betty has to trust him?

The two of them are talking like they have a whole load of stuff in common but it's about nothing important. We all know what's important is what's simmering away unsaid and it's making me nervous. Soon as I stub out my smoke, Tom says, 'Back to work,' and this is what steadies me. What's going on here is work, no more, no less. This is my job and I'm a professional.

Tom picks up the camera. I look into it. 'I'd like to find Barney Noble,' I say. 'I've been thinking it would be good to get in touch with my American past, whatever it is.' Tom keeps the camera trained on me so I know this thought interests him. 'He'll be able to tell me about my mother.' I take a deep breath. 'And also my father.'

'You never wanted to know about him before,' he says

'I think maybe having an American father . . .' I stop. 'Sorry I don't want to say that.'

'OK' he says.

'I think if I'm part American, if I have an American family, I should meet them. I never wanted to meet them because they had nothing to do with my life in England, but now I'm here, now I'm in Tennessee, I feel kind of close to them.' I shut my eyes while I absorb the sound of this thought and think it's fine. 'My father, whoever he is, can't be all bad and I don't think looking him up will be a betrayal of my mother's memory.'

Tom says, 'How are you going to find him?' I pull the letter out of my pocket and show it to the camera. 'It's ten years old but it's a start.' Tom gets me to put the letter on Betty's desk so he can film it.

Betty says, 'You have twenty minutes left.'

Tom says, 'Shit.' He gets me back into the floral chair. 'Heard from Dick or Jerrah?'

'I wrote the tribute Jerrah was interested in and played it to Merv but he thought it needed more heroics. I played it to Dick and he said listen to Merv.'

Tom says, 'Can we hear it?' I say sure. I get my guitar, fix my make-up, tune up and get myself arranged. It all takes time. Tom's going, 'Hurry up, Honey. Christ you don't need to fix your hair.'

I say, 'I still love this version,' and I get right into it.

'But God loves me Rita Mae
In heaven the angels will say . . .' and so on.

I finish. Tom puts his camera down. I wait for him to tell me it's the best thing I've written which I think it could be. 'Well?'

'Just no way Nashville's ever going to buy it,' he says and I want to burst into tears but am just not going to let myself.

He takes up the camera again and I know what's required of me. 'For me, it works. But a professional can't just be pleased with what works for her, she has to understand what works for everyone else. The music industry is market driven. I'm redoing it and I'm hoping to present a good alternative to Moonshine in person in a day or two.'

Saying this makes me feel sick because I don't believe it. I got that song right first time, I know it. If the person who produces the art likes the art, then other people not liking it doesn't make it less art.

I look across at Betty. 'That be OK with you? A trip into town?' I'm trying to sound normal but my voice is shaking because I really hate the kind of ignorant criticism I've just had from Tom. Betty looks embarrassed as the camera swings around to her and says she'll have to think about that.

Tom says, 'You given any thought to what will happen if this hearing goes all wrong for you?'

'I'm not giving any thought to what could happen if the hearing doesn't clear everything up for us because I am one hundred per cent positive it will. I know it, the label knows it.' Tom waves his arm to tell me to keep going and address the other possibility, so I do, because I am a professional. 'If we end up going to trial and if we end up getting convicted, Jerrah says Moonshine would have a big problem marketing a singer who's killed her banjo player. But that's not going to happen.'

Tom's still filming. He says, 'A love-crossed singer who might have been driven to murder has a weird kind of appeal, you know.' I say that's sick but he says sick doesn't bother marketing people unless their research shows it should. And I believe him. He knows the state of play better than anyone. He's been running between Merv and the people at Moonshine and all the TV and movie people and what he's been selling them is the idea that Rita's death is pure country and only adds to my appeal.

'I tell you what Spin said?' he asks, and he has, but I say what? I want Betty to hear how hard Tom works, how sincere he is, how much he deserves to do well. Spin's this radio consultant he's been cultivating who says we shouldn't be selling me as the new Kitty Wells. No one wants a new version of anyone that old. 'He says you're hillybilly's answer to Shania. He says the combination of Rita's banjo, your unusual voice, your looks and your story is making the whole industry sit up and rub their ears. He loves the death element.'

I say, 'Well maybe the industry's fed up with women who squeak and I remind them of what they loved all along. Like I'm this long forgotten chord buried under a pile of shiny sounds that took their fancy for a minute.'

'Right,' he says.

I turn to Betty. 'Can you believe that this guy knew nothing about country six months ago?' She says our hour is up.

Tom, who's been good as gold, looks at his watch and says, 'Hang on. I've only been here fifty minutes.' Betty says a full hour has passed. Tom says, 'Are you including setting-up time?' Betty says the arrangment was for one hour from the minute he arrived until the minute he left. Time is most definitely up. She says it in a way I know is going to rile him. He reacts badly to people putting their foot down. His face is hardening into mean and angry lines. His voice has gone all high.

'You know what I'm trying to do here. It's not like I'm doing Honey any harm.' He's furious, but just about holding it together. 'I'm here to promote her interests. This film could be the making of her. Why are you being so obstructive? So obstructive and so small minded.'

Betty says, 'Ah am not prepared to involve mahself in any discussion, Mr Sinclayah. You are in mah house at mah invitation and Ah expect you to honour the conditions.' She's the widder woman confronting the rustler from out of town whose ridden in to hound the poor. She picks up his camera and that's a mistake. His camera's as precious to him as my guitar is to me and Rita Mae's banjo was to her. He makes a grab for it and gives her a shove in the process.

'Stop it, Tom,' I yell, seeing only trouble here. He has the camera and he's out the study door and he's running through the house with the camera on his shoulder, grabbing images wherever he can of the place of our confinement. What an idiot. He must know the misery this will cause.

He's out the door and into the yard without watching where he's going, so he trips over the rope tying the goat to the tree. He stops himself from sprawling by tugging on the rope and strangling the goat.

Betty's calling, 'Abe, Abe, Ah need your help.' Abe's nowhere. Tom's half laughing but I'm panicking. I'm screaming at him to pull himself together then suddenly he runs smack into Stella Maria who all this time has been out behind the tool shed.

She's sitting at a table with a sketch book and some watercolours in front of her and she's painting a view of the mountain, like there's no rumpus happening in the house behind her and like she's just this brain-dead painter. I yell. It should've been Stella Maria who yelled, but she doesn't. She just stares at Tom as if he's wearing the body of Rita Mae.

He goes straight up to her to kiss her but she jumps away from him as if he's touched her with a cattle prod. He jumps back when she jumps back and for a second they just stare at each other. He says, 'Stella Maria, talk to me. Why won't you talk to me?' All the time he's filming. 'You haven't taken my calls. You won't return my messages. I want you to talk to me.'

She turns her back on the camera. She says 'Get away from me. I have nothing to say to you.' But he walks around her, continuing to film her.

He says, 'Not even thank you.'

'Thank you?' She can't believe what she's hearing.

He says, 'For getting you out of jail, for paying your rent for the last four months, for keeping you employed, for bringing you to Nashville, for giving you a life.'

I'm thinking, 'So maybe he doesn't love her.' Unless this is the verbal sparring that leads to intercourse. I don't know what Betty's thinking. She's just watching, saying nothing.

I say to Tom, 'You're a bloody idiot.' And I say to Betty, 'Sorry, Betty.'

Then Stella Maria speaks, all quiet and eerie like a pissed-off nun. She says, 'You made a promise to me and you've broken it. I owe you nothing. Honey owes you nothing and if she had any sense, she'd have nothing more to do with you.'

I say, 'I can speak for myself.'

She says, 'Well, listen to what comes out of your mouth when you do. You're a fool, Honey. You've put your life into his hands and you can't even see what he's doing with it.'

Tom says, 'That's rich, coming from the girl who sold me her best friend's life even when the best friend was saying she didn't want it sold.' His voice sounds squeaky and discordant after hers. It repels her. I can see she's repelled.

Abe arrives breathless and sweating but with no words on

his lips to soothe anyone. Except the goat. He says to the goat who's staggering around like someone's punched her, 'Well what have they done to you, little Marigold?' and he strokes her like she's a beaten woman.

Tom doesn't give a shit about Marigold. He says, 'Just one question I want to ask you Stella Maria. Just the one question I've been trying to ask you for weeks.' The camera's right up against her face. I think he's going to say 'Will you marry me?' He says, 'Did Honey kill Rita Mae?'

I nearly faint. I want to speak but no sound is in my throat and no air is in my lungs. Abe grabs Tom by the shirt and drags him into the house and through it. 'You are leavin',' he says. 'You are leavin' and you ain't ever comin' back.' Anger has given him words.

I wait until the rumble of the truck departing has faded into the hills, then I creep down to the bottom terrace, light a fag and sit on a log looking out into the valley, thinking Dollywood is about ten miles away. Created by Dolly Parton to prove the rags to riches story could happen to any old girl with a voice from heaven and iron in her heart. I used to love that story. Now I'm seeing how bitter it can be.

I want to get Stella Maria and shake her till she goes all limp. I want to say, 'Don't do this to me.' I want to smack Tom in the face and say, 'What are you doing? What makes you think you can say that sort of thing to my best friend and not see the trouble it will cause?' Because I know him. I know why he asked it. He wanted to punish Stella Maria, but only in a way that would work for him. Trouble works for him like nobody's business in a story he wants to end in triumph. Conflict he calls it. Story's life blood.

37

I nearly jump out of my skin at Betty's voice by my shoulder. 'Give your lungs a break, Honey,' she says. I immediately put out the cigarette, scoop up the dogends at my feet and shove them in my pocket.

I say, 'I'm sorry Tom went crazy, Ma'am. I think he was frustrated.'

She takes a seat and stares down into the valley. 'How much do you know about him, Honey? You ever thought about that?'

I say I know him better than I know most people. 'I guess Stella Maria has stopped loving him,' I say. She says it would seem that way. I say, 'Well that's not how love works for me. I love someone then I get over their bad behaviour.'

'That so?' she says. She has trouble with bad behaviour. I say well the thing about behaviour is you never get anyone who's all bad or all good and Tom's done so much for us, I can't believe Stella Maria's forgotten. 'Maybe what he's doing now cancels out everything he's done,' she says. And I think about that. I apply myself to that thought. I'm trying to zone in on that thought but my head is full of nothing. I look at the cherry tree all covered in leaves whose life is fruitless, title maybe, and when I force myself to concentrate, I think he's just doing what he said he was going to do. What we wanted him to do.

Betty says it sounds to her like the story he's telling, my story, the story of me cracking America, just gets better and better by the minute and what she's asking herself is how much he's contributing to that. I say no more than she is. No more than anyone is. She says well how can I defend a man who's just accused me of murder.

I have to laugh at that. 'That wasn't an accusation,' I tell her. 'That was him getting some good footage. Did you see Stella Maria's face?'

Betty says if that's what he was doing then it was cruel and cynical of him. 'Everything he does seems cynical, even if it isn't cruel.' And I know she has a point. I know Stella Maria has a point but they're both missing the real point. Which is that the story's unfolding the way it is because that's the story, the way it's meant to be.

'He can't control it. No one can control it,' I say. 'He didn't bring Rita Mae into our lives. He was right out of that chain.'

Betty sighs. She says she'd like to talk about Rita Mae and I'm happy to. She's barking up a fruitless tree the way she's thinking. 'Now there's cruel and cynical,' I say. 'There was no one more cruel or cynical than Rita Mae. Even that night at the Thai. She set out to make me like her and I couldn't help myself.'

'Three big deaths, a tragic love affair and you're not even twenty-one,' she said. I thought she was taking the piss but when I looked at her, she wasn't. I told her how one by one my mother, Stella Maria and Tom had built the road to Nashville for me and she couldn't believe things could work like this for anyone. It must have made her furious but she didn't let on. She just told me how hard it had been for her and how hard it was for most people. All that bar work, all that babysitting, all that waiting on tables.

She'd arrived in Nashville with enough money to last her three weeks and when that ran out all she'd had to keep her going through dead end job after dead end job was ambition. It was like this beast she fed off day in day out which gave her the strength to knock on doors and when they didn't open then to give them a good hard kick. Even so, she was getting nowhere. I could tell she was getting nowhere. She tried to talk herself up to me but on her own she just wasn't marketable.

'She'd be pleased she finally has a worldwide reputation.' I say to Betty. 'Even if it is for being the tragic all-American girl slaughtered by English girls in an alleged love triangle.'

'That how you see it?' Betty says, shocked.

'No,' I say, like no. 'But folks do, don't they? It's why Jerrah's panicking.' And even as I say it, I think well why's he panicking? Is everyone panicking? Should I be panicking? Stella Maria looks like she's panicking. And so does Tom.

What Rita couldn't fathom was why Tom had chosen me. 'You're a fine singer an' all,' she said, 'I love your voice bein' so deep. But you're a complete unknown and he isn't even a country fan.'

'It was just my lucky break,' I told her. 'He thought my story was interesting and my songs showed promise.' Her eyes were darting everywhere, looking anywhere but at me because if she looked at me I'd have seen the positively no sincerity in them. I said maybe her lucky break was Merv introducing us and she said she hoped so, she reckoned she deserved it.

'But you know something, Betty?' I say. 'I couldn't swear she loved her music. When she played, she had this expression on her face like she hated what she was doing. It always looked to me like she just couldn't forgive her banjo for being so out of favour.'

Betty has no thoughts on this. I don't even know if she's listening. She's weeding, picking this and that out of the new beds. There are many fine banjo pickers in Nashville and many fine artists who feature them on their records, but radio's not a banjo lover, doesn't matter how much an artist has spent on her teeth. Weird thing now, is a lot of what I know about Rita Mae is from what we discovered after her death. Main thing we discovered about her childhood was, it was dull. So dull it makes Stella Maria's look like a firestorm.

She had a younger brother and sister who thought she was great, she did well at school, she was a success at college. She had a pony, pocket money, clothes that didn't embarrass anyone and braces. Nashville would have been her first taste of failure. By the time we met her she'd been turned down by just about every record company in town. Merv was her final port of call.

I asked her about him. I said was he her boyfriend. She said come on, the guy had to be sixty. I said it looked to me as if he was in love with her. She said well of course he was, which is why she slept with him now and again but he was a business contact. She didn't mind sleeping with business contacts because it kept the relationship alive. She bet I slept with Tom. I bet I didn't. I wasn't going to tell that to someone I'd only just met. She said she didn't believe in love anyways.

'Do you get that?' I ask Betty. Betty replies that she isn't even sure what the statement means. I say nor me. Except it was Rita Mae's tragedy. To be so heartless. Her heartlessness showed in her music. She could make a banjo laugh and cry, yearn and thrill, which had to come from somewhere. But she never had words to describe how a body could feel in the midst of hardship because she'd never allowed herself to feel anything. Whenever I mourn Rita Mae, I mourn the loss of whatever it was that let her fingers dance.

Whatever Stella Maria came to think, I never felt comfortable with her when we weren't singing. Where Stella Maria is pure heat, Rita was ice and ice, is just about impossible to warm to. I try to explain this to Betty and she says, 'But you turned your back on Stella Maria so you could be her friend.'

I say, 'That's just not true, Betty. What's true is sometimes you need to like a person so badly you just won't let anything put you off and I really needed to like Rita Mae. She was homespun. I'm an import. No one was ever going to believe my music was authentic.'

We all needed Rita Mae. Even Stella Maria. Rita Mae knew the system inside out which we didn't. Whatever people say about new blood and exciting new talent, Nashville likes old talent better. Not dead-on-its-feet talent, but talent hungry enough to put up with shit that just feels a bit less shitty than the shit it's put up with since arriving.

I don't know this from personal experience, but from Rita's. She told me how it all worked and I could see it. She was desperate for a break. 'You want to know something, Betty?' I say. 'I thought she deserved a break too.'

She'd played on demos, done open mics til she could do 'em in her sleep, she'd hooked up with any number of hopeless dudes, she'd done any old thing to turn a buck. She'd slept with hundreds of guys she thought might help her, I reckon it was hundreds, and one or two had given her a tiny break in return. Some A&R guy had showcased her but no one had turned up. This can happen with showcases. If there's no buzz. There just never was a big buzz about Rita Mae. Didn't matter she was talented. You need a buzz to get people interested. Merv wasted no time getting a buzz going about me once he heard the sound I made.

Lovely Merv. He knew what she was like. He'd say, 'You don't want to go listening to Rita Mae, now. She's a hard woman, a little bit crazy. Must be to see anything in me.' He liked me because he thought I was ladylike and I am compared to Rita Mae who was, now I think of it, more like an ice pick than ice. 'In the end, sympathy was wasted on her. In the beginning too, mostly,' I say and Betty gets to her feet.

We walk back to the house in silence, both of us lost in thought. Happiness is hard to fathom, isn't it? Yesterday, or was it the day before, I was as contented as could be, even though there was tragedy all about us. Today I'm lower than low. I sat on the swing and I didn't even notice the mountains, which God made from pure delight, plus a bit of green to cheer the poor desperate souls in the valley below who could only sing for comfort.

38

'Dear Paddy.' I'm trying to think what I want to say but all I want is his arms about me. 'Dear Paddy, I'm sitting here on the bedroom floor and all I can think about is you.' Well I'm not sending that. Title – *Letter To My Lost Love*.

> *You are my dear but you're not here so I must say goodbye,*
> *I shortly go to fry. I have no alibi*
> *And where is Abe? My brand new babe*

Rhymes don't always do the sentiment you're striving for justice. My mobile's ringing but where is it? Don't hang up, don't hang up.

'Hey,' Tom says. 'Betty over it?' The man is unbelievable. I tell him Betty hates him, Stella Maria hates him and I definitely hate him. What was he doing pulling a stunt like that? 'Oh come on, Honey,' he says. 'I got some great stuff. Betty chasing me through the house. The sound of you chasing both of us. Stella Maria painting. Stella Maria's face when I asked her if you were a murderer. She looks rough, doesn't she?' I say I hadn't noticed. He says, 'She looks rank.'

'I thought you loved her,' I say.

He says, 'Yeah? Well. It's just you and me now, babe.' And he laughs. I think he's faking. Pretending to be an arsehole film-maker saying arsehole film-maker lines when really his heart's in pieces.

I say. 'She's never going to love you when you behave like a jerk. Why don't you stop behaving like a jerk and write to her? She loved you more than anything.'

'You want to know something?' he says. 'Maybe I never loved her. Maybe you talked me into it.' I tell him that's bollocks and he says, 'Maybe.' But it turns out this isn't what he wants to say anyway. 'I've been talking to Merv. He doesn't think you've cracked the tribute thing and he's getting some pressure from Dick and Jerry.'

'Really?'

'They need the right song or it's not going to work.' I say what's not going to work? 'Promoting you,' he says. I say well that's not new. He says, 'What's new is having a murder charge against you.' And it seems to me that this isn't the Tom I know and briefly loved. This is a different person with a different attitude. More of a rat than I'm comfortable to be around.

'Why are you sounding like such a creep?' I ask. 'Why are you carrying on like no one's got any feelings and all that counts is how it looks on your fucking film?' There's silence. 'You there?' I ask. I think, do I give a toss if he's not? No I don't.

'Sorry, Honey,' he says. 'Sorry. I'm knackered. That's all it is. Forget it. You don't need me to tell you how things are. I know you'll come up with something great.' Then he gets off the phone as fast as he can and now the room feels so empty, I have to call Merv, just to hear a friendly voice.

'Hello darlin',' he says and my heart warms to him because he is truly my friend. 'How's that song comin'?'

'Finished,' I say. Because it must be true if I've said it. It has to be true sooner or later.

'Do you like it?' he says. I tell him I love it. He says is it heroic? Is it sad? Is little Rita Mae in it from beginning to end and will the public love it? He's slurring his words so I don't need to hear the clink of the bottle to know how he is placed today.

'I think it's just what you want,' I say. 'Can I come and play it for you tomorrow?' He says nothing would give him greater pleasure. I say, how's he doing anyway? He says he's doing great. And I say, well see you about lunchtime. Then I go to find Betty to tell her.

She's in her study, talking I think to Stella Maria, but when I push open the door, I hear it's a tape of Stella Maria who's saying, like she's trying to make an excuse, 'Well she always kept stuff from me. Like her and Paddy. She never told . . .'

Fuck me! I'm desperate to hear what I never told her but Betty senses my presence and jumps to her feet, bashing the tape recorder to the ground in her haste to shut it up which she doesn't manage to do. 'Sorry,' I say. 'Sorry. I thought I heard you say come in.'

Betty's on all fours, trying to turn the thing off so the voice will stop but I hear 'and he's my brother for fuck's sake'. I store this information somewhere to deal with later, to join the information already in there which I'll deal with later.

She gets to her feet, flushed and looking none too happy. 'This is not a convenient time, Honey. Your session's in one hour ten. Can't it wait?' I tell her it can't, it's urgent and she says OK then, sit down, what's up?

'I've just been speaking to Merv. The label's getting jumpy about my tribute and I need your permission to go into Nashville.'

Betty's looking agitated. 'Forgit it, Honey,' she says. 'You need to do some serious thinkin' right now. Ah don't believe Merv, and Ah don't believe Dick or Jerrah or Tom or any of the guys who've been out to visit have any idea what's at stake here. Ah think those guys are distortin' your perspective. You and Stella Maria have a hearin' comin' up which will seal your fate in terms Ah don't believe you have even started to comprehend. On the basis of what happens, you might find yourselves on a chain gang while those guys forgit all about you and turn their minds to other people's songs.'

'Title,' I whisper.

'You gotta ask yourself. What matters right now? What's the most important thing in mah life right now? This hearin' is no small matter. It's a big matter. It may not be life or death. But it's a life or a life in jail. This is what you should be givin' time to. This is where your priorities should be. No way can I let you go anywhere until we have resolved your differences with Stella Maria.'

And she's standing up, going to the door to let me out when I know her thinking's all wrong. She's confusing the chance of a lifetime with an unfortunate hiccup that looks big but will be small when we get to look back on it. I don't get up. I say, 'But things are going real well with Stella Maria.' Hasn't she toned down her language? Isn't she painting to put herself in touch with her finer nature? And gardening?

'Not so well with you, though, Honey,' Betty says. And that surprises me but I tell her if it looks that way it's only because I have so much on my mind. If I don't get this song right, if I don't keep Dick and Jerrah sweet, then I might as well spend the rest of my life in jail.

I say, 'I have to go. That's how simple it is, Betty.'

Betty says, 'Well you can't. That's even simpler.' And I burst into tears. I sob and I sob with grief impossible to contain and she just hands me a tissue. Then she opens the door for me and lets me out and I hurry to my room where I continute to cry for a very long time because there is no one, no one in this whole world who understands the misery I'm in and for the time being I seem to have lost touch with my Mam.

'What am I going to do?' I whisper and all that happens is that the goat takes a run at the wall and tries to butt me through it. No way is Mammy that goat. Fuck it! I'm going anyway. If I leave now, I can walk to the interstate and hitch a lift.

I pick out a clean T-shirt and some knickers and a packet of fags and I stick them in my rucksack, then I climb out my window so no one will hear me in the hall. The goat runs at me but I chuck a handful of dogends at her and she stops. That goat will be Rita Mae. I look at her snuffling about the smokes with one eye on me and the thought terrifies me. I scarper, fast as I can, around to the front of the house and across into the jungle garden so I can hit the road out of sight of the house.

If I'd gone looking for Abe, would I have found him? I've run smack into him by not looking where I was going and he's stopping my way with his arms outstretched like I'm some runaway horse. 'You headin' out on a picnic?' he asks. And that's enough for me. I start to howl and I'm about to sink to the ground except he puts his gorgeous arms under mine and keeps me upright, not exactly holding me to him but supporting me in the manner of a rock or a mountain and I feel my heart melt, leave my body and crawl into his chest next to his. 'Y'all don't need to be cryin' now,' he says. 'Ah don't think Bet, ah'm sure Mizz Beecher wouldn't want you out here bein' so upset.' He takes a clean white handkerchief out of his pocket, shakes it and hands it to me. I blow my nose.

I try to explain to him why I'm not the idiot he'll be thinking I am. That I'm not running away because I'm some weakling who can't take the pressure of counselling but because I have overwhelming business commitments. I tell him how Dick and Jerrah will dump me, I might just as well not have come all this way, and I'm doing it for my mother who's dead. He leads me to a log where I can sit so he can watch me cry. 'There, now. You stay right here.'

258

He's going to get Betty, I know it, so I take off running through the jungle though not very fast as I have no real sense of direction and it's scary. Within seconds I hear him coming back and I hear Betty with him only it turns out not to be Betty but Stella Maria running so fast she's actually ahead of him. She brings me down by grabbing at my legs.

'You flipping eejit, where d'you think you're going?' I can't speak, so she gives me a thump on the back. 'Stop your blubbing,' she says. 'I'll sort it out. Thank you, Abraham. It's OK now.' She sulks till we get back to the house, then she says, 'Go to your room and wait.'

I lie on my bed looking at the ceiling thinking everything and nothing for five maybe ten minutes, then Betty knocks at the door. She doesn't come far into the room. She says, 'Stella Maria has been to see me and Ah have spoken to Abraham. You may go to Nashville but the conditions are these. Abraham will drive you there and back. You will leave here at 6 a.m. and I expect you back in this house by midday. Your session is in forty minutes.'

I'd like to hug her but it wouldn't be appreciated. Instead I say 'See you in forty,' even though it's the last thing I feel like, but Betty being all businesslike turns out to be kind of reassuring. We pick up where we left off. Trying to make progress on the matter of Rita Mae.

'How long did it take Rita Mae to turn on Stella Maria?' she wants to know. I don't even attempt to put another view. There isn't another point of view.

'Three weeks,' I say. 'Rita Mae said, "Dump her." Like it was an order.'

We were already getting interest from RCA, Arista and I think Warner and Rita Mae wanted us to get proper management. I said, 'Why? I'm happy with Stella Maria. She can talk her way through the gates of heaven.'

'Guess what, Honey?' Rita said. 'Nashville and Heaven have this much in common.' Which maybe she had reason to think. But what I was beginning to appreciate was just how bitter she was. She believed Nashville had done her wrong. She believed everyone had done her wrong. She hated everyone in Nashville who'd made it, everyone who hadn't made it, everyone who'd turned her down and everyone who hadn't made her a star. She was walking acrimony. I wouldn't budge. I said it wasn't just that she was my friend. Stella Maria was doing a fine job.

This was the truth. She could talk comfortably to lawyers, accountants, people at the CMA and ASCAP, and in the end, she came up with a great development deal. OK she had people helping her. Tom had his office look stuff over but she was the one speaking up for me and the only one I really trusted. Everyone says business advisors and lawyers will rip you off soon as look at you, but people didn't try to rip her off and she never tried to rip me off. She has a great brain on her. A really great brain and nerves of steel in the business sense.

But bit by bit, Rita Mae got to me. I began to see Stella Maria as Rita saw her. 'She can get on your wick, Betty, you have to admit that.' Betty has no comment. 'And Stella Maria wasn't exactly collapsing under the strain.' She wasn't. She was having a fine old time with Tom.

She had Tom. I had Rita Mae. Rita Mae and me would rehearse in the apartment and Stella Maria found an office for her and Tom. She put a bed in it. That's how cosy they were. Not sleeping together but so cosy that she reckoned any day they might. 'She was so wrapped up in Tom, I never thought she was too bothered by what Rita and I were up to.'

'And what was Mr Sinclayah making of it all?' Betty says. I say same as he always made of everything. He watched. He filmed. He interviewed. And he loved Stella Maria being so smart. He loved her running around after him, telling him when to wake up, when to eat and all the stuff that she does with me. I'd watch Rita watching them and the look in her eyes was so full of murder I told myself she had a vitamin deficiency.

She hated Stella Maria most for the deal she made her sign. We all had lawyers advising us but whoever Rita's was, he didn't give a tuppeny shite and ours was the best money could buy. They settled on a one-album deal with some clauses about touring and composition and complicated splits and I let them get on with it. But Rita always thought she'd been conned and Stella Maria loved it. 'Stella Maria's a great negotiator,' I say to Betty.

Betty says, 'You bet.' Having just had her arm twisted. Stella Maria can get on your wick but you'd have to go a long way to find a better manager.

39

We've been driving now for the best part of an hour and all Abe's said is, 'Too windy?' I ought to sleep having had none all night, but every nerve in my body is jangling and raring to go. I'm hearing the new tribute over and over in my head and trying to make it better, even now.

> Girl with dancing fingers and music in her soul
> All she wanted was to play the world her heart
> So she came to Tennessee with her banjo and her fiddle
> And she called to all she met oh let us sing.
> Let us sing, let us play, let us laugh, let us love,
> For we are young and free and God's above
>
> Chorus: She was the spirit of America
> Young and strong and brave
> Cut down before her time
> Like a soldier in his prime
> On the battlefield of life
> Oh let us sing
> La la la la la la la la la la. Tra la la la la la Tra lalalalalalalalala

It's like a march, like *When Johnnie Comes Marching Home Again*, and what I've done here is break free of the restrictions of rhyme and narrative and given myself to the spirit of the work. Also not stuck to the actual truth because even though Rita Mae was all American and her struggle to make it in Nashville was heroic, she was a cow. I couldn't write that, even if cow does go great with now, how and eyebrow.

Even as we pull up outside Merv's office on Music Row West, I'm toying with the idea of rhyming head with dead in the final verse as in '*A brick fell on her head, In a second she was dead*', but you lose the heroic thing in those two lines and if there's one thing Merv has impressed on me, it's the need for heroic.

'You got a mobile?' I say to Abe. He shakes his head. I say, 'Well you can't sit here all morning. You need to get yourself something to eat.' I give him my phone. 'I'll call you when I'm done.' I show him what to press to answer and what to press to end and he looks like he knows what I'm talking about. If this boy married Clover O'Shea they could start a new human race without the power of speech.

Oh God, I'm nervous. My palms are all sweaty and maybe I should've put on more antiperspirant because there's nothing less marketable in a guitar player than the suggestion of damp in the armpits. I hope I'm not going to go all sweaty on Merv. You don't want to deliver a song looking like this big leaking thing. It's the first time I've ever sung when it counted and not had Stella Maria by my side. But I'm twenty years old and I reckon that's old enough to do this.

It's 9.30 a.m. and already Nashville's steaming. Grey and hazy and damp, so I'm appreciating just how clean the mountain air is. 'Hey,' says the girl on the desk who's a Reba clone when no one should be a Reba clone. 'You're the last one in. Studio 2 this mornin'.'

'Who's everyone?' I say. But she opens the studio door and I see. Tom's in one corner, all set up with lights and so on.

Merv's sitting in another on a chair too small for him next to a table, looking like he doesn't know what's hit him to be up and about this time of the day, Dick's pacing and tugging his fingers until they click and Jerrah's just resting his bum on the table's edge, watching the door, waiting for me to arrive so he can not greet me.

'Honey!' Dick runs noisily towards me to make up for Jerrah not even moving an eyelash. 'Well you are lookin' so gorgeous, Ah don't know that Ah can keep mah hands off you.'

Merv gets to his feet and lumbers across to me, takin' his time, stretching, yawning. It's not such a big room, but he takes forever to cover the distance, like a man in slow motion, which maybe his life just is. 'You better keep your hands off her,' he says. 'She might break if you lay a finger on her, she's got so skinny.'

Tom laughs, all high pitched and mean. 'Hi,' I say to him. 'Didn't expect to see you here.' The sight of him makes me uncomfortable.

He says, 'Didn't expect to be here either. I only found out from Merv this was happening half an hour ago.' His hair's all sticking up and he needs a shave so he must've jumped out of bed and got here in seconds. His voice is clipped and unfriendly, which I'm not prepared for, since it didn't occur to me to tell him I was coming.

He's thinking I'm trying to cut him out of the frame and that's just not how it is. I was so taken up with getting here and so taken up with writing what I had to sing when I got here, it never crossed my mind to let him know I was coming. I give him a hug which I hope will sort things out. 'Howdy, Jerrah,' I say as I pass him. I say to Tom, 'I can't tell you how happy I am to see you.'

'Right,' he says, not believing me.

'You goin' to sing for us, or what?' Merv says. He's put his arm about my shoulder.

'Well, not or what,' I say.

'We're all mighty excited,' Dick says but I catch Jerrah's eye and see he's as excited as the table he's still leaning on. I take my guitar out, tune it, clear my throat, sing. Scared out of my wits and praying that the performer in me will take over because the person who isn't a performer is crap singing in public.

Merv's eyes are closed and he has his head tilted back so I can't be sure what he's thinking. I'm not even going to try to guess. I close my own eyes to lose myself in the spirit of a fine young woman marching off to some distant war to fight for freedom with her banjo but what I'm thinking is 'I'm sunk if they hate this one too.'

Finish, look up, look around me. Merv's staring at me with his eyes wide open and his mouth a little bit open but no words of praise are coming from it. Tom's eye is glued to the camera. He's saying nothing. Dick's looking at Jerrah and then at me, then back at Jerrah and when Jerrah doesn't speak he does. 'Well,' he says. 'Well. That's sure not what Ah was expectin'.'

Oh no! I say, 'I thought you were expecting something heroic. A kind of Rita Mae anthem.'

Merv says, 'What's missin' here, darlin', is the Hawksworth touch. I'm missin' your nice little rhymes here. Your quirky little phrases.'

Dick says, 'Ah know how much pressure you've been under but well, this just isn't what we had in mind. Ah'm sorry, Honey, but Ah don't think this is somethin' we can work with.'

The big wedge of the misery I know so well gathers in my throat and the big flood of wet I know is just waiting to overwhelm me gathers behind my eyes. I need Stella Maria. This is where Stella Maria would step in and tell them all to go to hell, I'm an artist and they have to respect my art for what it is. Closest thing to Stella Maria here is Tom and I look to him but he has this big smile on his face, like he's loving every minute of my torture.

'Well you didn't like the first version,' I say to Merv. Then I say to Dick, 'The first version had rhymes and my usual kind of phrasing. Do you want to hear the first version again?' And Dick's about to say might as well and I'm gathering my resources with breathing exercises when Jerrah raises his hand.

He says, 'Honey, can I ask you something? What is it you think you've got going for you that our own girls don't have?'

Merv says, 'Hell Jerrah, what kind of question is that?'

'One I want her to answer,' Jerrah says.

I say, 'I think I have my songs, my style of singing, my poetry which is mine and not the same as the next person's. My look.' It sounds pathetic. I hear myself sounding pathetic. Stella Maria is the person who sells me. Not me. Tom sells me. Not me. Tom's doing no selling today.

Jerrah gets up from his chair and walks around the table so he can stare across it. There's no natural light in this room. Just a big fluorescent strip down the middle of the ceiling, like in a jail. He says, 'The thing is this. To me, you are maybe an inch away from a novelty act. What makes you different from another girl blowing into town, from say Pennsylvania, is you are English. And that's novel. You have a feel for our music, I'm not denying that, but you are English, so you're no roots singer even though you sing like a roots singer. You understand the genre but really, you're mimicking. I don't have such a big problem with that. But what you need to understand here is that it turns you into a big, big risk, marketing wise. A novelty act, or someone an inch away from a novelty act, is a big, big risk.'

He isn't even pausing for breath. He wants me to suffer good and proper. My face is drenched. I'm wiping it with my hand but it's awash and my hand's absorbing none of it. 'A singer's not like a swimmer or a tennis player. You can't win

266

at singing. It's all down to taste and judgement and that's where the risk is. How many people's taste and judgement are you going to appeal to? My job is to minimise the risk.'

Oh shut up, you great fuck. Stella Maria would have told him to shut up ages ago.

'Now on top of your singing, which is OK, what you've got going for you is a great story and what we at Moonshine need ,to make that story work for us, is a great song. That song, that song you sang today, is to my mind, a great song. It needs banjo, it needs fiddle. But it's a great song. I can work with that song.'

Dick says, 'You bet. You bet.' Jerrah doesn't even shoot him half a glance.

'Just you don't go messing up your story by getting convicted of murder. Get yourself acquitted, or we don't have a deal.' Then he turns to the others. 'Gentlemen,' he says, 'we all know what we have to do,' and he leaves the room.

There's this stunned silence. I mean you couldn't pick any of us from mullets. No one moves except Tom who scuttles towards me with the camera trained on my face. 'Say something,' he says.

I say, 'I'm going to get myself acquitted.' Then I close my eyes and thank my mother for stepping in when I thought all was lost. I look for signs of her in the way of a moth or even a floating speck of dust but see nothing so guess she has taken to being with me in spirit only.

40

Merv and Dick walk me to the jeep. They're beside themselves with joy that Jerrah was so positive. They've never known Jerrah be so positive about any song ever and they keep trying to hug me and tell me how clever I am, what a great writer I am, what a fine singer and how I shouldn't worry too much about Jerrrah goin' on about me bein' foreign as I am no more foreign than say, than say . . . well Rita Mae wasn't local. 'That's just his way,' Dick says. 'He hates to look too emotional.'

I'm as overjoyed as it's possible to be. I went in there and I did that all on my own with no one on the sideline having any faith in me. But the minute I said I intended to get myself acquitted, Tom put down his camera and punched the air. 'Yes,' he yelled, like it was where his money was. And I knew how much I wanted his approval as well.

'Good song?' I asked.

He said, 'Jerry likes the song. That's what counts. He likes the song, he loves the film. He wants me to do the video.'

'You thought my luck had run out,' I said. He leant

towards me and pushed a strand of hair from my cheek where tears had glued it.

'Honey, you know as well as I do. We never have a clue which way it's going to run. We wait. And if you're me and you're behind a camera, you watch.'

Which could have upset me. I thought we were going all out for success. I thought we were working our arses off for success, not just waiting and watching and hoping it might fall into our lap. But I'm not dwelling on it, not today.

He's followed us out and is filming me saying goodbye to Dick and Merv. He wants me to come back to the apartment to say hi to Archie but I say no chance. 'The guys have gone. Work's finished. You won't run into Jed.'

If I wasn't so joyful, I'd whack him. I tell him I'm going back to Betty's because I promised her and I climb in beside Abe, who's understood exactly what's gone on from the way everyone was shouting and hugging each other and going 'Whoo!'

'Went well,' he says and I say it sure did and I sing all the way home. You sing and you think. When you know as many songs as I do, and I know hundreds from beginning to end plus several variations, then you can let your thoughts drift. Mine drift towards Paddy as they always do in a free moment, and I'm thinking how come Stella Maria knows about us. How come she told Tom? Why did she tell Tom? Then I'm thinking how come she knew about Jed when I didn't know about Jed? How come she didn't tell me everything she said to Tom? What was going on all that time between Stella Maria and Tom that he ended up knowing more about me than even I did? And what was going on between Stella Maria and me that she didn't tell me what she knew?

They'd be worrying thoughts if you were the worrying kind. I'm not even going to give them the time of day. Stella Maria is my friend. She was in love with a guy working his

269

bum off on my account and she was helping him as best she could. She's having trouble coming to terms with a tragic death when she's had no experience of tragic death but I know she'll be pleased our mission to crack America is back on track. Nashville doesn't just love my story and my voice, they love the song. Well Jerrah loves the song, marketing loves the song, and that's what counts.

I'm singing so loud and so happy and so infectious that as we head off the interstate, I put my arm around Abe's broad shoulders and rest my head on his arm. Big drops of rain slowly splatter against the windshield to accompany me and this so appeals to him that he joins me in the chorus of *Sally Was a Good Old Girl*. Best version Waylon Jennings, an all-time great who hasn't been in the charts since 1991.

Abe sings like Betty cooks. But when I look at him and he smiles at me, my cup practically runneth over. In the pit of my stomach, and lower if I'm honest, I feel the power of the connection we have made. It's not the connection I have with Paddy. It can never be. But should anything come of this, I'm confident that I'll have words enough for both of us.

We drive through Betty's gate at 11.55 and I yell 'yee ha' and throw my hat in the air. But the womenfolk don't come running to celebrate my triumph. No one comes running. Could be because we have a visitor. There's a Cadillac in the drive, and it's classy.

'Mr Siegal's car,' Abe says as he gives me a hand from the jeep. 'Oh,' he says. 'Took a call when I was in the coffee house.' So many words in a single sentence just about finish him.

'Who was it?'

'Puddy? Something like Puddy? He's callin' back.' My heart darn near explodes in my chest.

'Anything else?' Even if there had been Abe'd never have understood it. I want to say where is he? Is he on his way? Did you explain who you were? But what's the point. I couldn't be much happier.

Betty, Stella Maria and Harvey come through the fly screen door just as I hit the verandah steps and I'm about to yell, 'You'll never guess who's called. You won't believe what Jerrah said,' but they all look like they're heading off to a funeral so why waste the moment?

41

Harvey has beautiful skin, fine features and an elegant Southern drawl even though he was educated in Boston. You couldn't wish for a smarter person to argue the toss for you in court and he treats us with such courtesy you'd almost believe we were prominent ourselves. He shakes my hand. 'Had a good meeting?' he wants to know.

I tell him the best. I'm about to elaborate when Betty says, 'You want to freshen up before joining us?' I tell her I'm fresh enough, and Harvey holds the back of a chair for me before he takes a seat himself. Stella Maria's carried the big wicker job from the den, looking so tense you'd guess there was some wick or whatever up her bum. I give her foot a nudge so she'll look at me and when she does I give her the thumbs up. She looks away.

Once we're settled, Harvey clears his throat and I know from his expression that some sort of crunch has arrived and he's about to deliver it. Whatever it is, I can't imagine it diminishing the joy I feel right now. Professionally, I'm a success, love-wise I'm content, physically, I couldn't be more comfortable. A small breeze drifts through the jungle so lazy the trees barely part. The air smells wet and sweet. Harvey clasps his fingers in front of his chest and studies them before speaking, like he's preparing us for marriage.

I try to imagine him naked and on top of me but can't. His body appears to be in good condition but gentleness doesn't attract me. As he looks across at Stella Maria and me, I think maybe his fine brain would compensate.

'I've been explaining to Stella Maria and I want also to impress upon you, Honey, that the prosecution is going to go for us.' A trickle of moisture runs down my spine, making my back itch. I want to focus on his words but have some trouble when they have so little to do with my day so far. 'As they see it, you are two English girls, taking the easy route to stardom, who callously dropped a brick on to the head of a decent girl from a good Florida family. You not only killed her stone dead, you cruelly put an end to a talent yet to bloom. A talent she was sacrificing to serve yours.'

I look across to Stella Maria, but her eyes are glued to Harvey and I think she doesn't even look like Stella Maria. She looks like a blow-up Stella Maria doll. Harvey's gaze is as sweet as Florence Nightingale's. He says he knows this is not what happened. He'll be doing his darnedest to make sure the whole world knows it, but the law being what it is, the court won't take our word for it. And something has come to light which complicates our case: forensic evidence linking Stella Maria to the brick. A thread found on a tiny shard of the smashed brick among the matted blood in Rita Mae's deceased hair.

'It would appear to have come from the shirt Stella Maria was wearing on the day the brick fell. An English shirt, not dissimilar to, but not identical, to any shirt available in the USA. We must account for that.'

Of course we can account for it. Stella Maria was always lugging the bricks about and pulling threads off her clothes.

The bricks were part of her grand design. She would've touched and moved every single brick on that roof dozens of times. Got so Archie began to feel uneasy about it. He said, 'Stella Maria, Ah think you oughta stop messin' with the bricks as they are not your property and Ah have to account for them if there's an inspection.' She said to Archie, just wait, she was going to arrange them so they could be accounted for and also a thing of beauty. Archie said well the guys had been complainin'. Her garden was crampin' their style as it wasn't a garden and he didn't know if it should be. She said the guys could go hang themselves.

'Stella Maria was using the bricks to make a garden,' I say. 'They were just lying about before that.'

Harvey carries on as if my words haven't so much as dented his train of thought, just bounced off it. 'What we have to persuade the court,' he says, and he could be singing a gospel song so tuneful is his voice, 'is that although those workmen, Jed Wilcox, Henry Linklater and Marty Dodge, saw Stella Maria on the roof five minutes before Rita Mae's death, Stella Maria was elsewhere when Rita Mae died. As things stand, their evidence, the forensic evidence and the evidence of Stella Maria's undeniable motive, is enough to convict her. And, Honey, your evidence that she was with you, if it's proved to be fabricated, is enough to convict you of being an accessory.' A flush is moving up my throat. 'Do you both understand that?' Harvey says.

I nod. Stella Maria puts her head in her hands. Betty looks at her, changes her mind about saying something then looks back to Harvey. I look past Harvey into the jungle. The porch is dry, but the overhanging leaves are dripping on to the railings. Big fat drops are rolling to the edge of the leaves and falling with a loud splat. Like a brick on a head. I watch them while Harvey pushes on, counting them to keep my heart from beating so hard and so loud. He might be sounding sweet but what he's saying most definitely isn't.

274

What he has to do is a) account for Stella Maria's where-abouts all morning; b) explain Stella Maria's relationship with Tom; c) explain Rita Mae's relationship with Tom; d) explain Stella Maria's relationship with Rita and e) my relationship with all three. The brick's out of it. He isn't bothered about the brick apparently. He turns to Stella Maria, 'So Ma'am, where were you that morning?'

It's not like he doesn't know her position. Not like he isn't expecting the answer. But Stella Maria sits up in her chair, looking like a rabbit who's just realised the headlights she's in have a speeding car attached to them. She can't answer.

I say, 'She was with me.'

'I wasn't,' she says, still with her eyes on Harvey.

'You were. You've forgotten,' I say.

Betty gets up and stands behind Stella Maria's chair. She puts a hand on her shoulder. 'You were with Tom for some of the time,' she says.

'I was with Tom for some of the time,' Stella Maria repeats. I feel ill for her. Where has she gone? Where is Stella Maria of the loud mouth and brave talk? So crushed I wonder if someone hasn't steamrollered her brain. It dawns on me that wherever she was when Rita died, she must've seen or heard something so terrible she's unable to say because her wretchedness can't just be guilt that someone she wished dead all of a sudden was. I'm scrambling to find a position in my head for this thought but can't.

'We were both with Tom for some of the time,' I say. 'Up on the roof. When we came back from the office we went up to the roof for a fag, then Stella Maria and me went back down to our apartment. We stayed there going over schedules and that's where we were when Archie came and told us what had happened. Did you speak to Archie?' Harvey nods. All the while I'm speaking, I'm looking at Harvey but can see out of the corner of my eye Stella Maria shaking her head and she's going, 'No, it's not true.' And I flip.

'For Christ's sake, Stella Maria,' I yell. 'Just go with it. This is what happened. Not something you can't remember. Just this and you might as well accept it and admit it or it's curtains for you.'

I don't see her leave her chair. I just hear the ring of her scream in my ears. If I hear the sound of my head hitting the concrete lion, I don't remember.

Next thing, I'm lying on my bed, a doctor's been called, Harvey's in his car on his way back to town, Stella Maria's locked herself in her room, and Betty's sitting in a chair looking at me. Not smiling like Mammy would've been, but concerned and serious, saying how am I feeling.

I say 'Fine,' but I sit up and know I'm not fine so I lower myself back on to my pillow. I say to Betty to cancel the doctor. I don't need a doctor. She says of course I need a doctor. I've had a bad blow to the head and lost consciousness.

'Betty,' I say, 'I hate doctors. Please phone and tell him not to come.' She gets to her feet. 'Please, Betty. I mean it. I don't see doctors.' So out she goes to the phone but she's back in a minute to sit with me, unhappy as anything. I smile at her. She tries to smile back but it comes out a frown. We sit in silence. Only sound is the gentle rain on the porch. I say, 'Alright, Betty?'

'It can't go on like this,' she says.

'No,' I say. 'Someone's got to tell me why Stella Maria is so full of hate. I know I hurt her but she knows how sorry I am. All I want is for her to be happy and free.' Betty says it's all anyone wants. I say so what's her problem?

'I think you're not telling the truth about where she was. I don't think you understand you're making it worse for both of you,' Betty says.

'She was with me,' I say and I close my eyes. My head's throbbing. Bitching. I want to confide in Betty but what good would it do? She hates me, anyway. Because Rita Mae slept with Tom. Because I slept with Tom. Because I didn't stop Rita sleeping with Tom after I slept with Tom.

This is what Harvey wants to be clear about. Who slept with Tom, when, how and why? He wants to know about me and Stella Maria, me and Tom and me and Rita. I need to talk to Betty about Rita. I need to crack America. If I can clear my head of Rita Mae, my gloom will lift, my head won't ache and my world will be light again. Betty says I should rest. I say I can't with Rita on my mind.

She says, 'Willie Nelson.' I say who? She says *Rita On My Mind*. Willie Nelson.'

'Give up Betty,' I say, but she looks hurt so I add, 'Close though. *Gentle On My Mind*, words and music John Hartford, best version Glen Campbell. Can I tell you about Rita Mae?'

She's not going to say no, is she? I tell her there was nothing I could do. Once Rita had her sights set on Tom, there was nothing I could do. I saw what was happening, I knew why it was happening, but I couldn't control it, then suddenly it was disaster. Maybe I should've stopped it. Maybe if I'd spoken up, Rita would've backed off. It was like I'd been in this haze. But the haze lifted when Stella Maria and I were waiting to get arrested.

We were in her bed under the blankets, just like we were in the sleeping bag in Cockfosters, terrified out of our wits about what was coming but not knowing what it was. I kept saying why would we be arrested if it was an accident?

'How do you know it was an accident?' Stella Maria said. And she was right. It's not easy to prove an accident when there's so much hate flying about. The lightbulb hissed then popped in the bedside lamp, leaving us in darkness.

Stella Maria wept for Rita Mae. I said why was she so upset when our lives would be so much simpler with her out of the way? Stella Maria said I couldn't mean that, but I did. I was relieved it was over. We'd been bound together by the deal Stella Maria had overseen herself and there would have been no escaping her until the album was out and Tom had finished his film at least. It was only ever going to get worse, even if Rita Mae did have a knack of restoring herself in my eyes just when I thought I couldn't take her a minute more.

One thing I never understood, and still don't, is how someone as noble as Merv could care so much about her. Maybe he was in love with her dancing fingers. Nope. It would have been her vagina. Let's not kid ourselves. 'Betty, I need a glass of water,' I say. And off she goes and doesn't come back because Stella Maria's having a crisis in her locked bedroom.

42

I close my eyes but open them again real fast because the Rita Mae I see is this slimey, scaley monster spewing poison. She's crept out of some dark corner in my skull now. Betty's not here, but it's Betty who's unleashed her. Guiding me to her through the big cave in my head which is full of memories of all sorts but none as horrible as the Rita Mae I now see.

I keep my eyes open and tell the image to go fuck itself. Betty comes back into the room to see if I'm alive. She says maybe I should sleep now. I say no, my head is aching but I think it's Rita Mae, grabbing my brains and squeezing. If I can just get her out of there I'd feel better.

Betty says, 'You know somethin', Honey? I think the doctor has to come. A bad knock on the head needs a doctor.'

I say, 'OK, I'll sleep.' Betty sits on the chair with several days' clothes over the back. 'Is it raining again?' I say. Betty says nope, we had just the one big shower. I'm thinking I'll never sleep and I don't want to sleep in case I have a Rita Mae dream, but I suppose I nod off because one minute she's there, the next she's gone and the people in my head are Abraham and Paddy rolled into one, plus a tree.

I'm sheltering under the tree from pouring rain. The boys turn into the tree to shelter me. But there are big raindrops falling from the tree on to my head and they're really painful. 'Ouch,' I'm saying. 'It hurts. Stop it.'

And Stella Maria says, 'Want an aspirin?' I open my eyes to find she's sitting on my bed, squashing my legs which feels comfortable and safe, until I remember she wants me dead.

'I think I had one,' I say. She's turned into someone who not only hates me, but who's knocked me out. I stare at her, trying to decide if anything's changed but it doesn't look like it. Not from her eyes or her lips or her flat, flat voice.

She says, 'Sorry I pushed you over.'

'No worries,' I say.

'Everything go OK with Merv?'

'Merv and Dick and Jerrah,' I say, sticking only to the necessary words as I'm so tired. I nearly say Tom but stop myself. 'Jerrah said it was a great song. A really great song.' I want to sound more excited but don't have it in me. She has a little in her which is more than I'm expecting.

'That's great,' she says. And she sounds like she means it, so for a minute I confuse her with my old friend Stella Maria and tell her what else he said, even though every word hits the back, front and sides of my head before leaving it. 'Well isn't that fantastic?' she says. And you don't know bitter until you hear it in Stella Maria's voice. 'Just brilliant. He doesn't much care for you but he likes the song you've written about a girl who died in the process of getting the film that was being made about you turned into one about her.'

'That's not how it was,' I say.

'You know that's how it was.'

'It's not how they see it,' I say. 'Jerrah loves the song.' She gives this laugh with no humour in it.

'Honey,' she begins but I've had enough.

'They love my song, Stella Maria. Jerrah, who likes no one, loves my song and he's going to make it into a big hit which is what I want.'

She says, 'You are . . .' she can't think of a word. She's on her feet. My forehead's pounding. The desperation I felt before she ran at me rises in my chest all over again, gets my throat. 'Despicable,' she finally says. 'Paddy would be ashamed of you.' Outside I can hear this torrential rain, like all heaven's water has decided to leave the sky at once then rise like a mist into my body and come out through my eyes in one terrible flood.

'You know nothing about me and Paddy,' I say. 'You know nothing about us.'

'Blood's thicker than water, Honey. That never occur to you?' And now I'm going to be sick. Retching only, which I control, by filling my lungs with air. She's looking down at me, so full of hate I shiver. She's telling me that he loves her more than he loves me. That if he has to choose, he'll choose her, just like I've chosen Tom. A murderer. Then the room tilts on its side and out I go like one of the bulbs Mammy blows to alert me. And in the darkness horrible images come to find me.

When I wake the rain's still belting down. I can hear it against the leaves of the plants outside my window and wonder how the stupid goat is doing. Lucky goat. Only having to worry about food and trying to bash the house in by running at it.

I get out of bed, open the curtains Betty closed to keep out the light, and it's not raining. It's not sunny but it's not raining. Even so, I can hear it. I put my hands to my ears and I still hear it. The rain is in my head. Listening to it without seeing it makes the room spin again.

I get back into bed and close my eyes to focus on the sound and find I can make it soothing. Maybe I'm having a rain flashback. I try to recall a traumatic rain memory that Betty might have jogged but can't. I lie very still, waiting to see if it changes, if it comes with any wind or thunder or lightning, then I doze off again.

I keep my eyes closed when Betty comes into my room, puts a hand on my head, smoothes down my sheet and goes out again. And when the door opens and someone stands in the doorway before tiptoeing away. I stay semi-asleep until my mobile rings and I answer it.

Tom says, 'Guess where I am? I'm outside Barney Noble's.' I switch the phone off at once. I don't need news of Barney Noble. I don't want even to think about Barney Noble. Tom can have him all to himself. My thoughts are all of Rita Mae. They swarm out of my head and make my flesh crawl. Betty arrives bringing some herb tea on a tray with a cloth on it. I tell her I need to talk to her some more. She needs to hear. It's all pertinent. 'Also, there's rain in my ear,' I tell her.

'You mean it feels wet?' she says. She puts down the tray and pushes my hair back to take a look.

'Doesn't feel. Sounds wet.' I say. 'I can hear raining as loud as anything.' She says now she is calling the doctor. I say please could she sit with me. I'm so troubled. And she does because she's such a good woman she'd never refuse the request of any poor soul in need. I wish her happiness. I'd like to say to her, 'Betty, whoever broke your heart will burn in hell, but I'm pleased if you've experienced the pleasure of rewarding sex.'

Instead, I sit there holding my tea and looking at her. She says, 'Anything special?'

'Your book.'

'OK.' She sounds wary.

'What's it about again?'

'Why relationships fail.'

'Right. Well how do you know when they have?'

'When the pain they cause outweighs the pleasure they give,' she says, which tells me all I need to know. It's over between Stella Maria and me. Has to be. And if I ask myself where it leaves Rita Mae and Stella Maria, all I can say is that there never was a relationship. It failed the minute they clapped eyes on each other and went downhill after that.

We got together the morning after we met and Stella Maria went ploughing in which didn't help anything. 'First thing you need to know, Rita Mae, is Honey's a solo performer. If you want to perform with her, you gotta stand behind her at all times, play only when she says and sing only when she says. They're the rules. Take 'em or leave 'em.'

It was a crap choice whichever way you looked at it and not anyone extending any hand of friendship. Rita turned to me and said, 'Is this arsehole for real?'

'I'm for real, gobshite,' Stella Maria said. And next thing she was telling her she might as well know. She didn't see the point in any pissing banjo picker with a voice like a donkey's and a face like a horse's arse.

I pass this on to Betty for her consideration. She says, 'Some people attack when they're defending.'

Rita Mae didn't bother with either. She just decided there and then she was going to get rid of Stella Maria and that was it.

'And you didn't try to stop her,' Betty says. 'You saw clear through Rita Mae, knew just what she was up to but you didn't you try to stop it.' Her words are like gentle smacks to the side of my head, which wouldn't hurt if my head wasn't already a big ball of pain and if they weren't coming from nowhere. How could she think that? What sort of person does she think I am? Straightaway I realised that musically our harmony was perfect. Stella Maria could look after herself.

I sit myself up in the bed so I can look Betty in the eye better. She says would I like to stop but I tell her I'm feeling better. That tea has cured me except for the ear thing. 'This was a professional arrangement,' I say. 'Stella Maria wasn't my girlfriend or anything. We weren't lesbian lovers or anything. Professionally, I thought she could take care of herself.'

I'm not saying it didn't upset me they didn't get on but it was up to them to get over it. Only they didn't and pretty soon Rita Mae had the upper hand. She shoved Stella Maria to the back of the picture every chance she got. If we were walking along the street and he wasn't filming, she would stick her arm through Tom's. If we were all eating out together, she'd go straight to a table for three.

'Did you ever stand up to her?' Betty asks. I tell her all the time. Like over George Jones. Finest country voice ever, born with a broken arm in 1931, raised by a Christian mother and a drunkard father and at one time a busker on street corners, just like me.

I'm painting the picture for Betty when the phone rings and she jumps out of her skin, out of her chair, then out of the room like it's a call she's been waiting for all her life. She doesn't even bother to close to study door.

'Hullo?' she says, all breathless. She lowers her voice, but even so I hear her. 'Me too,' she's saying. 'Me too.' Then she tells the caller to wait and closes the door but I know already that this is a conversation riddled with hope and love and maybe sorrow.

'I've missed you,' I said to Paddy last time I saw him but, compared to now, I hardly knew the meaning of the words.

I've missed you. I never thought you'd call.
I'm sittin' here, right by the phone just staring at the wall.
And in the big blank spaces where your pictures used to be
I see only memories of you, well you and me.

George Jones will be in love with Tammy Wynette until the day he dies. Theirs was a romance doomed by tragic failing but fuelled by endless longing and I really want to know who's on the phone. I get out of bed but my head spins so I go back. *Rain In My Head.*

Rain in my head, like a storm at sea, tossin' my heart on the
waves
Surely you see, thunder or not, this is not how a true love
behaves.

Need my guitar. Bend over to get it from under the bed and crash! Down I go. When I come round this time I'm still on the floor, no sign of Betty but Stella Maria's looking down at me. I say, 'Did you hit me again?'

She calls real loud, 'Betty.'

I say, 'What happened?'

She says, 'You fell out of bed.' Then she screams. 'Betty come quick. Honey's had a fit or something.'

No sound of footsteps. I try to get myself off the floor but fall back down again and Stella Maria half sobs, 'Stay there, steaming git. You probably broke your back.' She goes to the door, watching me the whole time. 'Betttteeee,' she yells and now Betty does come and she's saying, 'What is it, what is it?' and Stella Maria says, 'Honey's collapsed. Call an ambulance.' So then I scream.

43

'No fucking ambulance!' I scream. 'I'm not going to any fucking hospital. I just tripped. I'm going to no fucking hospital.' I struggle to get to my feet but my legs buckle. Betty and Stella Maria tower over me with their great long arms coming down to pluck me or whatever long arms do when you're a tree and the last thing I hear over the rain is Stella Maria whispering, 'She hates hospitals.'

My eyes are closed, my lips are closed, there's a torrent of noise in my brain and I'm stuggling to explain to Betty how Rita said I didn't sound like George Jones. George is saying, 'Well Ah've been struggling with the demon drink all mah live long days but that don' mean a girl cain't sing like me.'

I'm trying to tell Betty how you take a syllable and split it into many parts then run them all together like the coffee, sugar and cream in George's voice, which Rita says makes me sound like the goddam duchess of intercourse. What a cow, Betty, I'm saying but my lips are closed. I force them open. I force my eyes open. Someone else is forcing my eyes open. First one, then the other to shine a light in them.

Not Betty. The doctor's here. 'Still raining?' he asks.

'Pissing,' I tell him.

Betty says, 'Honey is feelin' verra anxious about goin' to hospital.' She is here, then. Just not where I can see her. Over there somewhere.

'Now is that the truth, young lady?' says the doctor who's a middle-aged gent, not too attractive but quite friendly for someone with glasses that thick. His voice is warm. Velvet.

'I'm not going to hospital,' I say. 'No way.' He will know that people go to hospital to die so I don't spell it out for him.

'Not even for tests.'

'Not for tests.'

'Not even to get rid of the rain you can hear when there is no rain? Not even to see why you're falling down?'

'Not ever full stop,' I say. 'I'm just tired.' I am very tired and sick. I feel sick. I'm going to be sick. I am sick. All over the bed and floor and maybe him. 'Sorry. Sorry.'

They get me on to the chair, while Stella Maria who's turned up with a mop and a bucket, cleans around the place. Betty changes the bed while the doctor tells me how much better I'd be if he could just get me to see someone who knows about head injuries and could take a closer look at mine. I tell him. 'I'm not allowed to go to hospital, anyway.'

'Oh?' he says. 'And why's that?

'Because I killed someone.' He looks across at Betty who shakes her head.

'Ask her,' I say. Betty and the doctor both look at Stella Maria.

'She killed no one,' she says. 'She just doesn't want to go to hospital. You've got to go though, Honey. You have to. I'm your friend. I'm telling you.'

'You are not my friend,' I say. Then I get back into bed, roll on my side so I can go to sleep again and when I wake up I am in hospital because it turns out no one cares what I think.

I don't have hysterics or anything. I simply say to the

woman in my room could I please go back to Betty's house which is where I'm safe as there's nothing wrong with me that won't get better with a good rest and a couple of Panadol. All I had was a bang on the head.

The woman's all smiles. She says I'm probably right. They'll just keep me here for a day or two for observation and then they'll let me home. I ask the woman if she's a doctor. She's a nurse, fiddling about with charts at the bottom of my bed. I say well look, I really won't be staying, so I get out of bed and head for the door.

Christ knows what I'm wearing here. Some skimpy thing with my bum hanging out. She's going, 'Hey, just a minute.' I'm out the door and wandering down the corridor which is waving around like someone took the building from under it and then down I go. All the way to the ground. It takes many people to get me back to bed.

I'm saying, 'Let me out of here, let me out of here.' I'm trying to kick at them and hit at them and get them off me but I just don't have the energy. 'You arsewipes,' I yell.

'Shush,' they go. Someone gives me an injection.

Mammy's in the next bed. Her yellow hair is stuck to the pillow. Baby Jimmie is in her arms, all blue. I want to get into her bed. I want to be with them. I'm doing my best to get there and I'm crying and calling her but her bed gets further and further away. This weather is fucking terrible.

Now it's dark. There's a needle sticking in my hand attached to a tube attached to a bag hanging off a stand. I look across and see there is a shape in the next bed but she's way too fat for my mother. She makes this gurgling, dying noise. There's no air in the room. I can't breathe. I scream. Real loud. No one comes. I thought I screamed. Maybe I didn't scream. 'Nurse,' I call. 'Nurse.'

A man comes. He says he's a nurse. I say I want to go home. He says I can't. It's too dark out there. He's whispering. I ask him why. He says the woman in the next bed is very sick. I look across and sure enough in the next bed the woman has died. 'She's dead,' I tell him. He looks surprised. He goes over to look at her then comes back.

He says she's not dead. I say she's definitely dead. I've seen a dead woman before. My Mammy. And this time I do scream so he gives me another injection.

Now I'm in a room all by myself. There is sun coming into the room through a big window which looks out across a car park where people are coming and going, visiting dying people and so on. I'm no longer wanting to scream. I'm no longer wanting anything much. I have no feelings I can recognise.

What I've been doing ever since I woke up hours ago is listening. There are so many hospital noises in the dead of night and I've been straining to hear them over the rain. Hospital sounds are desperate. Clanging and murmuring. The last sounds Mammy heard and the only sounds in the world that Jimmie knew.

No. I expect Mam hummed to him. I expect she did when she could. I pray that when she held him she found the strength to give him just one melody. Then he'd have known there was a heavenly pleasure right there in his Mammy's throat and maybe the music carried his soul to heaven. That's what music can do. Even when the soul's a little one.

I hum to myself but the sound is muffled by the rain and I think about the power of music. It was the music that bound Rita Mae and me and it's the music that has driven Stella Maria and me apart. I know now that we are apart. And I think that we will stay apart. Now she's tried to kill me, despite the good in my heart for her. I'm not dying though. The nurse told me I'm not dying. They thought there was a clot in my brain caused by Stella Maria but it's just a fractured skull.

'Doctors killed my mother,' I told the nurse.

'No one here, I hope,' he said. And I said no, it was no one here but what difference did that make? I've been thinking

289

what to do. Even if Stella Maria wanted my friendship, and she doesn't, have I got any left to give? Wasn't she always telling me I shouldn't put up with Micky slapping me about? Wasn't she always saying that? You shouldn't put up with anyone slapping you about.

If she wants to say she was sitting on the brick that landed on Rita's head she can. I don't know where she was when the brick fell and now I don't care. Here's something else. I'm not going to feel guilty about her anymore. We came to America together to crack it and we came with open eyes. We worked out what we had to do, she did as well as me, and what we had to do was involve someone like Rita Mae who turned out to be Rita Mae. I don't want to see her any more. I have nothing to say to her. I'd rather stay here than go back to see her. I'm thinking if I owe anyone anything, it's poor dead Rita Mae. If we're talking about luck, who's luckiest? Stella Maria and me are alive.

In my head I try to hear the music we made. I can't. But I remember that it was beautiful. I'd pick up my guitar, she'd pick up her banjo, we'd tune them, I'd start to sing and we'd be transported, I swear, to some place where there was no hate, no jealousy, no resentment, no bad feeling at all. I still don't know how this could be.

We didn't speak much but we made a lot of eye contact. I'd sing and play, she'd play along and harmonise. I'd hear something wrong and stop. She'd try an improvement. I'd nod and ease myself into it. It was pure instinct. I never knew anything could be so fine. And what were the odds of it happening when I'd never worked with anyone ever before and she'd worked with everyone and failed?

I suppose it was like sex. Maybe if I'd found love with the man for me, I wouldn't have had room for Rita. But if I hadn't had room for Rita Mae, I'd never have experienced the joy. That is the memory of her I will keep and treasure forever. Stella Maria has next to no music in her.

They never got poor Rita Mae to hospital. She died where she fell with bits of her brain on the woman who'd been walking behind her. I don't believe she suffered. She was just walking along, food rattling around inside her, not caring whether this breath was her last, and then she knew no more. It was a freakish accident. That brick could have landed anywhere. How was anyone to know that a brick could travel so far and arrive at the same spot as someone's head at the exact time? Rita Mae couldn't have and now she's too dead to care.

Too Dead To Care (with bending syllables in the manner of George Jones): I sing loudly to hear myself above the inclement weather.

> *'She's too dead to care*
> *She's too day-id to care.*
> *Shee-ee-ee-ee Ee-ee-ee-*
> *Ee-ee's too dead to ca-ar-are.*
> *And she's too dead to care. Oh yes*
> *Too day-id to care . . .'*

Her family didn't want to meet me even though I was her next to last friend on earth. They met Tom and he said they were quite pleasant.

'. . . Too fucking day-id to care.'

A nurse comes in. A new nurse. She says could I please keep the noise down. There's a very sick woman over the corridor. I say sorry. I say I am truly sorry and the nurse smiles and said well that's OK then and maybe a more cheerful song would be better.

'What's wrong with the lady over the corridor?' I say.

'She had a major operation.'

'What operation?'

'A Caesarian section.'

'Where's her baby?' The nurse pours water into my jug to give herself something to do.

'She lost her baby,' she says. But I already knew.

I say what were the odds of that happening? The nurse says, 'It's a tragedy.' I say is the lady going to die? The nurse says no, she's recovering but I know she'll never recover and my whole body aches for her loss.

That's when Betty puts her head around the door. Smiling in a tragic moment. I'm not so pleased to see her. She says may she visit? The nurse says why of couse, now is a good time as I need cheering up and Betty says she has with her just the person to do it. I fear it will be Stella Maria. 'Alright, Honey?' Paddy says.

44

Betty's smiling so hard her face looks like splitting. 'How about that?' she says. 'I don't know what she thinks Paddy is to me, but I suppose it's whatever Stella Maria has told her, so I don't hold back. When he kisses me on the cheek, I put my arms about his neck and cling to him. His face is so cool on mine I never want to let it go.

He whispers in my ear, 'Don't cry there, Honey. Stop crying now.' He removes my hands from his neck. He turns to Betty and says, 'You'd never know she was pleased to see me.'

She laughs. She laughs like a girl half her age who's noticed how very attractive my true love is. So attractive I want to pull him into the bed with me. I want him holding me in this very bed, bringing me comfort and love because there's been so little of it in my life lately. I say to Betty, 'Have you come to take me home?' The smile dies in her eyes.

Paddy says, 'Now Honey, don't say that. I'm not having you fade away on me when I've come all this way.'

Betty says she'll just pop out for a minute to see a friend

who works in the psychiatric unit. And now we're alone, Paddy sits on the edge of my bed. I take his hand and I know that all I want is to have him by my side forever. I think from his face this is what he wants as well. I tell him I'm so happy he's here. He doesn't know what it means to me that he's here. I love him so much. 'I love you,' I say. He kisses my hand like he loves me too.

He says, 'You've had a rough time.' I say it's been demented. One minute really great stuff happening, then really bad.

'You know from my letters, anyway,' I say.

He laughs then stops when he sees it's not funny. 'What letters?' I tell him the letters I've been writing him non stop since I left London. He says well he got no letters. This pleases me and upsets me all at once just like most things.

'Well what did you think when you didn't hear from me?'

He looks into my eyes, then looks away. 'I thought we didn't have much to say to each other.' I take my hands away from his. He takes them back. He says, 'I'm here now.'

'So why did you come?'

'Honey, are you serious? '

I say I think I am. I don't see a joke. He says, 'My sister is charged with murder. Do you think her family would turn its back on her?'

'She thought you had. She told me you had.'

'She was having you on.' He's making it sound like it's nothing. But we both know it's huge. He says, 'She's very sorry she pushed you over. She's got a terrible temper on her.'

'You never told me she knew about us. I thought we were a secret.'

'She's my sister, Honey. She guessed. It doesn't matter now anyway.' And I don't know what he means by that but I don't want to ask him either. 'I'd say there were bigger things to worry about right at this moment,' he says. 'It's a terrible business for a poor girl to die.'

'I know,' I tell him and I'd say more except my voice starts to give out on me.

'Don't distress yourself, Honey,' he says. As if I could help myself. He puts his arms about me. He strokes my hair and he murmurs stuff I can't appreciate because he mumbles and I can't hear so well.

'It wasn't your fault,' he says. I say I know it wasn't. He says I mustn't blame myself. I say I don't. He says ambition can change a person, he knows that himself.

I agree with him. 'Look what it did to Rita Mae and Stella Maria,' I say.

He puts me gently at arm's distance as he appears not to understand but thinks he will if he looks hard at my horrible, blotchy face. 'I mean you, Honey,' he says.

The insult rips into my soul. He's been talking to Stella Maria and she's blamed me for everything. I yell at him. 'You don't know what you're talking about. I just got on with my work. They hated each other on sight. They wanted each other dead. I was just the bystander.'

He says, 'No one's saying you killed her. All I'm saying is you let things get out of control.' The man's in misery. I can see he's in misery but he can fuck right off. They can all fuck right off. 'All I'm saying is you need to take responsibility for the mess you're in,' he says.

'Do you mean as well as writing songs, recording them, singing them about town to cretins who don't care whether I live or die so we can all . . .'

'Shut up, Honey,' he says, angry now, shocking me with his anger. 'Have you ever asked yourself what you did to Stella Maria? Has it ever crossed your mind the damage you did to her while you were so busy being a star?'

'I know what damage I did,' I say, 'and I said I was sorry.' I'm so angry myself I can barely catch my breath.

'Sorry,' he repeats. 'Sorry. That's all you are. You destroyed her.' He spits it out. He can't disguise the contempt he has for me. 'You stopped loving her Honey. When she'd loved you so much.'

'Fuck off!' I yell at him. 'Fuck off, you know nothing.' I turn my back to him so's not to see his disgust.

'And you destroyed yourself into the bargain,' he says. Then he goes. When Betty comes back to say goodbye I pretend to be asleep. I want to be asleep. I never want to wake up again.

45

As soon as the door closes behind her I know I'll never sleep again unless I can explain to someone that it wasn't how it looks. We were happy. We were on course. We knew what we had to do, her, Tom and me, and we just got on with doing it. Did Stella Maria tell Paddy that? No. All she can remember is how it was the day Rita Mae died and the heavens went black for her.

Her problem, the problem that had nothing to do with me, was hating Rita Mae on sight. She never got over the fact that Rita Mae wanted to conquer Nashville just as much as we did and she wanted to throw her hand in with us. What was I supposed to say to her – bugger off? She was taking her chance same as the rest of us and we were her last hope. Merv got it. Tom got it. I got it. There was no explaining it to Stella Maria. All she saw was rejection. Me rejecting her. But I was never going to spend as much time with her once I had a deal with a label. She knew that. She knew I had to work every minute.

It was OK for Tom saying he wanted success to happen in

the blink of an eye but an album just doesn't happen in any blink. Merv was sifting through all my tapes looking for nuggets from my early work to rearrange and I was writing a whole pile of new stuff for Rita Mae to muck around with. It took ages, tossing stuff back and forth until we had something we liked. I'm not saying I didn't know there was tension, but I tried to take it in my stride because how else could I take it?

Tom was recording all the ups and downs of my new musical partnership and the way it was affecting Stella Maria and me, but he was more interested in finding me a love interest. He tried to set me up with Merv. 'Do you want me dead?' I said. 'Merv is Rita Mae's.'

Everyone was Rita Mae's. Even Tom was warming to her. He liked her arsey remarks. To the film-maker, a character with a vile temperament is a real gift. That didn't help Stella Maria much. She was miserable the night Tom and I agreed Rita Mae could come to our daily catch-up sessions. 'It's not in her contract,' she said.

I said, 'Forget the contract.' But she wanted to argue. She said did we have any idea what we were letting ourselves in for? We were only putting up with the girl because of her flipping banjo. She'd ruin everything. An intruder with her great loud mouth and pushy fucking manner. The deal was between the three of us, our pact was private. She wanted to tear up the contract and get shot of her before the rot really set in. I said, 'Stella Maria. This is going to happen.'

It had to happen. Rita Mae had been on my back so hard. She'd been on and on at me, and when I'd ignored her she'd gone on and on at Tom. Tom had told her to talk to Stella Maria and that just sent Rita Mae straight back to me. She knew my weaknesses and she chipped and chipped away. Pretty soon, I collapsed. I had misgivings but I thought we could muddle through. Personality clashes didn't have to be the end of the world.

Stella Maria was right. An icepick was never going to sit comfortably in something as cosy as a bowl of soup. Every night, the three of us had always cuddled up on the couch with our Buds to plot where we were, where we'd been and where we were going and we didn't need any help or interference from anyone else.

Stella Maria was the general who lined up guns from all the important positions and she was the one who decided which ones to fire. Tom would draw the explosions as she set them off, one by one, so our lives looked like a comic strip in a war magazine.

First night Rita Mae turned up, she shoved herself between Stella Maria and Tom so Stella Maria had to sit on the floor and she helped herself to Stella Maria's information sheets like they were bus timetables. Stella Maria told her to keep her filthy mitts off stuff that didn't belong to her and to move her great arse as she was taking up so much space no one else could move. It was stupid. Insults were gifts to Rita. She'd just catch them, polish them and hurl them back harder, faster and closer to the bone. Not at once. When she was good and ready. Stella Maria wasn't much of a general in warfare of the heart, more's the pity.

I was as rattled as she was by the disgusting way Rita Mae sucked up to Tom. It was so repulsive that under normal circumstances I would've wanted to sock her myself. But these weren't normal circumstances. The reward was in sight so I was treading much more carefully than I'd ever done and Stella Maria, to her credit, was learning to bite her tongue as well.

'Hope ya'll don't mind me buttin' in like this,' Rita would say. She'd have her arm draped around Tom's neck. She was always touching him, always consulting him like he was this big business oracle, and soon he was falling for it. He started asking himself if he was making a mistake, skimming across the surface of the country music industry when so much lay beneath, and wondering if maybe it wouldn't be a better story if I paid a few dues.

You'd think this might have thrown Stella Maria and me back together again. It drove us further apart. She clung as close to Tom as she could, trying to fend off Rita Mae, and I clung to Rita Mae because I wanted her with me, not him. I went out of my way to make her like me more and if sometimes that meant being meaner than I'd normally have been to Stella Maria, then I did that. What else could I do?

She wormed her way into our lives little bit by little bit and after a few weeks, there was no way neither Stella Maria nor I had any control over it. Nothing we said or did would have kept her away from the meeting Stella Maria had lined up with Moonshine. It was a make-or-break meeting. They'd loved the demo. What they wanted to see was the strength of the talent.

Rita Mae was in there faster than a snake in a hen house and Stella Maria and me just sat there like hens who'd never seen a snake before. I wanted to yell in their faces, 'Hey, she's just the banjo picker I might sack.' But instead, I went along with her, taking the piss out of *Wormwood Scrubs* even though that song has always been precious to me. I sang it to kick the meeting off so's the suits could all see how little my Englishness mattered.

Hard men go to the Scrubs to die,
Turn their face to the wall, say they'd sooner fry
But Micky O'Shea said, 'Not me baby
I'll never give in and I don't mean maybe.'
Micky O'Shea, Micky O'Shea
Micky O'Shea yodel ay-ee-ay.

I called him Micky O'Shea because you can't get a yodel to rhyme with Besant. It's a bit of a joke but not that big a joke. Rita, on her fiddle, played it for laughs leaving me no choice but to laugh along as well and it worked a treat. I could sing it real low. The harder those Moonshine executives laughed, the lower I sang and soon the whole boardroom was rocking. They loved the notion of me as a performer whose song-writing partner was pure part Native American. They thought we were hysterical together. Which is why I did it. Which is why I said what I said. No choice.

What I said was, 'Local sounds good.' Sounds innocent, I wanted it to be innocent, but Rita Mae made sure it wasn't. She meant to get rid of Stella Maria and she meant to do it in public so it would be final. I know that now. But what was I supposed to do? Ruin the whole thing when it was going so well?

I had to sacrifice Stella Maria and I didn't feel so bad about it because I knew it wouldn't be permanent. I knew I'd be able to explain to her afterwards that it was only for show and we could sort it out between ourselves behind the scenes. But she said, 'Who are you kidding, Honey?'

On the rushes I could see maybe she had a point. We finished singing and Tom took Rita Mae by the arm and sat her at the table bang opposite Stella Maria. That looked innocent as well but it wasn't. He did it so they'd both be in his field of vision, like he knew what was coming, like Rita had warned him. She understood what he was after film-wise better even than Stella Maria.

I was sitting next to Stella Maria. Merv was next to Rita who was acting cocky because we'd been such a success. She knew these guys were worried about me being English and she guessed they wouldn't be happy about Stella Maria being so young and inexperienced. Also, having been to our planning meetings, she knew Stella Maria's limitations. There are holes in her technical knowledge. Sometimes we'd ask her something, she wouldn't know the answer and she'd go, 'Yeah, blah blah blah . . . I'll wing that.' Never bothered Tom or me.

Everyone in the room knew this whole thing was about seeing how far I could get in an industry that might have been closed to me on account of my place of birth. And Rita Mae knew that while the industry looked like welcoming me with open arms, it had no reason to welcome Stella Maria who was throwing her weight around on the strength of nothing. Maybe Stella Maria did walk into that meeting not as well prepared as she should've been. But she'd have been fine if she hadn't let Rita Mae upset her.

Every time she opened her mouth, Rita'd go, 'Pardon me, I didn't get that,' or 'Come again. I don't understand the sense of it.' And sometimes she repeated what Stella Maria had just said in a silly English accent, as if she couldn't possibly have heard anything so stupid. It didn't take long for Stella Maria to lose her nerve.

I'd have expected her to tell everyone to drop dead, we didn't need them and they knew what they could do with their contract, but it was like she'd forgotten that script. She started stuttering and stammering and getting all sorts of facts wrong, losing bits of paper, calling people by the wrong name, mixing up musical terms, not getting references to other musicians. And it was funny. People were laughing. Even Tom was having a laugh because Rita Mae could be funny at other people's expense.

Rita wasn't laughing. Just smiling and pretending to be good-natured in her charming Tennessee accent which was as natural as mine. I laughed because I wanted it to look like it was good-natured and so did Merv, but we both knew Rita's dagger was drawn. Stella Maria tried to laugh as well but in the end she was crying. I knew because I know her crying face. It's a smile with heartbreak in the corners.

I was desperate for her. I hated what Rita Mae was doing. But this is a tough world. So when Rita said at the end of the meeting, while Stella Maria was packing her files away, 'I think Honey should git herself some local management, what do you guys think?' she must have known she had me. She said, 'What do you think, Honey?'

That whole room went silent. Tom had the camera on his shoulder, and was shuffling backwards to get us all in. I looked at Stella Maria whose eyes were wide with disbelief, willing me to betray her. And I looked at Rita, her slitty eyes shooting death rays in my direction, and I called for Mammy to guide me. She sent a beam of sunshine to play on Rita's face. It was that cut and dried. 'Local sounds good.' I said.

But I didn't get rid of Stella Maria, did I? I only said maybe, to save face all round. That was what Mammy had meant by the sunshine. It was never my intention to get rid of Stella Maria who had come with me to Nashville with so much hope in her heart. And I apologised at once. Naturally. And Stella Maria accepted.

Rita Mae said later if she'd had any pride, she'd have resigned on the spot. But Rita knew nothing. Stella Maria was in love with Tom and Stella Maria wanted to be rich. OK, she felt like shit and wanted to go home. Definitely she said she wasn't going to hang round and be humiliated like she was some lower form of life. But Tom and I persuaded her. Tom said he needed her. She was his girl. I said I needed her. She was my manager, whatever Rita Mae said. We both said her garden needed her. The grand design would wither and die without her. She said for her, it already had. But she stayed.

All she had to do was see Rita out. That was what I advised her when we were in bed that night, though she wouldn't even acknowledge my presence. And isn't that what she has done?

I want Paddy to know this. I want him to understand this. You set out to crack something and there have to be sacrifices. You want an outcome, you have to consider all the possibilities. You want a reward, you have to take risks. If I've learnt anything since I've been here, I've learnt that.

46

The breakfast trolley's rumbling down the corridor and I'm getting out of here. I'm going back to Betty's to tell Paddy my side of the story. My head's clear even if there is still a stupid noise inside it. I slide from the bed and test my legs on the cool floor. They're wobbly. I edge my way to the locker to see what clothes are in it but there's just a pair of knickers and a T-shirt. I'm wearing a nightie Betty brought in. Just about covers my bum which is saying something about Betty I'd never have guessed. No legging it in this. I need a phone.

There's no one in the corridor. Not a soul. I can't even see any trolley so where did that go? There's a chair outside my door which I grab to steady myself. In the room across the hall, the lady who's lost her baby is sitting up looking at the wall. Her face has no life in it. The baby must have taken it. I stand in her doorway. I want to say something to her.

'Hi,' I say. I'm thinking I could tell her I know her pain, but that's not an easy thing to say to a stranger. I want to tell her the baby's journey on earth was only ever meant to be a short one and hers hasn't finished yet.

She turns. 'You the girl 'cross the way there?' I say I am. She says, 'Mah horse sings better'n you.'

I walk as normally as I can along the corridor, through two sets of swing doors, past rooms which have patients in them and one or two which don't until I get to a desk with a nurse behind it. A police officer's saying he's Officer Hicks and he's come to relieve his pardner. The nurse says sure, his pardner just this minute left. It's through two sets of swing doors and second room on the left. My room. They're speaking real soft but I hear them and I know what they talking about. I've been under police guard.

I say, 'You've come to guard me but you don't need to because I'm going home.' The nurse is on his feet and coming round the desk. I put my hand out to ward him off and take a couple of steps back. I yell, 'Y'all don' wanna make this a problem, you hear? Ah'm goin' home. A single minute more in this place and Ah'll have a nervous breakdown, Ah swear Ah will, an' you won't know what to do with y'all selves.' It does the trick. They know I mean it.

Everyone gets on the phone, a doctor arrives, Betty's consulted, Harvey's traced, and two hours later I'm on the way home, driven by Officer Hicks. I say it's better than sittin' in some dumb chair all day isn't it, and he agrees but that's all I say to him. I don't talk to the police without a lawyer present.

I pretend to be asleep so's not to hurt his feelings and every now and then I snore for verisimilitude. I like verisimilitude, a word I discovered when I looked up another word for truth. I've never put it in a song though truth often crops up in lyrics about love. Love and truth, love and deceipt, love and treachery. In my head I rehearse the scene ahead with Paddy. I'll tell him that Stella Maria and I are estranged but I want him to know the truth.

Rita Mae and Tom would have had sex with each other no matter what I did or didn't do. She used every trick in the book. She even said she was falling in love with him. But she didn't do love. She told me so herself, not once but many times, and when I said I didn't believe her, she said, 'Do I look like someone who'd give up my destiny so easily?' And she didn't. Did love fail Rita Mae or did Rita Mae fail love?

Did love fail Rita or did Rita fail love
In the end what she said was 'A sign from above
Will make it plain,
One way or the other
Whether I love you, like a man or a brother'
But she died.

I hear a melody for that clear as can be. 'You say somethin'?' asks Officer Hicks.

'Nope,' I say.

I'm feeling anxious about seeing Stella Maria. Her hate for me is a heavy load to carry when your head's all battered. I know I hurt her, but I couldn't have been more sorry. I knew at once I had to make amends and I will but I can't stand any more scenes.

Rita Mae didn't do love because she thought if you gave even a little bit of yourself to someone you'd be less of a person. Anyone who's truly loved knows the opposite is the case. Whatever she had for Tom never looked like love anyway. It looked like grabbing. But one thing she underestimated was how little interest Tom had in her body.

His attitude to sex is if someone's sitting on his penis he might as well move, which was unfortunate for Rita Mae because her only weapon was making men fancy her. She presumed Tom did, but Tom was more attracted to the dues she'd paid to the music industry. I knew it but maybe I was the only one who did. He could see that, just like I'd tried to tell him the day we found the apartment, dues would give my story depth. I said I told you so when he said how much he admired Rita for hers. 'I know, I know' he said.

When he didn't jump into bed with her as soon as she

asked him, she was truly shaken. The excuse he gave was it wouldn't be appropriate. Which to me is the same as saying, 'Local sounds good.' Rita Mae said all Tom needed was time. She completely blocked out the idea that his interest might have been elsewhere. She completely blocked out Stella Maria full stop. And with persistence, slowly, slowly, slowly, she wooed him away from us. Stella Maria should have moved faster.

Stella Maria's argument is all I had to do was tell Tom I hated it. But that was just not correct. It didn't do to cross Rita Mae. Not when you needed her. So what I ended up telling myself was that she and Tom could get up to anything they liked. If Tom was going to fall for the likes of her, he didn't deserve Stella Maria. But all the while, I was being sucked into Rita's devilry.

There's no sign of Paddy or Stella Maria when we pull up at the gate. Betty's there. And Tom. Why's he here? He's wearing a huge smile as he opens the car door and helps me out. I'm wearing the Betty nightie over my T-shirt and knickers so I feel pretty stupid. He says, 'You won't believe . . .'

Betty cuts across him real sharp, 'You feelin' OK, Honey, after your journey? You come right in now and put your feet up.'

I hug both Tom and Betty. I say 'Where's Paddy?' And Stella Maria who's appeared at the top of the porch steps says Nashville, getting ready to go home and I stun everyone by not producing a torrent of tears. Maybe I'm relieved. I rehearsed that scene with him so long I'm tuckered out. I thank Officer Hicks, who won't come in as he's been so bored shitless, then Betty takes my elbow like I'm a Vietnam vet and supports me all the way up the path to the porch, making Tom walk behind.

The day is overcast so the jungle's looking darker and greener than ever, but it does me good just looking into its secret glades and up at the hills. Betty says, 'Stella Maria has made you a cake.'

'How come you're here?' I say to Tom. He's watching me. Betty's watching me. Something's up. I can feel it. Am I dying? Betty says why don't I get some clothes on and join them out the front. Something's up for sure. I try to imagine what it can be while I pull on jeans and a shirt.

'What's up?' I say when I'm back on the porch. They look at each other. Tom's happy as Larry. Betty isn't.

'Honey,' Betty begins, but Tom can't keep his lips buttoned a second longer.

'I've found your father. Barney Noble's your Dad. He wants to see you. He wants to see you tomorrow. Jerry's over the moon.'

This will be what it's like to die of hypothermia. The cold creeps into you and you shiver and shake and then you feel nothing. Your blood is ice. 'Jerrah,' I say. I don't know what else is said but it's not much. I go back to my room and close the door. Someone's put flowers next to my bed. The rain has become a waterfall so loud I can't even hear myself think. I want someone or something and I suppose it's Mammy or Paddy or Stella Maria. Whoever it is, I can't have them.

47

A day has passed. In bed, mostly asleep, because I can't stand to be awake. When I'm awake the thought that troubles me is this. What is good? What is bad? And I have no answer.

Was it bad to want to crack America? Was it bad to turn my back on Stella Maria? Was it bad to want Rita Mae dead? Is Tom bad for watching it all unravel and saying nothing? What's honest? I just can't figure it out. We came here with honest intentions, all three of us, and what have they become? What have we become? Stella Maria says killers. Can you kill without an honest intention?

I hear Tom's voice in my head asking me to repeat such a fine line for the camera. I see his scheming face and I hate it for letting Jerrah into my life. My father is between me and Mammy and no one else. Tom knows that. He know it's no place he should go trampling and he's trampling with Jerrah. Well he can sod off. Stella Maria is right. He should sod right off. He's taking liberties now. But wasn't sending him to find Barney Noble just a roll of the dice? Didn't I say that? Didn't

Mammy tell me that? Roll those dice and see what comes up. That's what she said.

Sometime yesterday Betty came in with food. There was meat and so on, so I ate a bit. She said, 'You don't have to see your father, Honey.'

I said, 'I think I do, Betty. I think Mammy must want me to.' Then I put the pillow back over my head and made myself go back to sleep.

And this morning I woke up early, the sun was rising, the light was gorgeous on the hills and what came to me was this. You can drown in a sea of uncertainty or you can swim towards the shore called hope which is a thought I know I will one day put to music.

People are leaving my life in droves but Mammy's sending me a father to take their place. Paddy has turned his back on me, but Josie's pointing me in the direction of a man who never will.

I'm going to have a shower, put on make-up, brush my auburn hair till it shines like a flame down my back, then I'm going to lay my cards on the table because I've got nothing to lose. Abe has a sweet and loving nature which he expresses through his devotion to plant life and only a fool would let him slip through her fingers. If I get slung into jail without telling him how things are, he'll never know he was the man for me and I'd regret it to my dying day.

It's scary though. Almost as scary as meeting a man who says he's my father though he never knew for sure I existed. That's what Tom told me before Betty shut him up and just as well. I'd rather hear about him from his own mouth. No point in us sitting there at our very first meeting with me going, 'I know.'

Betty says, 'Well don't you look a treat?' when I meet her on the porch. 'How's your poor old head?''

'OK,' I say. I look about for Stella Maria who's made herself scarce since I came back from the hospital. 'Know where the gardener is?'

Betty looks startled. 'Well let me think. Is he in today? Why of course he is. Ah believe Ah saw him only minutes ago. Did Ah see him? Yes Ah did. Ah asked him to look at the fungus in the . . .' Then I see his back, disappearing into the jungle and I hurry to catch him quickly, in case her confusion is caused by the thought that I'm about to have it off with him in the shrubbery.

He doesn't hear me coming he's so involved with whatever he's found at the foot of the skinny tree he's prodding. 'Fungus?' I say. He gets to his feet and says it looks that way.

'Nothin' worryin',' he says. There's sweat on his forehead and the back of his shirt is damp. I tell him I'm not worried about it. He says, no Ma'am. His eyes are everywhere but on me. I don't know how to get from fungus to passion. The silence is getting too long for comfort when his southern manners rescue us. 'You better?'

I tell him I'm fine. Just have this weirdo ringing in my ears. 'Like rain,' I say. 'It's hysterical when it does rain.' That stumps him. I ask him if he likes rain.

'Some rain,' he says. I ask him where he learnt about plants. 'From Miz Beecher,' he says. He's moving on, from one tree to another, sniffing, which must be a gardener's trick for fungus hunting, and I say I don't know anything about gardening. He says, 'Just ask Stella Maria.' I say she doesn't know much either. He says, 'She knows plenty.' And I think well this is completely the wrong way to seduce anyone. A man of few words is probably best with none at all.

I stand next to him in silence for as long as I can manage, then when he turns to move to the next mouldy old tree, I take a step towards him. 'I want to tell you something,' I say. 'Ask you something, if you don't mind.' I hope my eyes are sparkling with the interest I have in him. I hope something about my body is doing the job not being done by the words coming out of it. This isn't how it usually is. Paddy just tilted my chin and kissed me because he'd wanted to for so long.

311

Abraham's studying his feet as if he knows what's coming, but his shyness tells me nothing. I don't know if shyness comes with revulsion, or before it or instead of it. It's humid in this garden. 'I wanted to ask you this.' Before he can leap away, I put my hand around his neck, I pull his head to mine and kiss him as gently but as meaningfully as it is possible to kiss anyone not expecting to be kissed. Not expecting it. And not wanting it even a bit.

He doesn't seem sure of the manners for stopping. He keeps his lips buttoned and then he pulls back and he squeaks, all quavery and frightened, 'Betty and me . . .'

'You and Betty what?' I say. His face is the colour of my hair, burnished red.

'We're . . .' He just can't think of another word and doesn't need to. Oh God. It's the worst. Him and Betty.

'Sorry,' I say. 'Sorry. I made a mistake.' I try to walk away as if that's all it was but soon I have to run because of the humiliation which would be funny if it wasn't so shocking. I slow down when I see Betty and Stella Maria heaving painting gear onto the porch but I don't speak to them. 'You OK there?' Betty asks as I pass her.

In my room, I put on a tape, any tape and play it as loud as I can so I can hear and think nothing, except the sound of someone who turns out to be Dolly on the subject of love being like a butterfly to the accompaniment of heavily falling rain. He's Betty's boyfriend. Oh God, oh God, oh God. Betty must have come to a special arrangement with Jesus about her sex life. Oh God. I ignore the tapping at the door. Betty's asking if she can come in and I'm pretending to be dead. Stella Maria's pushing open the door but I'm lying face down in the pillow not moving so she panics.

'Shit. Betteee,' she yells just like before, thinking I suppose that this time I'm dead. I sit up.

'What is it? What is it?' Betty says.

'Nothing,' I say. 'Nothing.' But I can't stand it. I have to say. I tell her I'm sorry. I didn't know about her and Abraham. I kissed him. Betty's mouth has fallen open. She says she doesn't know what I mean. There's nothing to know about her and Abraham. Nothing that could possibly be my business. I say I know it's not my business. It was an accident.

'An accidental kiss?' Stella Maria says.

'Song,' I go. Which hardens Betty towards me, I see it.

'Speaking of accidents,' she says, and I have never heard her voice sound so cold or distant. 'As you are feeling so much stronger, could you please apply your mind to the small matter of Rita's death as we have next to no time to reach the truth.' They leave. They leave me lying in a pool of self-disgust. I think I would now like to be dead.

Papa will you come and take me home with you
Take me from the valley to the mountains where the sky is blue
Take me from the misery and take me from the pain
Papa will you come and stop the rain.
Papa will you come and take me home with you

48

The porch door slams and I know from the silence the house is empty. An empty house when love has been withdrawn is the saddest sound there is. I wander through it, hearing my loneliness, hearing the goat running at the wall and butting it and I'm looking for some kind of sign that everything's going to be alright. Some shaft of light, some breath of wind, some anything. But this is Betty's house. Everything in it is Betty's and it speaks to Betty not to me. The only comfort I've had in it has been her kindness which I'll never know again.

I open the door to Stella Maria's room in the hope of finding something familiar to comfort me and blow me. It's a mess like you would not believe. Piles and piles of scrunched up sheets of paper all over the floor and the bed, covered in her funny square writing. Lined yellow paper torn from a pad.

Mammy's saying, 'Go in, go in.' So I do. I close the door, tiptoe across to the bed and see at once what she's been doing. She's been figuring how to describe the day of the death. All these versions are laid out about the room so she can decide which works best. She doesn't like any of them by the look of it.

I sit on the floor and smooth them, one by one. If she finds me here I'm dead, definitely dead. But I'm as good as anyway, is how I see it. I flip through the pages, snatching images and there's no escaping it. My hands grow clammy and my mouth goes all dry. What I did was bad. The pit of my stomach will not allow anything about it to be good.

All her versions start with the dentist. She came with me to the dentist like she always did because she never trusted me to go on my own. The dentist is how I remember it. I'd said to Rita Mae, 'Tuesday mornings she comes with me to the dentist.'

It was a Tuesday morning. After the dentist I had charm school. We'd pretty well finished in the studio and I was mostly tied up with the promotions people who could take or leave Rita Mae. She said charm school sucked but she needed it far more than I did, given her bland past. That's what they teach you to handle. Media enquiries into a past you'd rather not reveal.

'Honey's teeth v. good. Dentist happy. Headgear every night. No cheating. Left dentist. Took cab to Starlight and dropped H off.' Starlight was the charm school. 'Took cab on to office. Expected to find Tom there but door still locked. Presumed Tom was at Moonshine.'

But he wasn't. I knew he wasn't. Rita Mae had said all she needed was an hour alone with him. I told her the dentist took an hour. I knew Tom was Stella Maria's, but I set him up for Rita Mae because I needed Rita Mae more than I needed Stella Maria at that time.

You can make a bad thing sound good if your life depends on it. I told myself it was Stella Maria's own fault if she hadn't made a move while she had the chance, that it was Tom's choice and not mine. If it was meant to be, it was meant to be. I knew Rita Mae wanted Stella Maria to discover them. She wanted to break Stella Maria's heart because she wanted Stella Maria to run back to England and leave half the field clear for her and so far all her schemes had failed.

In the cab I said to Stella Maria, 'Wonder where Rita Mae is?' Stella Maria hoped she was dead. It didn't cross my mind to warn her. Hadn't Mammy sent me dental appointments on a Tuesday?

Stella Maria dropped me off and I waved to her. We were both smiling because she'd forgiven me for the Moonshine meeting and she'd forgiven me for sleeping with Tom which she understood was an accident of fate. But ten minutes into my lesson on The Awkward Question, I saw the pain ahead of her. It hit me full blast in the conscience.

I said to Angel Bonzo, whatever her name was, I had to go, sorry, and I grabbed my things and headed for the door, before she could say well this wasn't very professional. I hit the road running, trying to dial Stella Maria on my phone and hail a cab at the same time. I was saying, 'Pick up, pick up,' but she wouldn't. The number rang and rang. I dialled the office to warn Tom that Stella Maria was on her way but they'd taken the phone off the hook and his mobile was switched off. I ran for all I was worth the three blocks to save my friend. And I arrived too late.

Stella Maria's account keeps stopping here. She can't get past the locked office door. I can feel her rearing away from it. A wide-jawed monster breathing fire. She doesn't want to look at it and I don't blame her. 'Let myself in. Saw the bed.'

There were two bodies in it. One Rita's. Wearing nothing. Other was Tom's, wearing nothing. Rita was grinning up at her, expecting her, thrilled with herself. Tom was clutching clothes to himself, not believing what was happening, shouting at Rita to cover herself up, didn't she have any shame? Which of course she didn't.

I'm amazed, I now realise, he didn't grab his camera. Stella Maria took it all in. Horrible, evil, cruel Rita pretending to be embarrassed. Stupid, weak Tom wondering how come he was in this position.

Rita Mae had stretched long and hard although she was naked and she'd smiled up at Stella Maria whose world had just collapsed on to those stinky old sheets. 'Whoops,' she said. 'Bad timing!' Stella had whacked her across the face and Rita had screamed. Then Stella Maria had run.

I keep smoothing the bits of paper but I'm not reading. I'm seeing it like it's happening here and now. I got there just in time to see Stella Maria tearing down the street and around the corner, and I knew at once what had happened and took off after her.

She had no idea of the part I'd played but still, she didn't want to be caught. She thought she could run all the way back to Cockfosters and maybe she'd have made it to Virginia but this cute man in the street stopped her, seeing I was trying to catch her, seeing she was running full pelt and stumbling and in danger of crashing headlong into a wall. A seriously cute guy in a stetson. He said, 'Whoa there! Have you stolen somethin' or does she jest wanna kill you?' How was that for a remark from nowhere?

Stella Maria said, 'Get off, get off.' She struggled with the guy who cottoned on to the idea that this wasn't a fun run and let her go. But he'd slowed her up and soon I was able to grab at her by the shirt with the threads that ended up on the brick. She was wriggling and kicking at me and she was letting me have it for all she was worth. She was in loud, ugly tears of agony which drenched my heart. So then we were both sobbing. She was punching and kicking and sobbing, so finally I slapped her face as hard as I could and she slapped me back as hard as she could.

Maybe we'd have killed each other if she hadn't suddenly lost all her fight and dropped to the gutter, bawling her eyes out, beating her head with her fists. And maybe I'd have had to leave her there if Tom hadn't come hurtling along in his truck. I dived in front of him and he stood on his brakes. 'You nearly killed me,' I said but he wasn't interested in me.

He picked Stella Maria up from the gutter, like she was this accident victim and he carried her to the truck and placed her gently on the seat next to him. He just about waited while I got in next to her then he drove us home like he was driving an ambulance with a dying person in it. He had one arm around her, to protect her, but she was rigid, like a corpse, staring straight ahead, white as a ghost. Even now I think it was so fucking romantic.

He picked her from the gutter, a sad and sorry sight,
He told her how he loved her, and could he hold her tight?
He'd loved her from the first day that he'd seen her by the
*   stream*
And now his heart was breaking and aching for the dream
But she said the dream was gone
Wherever bad dreams go
And although she loved him truly she didn't want to know
*   him anymore.*

Never sang that to anyone. Probably never will. There's no poetry in Stella Maria's account. None at all. Just hard little facts.

Christ. The door. I'm under the bed so fast and my heart's pumping so fast I expect blood to gush from my mouth. No one comes so I crawl out again and unscrunch more papers, looking for one which tells me what I have only been guessing. And here it is.

'Couldn't face room. Ran up back stairs to roof. Tom followed. I told him to get away. I said go back to Rita. He said never. He never wanted to see her again. He loved me.' I'm scrabbling through these bits of paper. I hear the gate swing closed. I'm reading as fast as I can. I should get out while I can. Tom took her hand. He said please would she forgive him. 'I'm a shallow man, Stella Maria. You know I am.'

She said, 'She wants me out of the picture, doesn't she?'

'And Honey,' he said

And that's when I make a dash for my room where I get under the covers so I can be alone with all I need to think. The feeling I'm recalling is like gravel in my blood, the feeling that I'd sacrificed my oldest friend, my next of kin, for a scheming rat of a girl who cared only about her own glory. Hiding on that roof behind the chimney stack where no one could see me, it had all but overwhelmed me.

49

Stella Maria opens my door without knocking and says, 'You've got to come to the study now.' And I know I do. Or where else will I go ever again?

She doesn't follow me in but I say to Betty, I want her with me and Betty says, 'OK by you Stella Maria?' Stella Maria doesn't know whether it is or not. She looks at me hard before giving me the benefit of the doubt.

I sit in the floral chair, Stella Maria lounges by the door, not sitting. I say, 'Betty, I am really, really sorry.'

She says, 'Honey, don't be. Ah should have said. Abraham's an attractive man and Ah know you are lookin' for love.' Which makes me feel like a sad fuck but I'm grateful anyway. I say I also want to apologise to Stella Maria, who's been such a friend to me even though she's been pretty mean of late.

'Well now,' says Betty sounding both surprised and relieved.

Stella Maria asks, 'Why?'

And I can't tell her. I can't bring myself to admit what I did when she already has such a low opinion of me, even though I am full of bitter remorse. Betty's offering us tea but I say no and Stella Maria says no, so Betty says she can do without as well which is sensible when I'm struggling. I say I want to be honest with myself now but it's not easy because what I wish I'd felt and done is so messed up with what I actually felt and did.

I say, 'Betty, Rita Mae was this parcel bomb fate sent us through the post, only we never knew that's what she was because when we shook her she made a sound like music from heaven.' I can't look at Stella Maria. 'I don't think I'm weak,' I say. 'I don't believe me being weak was the problem because it took every bit of my strength to survive her. It just felt to me at the time that I didn't have a choice.'

Stella Maria still doesn't utter a peep. Nor does Betty. Like they're going to let me get through this on my own, whatever it is. 'I just wanted my music to work so bad and I told myself anyone who played like that had to have beauty in her somewhere. But she didn't. That's what it boiled down to.' I sneak a look across the room where Stella Maria's standing still as a rock. The blood has left her lips. She's so white she could pass for a snowman. 'It was really bad of me. I know it.'

My clothes are feeling prickly on my body. I can't look at either of them.

'Did you think about the effect this was having on Stella Maria?' Betty asks.

'No,' I say and I know how sick this must make Stella Maria. 'I thought we'd just drifted apart. I thought we'd come to Nashville which was like home to me and I fitted in but Stella Maria didn't.'

Betty asks did I know that Rita was in bed with Tom the morning she died. I say, 'Yes.' A loud sigh escapes Stella Maria. 'She asked me to help her set it up but I wouldn't. I just told her Tuesday morning would work for her. I'm really really sorry, Stella Maria.'

Betty sighs now. Her eyes are sad. She has nothing to say.

'I thought if I let Rita Mae get rid of Stella Maria, I could head her off before she got to me. And that's what happened.'

Stella Maria says, 'How sorry are you?'

'More sorry than I can tell you.'

'Then quit the film,' she says.

But why? To punish me? To punish Tom. I say, 'I would Stella Maria if it made any sense but it doesn't. The best thing we can do is finish what we set out to do. To make all this garbage worthwhile.'

Her face is pinched and unhappy and I want to please her but not this way. I just can't. I won't. And I want this conversation to end right now but Betty's not having it.

'Honey,' she says. 'You're makin' great headway. Really great headway. Acceptin' responsibility and seekin' reconciliation. It is a big, big step. But you two are talkin' in circles and what would help here is if we got down to some specifics. Like, were you at any time on the roof with Stella Maria the mornin' Rita Mae died?'

And I think well I don't know how much truth they can handle here. 'Tom and Stella Maria had a lot to say to each other and I had a lot of thinking to do. I was digusted with Rita Mae and I was disgusted with myself. I wanted her off the gig.'

'But were you on the roof?' says Betty.

I'm remembering. 'Stella Maria and Tom got in the lift together. I stayed in the lobby talking to Archie.' Which is true. Archie was in a worse state than I was, so upset he didn't even notice Stella Maria's condition. All he wanted to know was whether she was headed for the roof because if she was, she was going to find her pot plants smashed into tiny pieces. He'd been arsing about with the workmen, chucking a baseball about, he'd missed and a pot was smashed. Then the guys had set to work on all the other pots. Archie was well and truly over the idea of the roof as a horticultural haven.

'Oh Lordie,' he said. 'What am Ah goin' to tell her?'

'When I left Archie I went to the apartment,' I tell Betty. Which isn't true. I went to the roof.

'Verra good,' she says. 'Now Stella Maria why don't you explain to Honey what went on up there? Tell the truth here now.' And I'm relieved to hear Betty doesn't think Stella Maria is always the truth teller.

The picture Stella Maria paints is so clear, I see it like I'm sitting right on the edge there, looking down the street and back to where she and Tom are fighting by the fire stairs. The pots are smashed, her plants are all bent and broken and the workmen are still chucking their stupid ball all over the place, like they're putting the final nail in the coffin that was her dream.

She isn't angry. Who wants a dream that's a coffin? She just picked up the ball and chucked it over the roof, not out on to the street where Rita Mae was about to meet her doom, but over the back to where the dustbins were. The guys went, 'Lady, you are nuts!'

They looked like they were going to make something of it but Tom said, 'Get out of here. Go on. Piss off. You've done enough damage.' As if they'd made him sleep with Rita Mae. And he must've looked pretty fierce because they went. Tom tried to hold Stella Maria, like she was going to want any arms about her with Rita Mae still on them.

She shook him off, she wanted nothing more to do with him. Nothing more to do with me. Nothing more to do with Nashville. She was going home. Tom begged her. He said please would she stay. We'd come here together and we were going to make it together. Rita Mae meant nothing to him. Went down like a glass of arsenic. Stella Maria said she believed him. No one meant anything to him. Not Honey, not her. She was going to have it out with me and she knew I'd see it her way. She told him we'd be going home together.

I know she said that. I heard her. He was pleading for his

life. 'Please, Stella Maria, please. I love you. You have to trust me. I love you.' But why would she trust him when he'd had months to tell her he'd loved her and hadn't?

She couldn't stand a minute more in his company. She pushed him away and left him staring after her. Feeble gobshite that he is. That was the last she saw of him for hours. Except from where she was sitting in the stairwell, avoiding me and him, she could hear someone padding about among the broken pots and she thought it was him so she stayed very still in case he came to find her.

She heard the scream. Not Rita Mae's but the scream of the woman walking behind her who was splattered with bits of Rita Mae's head. 'I thought it was nothing. People scream for anything. I just thought, "That's it, I'm going," and I went to the apartment to pack.'

'That sound right to you?' Betty says and I say it does. That sounds like the truth.

50

It's fine up here. I'm way, way up. Through the trees I can look down and see the house but I try not to because I hate heights and even though I know I can't fall, my body feels like it wants to. I'm just lying on my back looking up to where the mountain meets the sky and I'm watching the dark clouds gathering, preparing for a storm. I want it all to seep into my heart and into my skin and into my soul so it will be with me for ever. I'll be going to jail. Don't see how I won't.

People are yelling for me. First Betty. Then Stella Maria. Then Abraham. And a long time later, Tom. I saw his truck chugging up the track followed by a big white car. I know my father's waiting but I can't stand to see him or anyone.

I said to Betty could I go for a walk to clear my head and she said sure. She said she understood it must need clearing. She wanted me to know how pleased she was with me for confronting such a difficult truth. She doesn't get how hopeless it is. How can it help anyone, now Stella Maria has no alibi?

I reckon Stella Maria must think Tom threw the brick and

she must think I'm protecting him. She'll have figured, he chucks the brick, we get the blame, he gets a movie way beyond the possibilities of Kurt and Courtney. Orphan girl on brink of making it in Nashville kills poor banjo picker in a tragic love triangle, finds her long lost father and dies in jail.

Up here, no one killed anyone, I had nothing to do with betrayal or pushing my luck so far I killed someone and there's no punishment coming my way. If I had a father, he died before I knew him but he loved me with all his might. There's a boy who loves me more than life itself whose name isn't Abraham. Up here, I can be at peace forever and always and I don't have to pretend anything to anyone. It's bloody dark though. To keep my spirits up, I've written a song for Mammy.

Do you hear me Mama, do you hear me loud and clear?
Put your arms about me Mama, I'm so tired and full of fear.
Walk higher up the mountain, in the soft sweet air,
My poor heart is achin' but I know I'll find you there.
Do you hear me Mama, do you hear me loud and clear?

The melody is high and piercing, a fiddle accompanying someone in deepest sorrow. But I've been thinking that maybe, when I'm twenty-one, I'll be too old to ask for guidance. Maybe even the best mothers want a break from their children endlessly asking. I say to Mammy, 'I'll leave you in peace when I'm twenty-one.' But I'm not twenty-one yet. 'Do you want me to see my father?' I ask. And, without hesitating, she takes the rain out of my head. She doesn't leave even the faintest pitter patter. I hear nothing apart from the birds singing good night to each other and the leaves rustling in the early evening air.

I hum the new song as loud as I can to make my skull vibrate, in case the noise is just waiting to be disturbed but it's not. I sing louder and louder, louder and louder and I'm singing my heart out when Stella Maria, right next to my head, says 'Get your arse down the hill. Your father's here and he hasn't got all night.' She pulls me to my feet and gives me a shove in the direction of the house. Taking charge. Sounding normal. 'Stupid git, buggering off,' she says.

'Is Betty cross?' I say.

'No,' says Stella Maria.

'What's he like?' We're running together along the little lane.

'Alright,' she says. 'Big hooter.'

'Will I like him?'

'How the fuck would I know?'

We're talking about everyday matters, almost everyday matters, as if the last thing I said to her wasn't 'I sacrificed your happiness for my own selfish ends'. I stop before we get to the gate. 'Stella Maria,' I say.

She turns and I look for signs of friendship in her gaze but find none. Her eyes are looking for trouble.

'Will you forgive me for what I did?'

'Why should I?' she says.

'Because I'm begging you to. You don't know how much I regret it.'

'I don't know,' she says. She gives me a shove through the gate towards the house and now I'm filled with panic.

I don't even know his name. 'What's his name?' I say to Stella Maria.

'Daddy,' she says. It's a notion so powerful I nearly gag on it. I try to grab it, pin it down, push and pull it into some kind of shape I can handle, but I find I'm feeling nothing and have no thoughts about anything. I stare up at the porch where three people are in a huddle.

Stella Maria says, 'He's not staying long. He's rented a car to take him home.' She heads along the path. But I'm stuck. Can't move. Can't move into the bit of my life which will be so different from the bit I've just left when I only had a mother.

I brush myself down. There are twigs in my hair. I remember to breathe. Then I follow Stella Maria to the porch where everyone is waiting, where Tom has his camera up to his shoulder. That's what I see. I know Betty's there. I know there's a man standing behind Betty, towering over her, looking at me without rancour, ready to move towards me. But all my attention goes to Tom with his camera and I'm full of fury.

'Put the camera down,' I say. 'I don't want this in the film.'

He says, 'Honey, how can I leave it out?'

'By not putting it in,' I say. 'This isn't *Surprise Surprise*. It's private.'

'Take the camera inside, Mr Sinclayuh,' Betty says.

Tom looks as if he might burst into tears. 'No,' he says. 'No, please, Honey. You know how important this is.' He keeps the camera rolling. He ignores Betty. 'Please trust me, Honey. It's a really huge moment.' And I'm thinking who for? Who for?

I'm about to ask him when my father reminds me. He steps forward and says like he's my new dentist, 'Honey, I'm Bill Whitecross.' He shakes my hand, studying me like I have an interesting gum disease. 'Tall and slender, just like your mother. I'm very pleased to meet you.'

I say, 'Hello.' He's as at ease as could be. Probably from so many years of conducting an orchestra in front of an audience. Part of me is hurt that he hasn't immediately crushed me in the hug of twenty empty years but I think it's just as well. I probably stink.

He doesn't take a scrap of notice of Tom but looks to Betty who says would anyone like something to drink. Bill Whitecross says he's drunk plenty already and what he'd really like, if I didn't mind and she didn't mind and nobody minded, would be if he and I could have a little while alone together. We had many things to say to each other and not all that much time left.

'Sorry,' I say. I can't take my eyes off him. There's a look of me in his face, no getting away from that, but what it is I couldn't tell you. He's a man about Merv's age, well off for sure and with a manner that would definitely have worked on Mam. He smiles at me with such warmth and friendliness I can only smile back and my heart softens for him.

I see myself moving into his rambling white house on the prairie and him buying me clothes, introducing me to his friends and to the family he once had but has had to leave as he only ever had one love who was my mother. I hear him saying that to have found me is like a gift from God he never expected in his declining years. I'm dead relieved he's not some fat-bellied dead beat.

Betty says, 'Use my study.'

He takes my elbow. Tom follows us to the door but Bill Whitecross says, 'Not for this bit, Tom,' and closes it in his face. He sits at Betty's desk. I take the chair. 'Did you have a pleasant journey?' I enquire.

He laughs. He has an excellent laugh. Deep and low. He says Tom's a fine young man but his truck is not a fine young truck so he transferred to a rented car once they hit Nashville and that will take him home. When he laughs, his eyes disappear into many folds of brown skin. His nose isn't that big but it is hooked. His face is an outdoor face, not a musician's face. It's quite close to mine, leaning forward, expecting me to speak.

'Thank you for all the books. Mammy loved them. I love them too. I read them all the time.'

He says they were his pleasure. He knew what a big country fan she was. 'Not my taste, I have to admit, but hers. And yours, I understand.'

I say country music is my passion. He says and why not. Then he says what a shock this must be for me and I say yes and what a shock for him and he says yes and then he says he'd like to tell me a little bit about himself. I say I'd like that.

329

He says, 'You sound just like your mother. Same pretty lilt exactly.' I say really? I wanted to say something cleverer but could only think of really.

He's been married three times. Once before Mammy, twice since. He wanted to marry Mammy but she wouldn't agree. I say why? He says why does a woman do anything and I say because their mother tells them and he laughs but he doesn't have a clue what I'm talking about. After her cruel rejection, he was unlucky again but now he believes he's found the right woman for whom he thanks the Good Lord every day, and I see a dumpy little apple-cheeked country woman like the woman at the Post Office.

'She's a lovely young lady, no more than five or six years older than you,' he says. They're expecting their first baby any day, which means he'll then have seven children and that is a great many children to keep clothed, fed, educated and in the luxury goods they seem to need.

I tell him, well, he's saving money on me. He says he wasn't actually including me but yes I have been a saving and he laughs again. I laugh too but my heart is sinking. I've wanted a father for just three minutes, and already he's dashing my hopes. He says just as well he gave up music or they'd be poor as church mice. He's made his money from farm machinery and he thanks the Good Lord for that as well.

'Any questions so far?' he says. I tell him only fifty billion and he says they'll have to wait as he has to get back to Kentucky but there's something he wants to say to me that can't wait. It's the reason he hot-tailed it to my door the minute Tom informed him of my existence and of the predicament I'm in. Which he deeply regrets.

'You mean the court case,' I say. He nods. He's looking solemn and wise and kind and I know what's coming and I feel this weight fall from me and slide across to him where it just vanishes. I smile because I can't help myself. He's going to say leave it all to him. He'll talk to people who know people and he'll stop the court case before we even have any crappy old hearing. It's the least a father can do for a daughter who's asked nothing of him for twenty years.

'Politics are what interest me these days. I don't suppose they interest to you.' I begin to tell him I rate them higher than anything and intend to devote my life to them the minute I've cracked America.

'No.' I say.

He says, that's smart. He can see how smart I am. He knows I'll understand the importance of what he's about to say. He's running for Mayor. It's a difficult campaign. He can't afford any scandal.

Out the window, Mammy sends a bolt of lightning into the jungle. There's an almighty crash of thunder. Bill Whitecross is speaking but I can't hear him above the rain that's plummeting on to the roof and gusting across the porch but no longer in my head. He's just not in a position to have any scandal in his life right now and this case has attracted a huge amount of media attention. He is all for media attention. Just not this sort.

'It's not as if you've ever depended on me. You said so yourself. Tom says you're well provided for. Your mother chose not to tell me of your existence and my feeling is we should respect her wishes and leave things exactly as they are. Were.'

He's on his feet and preparing to leave. He puts his hand out to shake mine. 'I'm very pleased to have made your acquaintance. I know you'll understand why this must be the beginning and end of it. I was very fond of your mother. May she rest in peace.'

'No,' I say. 'No. She's not in peace.' This startles him. There's another loud clap of thunder. 'She's not at peace. She hates you. She always hated you and now I know why she hated you.' I'm smiling at him. He opens the door. Betty, Tom and Stella Maria are all outside. The camera's rolling. They're all smiling too.

Bill Whitecross shakes his head. 'Thanks for your hospitality.' And he runs. I'm not crying. My body is too dry to cry. All the fluid has dried to nothing, even though all that's happened is I've lost a father I never even found.

'You shit,' Stella Maria spits at him as he passes. She understands exactly what's gone on. Bill Whitecross runs. Down the gravel path, running, running, running to escape from me. But maybe because it's raining. Maybe he'll turn, change his mind, think how he loved my mother truly and so will come to love me. He'll say his heart could never be so hard.

But then I hear the sound of his car engine, the sound of a man Stella Maria will forever call coward of the county telling me once an orphan, always an orphan. And now I cry. I cry because the scars of my heart have ripped apart and will never ever recover.

51

Betty and Tom are yelling at each other. Not like Stella Maria and I yell but trying to stay polite and speaking very fast, with Tom, every now and then, banging his hand on the porch rail. He started it, by filming me in my state of shock. Betty said how dare he! How dare he take advantage of me!

Stella Maria and I are lying on her bed in the dark, where we can hear them but don't have to look at them and they don't have to see me being a snot-soaked wreck. Which I'm trying not to be. I never even liked the stupid man. I can't stop shaking. It must be rage. I'm angry with Bill Whitecross, but I'm so angry with Tom I could smash his thieving camera into a million tiny pieces. That camera stole my life.

They're not arguing about me anymore, anyway. They're on about the gambling, not for money but with people's lives. Betty has said Tom has no conscience. Tom's saying is she stupid? The whole of life is a gamble. Us coming to America. Her taking us in. Bill Whitecross coming to meet his long lost daughter. He's trying to say him coming here was no different from him buying a raffle ticket. But the difference between him buying a raffle ticket and finding me is this. When he chucks the ticket in the rubbish, no one gets hurt.

'And what would his gamble have been?' Stella Maria pipes up from the bed next to me.

Tom says, 'If you're talking to me now Stella Maria, I'd appreciate being able to see you.' His voice has softened. He says he doesn't love her but listen to his voice. He loves her. I look at her face to see if she's noticed but in the half light from the porch all I see is she's as angry as me.

She says, 'What risk was the man taking? He was only seeing his daughter for the first time.'

'She mightn't have agreed to his terms,' he says.

And Betty's on him in a flash. 'You brought him here knowin' he was going to reject her and knowin' the pain that would cause?' She can't believe anyone calling himself a human being could do anything so low. Tom has nowhere to go with it. He has to admit it's the truth. But what could he do? Bill Whitecross had agreed I was his daughter before he knew I was the girl in the English murder trial.

'There he was, in the middle of his life, running for Mayor, and suddenly I'm on his doorstep and about to upset the applecart,' Tom's saying. 'He needed some assurances.' Stella Maria says well why didn't he offer to come back for me once he was Mayor? And there was no answer except the man's as big a shite as all the other shites in my mother's life. 'Come out, Stella Maria. Come out so I can see you,' Tom calls.

She thinks about it for a minute, then she gets up and I follow her. Betty's sitting on her little table, her pipe unlit in her hand, which says to me she's tense, and Tom's standing at the bottom of the porch steps. His eyes have sunk into pale mauve pools above his cheekbones. He looks shrunk in body and his spirit seems shrunk. Yesterday I would have been sorry for him.

He slides his camera off his shoulder and places it on the

ground as we appear. He walks right up to Stella Maria and says, 'Please can we talk?'

She says 'You broke your word. You promised you'd stop filming. I begged you and you promised.'

'You weren't yourself,' he says.

'A girl had died. She'd died and you'd filmed her death like you'd written the script.'

'I didn't make it happen, Stella Maria. If that's what you're suggesting. I'm a film-maker, not a murderer.' His voice is shaking but he's keeping cool.

'You made everything happen,' says Stella Maria.

'You pursued me, Stella Maria. You sold me the story. You knew the terms. Whatever happened – that was the agreement. They were your very own words.' And they were.

'You draw the line somewhere,' she flashes back. 'Unless you're a psychopath.'

Tom gasps, like she's punched him in the stomach. 'I said I'd stop if Honey asked me to, and she hasn't.'

This is big news to me. 'Did he?' I ask. Stella Maria nods. 'Then why didn't you say?'

'Honey,' she says, 'I've been saying it for three weeks. I asked you over and over again.' I can't argue with her.

'I want my life back,' I say to Tom. 'You turned it into something it should never have been.'

He drops to the porch steps. 'I didn't,' he said. 'You chose to come with me and what's happened is the consequence of your choice. I didn't turn anything into anything.'

I remind him. 'You slept with me, you slept with Rita Mae, you let Rita Mae . . . you know what you did . . . Now we're going to jail and you can't say it's not your fault.'

He and Stella Maria exchange a look so fast I'd have missed it if I'd blinked. 'I'm not,' she says.

'You might,' I say.

'She won't,' Tom says. 'Tell her Stella Maria. If you don't, I will.'

'Tell me what?'

'We know who threw the brick,' Tom says. I have to steady myself on the porch rail. His mouth is open, with the name on his lips but Stella Maria beats him to it.

'Jed,' she says. 'We saw him.'

Tom closes his mouth real tight. And Betty goes, 'Holy shit. You kids don't have any ideah at all the size of the trouble you're in.' And I'm seeing her point because what in Jesus's name are they playing at? I can't even stand to look at them. Nor can Betty. I light a fag, she lights her pipe and we sit on the porch steps looking out into the garden while Stella Maria explains her very shaky case.

She says she didn't go into the stairwell to sulk. She was going to, but she didn't. Tom had stormed off and she was storming off when the guys came back on to the roof without their ball which was lost. To rile her, they said, 'We don't need a ball. We gotta brick.' And they picked up a brick from one of Stella Maria's pot stands and started to throw it about, going catch, catch, stupid faggot, catch.

Then Jed said catch and chucked it so hard the guy doing the catching let it go sailing over his head. And Tom, who was on the fire stairs filming Rita Mae waving up at him, also caught in the frame the brick dropping over the roof's edge and on to her head.

Stella Maria heard the scream. So did Jed Wilcox, Henry Linklater and Marty Dodge who took one look and scarpered. Stella Maria stayed where she was, not knowing who'd screamed, but sick to her stomach that anyone had had reason to. She crept into the stairwell and stayed there. Not sulking. Hiding. Tom was down the stairs and out of sight, thinking he could revive poor Rita Mae, may she rest in peace, but he couldn't. She was dead.

'Why didn't you tell me?' I say to Stella Maria even though I know the story's a lie. 'Why've you put us all through this misery when you didn't have to?'

'To make you see sense. To make you see what was happening. What a mistake we'd made.'

'What mistake?' I say.

'Trusting him', she says nodding at Tom. 'It wasn't about you making it as a singer. It was about you making it, whatever happened. A death had happened and it was obscene. You see that now, don't you?'

And I'm thinking I do but what else am I seeing? Stella Maria making up a pack of lies to save whose skin. Tom's? Does she think she's saving Tom's?

'And why didn't you say anything?' I say to Tom, who knows his skin doesn't need saving. All he does is shrug. He leans back against the porch rail, closes his eyes and shrugs.

Stella Maria says, 'I thought you'd make him stop the film if I was charged with murder. But you told the flipping lie instead and I couldn't get you to untell it.' My hand is shaking so much I have to put my smoke out. I think I'm going to puke from exhaustion. 'It's over now, anyway,' Stella Maria says.

'Well you've got that wrong,' Betty says. 'You have a hearin' day after tomorrow. And you got three witnesses all sayin' they saw you on the roof near the brick and with a motive.'

Tom has picked up his camera and is filming. Must be habit. I say, 'Put the camera down Tom and piss off. I can't stand the sight of you.' He puts the camera down. No fight left in him either.

He says, 'One thing you need to know, Honey. And I really want you to think about it. No film, no record deal.'

Betty says, 'You still not asked yourself when the price of success is too high, Mr Sinclayuh?' He doesn't answer. She says, 'Kindly go away. You are upsetting mah plants.'

He speaks only to Stella Maria before he heads back to the truck. 'You sure it was Jed?' he says. She ignores him.

You'll never see anything as eerie as a white goat in the

337

moonlight. I'm watching her through my window and trying to arrange my thoughts before getting into bed. When is the price of success too high? Well, I guess now would be the answer. Everything feels too high to me right now. Look at that goat butting its head against this wall over and over. One day it's going to occur to her there are better things to do with her life and then she'll give up, just like I am.

52

Betty's had us up since the crack of dawn because Harvey's arriving first thing. She's wanting us all neat and tidy and sounding sensible as the last time he saw us, Stella Maria was looking crazy and I was looking unconscious. And now, she says, he's none too pleased to find he's been deliberately misled. I can see it's a bugger for him but it's about to get a whole lot worse.

Speaking for myself, I'm lighter of spirit than I ever hoped to be the day after being rejected by my father. This will be the consequence of deciding to tell the truth come what may. But Betty's on edge and Stella Maria's on edge and it doesn't help that Betty has cooked eggs for breakfast. They are the worst. The very worst. Big dollops of runny yolk mixed up with hard lumps of scrambled stuff. Not even the goat deserves it.

Stella Maria stares at her plate, green-faced and miserable. I say, 'Betty, we're too nervous to eat.' And she says, well that's mighty disappointin' as she'd been hoping to serve us somethin' fillin' when we ate so little yesterday. She's not touching them herself I notice.

We're saved only by the sound of Harvey's car on the gravel as he pulls off the track and into the yard. Abe calls from the porch, 'He's here,' and we all jump up and run various places for no reason, like he's yelled, 'Bomb!' Abe was about the place so early I wouldn't be surprised he didn't stay the night. I can't believe he and Betty had sex. She'd have had so much on her mind. This morning she's done her hair up into a bun. Does that say sex or no sex? I can't read her anymore. Like everyone else, she isn't who I thought she was or doing what I thought she did.

She shows Harvey into the study and then calls us in. He's brought that Morris with him. I could do without Morris, leering before we're in the room.

I say to Stella Maria, 'He'll have a dick like a conker.'

'Like a bean,' she says. 'Baked.' Which might mean she has forgiven me or it might not.

Abe's brought chairs from all over the house so no one has to sit on the floor. 'Good morning, ladies,' Harvey says. Gracious as always, only looking less sympathetic now he thinks we've brought this trouble on ourselves. You take the sympathy out of a gracious man and you get something terrifying. Betty's doing her best to keep things on an even keel, pouring coffee for everyone and being hospitable. They don't know how lucky they are she's not offering them eggs. Morris has a whole pile of files with him which he puts on the floor. He has a tape recorder, same as Betty's, and a big yellow pad so he can take notes. I'm half expecting pictures of nude women to fall from it. I sit between him and Stella Maria, nervous in case there's a scene but not fearful. I have come to terms with my fate.

Harvey's not beating about the bush here. 'As I understand it, you were a witness to the brick being thrown,' he says to Stella Maria. 'But you were not,' he says to me. Stella Maria says this is correct. She says she wants to say how sorry she is for not telling him the truth but she was desperate. She had found herself in a morally desperate situation.

This is Stella Maria as I've always known her, gabby and confident, not the miserable cow she was as recently as yesterday. Harvey is interested in her moral dilemma and also in mine. He wants to know why I lied. I say, 'To give my friend an alibi.'

He says 'So you were giving an alibi to the friend who wasn't telling you she didn't need one as she was trying to force you to appreciate the extent of your moral peril at the hands of Tom Sinclair?'

'Right,' I say. I still don't see peril. I just see mess. I see mess before, around and ahead. What will Merv say? What will Dick say? Jerrah can go fuck himself.

Harvey's talking us over and over the same ground, what went on, why it went on, where it went on and soon I'm sweating because I know what I have to say but can't say it. I'm letting him work on the new story even if it's as big a lie as the old one just to play for time. I want to ask Mammy for help but I've been trying not to. I'm hoping she'll just guess, without me saying anything, that I'm in dire need here. And maybe she does.

Harvey is just asking Stella Maria about the trajectory of the ball she threw when we hear another car crunch on to the gravel and Abe calling, 'More visitors.' Betty excuses herself and I try to see who it is but can't. In the end, we hear Dick before we see him. He's saying, 'Ah know this is uncivilised, arrivin' unannounced, but we had a most alarmin' conversation with young Tom last night and we figured least damage'd be done if we got out here soon as we could.'

Betty's saying, 'Well Ah don't know what could have alarmed you and Ah'm sorry you've driven all the way out here. Stella Maria and Honey are not available this mornin' as they're with their lawyers. But the least Ah can offer you is a drink after your long drive.'

Jerrah says, 'If they're not available now, we'll wait.'

Dick's sayin', 'Ah don't think you've met Angel Merryweather,' and Betty's saying she's pleased to meet her. I'm thinking what's she here for?

Betty says, 'You may be waitin' some time. If you'd like to avail yourselves of the porch, you will find it cooler than hangin' around out here in the yard.'

This isn't a great move because from the porch you can hear everything being said in the study and the other way round, so those of us inside are so totally aware of those who are outside that positively nothing further is going to be cleared up legal wise unless we're all together. Which Harvey pretty quickly figures. We adjourn to the porch with all the chairs and the coffee and so on and everyone greets everyone else. Jerrah says to Harvey, 'Gather there have been some developments here.'

Harvey says, 'Some. We now have two defendants agreeing where they were but an allegation that the brick was thrown by a prosecution witness.' 'Uh huh,' says Jerrah.

'What's that mean precisely?' says Dick.

'It means no love angle for the film and less reason to mourn the passing of Rita Mae,' Jerrah says.

I say, 'There is no film, Jerrah.'

He says, 'Sure there's a film. It's less . . . dramatic . . . now your best friend didn't kill Rita Mae in a jealous rage, but you have a fascinating story to tell and I've been greatly encouraged by Hollywood's interest in it. You don't need to worry about the film, Honey. We love your song.'

I say, 'I don't give a monkey's whether Hollywood's interested or Moses is interested, there's no film because I withdraw myself from it and I am the subject.'

Harvey says, 'If I could just remind everyone. The film is not the prime cause for concern right now. Our problem for the hearing tomorrow remains the same. Although you young ladies are now in agreement as to where you were, we have no one to support your claim and the circumstantial evidence of your motive and the forensic evidence still exists. I will naturally be applying all my efforts to getting admissions from Jed Wilcox, Henry Linklater and Marty Dodge but we have no guarantees. If those boys stick together then what we have is your word against theirs and the truth is, they are home-grown boys without a motive.'

Dick whispers to me, 'Honey you gotta stick to your story that you were not with Stella Maria at the time. That's the story you should've told all along.'

'Stella Maria needed an alibi,' I say to him and he nods.

'Ah know that, Ah know,' he says, 'but Ah cannot impress it upon you too strongly. Your liddle song is goin' to make your fortune provided you don't blow it by sayin' somethin' silly.'

I tell him I don't know what he's on about but I do and it's sickening me. It's doing worse than that to poor Stella Maria who went into a decline the minute she heard Jerrah's voice. She's as quiet as those bells in the valley on a Monday and I can see the full weight of the risk she's taken bearing down on her. I take her hand.

'OK?' I say.

She pulls her hand away. She's not a big handholder. 'I'm OK.'

Harvey is talking to Betty and to Morris, and Jerrah is leaning into their conversation and commenting now and again and I'm straining to hear what's being said as last thing I want is for any decision to be made about me that I have no part in. But Dick goes, 'Psst. Honey. You remember Angel. She's goin' to help you through tomorrow. Give you some pointers about handlin' the press.'

I say, 'Dick, I won't be speaking to any press. Way things are goin' . . . well I don't know who I'll be speaking to.' And then we all look up because another car is approaching, like the whole world is converging on Betty's because it's heard she's selling used and broken dreams.

The sun's bouncing off the windscreen so I can't tell who it is. It's no car I recognise. I'm straining to see who it is. More than one person anyway. First person out could be anyone and I'm about to ask Betty who she's expecting when I see. Shoot! It's Archie. Archie and Tom, driven by Paddy. I'm on my feet and I'm running towards Paddy because I have always loved him but never more than I do right now.

Abe says, 'Come back,' and runs after me, thinking I'm legging it again. He runs smack into my back when I jump into Paddy's arms and it's only because Paddy is a rock that we don't fall. I kiss my boy on the lips in full view of everyone because now it doesn't matter who knows. He holds me to him, kisses my hair, then says, 'This the gardener boy?' And I wonder what Stella Maria has told him.

Tom hasn't bothered even to say hello. He's marching up to the house with Archie tagging behind and from the back he looks smaller than he's ever looked, punier, less impressive, even if he is striding in a purposeful manner. The difference, I realise, is he isn't carrying his camera which has always been like an extra bit of him. The bit of him that contains his strength and vigour.

Here is the biggest scene of my story so far maybe and he doesn't have his camera on him. 'Back so soon, Mr Sinclayah?' Betty says coolly, thinking maybe Tom is out of his mind.

Tom says to Archie, 'I think everyone is here who counts. You all know Archie Brown.' Archie's looking like he would rather kiss a rattler than do what he now has to do and I guess he's about to tell Stella Maria that he's thrown away the remains of her garden. She's giving him a look that says this is what she thinks as well. Somewhere between a scream and a whack with just a dash of a sob.

'Don't Archie,' she says. 'You don't have to.' But he does.

He says, 'I threw the brick that killed poor Rita Mae Pinkerton, may she rest in peace. I am prepared to say so to a

police officer and in a court of law.' Then he gives Stella Maria
such a look that I don't know what's gone on between them
but anyway, it frees my tongue and I get to my feet. Archie is
an old and good man.

'He's lying,' I say. 'I killed Rita Mae.'

You know in films when everyone gasps. Well everyone
gasped, including me and in mine goes all the poison that's
been gathering in me since God knows when. It seems to hit
Angel full in the face because she covers it with her hand.

Stella Maria says, 'She's making it up.' But comes to stand
next to me.

Harvey says, 'Honey, I'm getting a little weary of this.'

I say he will have to hear me out. 'This is what happened,'
I say and I tell them the truth.

After I spoke to Archie in the lobby, I didn't go to the
apartment. I followed Tom and Stella Maria up on to the roof
and I heard them in a conversation I knew was never meant
to include me. It ended exactly as Stella Maria said it did
before she started lying. She went into the stairwell to sulk.

I came out from behind the chimney and Tom had
disappeared. I couldn't see the fire escape from where I was.
I went to the edge of the roof to see if he was in the street but
he wasn't. No one was. Not a soul in sight. I wasn't expecting
to see Rita Mae and I didn't. At this moment I was wanting
her dead.

'Now Honey,' Dick says, but everyone goes 'Shush.'

'I hated her for what she'd done to Stella Maria. I hated
what I'd become from knowing her.' Jerrah's face has turned
to stone.

'But I was a mess. Stella Maria was going to ask me to go
home with her. I didn't blame her but I just didn't want to go.
We were so close to making it. I wanted to make it. I'd
worked so hard. On the other hand, I knew I couldn't fail her
again.'

I was tossing this brick from hand to hand. It wasn't any

special brick. Just a brick that had been lying on the ground with loads of others. And I thought well I'll let fate decide. I'd toss this brick as high as I could into the air and see how it fell. If it landed on something soft and didn't break, I'd stay. If it smashed, that'd be it. Dream over.

'Then I heard Tom call to someone in the street. I didn't know who . . . Maybe for a tiny split of a second I knew it was Rita Mae but maybe I didn't. I chucked the brick, anyway. I threw it as high as I could out over the wall towards the grass verge. It didn't get anywhere near as far as the verge. It just went straight up and almost straight down and while it was falling Rita Mae turned the corner and it landed on her head. That's the truth.'

There's a silence like after a performance that's been either so, so good or so bad. Then Archie laughs so loud he could be a mad man. The words everyone has on their lips freeze, giving way to this laugh which could mean anything.

'You are so rich, Honey darlin'. That's the best story Ah ever heard and Ah thank you for it. But you don't have to tell it to save old Archie. Ah ain't afraid of the consequences of mah act. You got to ignore her folks. She's as brave a little person as you'll ever come across but that's a made-up story or my name's not Archie Mason.'

'Brown,' says Tom.

Archie's still laughing. 'Ah know. Just teasin'. Brown.'

53

Talk about possibilities and outcomes. Here were two stories, one true, the other one not and the one they plumped for was the one that was not. Harvey took Archie all the way back into town so he could confess to the investigating officers and they kept him in a cell overnight which was a scandal, a man that age, when he'd never have done a runner. I fretted all night long.

No one believed my version of events except Stella Maria and Tom and it had been a revelation to them. They'd been so busy suspecting each other it hadn't occurred to them that I was the murderer. 'Except it wasn't murder,' Stella Maria said. 'I've never heard a clearer case of accident.'

She'd had a lot of explaining to do for telling a second whopper straight after admitting the first but everyone guessed she'd been trying to save Archie, same as they assumed I'd been doing. Harvey said, 'Well I don't know what to believe,' so Stella Maria had helped him out.

She said, 'Honey couldn't have done it because she was with me in our bedroom, just like she was saying all along.'

So this was the story everyone settled for in the end and the one Harvey told the judge.

Stella Maria had left the roof and was heading back to our apartment when she'd heard Archie creeping about outside, trying to clear up the mess in the hope that she hadn't seen it. Then she'd heard the workmen come back, and she'd thought well who cares? She'd listened to Archie yelling at them to stop their vandalism, she'd heard them laughing and throwing bricks between them to torment him, and she'd had to admit, she did. She cared.

She'd charged out of that stairwell like a madwoman, yelling obscenities and threatening violence, and they'd been so shocked they'd slunk off, leaving Archie not knowing whether to slink after them or not. He began clearing as fast as he could, not looking her in the eye, not speaking, gathering all the bricks into a pile, and in his panic, that's all it was, he'd chucked one brick to the left instead of the right and it went sailing off the roof and on to the head of Rita Mae Rainbow or Pinkerton. Killing her stone dead.

The judge made him demonstrate how it could possibly have happened and, pretty soon everyone could see. A man in a panic, turning this way and that, especially a man who's useless at the wheel of a car, can get confused. Which Archie had. It was understandable but not excusable, the judge said. He delivered us a lecture that was as fascinating as anything Tom ever had to tell me on the matter of luck, plus acts and their consequences.

He said, 'What this court must address is the concept of responsibility. A brick, thrown carelessly, has ended the days of a young woman who could reasonably have expected to live another fifty or sixty years. We can only guess at the quality of this life but my understanding is that this was a young woman possessed of a unique talent. She may well have been deprived of international acclaim by the brick. Was she just unfortunate? Was bad luck to blame for her tragic end? Is anything purely the result of luck? It is the view of this court that it is not and nothing happens without someone or something causing it.'

I looked over my shoulder to where Tom was sitting but he was staring at his hands, not at the judge, so's I couldn't decide what he was making of it. All I could read from his expression was sadness. That's how he looked. As sad as a body could look and my heart went out to him. But I was struck by the judge's words. I wanted to yell wait up! It had to be luck that Rita Mae was where she was when the brick fell. She could've been one step ahead or one step behind but she wasn't. Luck took her to be right under the brick. It was her destiny.

Harvey says the view of that judge might not be the view of another, and he will be hoping for this when Archie comes up for trial, which he will in due course, on the same charge that was laid against Stella Maria for which he is currently on bail. Harvey says Stella Maria and I were lucky not to find ourselves at the mercy of such a hard man. He expects Archie will get an easier time on account of his age and him being localish. I hope so. I truly hope so. As they took him away to be charged he winked at me and my heart just about broke. I owe him a debt bigger than the mountain outside Betty's door.

The judge said Stella Maria and I were free to go. We'd murdered no one and weren't even party to any murder. The judge was extremely unhappy about the way we'd misled the court and warned us we could be charged in connection with that matter but that doesn't bother me. Not with Harvey on our case. I feel a great sorrow for all those who've been accused of a crime and represented by morons. I've been playing around with my tribute to their terrible luck.

Down and out in the Nashville County Courthouse,
Fate in the hands of a man who wants his dinner,

What's it to him if I live or die.
He gets paid
I get hung for a sinner.

Needs work.

We didn't hang about. Once the judge said we were free to go, the Moonshine people hurried us out the back entrance to avoid the media who'd been hoping for something more spectacular. Angel was saying better we do a press conference tomorrow and Jerrah was saying right, right and Dick was saying he was hungry. I know because they formed this huddle about me even though Paddy was there to protect me.

I said, 'Let's celebrate with a Cracker lunch. In honour of Archie.' Everyone went, 'whey hey' but Dick mostly. Jerrah had never been to a Cracker and he tried real hard to join in because all of a sudden, he needed me to like him. So we all went. Stella Maria, me, Tom, Paddy, Merv, him, Dick and Angel jumped straight into waiting limos and Betty and Abe followed in the jeep.

I can't say these were a bunch of people you'd usually invite to the same party but anyway, there we were, and though I was desperate to talk to Stella Maria to see where we currently stood on Tom, I only truly had time for Paddy. And I didn't even have time for him because the Moonshine people wanted to do business and we had to do business as we still had a contract.

Jerrah made sure he sat one side of me and Dick on the other, with Angel across from me and Paddy next to her. I thought if I was a blind person and knew that Jerrah and Paddy were sitting across from each other, I'd say to the seeing folk, 'Here you have love and hate.' I'd hardly finished my meatloaf when Jerrah made this speech.

'Honey, I can't tell you how delighted I am by today's outcome and how impressed I was by your bravery yesterday. In attempting to take the blame for an old guy like

Archie, you acted in the very best Moonshine spirit. We have organised a little celebration to show just how proud of you we are.' He paused here, expecting rapture but I only gave him moderate interest. He pressed on. 'We have organised a showcase to present you to the most important people in the industry – they will be descending on our office at 2.00 p.m. tomorrow and we couldn't be more excited. How about that?'

No one went 'Woo!' or 'Wow!'' Not even Merv. I said, 'Jerrah you know what? I have to think about it.' And he turned mean in an instant.

He said, 'Don't think about it too long, Honey. Opportunities like this don't come your way every day.' Then he slid out from the booth hardly touching his Country Fried Chicken and Angel nearly ruptured herself trying to climb over Paddy to follow him. 'You comin' Dick?' Jerrah called. And naturally Dick was because he had no choice even though he was only halfway through his platter.

54

You know what it's like after years of secrecy and sorrow to lie between good clean sheets in a proper sized bed with the man you love better than life itself? It's like the finest melody you ever heard carrying you all the way to heaven.

Paddy and I spent the night in the Vanderbilt Plaza on West End Ave. It's one of the finest this town has to offer and costs an arm and a leg but Paddy said only the best would do. If he was expecting intercourse, it never happened. I spent all night pouring my heart out to him and he loved me enough to stay awake to listen.

It was in the perfect calm of his arms that I could think clearly for the first time in months or maybe it was the questions he was asking, like 'Honey what's going on with your teeth?' But I looked at my life through his eyes and wondered as he did, 'All those people injured and dead and for what?'

'For their dreams,' I said.

He said, 'Dreams are fine, Honey, but you have to keep your feet on the ground. You threw a fucking great rock in the air and didn't even think it could land on someone's head.'

'It was an accident,' I said. 'Accidents are God's way of reminding us our lives are in His hands.'

'Bollocks,' he said. 'Never throw rocks.' And thank God he was there because last night, for the first time, I saw what Stella Maria had been seeing for weeks. The poor smashed body of a girl who died a sad wretch. I cried myself sick. In the end Paddy said, 'She sounds horrible.'

'She might have improved with time,' I said.

It's less than two weeks since we first set eyes on Betty's mountain home but it feels like a lifetime. The bit of me that went missing the day we arrived has been replaced by another bit which is older and wiser, if wiser is when you feel like someone's taken out your innards, rearranged them and put them back again.

This morning Archie drove Stella Maria and me out to the Cumberland Plateau to fetch our belongings, bright as a button for a man on a murder charge. He's making all sorts of plans for the windfall he's come into just lately.

Saying goodbye to Betty wasn't easy. I didn't find it easy. We walked down to the bottom terrace together, just her and me as this was our special place, and I said how grateful I would always be to her for seeing me safely through this treacherous time.

She said, 'Not as treacherous as we thought in some respects, more treacherous than we thought in others.' I wasn't sure what she meant so I said about feeling more grown up and she said, 'Takin' responsibility for the choices you make is a grown-up thing to do. I'm hoping Archie appreciates this.'

She looked at me in her Betty way and I said, 'Me too.' We didn't hug or anything.

Leaving her was a wrench but worst of all was leaving the hills where I laid the ghost of my mother. I walked a little bit up the mountain and stood very still so she could make her presence felt if she wanted to but I guess she didn't. I took some deep breaths of the cool, clear air to sustain me for the journey ahead wherever it takes me.

Abe loaded our bags in the back of Archie's car then shook our hands. We both shook Betty by the hand. Betty said to Stella Maria, 'You keep on with the paintin'. You show real promise.'

I laughed. Well I did because when has she ever painted before? And Betty said to me, 'Honey, you haven't been feedin' Marigold have you? She's been lookin' off colour and Ah just cain't make it out.'

I don't know how we made it down the mountain track because my eyes were closed. If we'd struck anything coming up, it would've been curtains for the lot of us. I was so happy to make it out alive. I've been singing all the way back into Nashville. Stella Maria's been staring out the window. Archie's joined in some choruses which is a tribute to his fortitude.

We're headed for the showcase. Stella Maria and me talked it over and agreed I should attend, I should perform and she should accompany me as my manager, reason being, we couldn't not, owing to my contract, which she signed herself. It has a clause allowing Moonshine to get out of it if I sully the good name of the label by any extraordinary act – like going to jail – but no such reciprocal clause applies to them.

Anyway, why wouldn't I go? I'm still a country singer and why pass up the chance to impress Nashville's toughest audience? I don't mind admitting I'm nervous. Performing's great but you have to steel yourself. I'm not sure about the T-shirt I'm wearing. Doesn't feel tight enough.

Stella Maria's very silent and I know she's thinking about Tom. She doesn't know if the damage he did to her love for him can ever be repaired. I say well she's forgiven me, hasn't she? She turns to look at me and from her face I'd swear that she hadn't. She says forgiving Tom isn't the same as forgiving me.

'Why?' I ask.

'You're family. Forgiveness doesn't come into it.'

Then she looks back out the window though I'm so moved I could kiss her and I would, except we've pulled up outside Moonshine and there's a welcome party. 'Yikes,' I say instead.

Paddy's chatting to Dick and Merv and the sight of him steadies me. He says, 'How you feelin'?'

'Nervous.'

He says, 'You'll be great.' He takes my guitar, like I mightn't be strong enough to carry it, and we all trail into the building.

Merv and Dick are sweating like big fat leaking hoses. 'You decided what you're singing?' Merv wants to know.

I tell him *Roaring Into Town On A Train Going Nowhere, Bettin' On Your Cheatin' Heart* and *Rita Mae.*'

He says, 'Which version?'

'Relax Merv,' I say.

He says, 'Maybe the first one's better.'

I say, 'Don't you know?'

He says, 'This stage of the game darlin', Ah never know anything.'

The boardroom's all been moved around. The table's gone and there's rows of chairs full of suits who don't smile even though this is the music industry. In the middle of the chairs is a mic and in the corner of the room is Tom, with a camera on his shoulder.

Stella Maria says, 'What do you think you're doin'?'

He says, 'Jerry asked.'

She says, 'What's flamin' Jerry got to do with it?'

He says, 'Jerry owns the film rights. I gave them to him so he'd stand bail.'

'He got his bail back,' Stella Maria reminds him. And I can see a brawl in the offing which I don't need right now and I say could they give me a break. I want to get on with this. They can sort it out once I'm done.

But it's preying on my mind the whole time I'm singing

and I'm thinking what did Tom sell and why? And the same thought must be running through Stella Maria's head as well because her eyes keep wandering back to him even though she's trying to keep them on me. I'm looking at her looking at him and I'm thinking Tom sold the rights to his dream to keep us out of jail and then to pay Archie to keep us out of jail even though a judge might never have sent me to jail. Where's the gamble there, for a gambling man?

So maybe I haven't given *Roarin' Into Town* my all. But I've done my best and when I finish, I hear this loud cheering and as I bow I think, 'They love it!' Then I look up and see the cheering's coming from Paddy, Merv, Stella Maria and Dick. Same thing happens with *Your Cheatin' Heart.* My friends love it. The industry, no getting away from it, doesn't. I want to be sick. I almost don't bother with *Rita Mae.* I almost can't stand the strain of it. But a professional would go on, whatever the audience and I owe it to Rita Mae who's dead and gone but who merits at least an outing with the industry which appreciated her too late and mostly not at all.

'Thank you,' I say. 'I'd like to sing for you a song dedicated to a friend of mine, Rita Mae Rainbow. She died tragically in an accident that could have happened to any of us. She was a great banjo picker. She had fingers that danced.'

And as I sing, you know, my heart does ache for her. She was a cow but it's tragic when life goes on without you. And the world's a poorer place without her music. I sing with every bit of feeling I can muster for the girl and when I finish, there's not much cheering from my friends. But after a second's silence, the industry claps its heart out, people are on their feet and from the back of the room someone yells 'Woo-hoo!'

Jerrah runs the full length of the room to put his arm about my shoulder which feels like a dead weight. 'Isn't she great? Isn't she just great? A star in the making you'll all agree, even if she is from London.' And everyone claps again.

It's a moment I've imagined so often it's practically a joke and even though I know he's not expecting it, I'm going to grab it and run with it. 'Can I speak?' I say to Jerrah. The look on his face says no way.

'Sure' he says. 'Go right ahead. Ladies and gentlemen, I give you Miss Honey Hawksworth.'

'Thank you,' I say. 'I'm pleased you liked my song but it's not just my song. I have people to thank. Rita Mae Rainbow and our producer Merv Pickett. I also want to thank my two travelling companions, Stella Maria O'Shea and Tom Sinclair.' I point to them and the audience turns and gives them a cheer without knowing why. 'But more than anyone I want to thank my mother Toni Hawksworth, may she rest in peace, who taught me to have faith. What I've had to decide for myself is where to place it.' Those suits are thinking she needs more charm school but I couldn't give a damn. 'It won't be in this town whose product I'll love till I die.' Jerrah's grip has tightened around my shoulders but I shake it off. 'I'm settling for the love of a good man. It's the biggest gamble of my life but I'm goin' to take it. I thank you all for your kind attention.'

I'm half way down the room. I kiss Merv as I pass him. Stella Maria's one step ahead of me and Tom's one step behind with his camera to his shoulder. Paddy's waiting by the door. We don't look back, not even once. We hit the road laughing. Title.